So What?

4

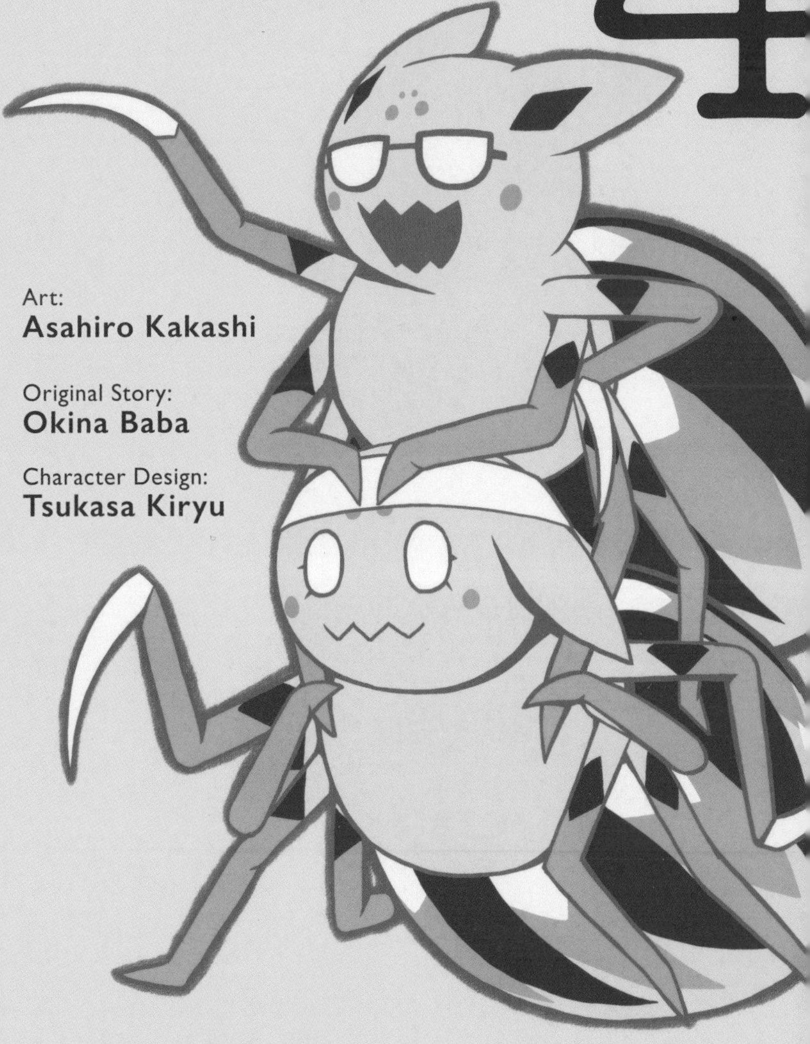

Art:
Asahiro Kakashi

Original Story:
Okina Baba

Character Design:
Tsukasa Kiryu

So I'm a Spider, So What?

CONTENTS

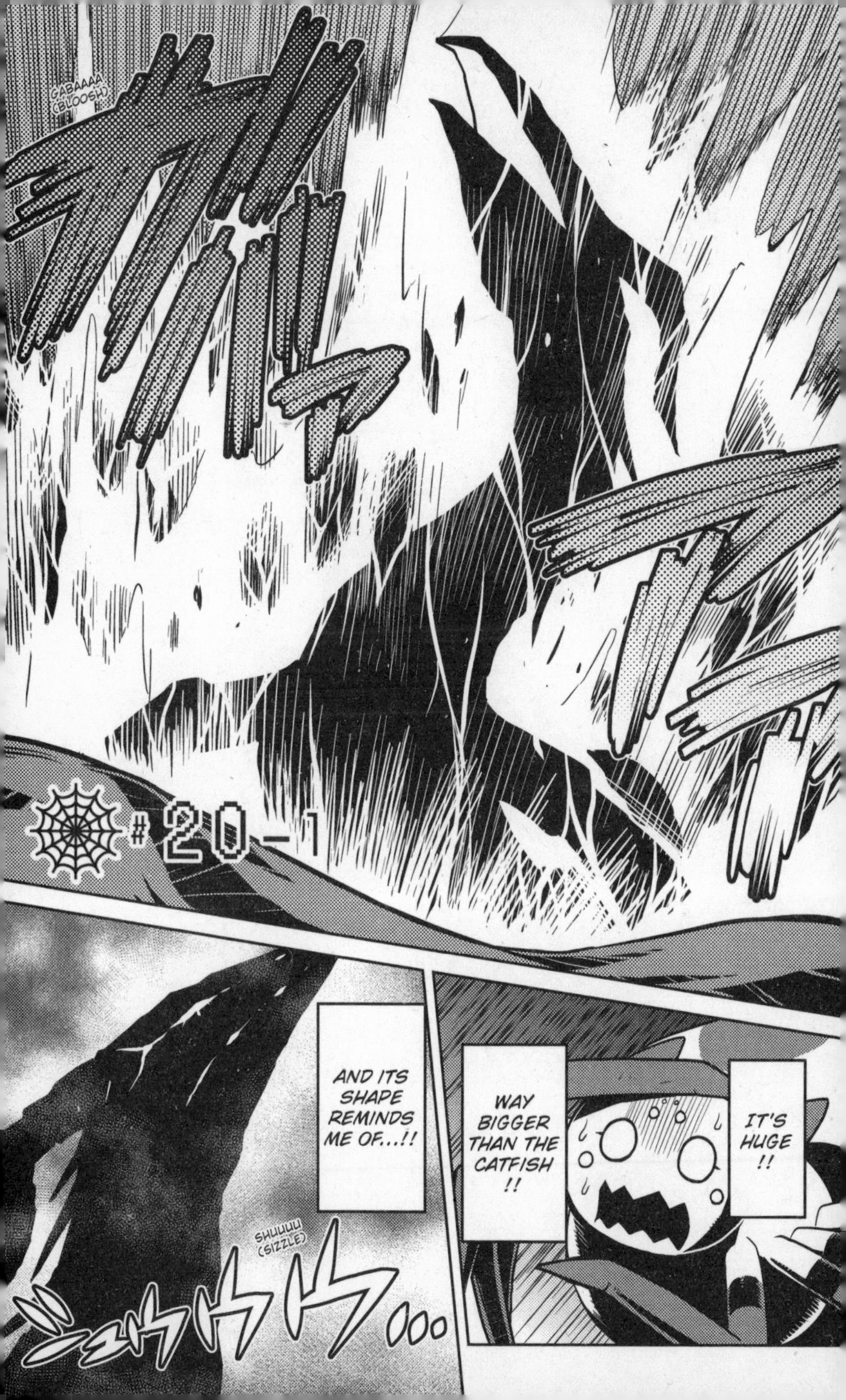
CABAAAA (BLOOSH)
#20-1
IT'S HUGE!!
WAY BIGGER THAN THE CATFISH!!
AND ITS SHAPE REMINDS ME OF...!!
SHUUUUU (SIZZLE)

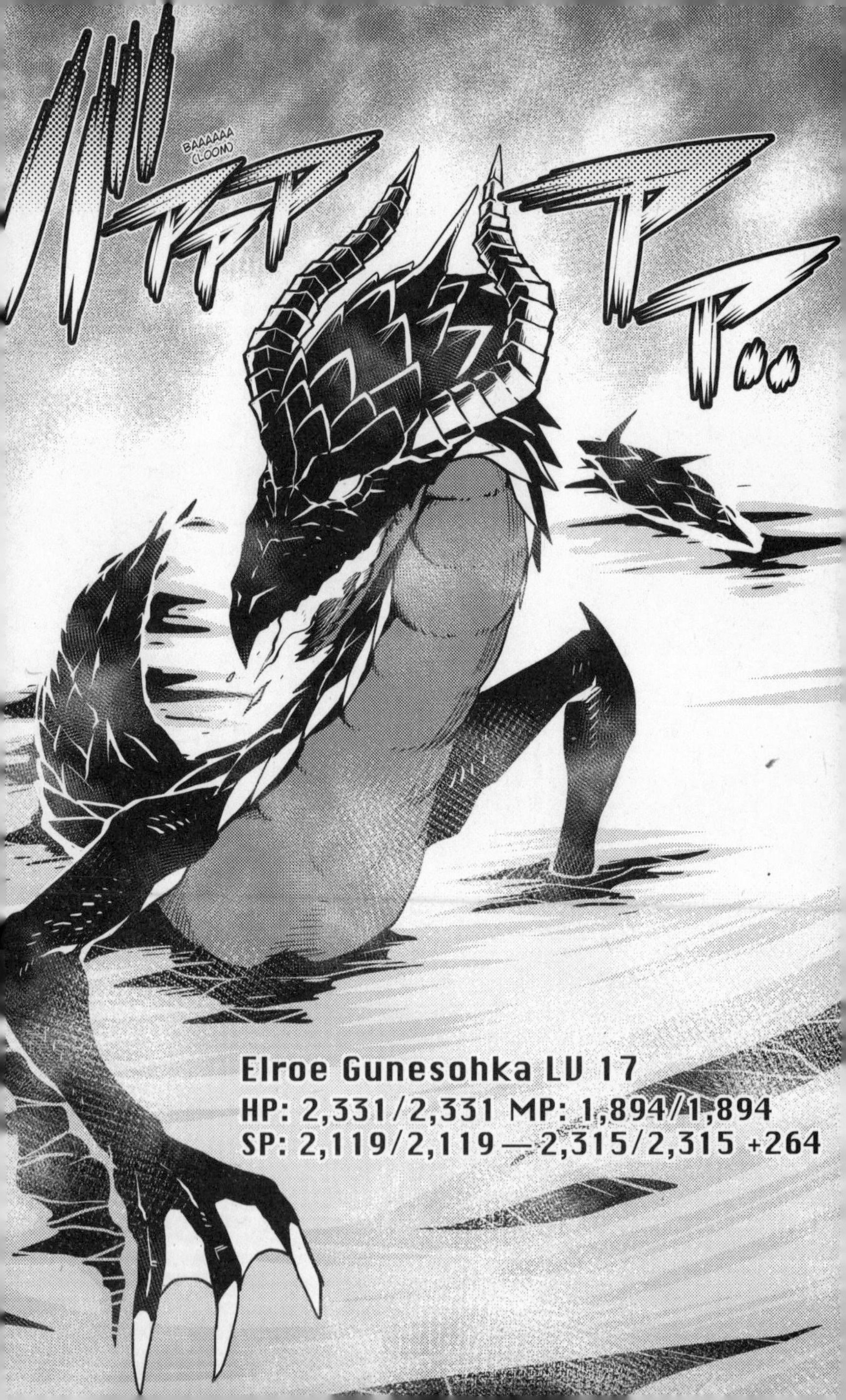
BAAAAAA
(LOOM)
Elroe Gunesohka LV 17
HP: 2,331/2,331 MP: 1,894/1,894
SP: 2,119/2,119 — 2,315/2,315 +264

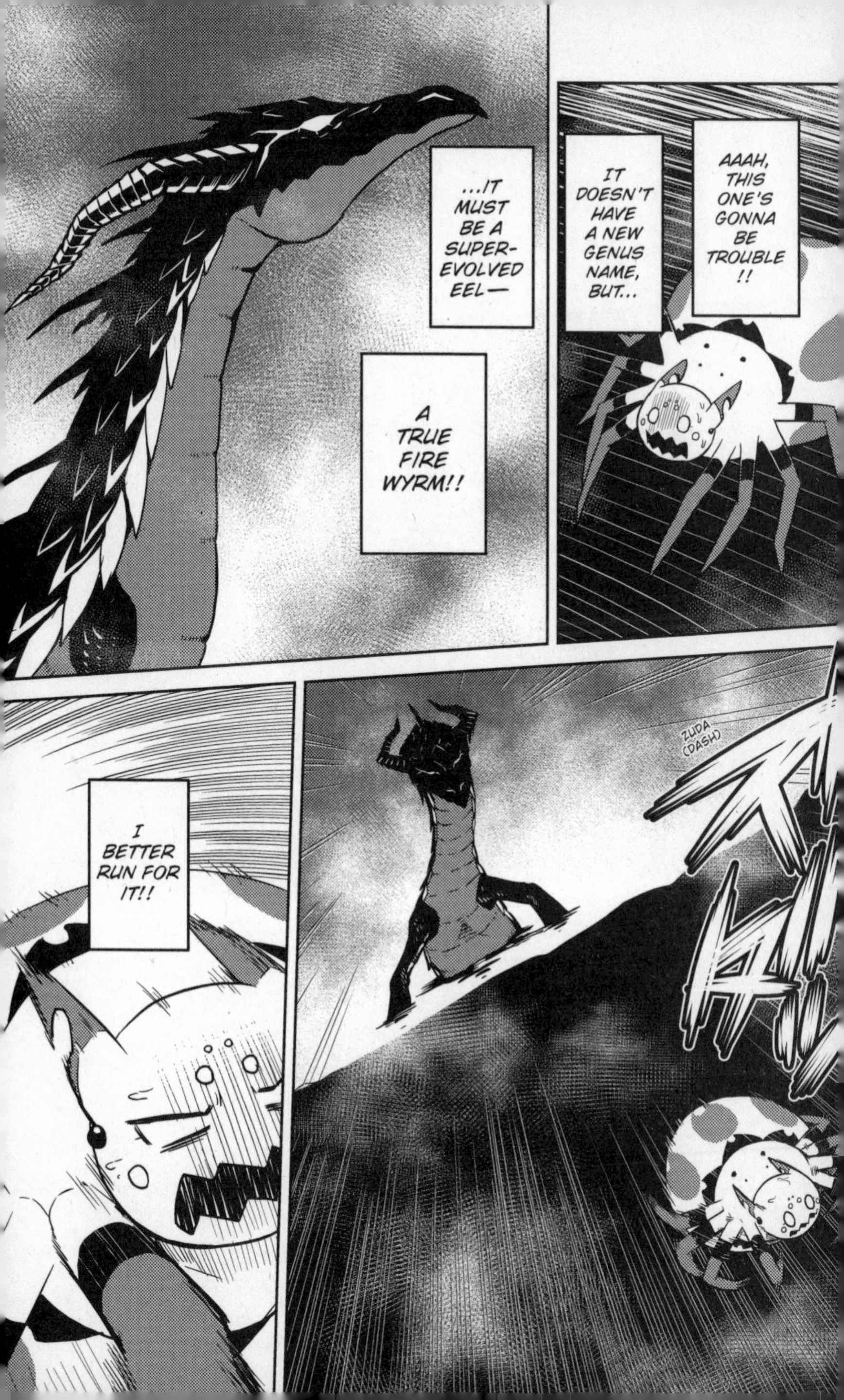
AAAH, THIS ONE'S GONNA BE TROUBLE!!
IT DOESN'T HAVE A NEW GENUS NAME, BUT...
...IT MUST BE A SUPER-EVOLVED EEL—
A TRUE FIRE WYRM!!
ZUDA (DASH)
I BETTER RUN FOR IT!!

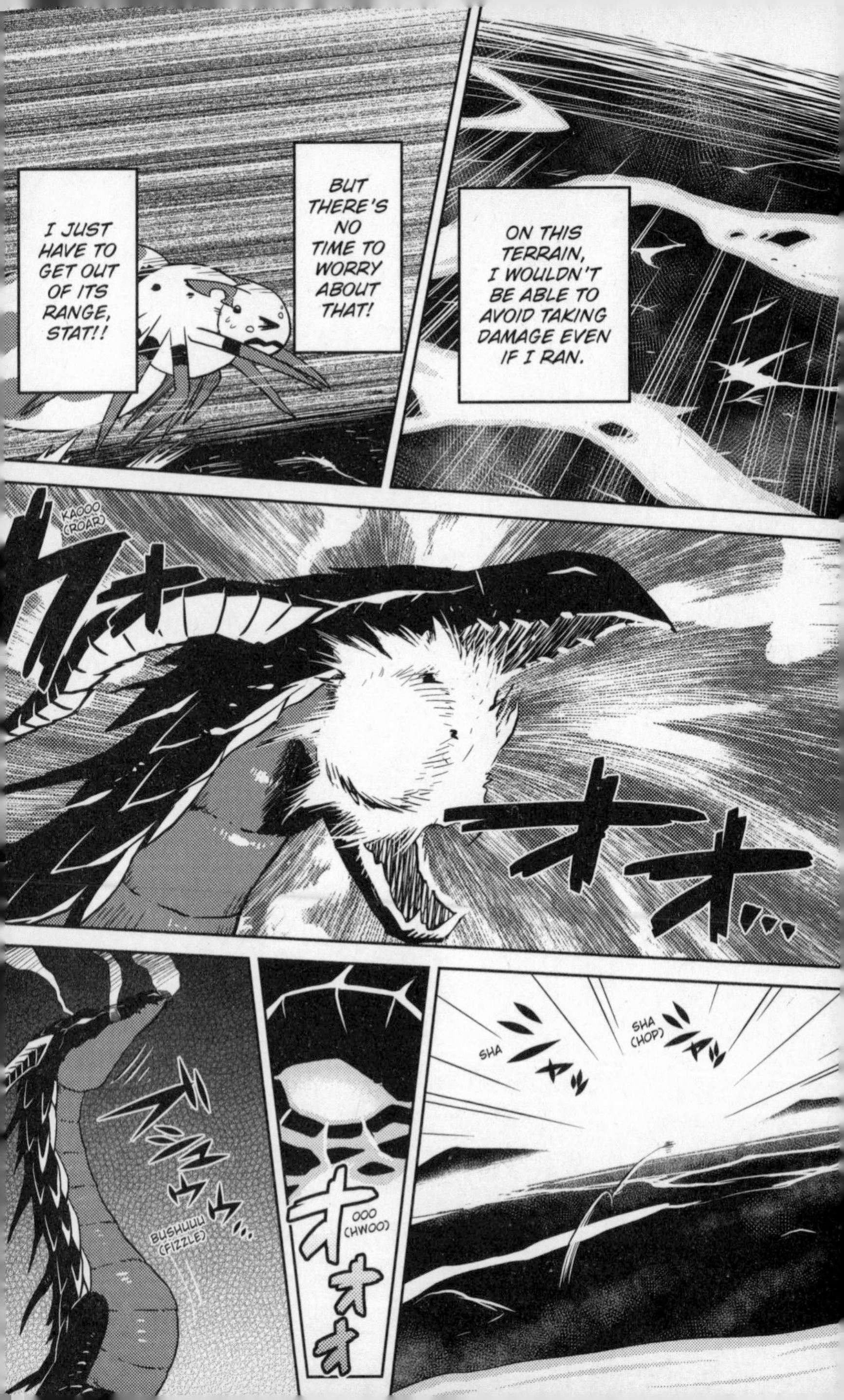
ON THIS TERRAIN, I WOULDN'T BE ABLE TO AVOID TAKING DAMAGE EVEN IF I RAN.
BUT THERE'S NO TIME TO WORRY ABOUT THAT!
I JUST HAVE TO GET OUT OF ITS RANGE, STAT!!
KAOOO (ROAR)
SHA (HOP)
SHA
OOO (HWOO)
BUSHUUU (FIZZLE)

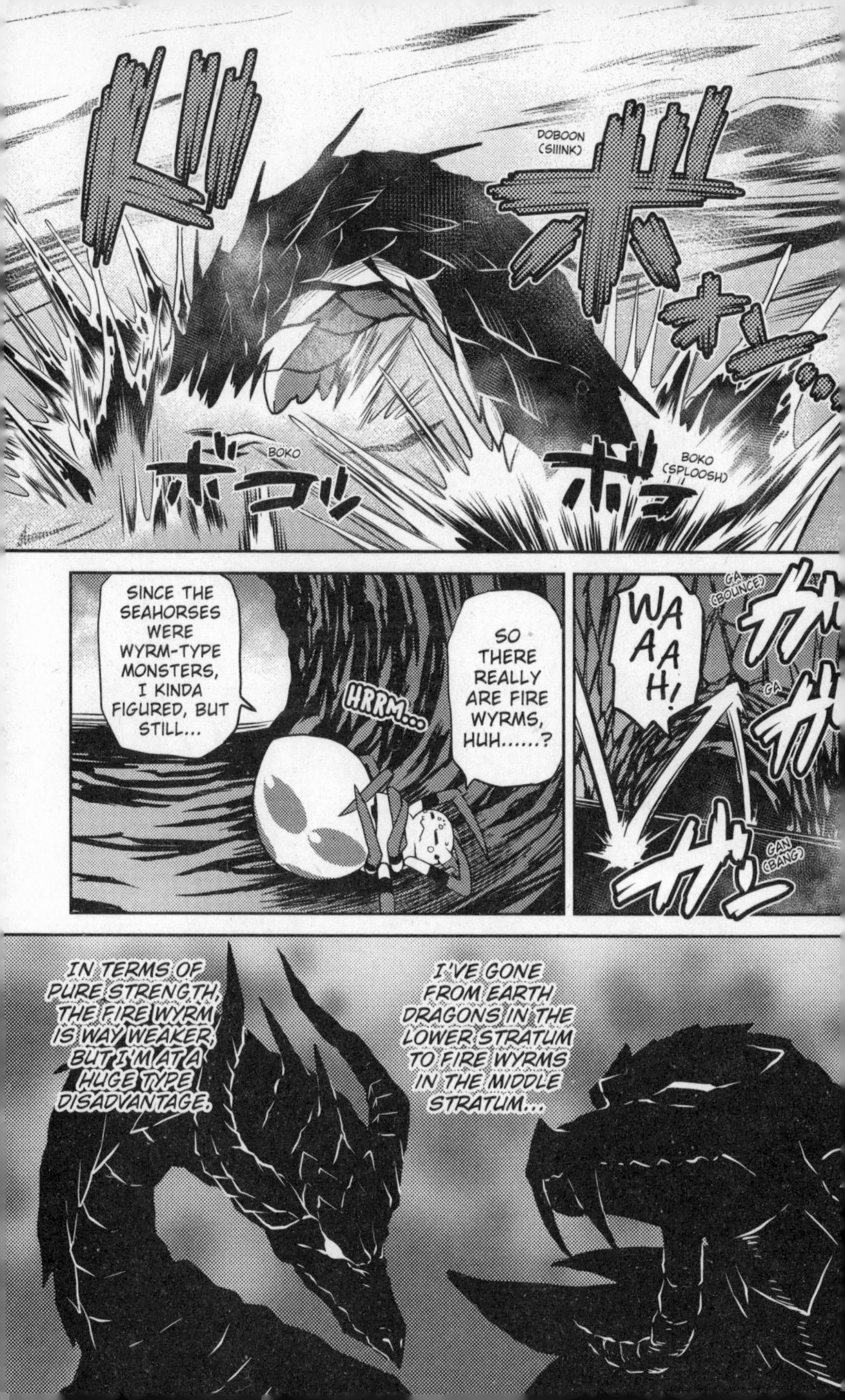
DOBOON (SIIINK)
BOKO (SPLOOSH)
BOKO
GA (BOUNCE)
WAAAH!
GA
GAN (BANG)
SO THERE REALLY ARE FIRE WYRMS, HUH......?
HRRM...
SINCE THE SEAHORSES WERE WYRM-TYPE MONSTERS, I KINDA FIGURED, BUT STILL...
I'VE GONE FROM EARTH DRAGONS IN THE LOWER STRATUM TO FIRE WYRMS IN THE MIDDLE STRATUM...
IN TERMS OF PURE STRENGTH, THE FIRE WYRM IS WAY WEAKER, BUT I'M AT A HUGE TYPE DISADVANTAGE.

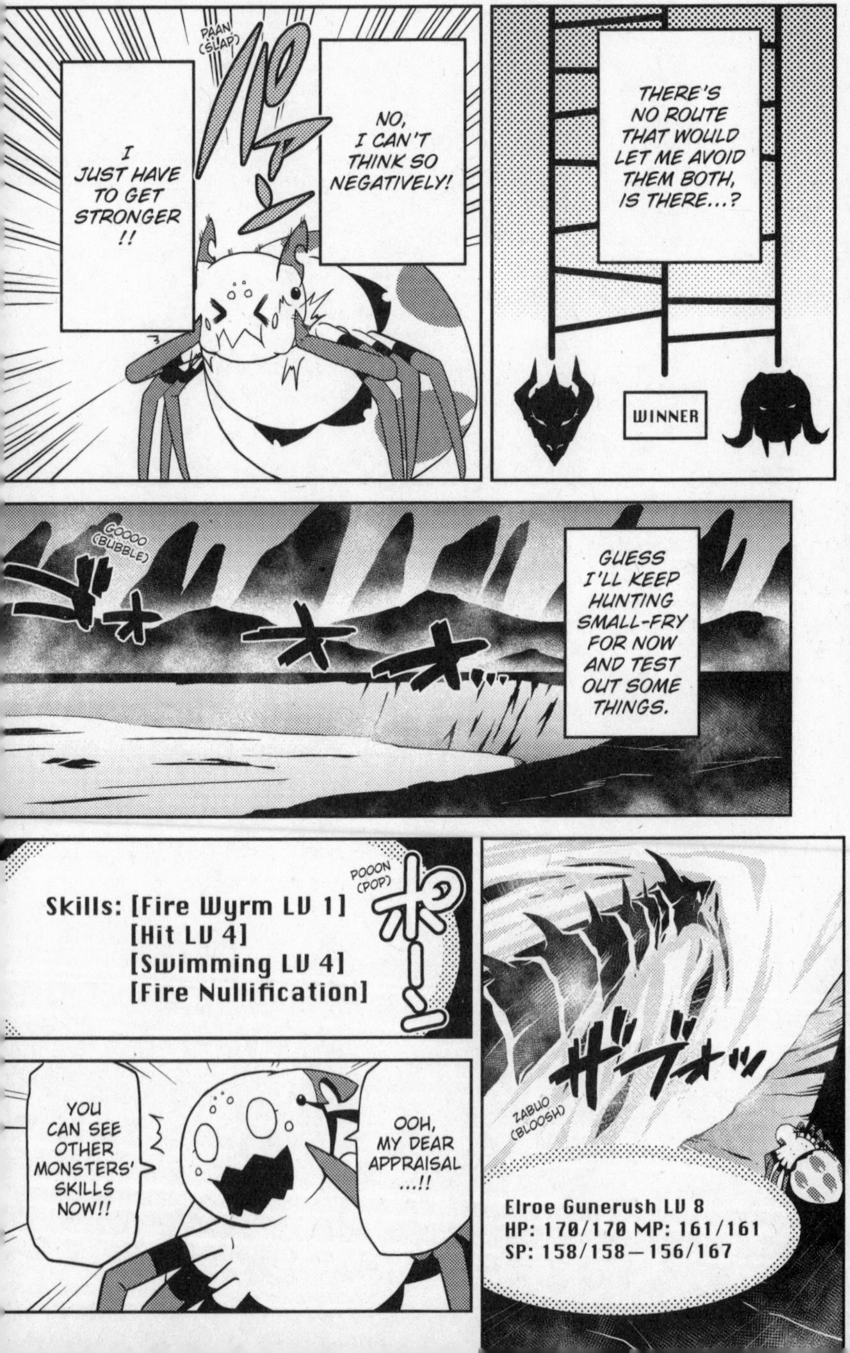
THERE'S NO ROUTE THAT WOULD LET ME AVOID THEM BOTH, IS THERE...?
WINNER
PAAN (SLAP)
NO, I CAN'T THINK SO NEGATIVELY!
I JUST HAVE TO GET STRONGER!!
GUESS I'LL KEEP HUNTING SMALL-FRY FOR NOW AND TEST OUT SOME THINGS.
GOOOO (BUBBLE)
ZABUO (BLOOSH)
Elroe Gunerush LV 8
HP: 170/170 MP: 161/161
SP: 158/158—156/167
POOON (POP)
Skills: [Fire Wyrm LV 1]
[Hit LV 4]
[Swimming LV 4]
[Fire Nullification]
OOH, MY DEAR APPRAISAL...!!
YOU CAN SEE OTHER MONSTERS' SKILLS NOW!!

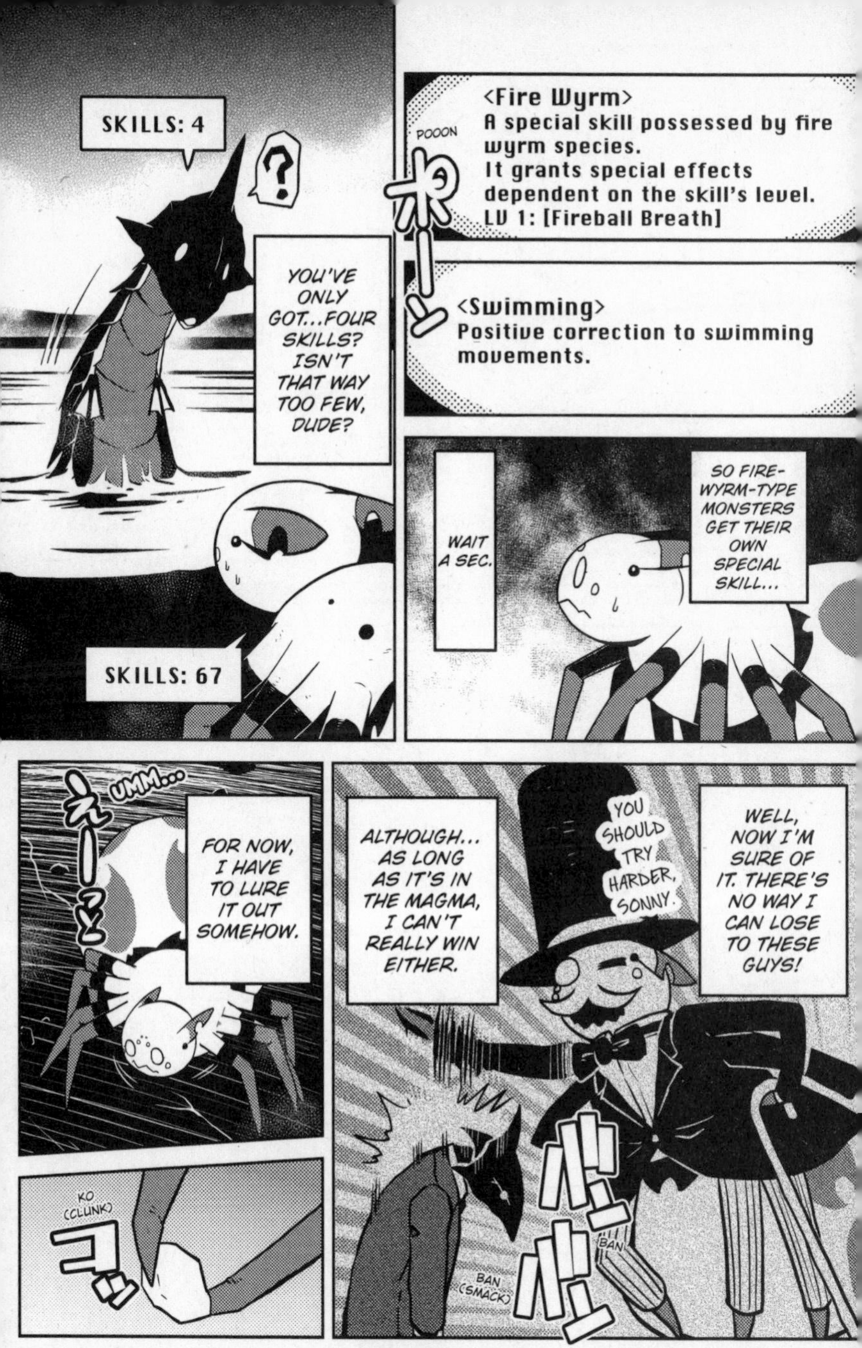
POOON
<Fire Wyrm>
A special skill possessed by fire wyrm species.
It grants special effects dependent on the skill's level.
LV 1: [Fireball Breath]
<Swimming>
Positive correction to swimming movements.
SO FIRE-WYRM-TYPE MONSTERS GET THEIR OWN SPECIAL SKILL...
WAIT A SEC.
SKILLS: 4
YOU'VE ONLY GOT...FOUR SKILLS? ISN'T THAT WAY TOO FEW, DUDE?
SKILLS: 67
WELL, NOW I'M SURE OF IT. THERE'S NO WAY I CAN LOSE TO THESE GUYS!
YOU SHOULD TRY HARDER, SONNY.
ALTHOUGH... AS LONG AS IT'S IN THE MAGMA, I CAN'T REALLY WIN EITHER.
BAN
BAN (SMACK)
UMM...
FOR NOW, I HAVE TO LURE IT OUT SOMEHOW.
KO (CLUNK)

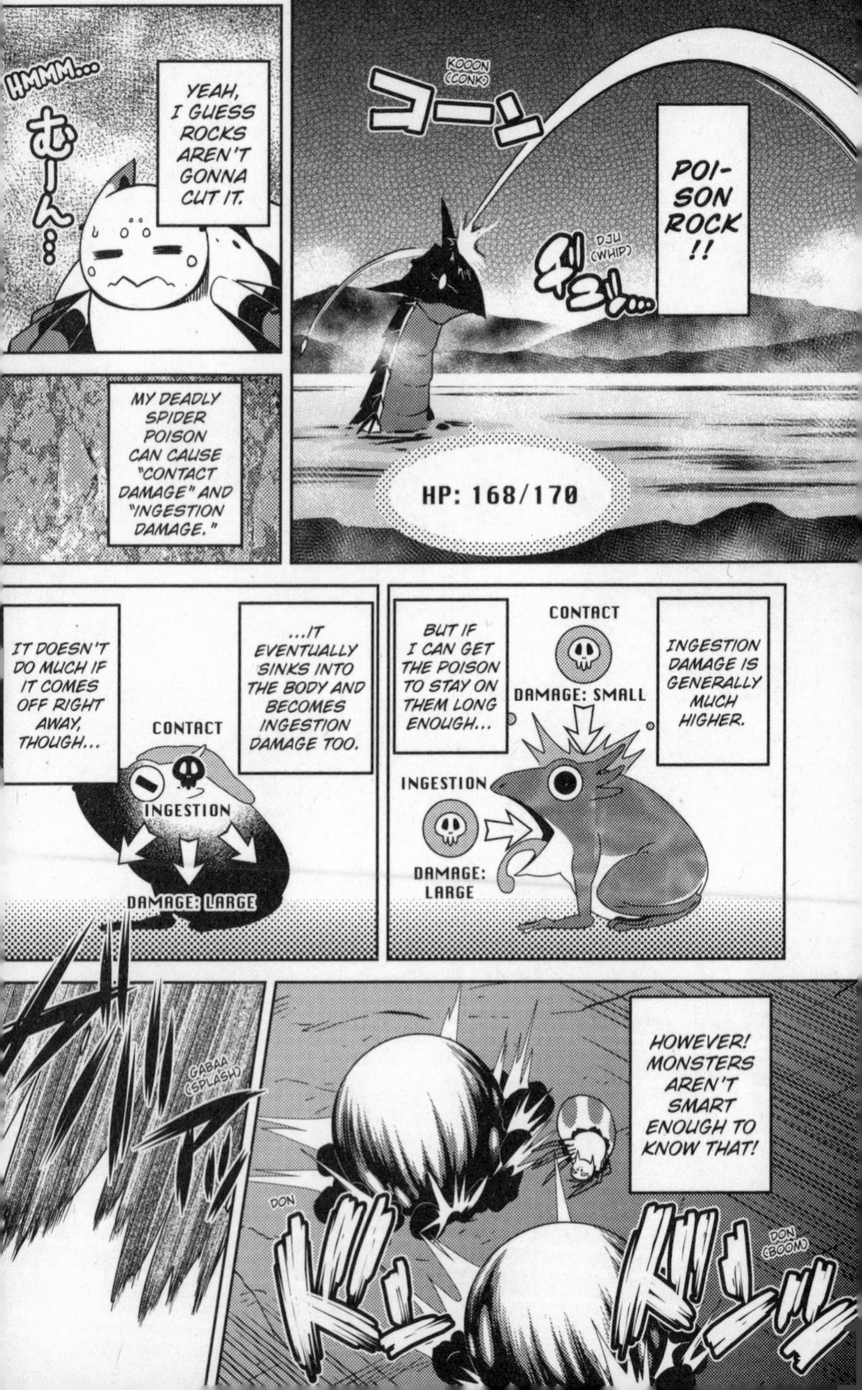
KOOON (CONK)
POI-SON ROCK!!
DJU (WHIP)
HP: 168/170
HMMM...
むーん…
YEAH, I GUESS ROCKS AREN'T GONNA CUT IT.
MY DEADLY SPIDER POISON CAN CAUSE "CONTACT DAMAGE" AND "INGESTION DAMAGE."
INGESTION DAMAGE IS GENERALLY MUCH HIGHER.
CONTACT
DAMAGE: SMALL
BUT IF I CAN GET THE POISON TO STAY ON THEM LONG ENOUGH...
INGESTION
DAMAGE: LARGE
...IT EVENTUALLY SINKS INTO THE BODY AND BECOMES INGESTION DAMAGE TOO.
CONTACT
IT DOESN'T DO MUCH IF IT COMES OFF RIGHT AWAY, THOUGH...
INGESTION
DAMAGE: LARGE
HOWEVER! MONSTERS AREN'T SMART ENOUGH TO KNOW THAT!
DON (BOOM)
DON
GABAA (SPLASH)

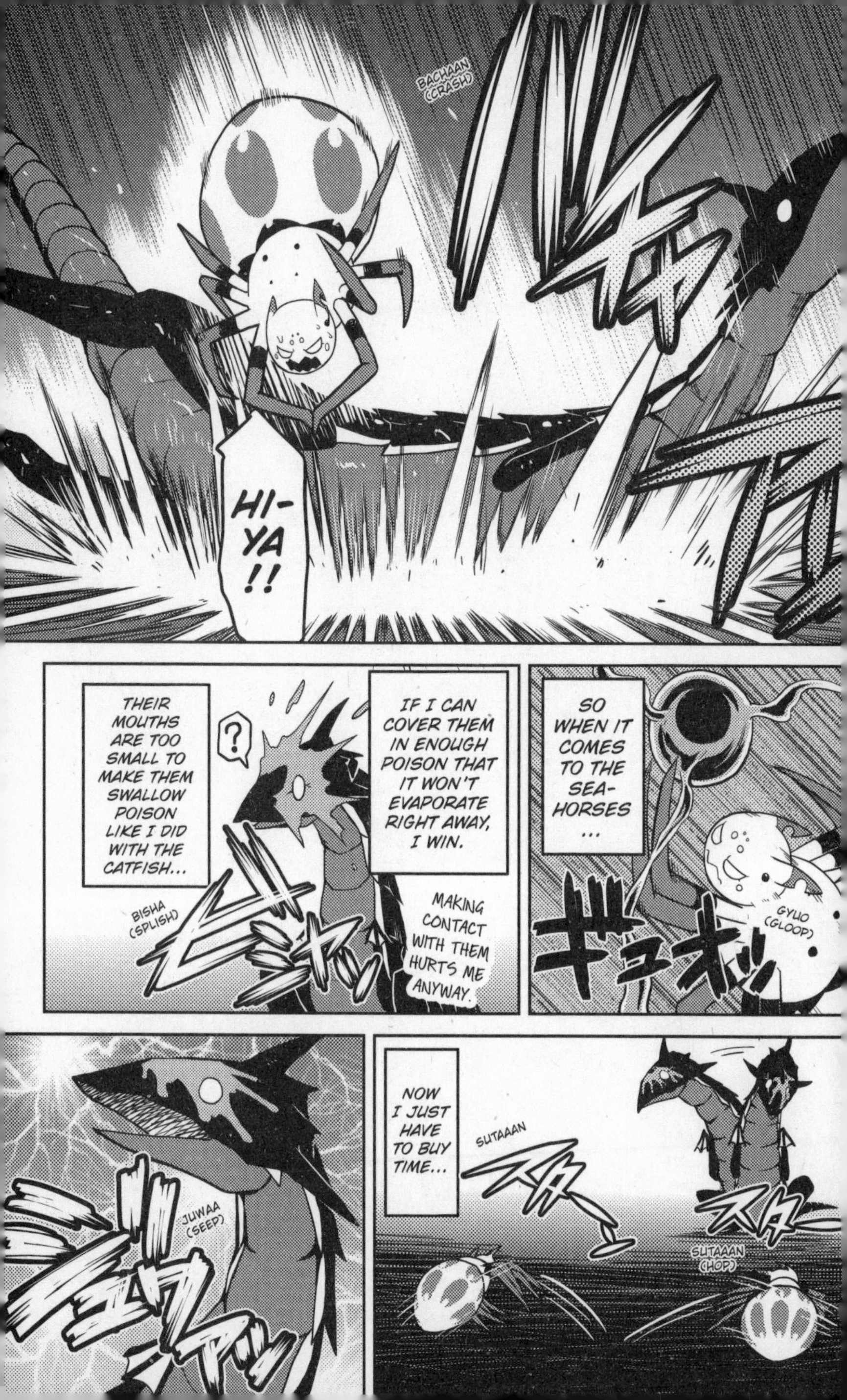
BACHAAN (CRASH)
HI-YA!!
SO WHEN IT COMES TO THE SEA-HORSES...
GYUO (GLOOP)
THEIR MOUTHS ARE TOO SMALL TO MAKE THEM SWALLOW POISON LIKE I DID WITH THE CATFISH...
?
IF I CAN COVER THEM IN ENOUGH POISON THAT IT WON'T EVAPORATE RIGHT AWAY, I WIN.
MAKING CONTACT WITH THEM HURTS ME ANYWAY.
BISHA (SPLISH)
NOW I JUST HAVE TO BUY TIME...
SUTAAAN
SUTAAAN (HOP)
JUWAA (SEEP)

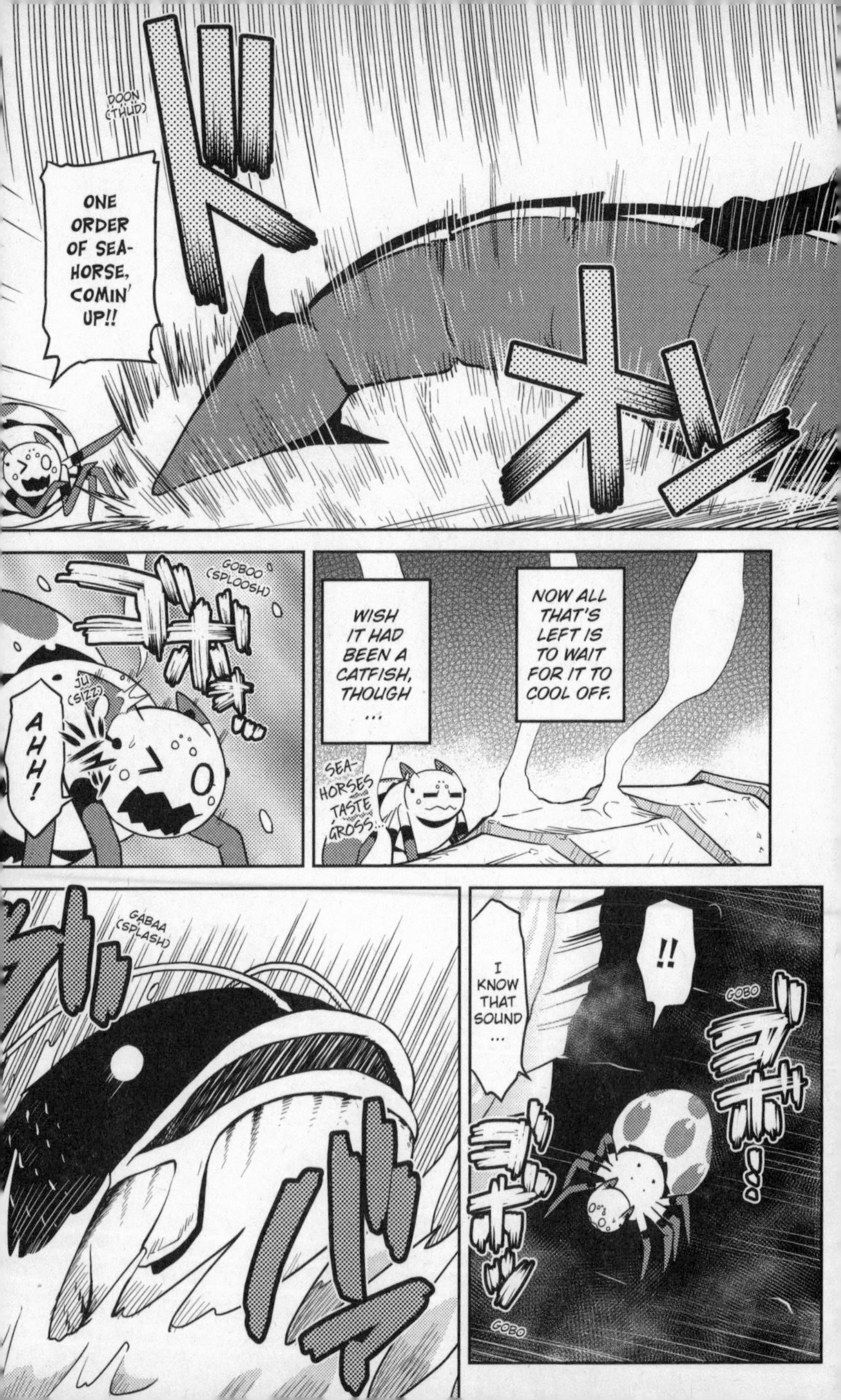
DOON (THUD)
ONE ORDER OF SEA-HORSE, COMIN' UP!!
NOW ALL THAT'S LEFT IS TO WAIT FOR IT TO COOL OFF.
WISH IT HAD BEEN A CATFISH, THOUGH ...
SEA-HORSES TASTE GROSS...
GOBOO (SPLOOSH)
JU (SIZZ)
AHH!
!!
I KNOW THAT SOUND ...
GOBO
GOBO
GABAA (SPLASH)

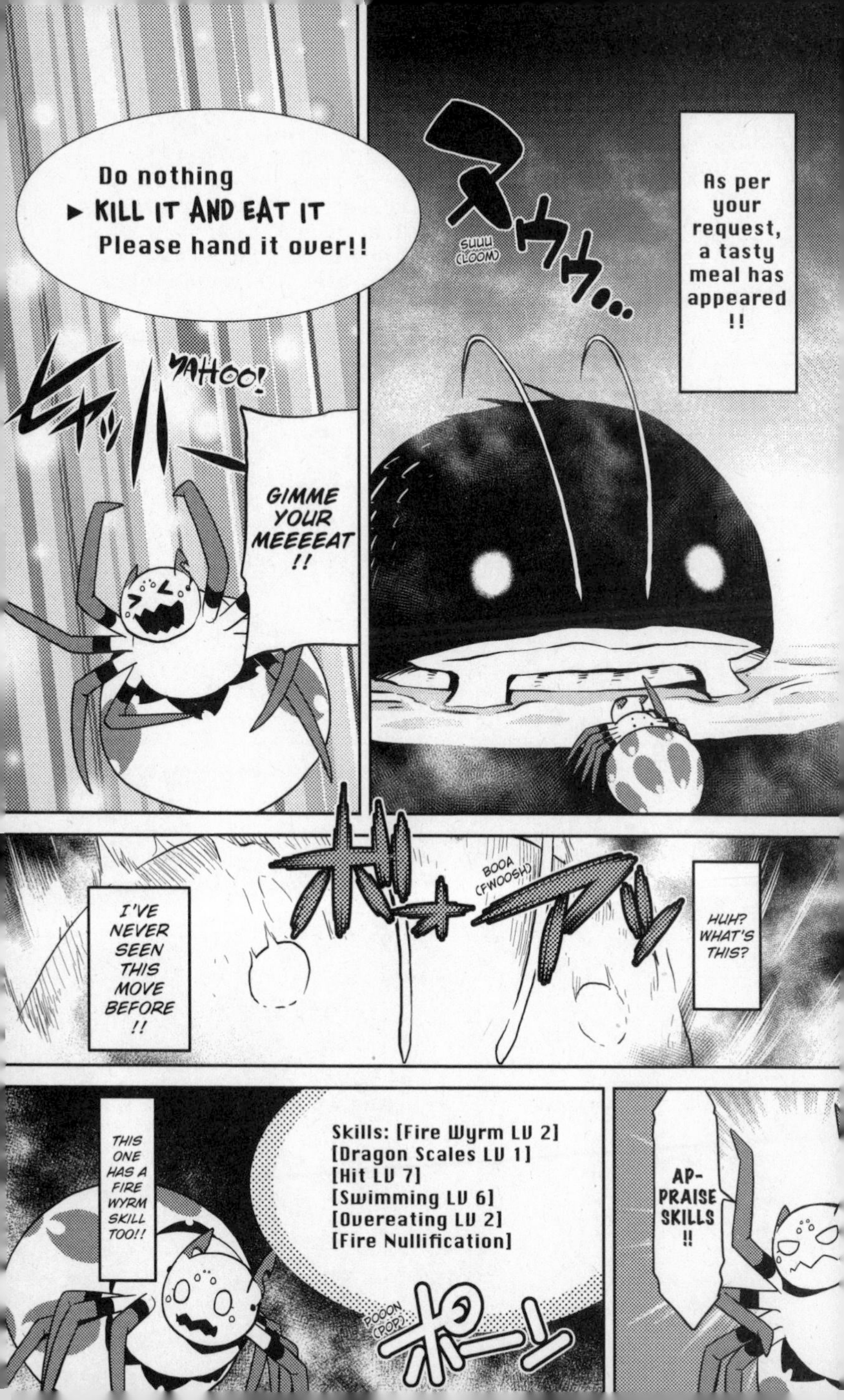
As per your request, a tasty meal has appeared!!
SUUU (LOOM)
Do nothing
▶ KILL IT AND EAT IT
Please hand it over!!
YAHOO!
GIMME YOUR MEEEEAT!!
HUH? WHAT'S THIS?
BOOA (FWOOSH)
I'VE NEVER SEEN THIS MOVE BEFORE!!
AP-PRAISE SKILLS!!
Skills: [Fire Wyrm LV 2]
[Dragon Scales LV 1]
[Hit LV 7]
[Swimming LV 6]
[Overeating LV 2]
[Fire Nullification]
POOON (POP)
THIS ONE HAS A FIRE WYRM SKILL TOO!!

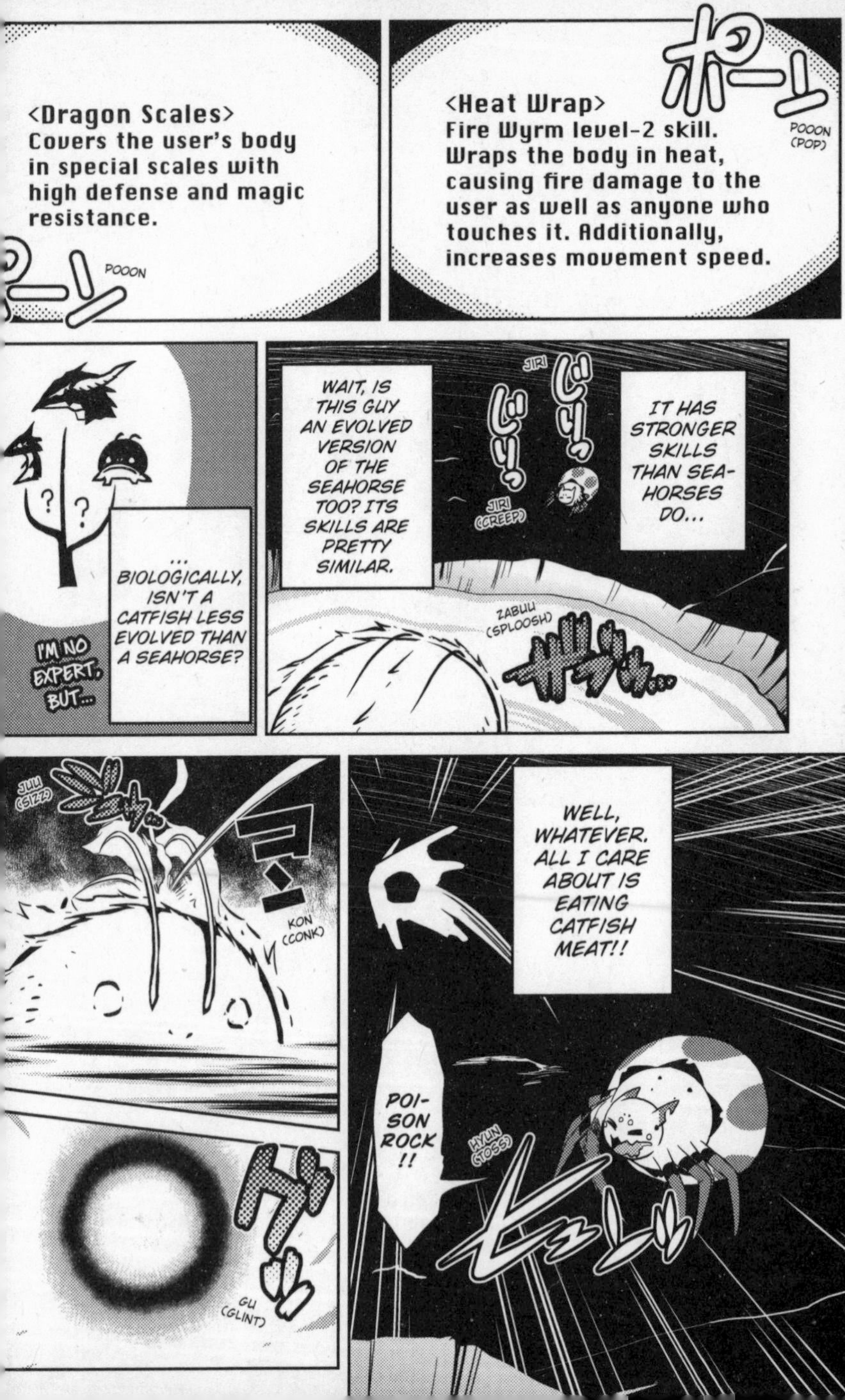

<Heat Wrap>
Fire Wyrm level-2 skill. Wraps the body in heat, causing fire damage to the user as well as anyone who touches it. Additionally, increases movement speed.
POOON (POP)
<Dragon Scales>
Covers the user's body in special scales with high defense and magic resistance.
POOON
IT HAS STRONGER SKILLS THAN SEA-HORSES DO...
JIRI
JIRI (CREEP)
WAIT, IS THIS GUY AN EVOLVED VERSION OF THE SEAHORSE TOO? ITS SKILLS ARE PRETTY SIMILAR.
ZABUU (SPLOOSH)
...BIOLOGICALLY, ISN'T A CATFISH LESS EVOLVED THAN A SEAHORSE?
I'M NO EXPERT, BUT...
WELL, WHATEVER. ALL I CARE ABOUT IS EATING CATFISH MEAT!!
POI-SON ROCK!!
HYUN (TOSS)
JUU (SIZZ)
KON (CONK)
GU (GLINT)

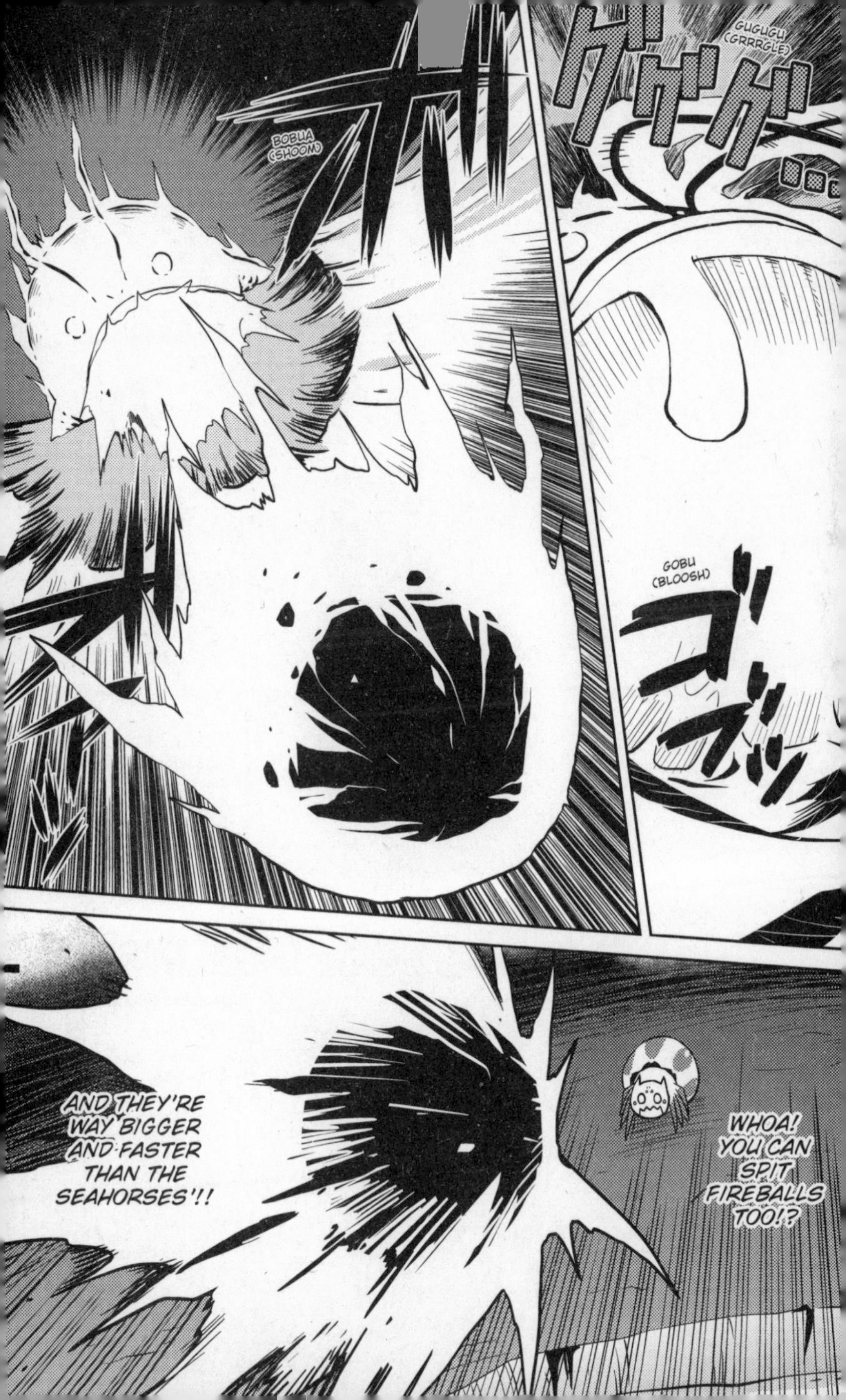
GUGUGU (GRRRGLE)
GOBU (BLOOSH)
BOBUA (SHOOM)
WHOA! YOU CAN SPIT FIREBALLS TOO!?
AND THEY'RE WAY BIGGER AND FASTER THAN THE SEAHORSES'!!

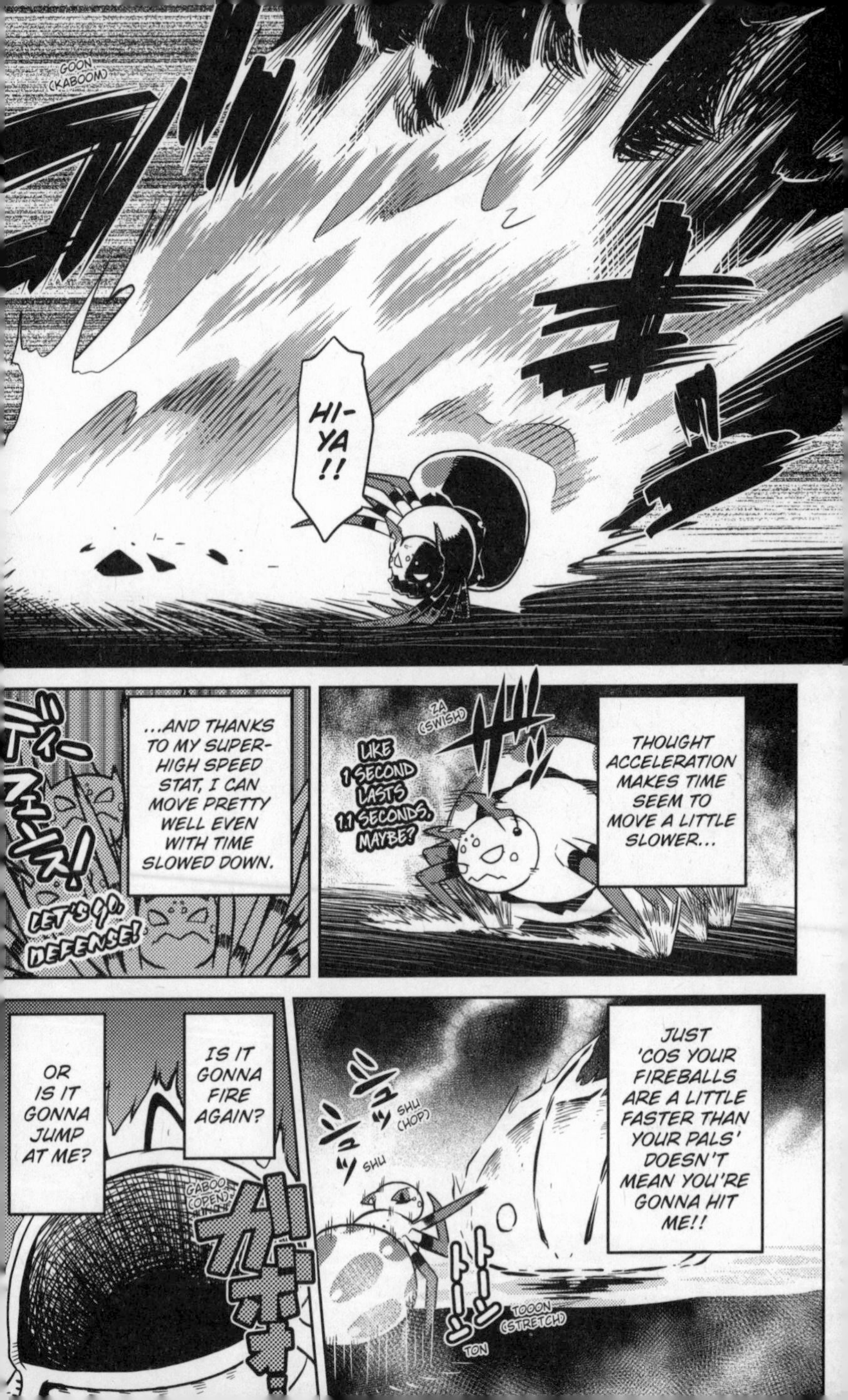
GOON (KABOOM)
HI-YA!!
ZA (SWISH)
THOUGHT ACCELERATION MAKES TIME SEEM TO MOVE A LITTLE SLOWER...
LIKE 1 SECOND LASTS 1.1 SECONDS, MAYBE?
...AND THANKS TO MY SUPER-HIGH SPEED STAT, I CAN MOVE PRETTY WELL EVEN WITH TIME SLOWED DOWN.
LET'S GO, DEFENSE!
JUST 'COS YOUR FIREBALLS ARE A LITTLE FASTER THAN YOUR PALS' DOESN'T MEAN YOU'RE GONNA HIT ME!!
SHU (HOP)
SHU
TOOON (STRETCH)
TON
IS IT GONNA FIRE AGAIN?
OR IS IT GONNA JUMP AT ME?
GABOO (OPEN)

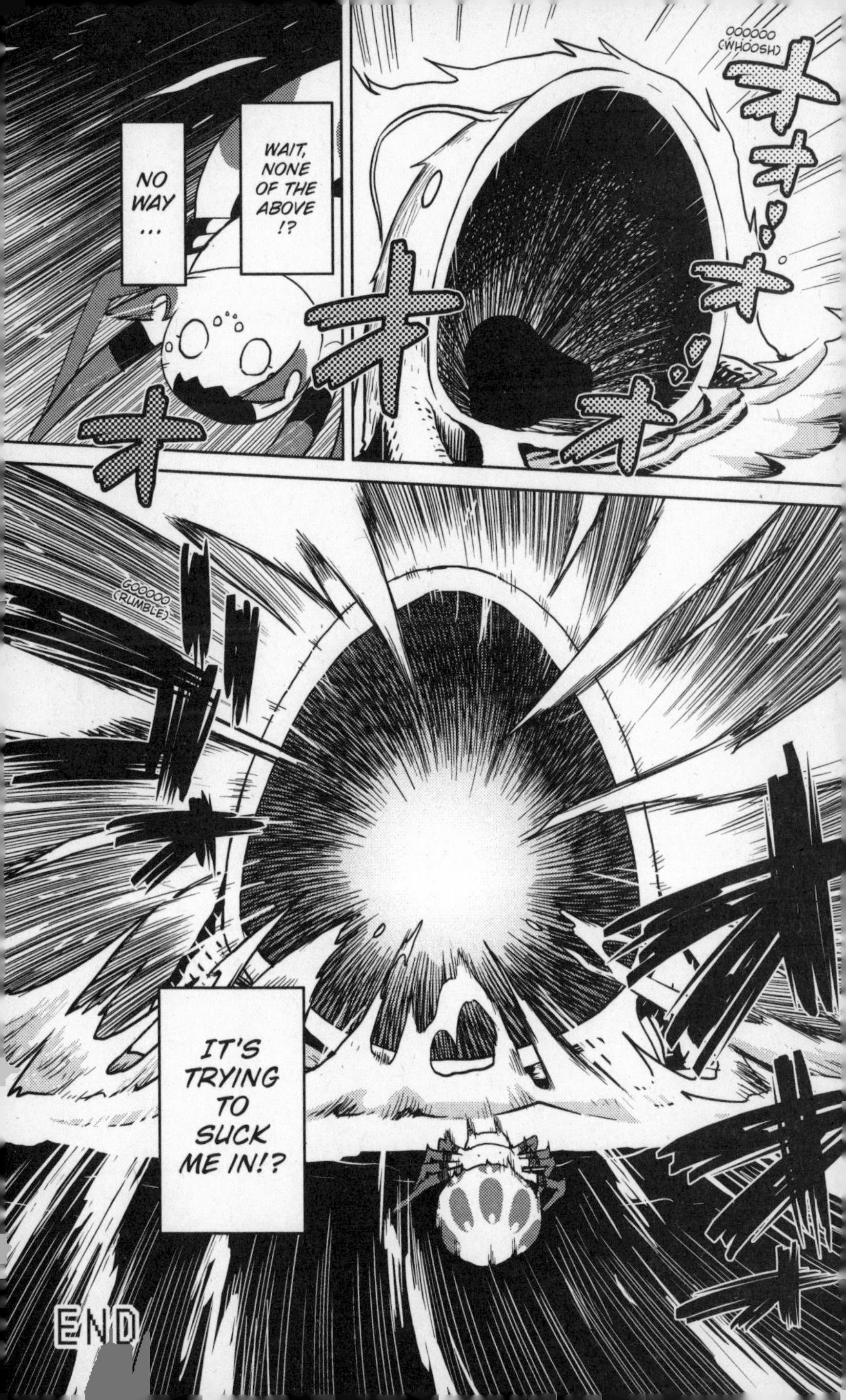
OOOOOO
(WHOOSH)
WAIT, NONE OF THE ABOVE !?
NO WAY ...
GOOOOO
(RUMBLE)
IT'S TRYING TO SUCK ME IN!?
END

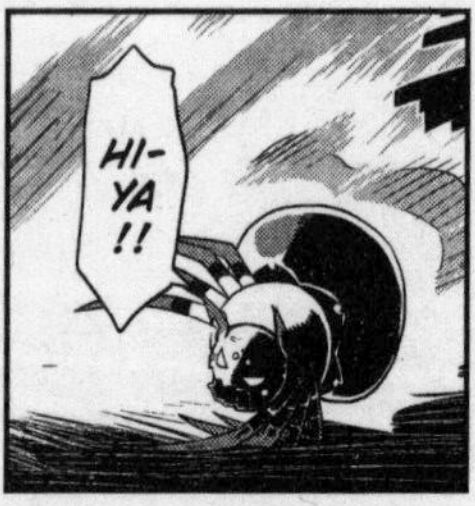
HI-YA!!

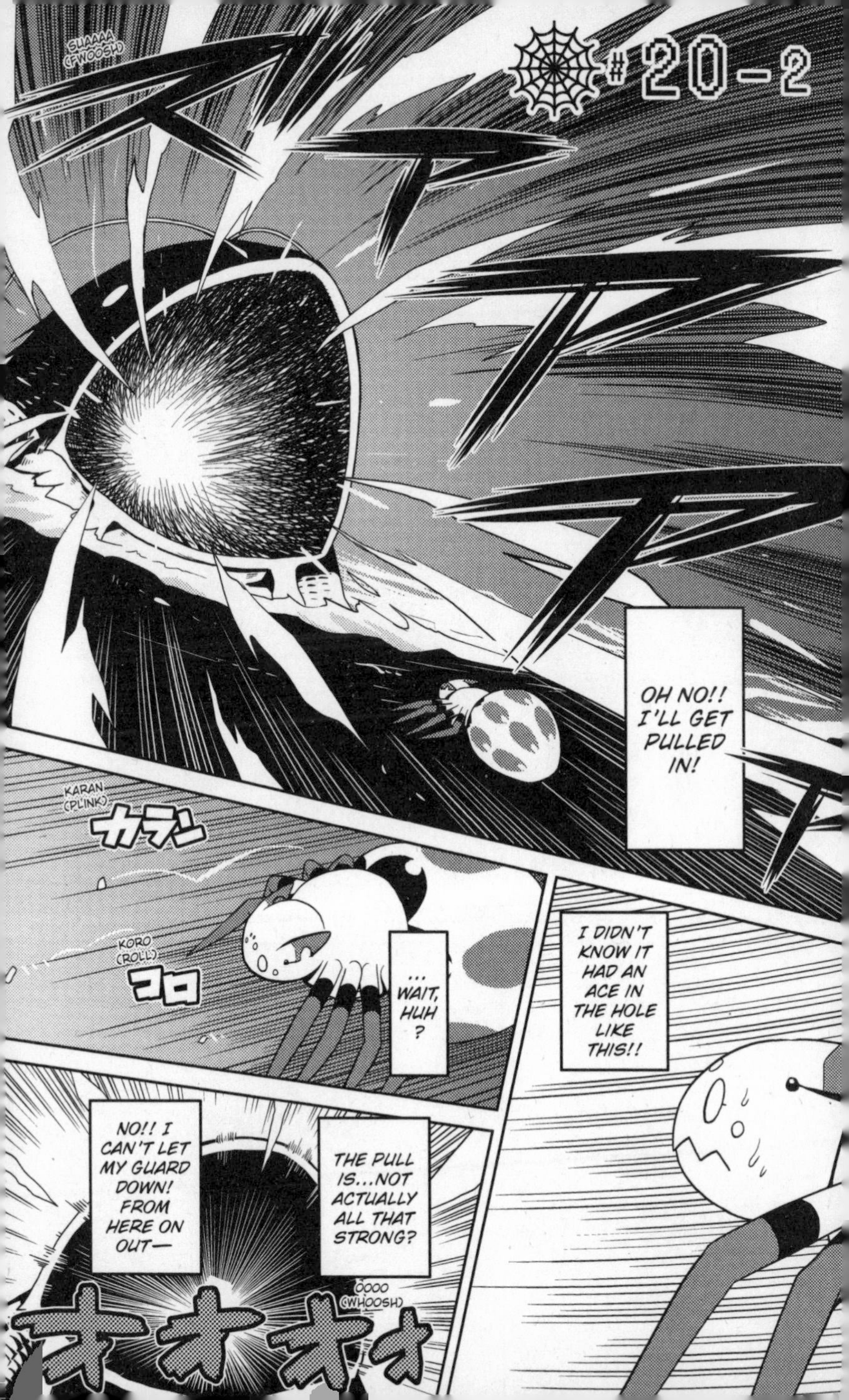
#20-2
OH NO!! I'LL GET PULLED IN!
SUAAAA (FWOOSH)
I DIDN'T KNOW IT HAD AN ACE IN THE HOLE LIKE THIS!!
KARAN (PLINK) カラン
...WAIT, HUH?
KORO (ROLL) コロ
THE PULL IS...NOT ACTUALLY ALL THAT STRONG?
NO!! I CAN'T LET MY GUARD DOWN! FROM HERE ON OUT—
OOOO (WHOOSH) オオオオ

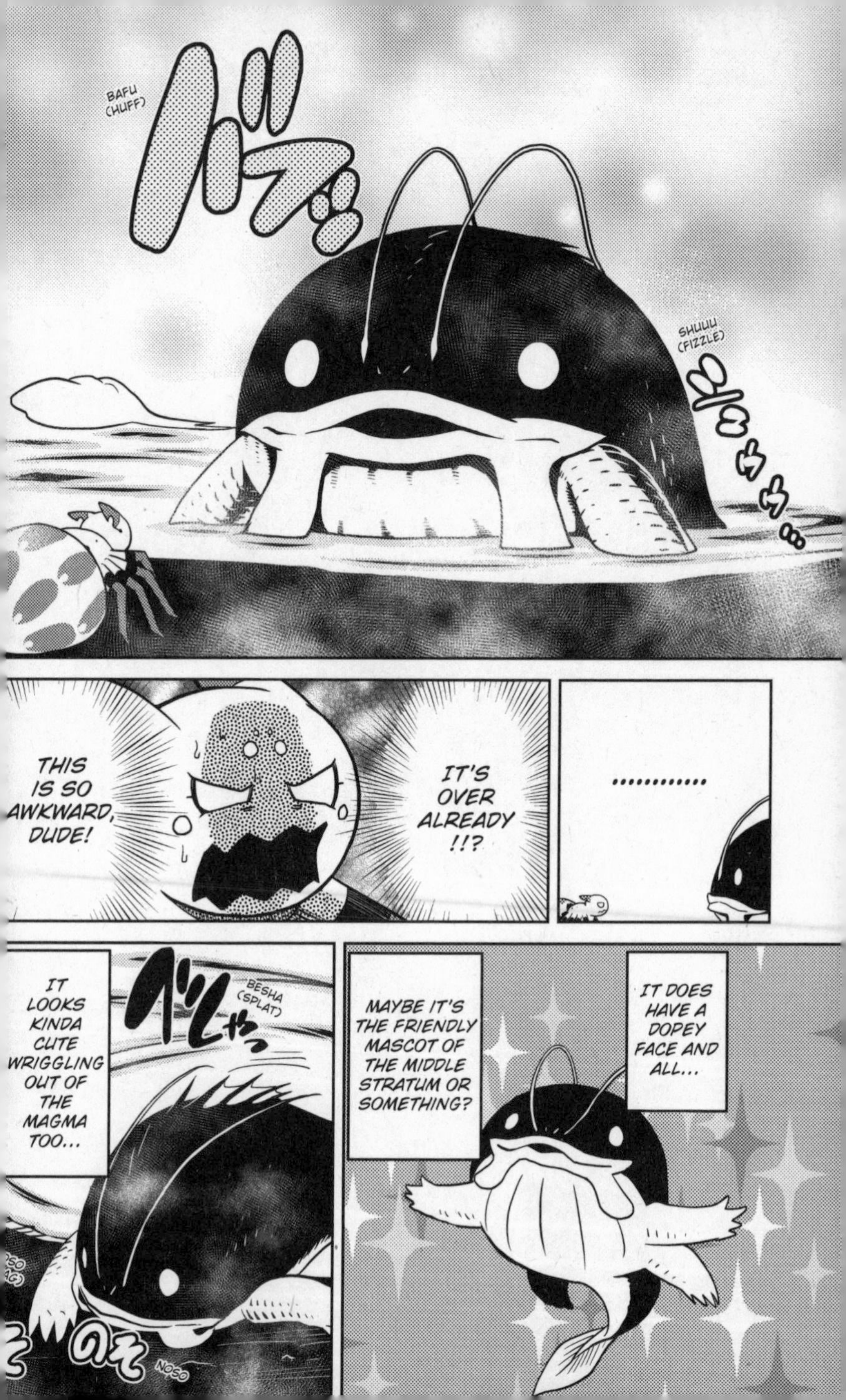
BAFU (HUFF)
SHUUU (FIZZLE)
....
IT'S OVER ALREADY !!?
THIS IS SO AWKWARD, DUDE!
IT DOES HAVE A DOPEY FACE AND ALL...
MAYBE IT'S THE FRIENDLY MASCOT OF THE MIDDLE STRATUM OR SOMETHING?
BESHA (SPLAT)
IT LOOKS KINDA CUTE WRIGGLING OUT OF THE MAGMA TOO...
NOSO

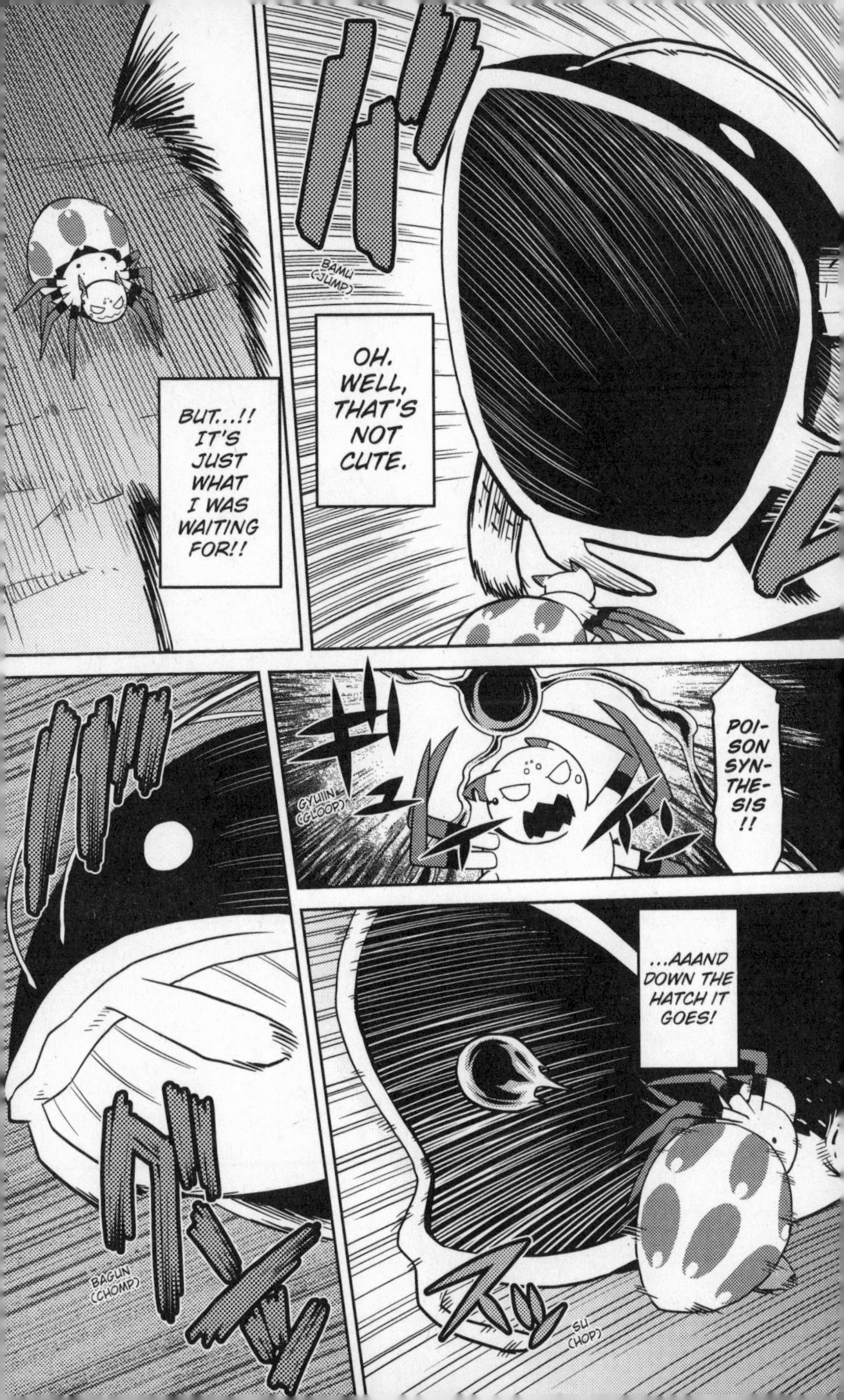
BAMU (JUMP)
OH. WELL, THAT'S NOT CUTE.
BUT...!! IT'S JUST WHAT I WAS WAITING FOR!!
POI-SON SYN-THE-SIS!!
GYUIIN (GLOOP)
...AAAND DOWN THE HATCH IT GOES!
SU (HOP)
BAGUN (CHOMP)

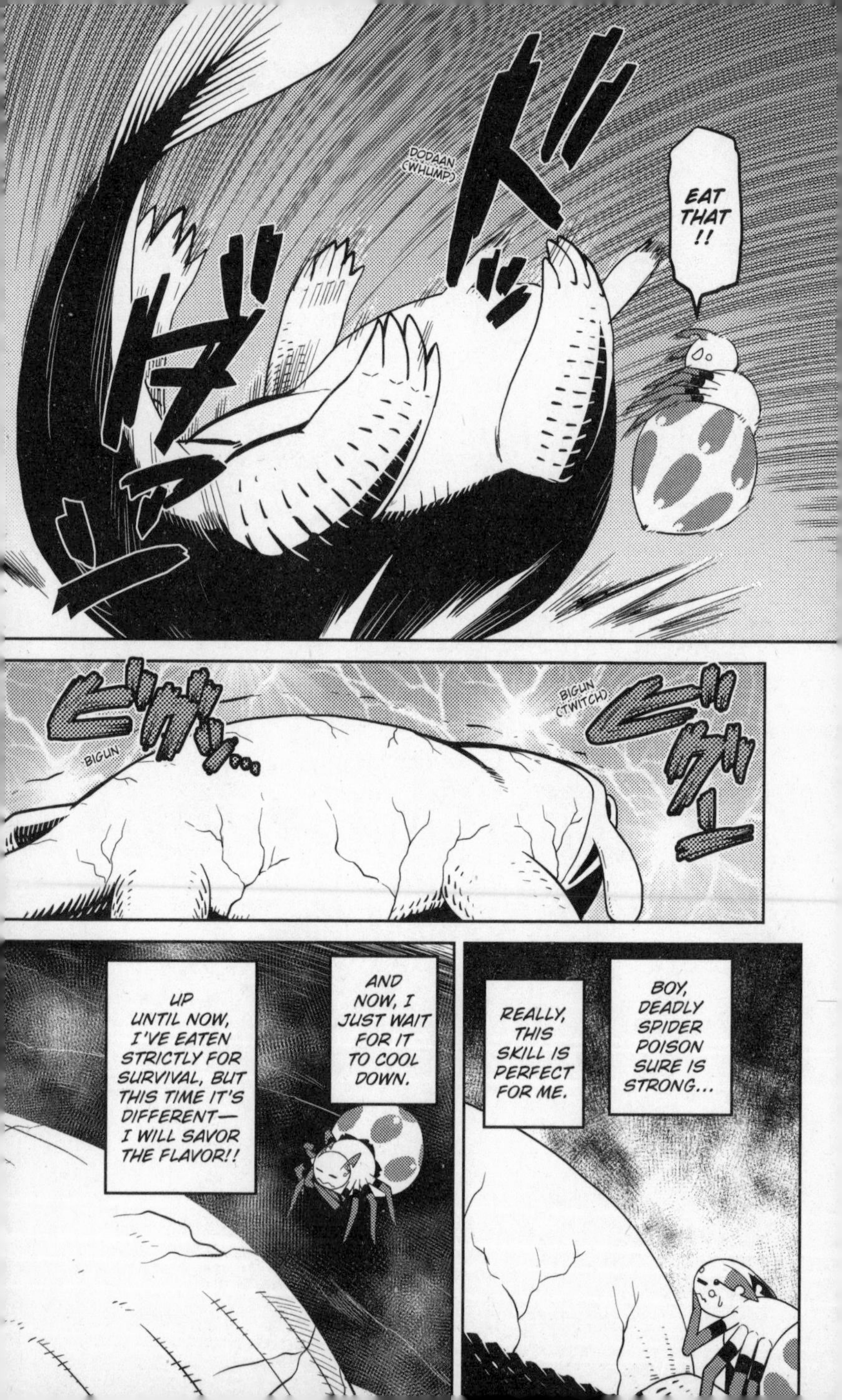
DODAAN (WHUMP)
EAT THAT!!
BIGUN (TWITCH)
BIGUN
BOY, DEADLY SPIDER POISON SURE IS STRONG...
REALLY, THIS SKILL IS PERFECT FOR ME.
AND NOW, I JUST WAIT FOR IT TO COOL DOWN.
UP UNTIL NOW, I'VE EATEN STRICTLY FOR SURVIVAL, BUT THIS TIME IT'S DIFFERENT— I WILL SAVOR THE FLAVOR!!

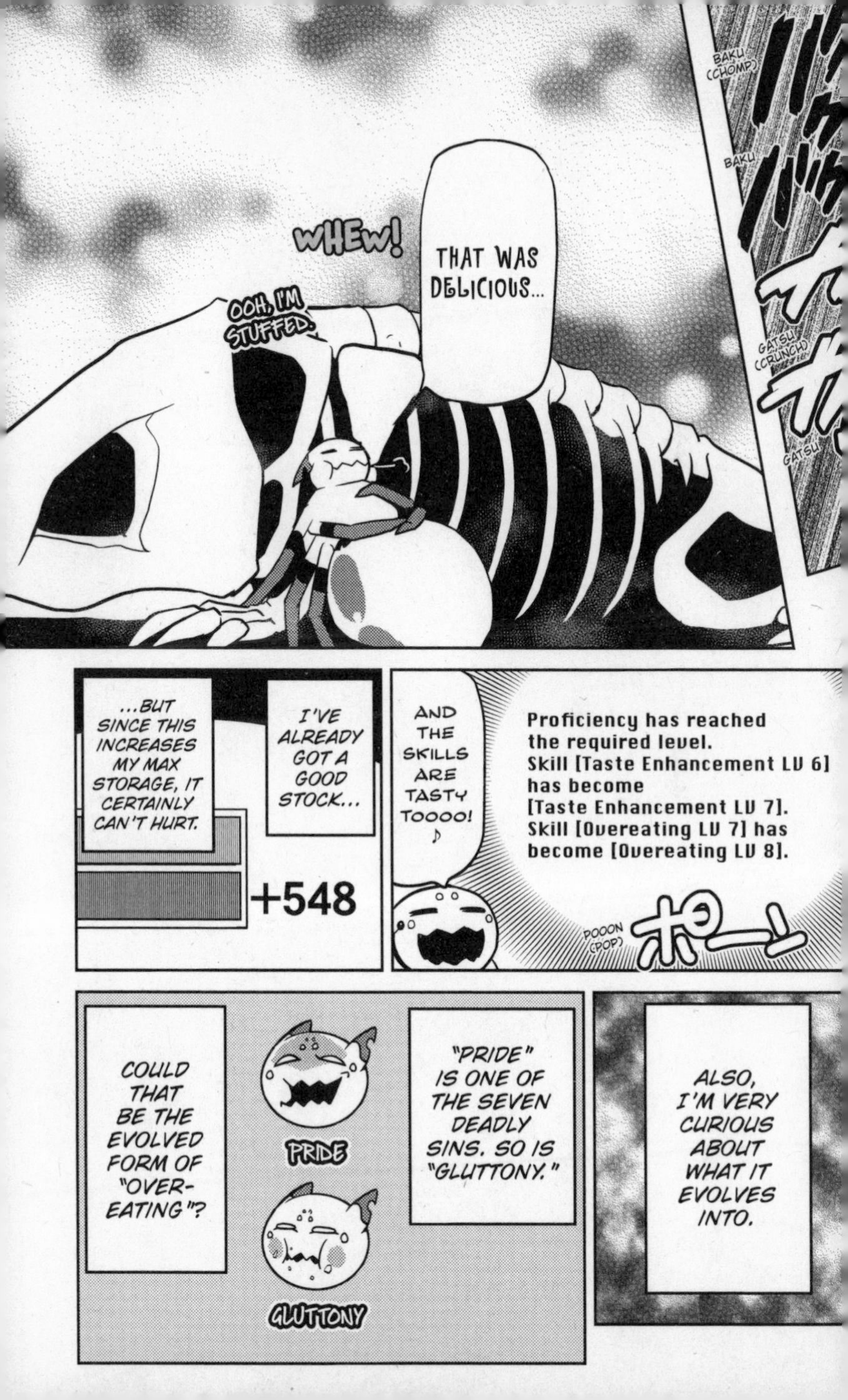
BAKU (CHOMP)
BAKU
GATSU (CRUNCH)
GATSU
THAT WAS DELICIOUS...
WHEW!
OOH, I'M STUFFED.
Proficiency has reached the required level.
Skill [Taste Enhancement LV 6] has become [Taste Enhancement LV 7].
Skill [Overeating LV 7] has become [Overeating LV 8].
AND THE SKILLS ARE TASTY TOOOO! ♪
POOON (POP)
I'VE ALREADY GOT A GOOD STOCK...
...BUT SINCE THIS INCREASES MY MAX STORAGE, IT CERTAINLY CAN'T HURT.
+548
ALSO, I'M VERY CURIOUS ABOUT WHAT IT EVOLVES INTO.
"PRIDE" IS ONE OF THE SEVEN DEADLY SINS. SO IS "GLUTTONY."
PRIDE
GLUTTONY
COULD THAT BE THE EVOLVED FORM OF "OVER-EATING"?

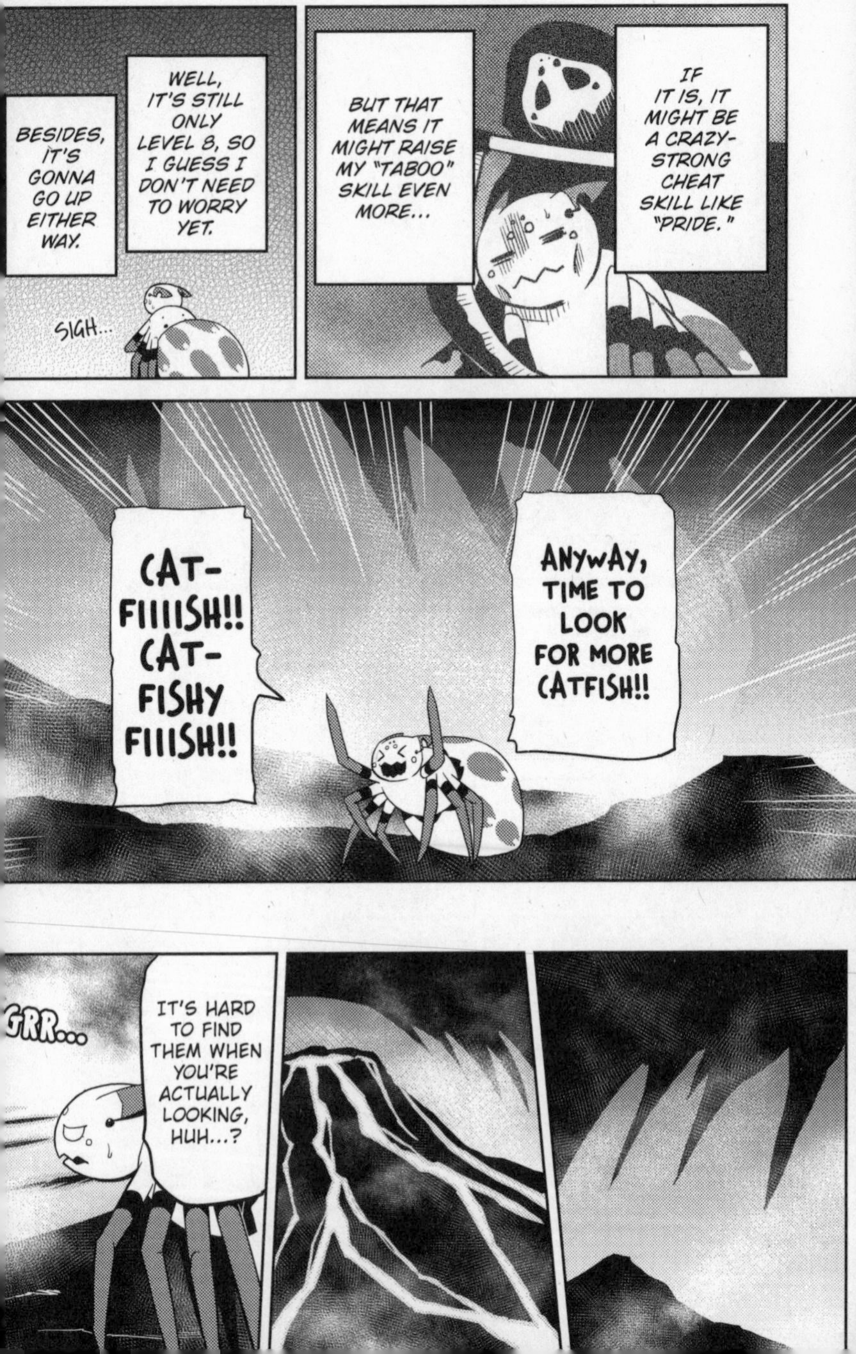
IF IT IS, IT MIGHT BE A CRAZY-STRONG CHEAT SKILL LIKE "PRIDE."
BUT THAT MEANS IT MIGHT RAISE MY "TABOO" SKILL EVEN MORE...
WELL, IT'S STILL ONLY LEVEL 8, SO I GUESS I DON'T NEED TO WORRY YET.
BESIDES, IT'S GONNA GO UP EITHER WAY.
SIGH...
ANYWAY, TIME TO LOOK FOR MORE CATFISH!!
CAT-FIIIISH!! CAT-FISHY FIIISH!!
IT'S HARD TO FIND THEM WHEN YOU'RE ACTUALLY LOOKING, HUH...?
GRR...

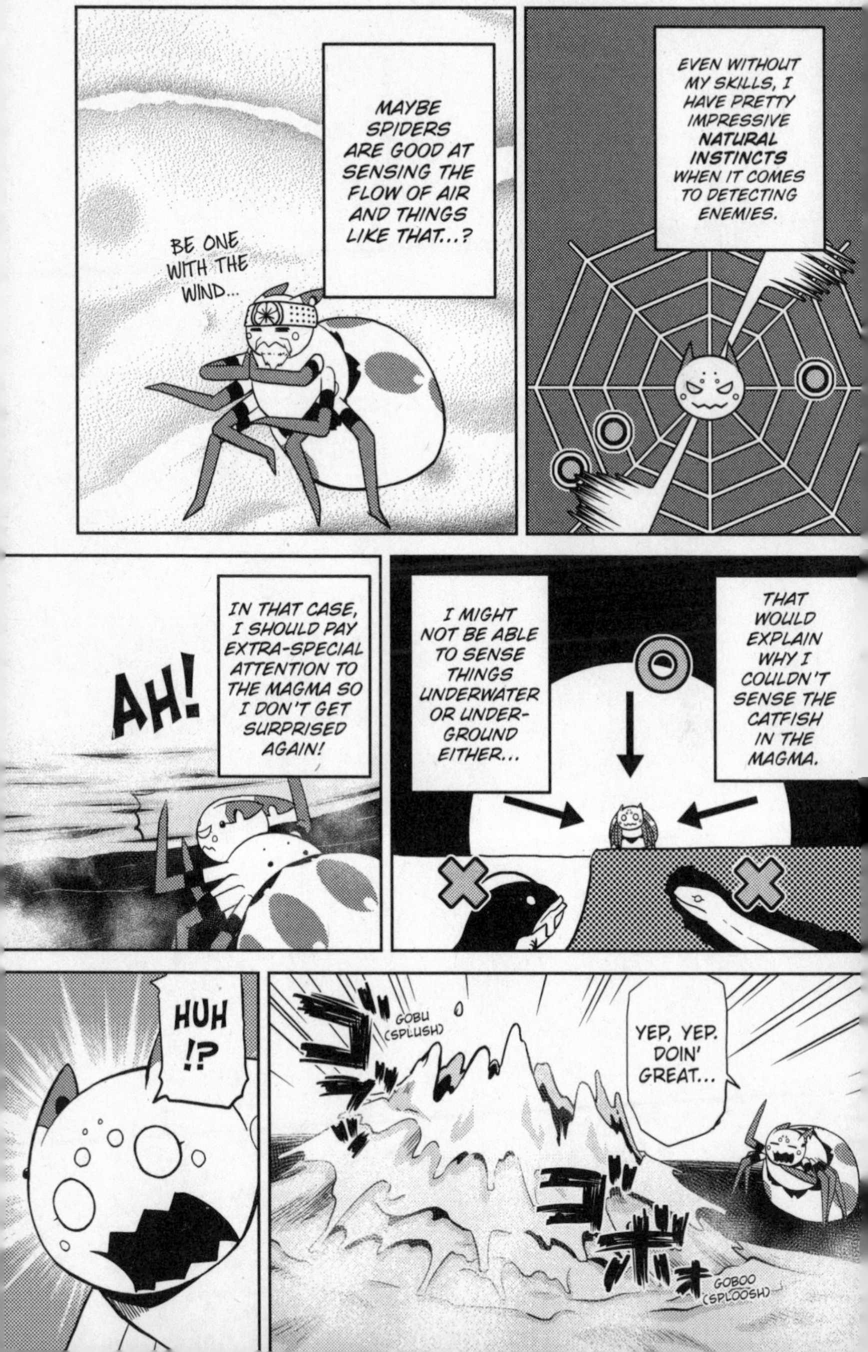
EVEN WITHOUT MY SKILLS, I HAVE PRETTY IMPRESSIVE **NATURAL INSTINCTS** WHEN IT COMES TO DETECTING ENEMIES.
MAYBE SPIDERS ARE GOOD AT SENSING THE FLOW OF AIR AND THINGS LIKE THAT...?
BE ONE WITH THE WIND...
THAT WOULD EXPLAIN WHY I COULDN'T SENSE THE CATFISH IN THE MAGMA.
I MIGHT NOT BE ABLE TO SENSE THINGS UNDERWATER OR UNDER-GROUND EITHER...
IN THAT CASE, I SHOULD PAY EXTRA-SPECIAL ATTENTION TO THE MAGMA SO I DON'T GET SURPRISED AGAIN!
AH!
YEP, YEP. DOIN' GREAT...
GOBU (SPLUSH)
GOBOO (SPLOOSH)
HUH !?

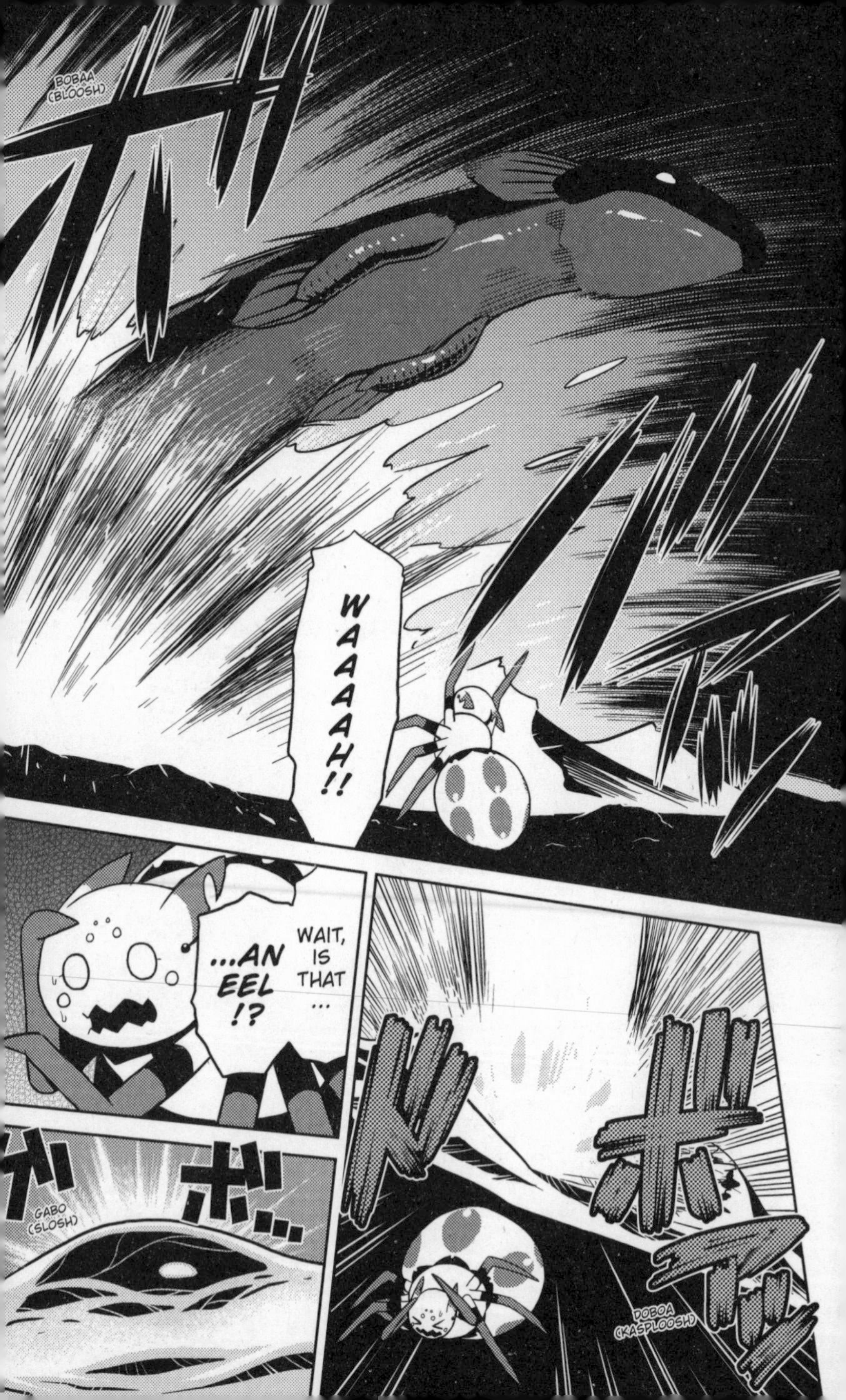
BOBAA (BLOOSH)
WAAAAAH!!
DOBOA (KASPLOOSH)
WAIT, IS THAT ...
...AN EEL !?
GABO (SLOSH)

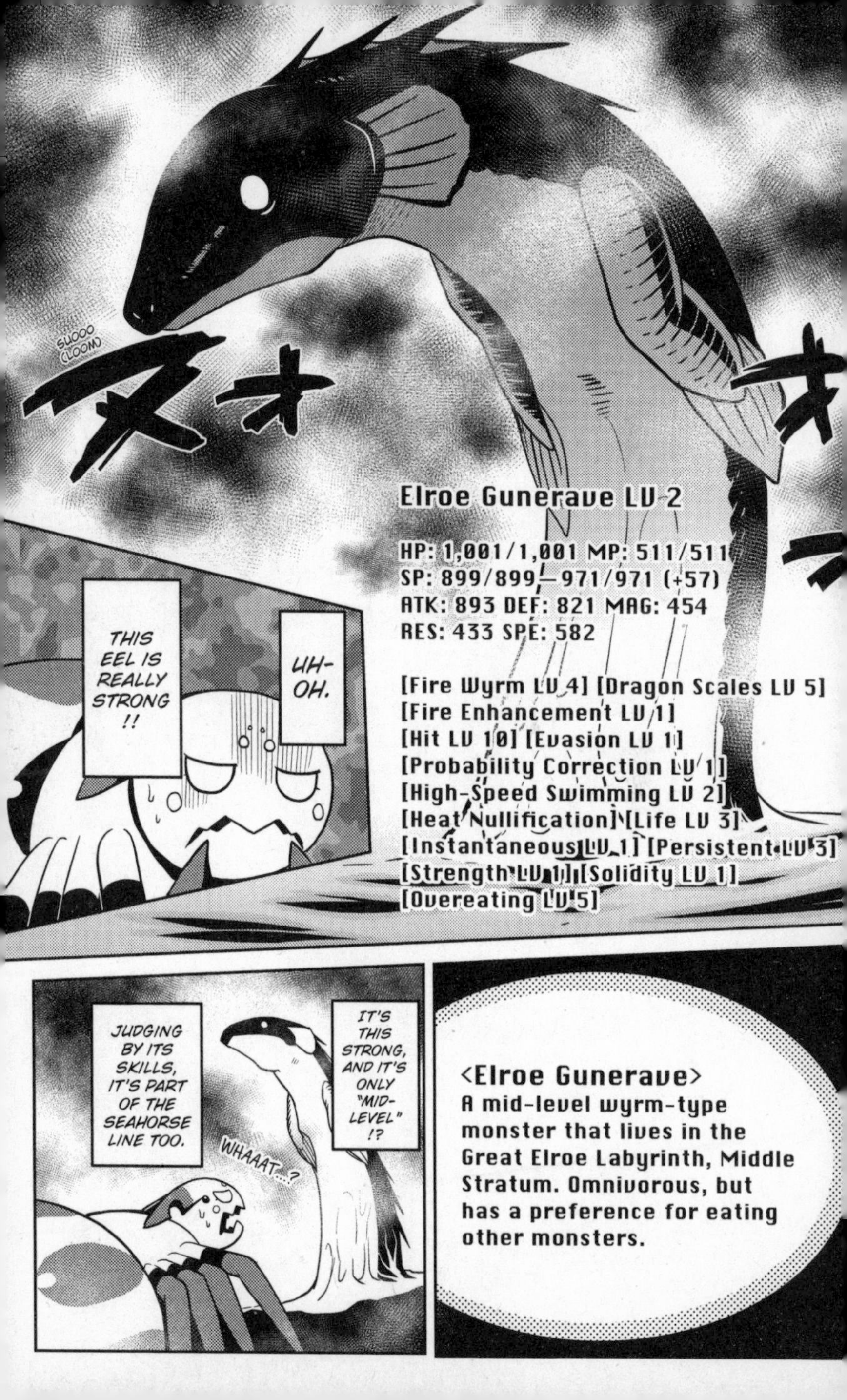
SWOOO (LOOM)
Elroe Gunerave LV 2
HP: 1,001/1,001 MP: 511/511
SP: 899/899 — 971/971 (+57)
ATK: 893 DEF: 821 MAG: 454
RES: 433 SPE: 582
[Fire Wyrm LV 4] [Dragon Scales LV 5]
[Fire Enhancement LV 1]
[Hit LV 10] [Evasion LV 1]
[Probability Correction LV 1]
[High-Speed Swimming LV 2]
[Heat Nullification] [Life LV 3]
[Instantaneous LV 1] [Persistent LV 3]
[Strength LV 1] [Solidity LV 1]
[Overeating LV 5]
UH-OH.
THIS EEL IS REALLY STRONG!!
<Elroe Gunerave>
A mid-level wyrm-type monster that lives in the Great Elroe Labyrinth, Middle Stratum. Omnivorous, but has a preference for eating other monsters.
IT'S THIS STRONG, AND IT'S ONLY "MID-LEVEL"!?
JUDGING BY ITS SKILLS, IT'S PART OF THE SEAHORSE LINE TOO.
WHAAAT...?

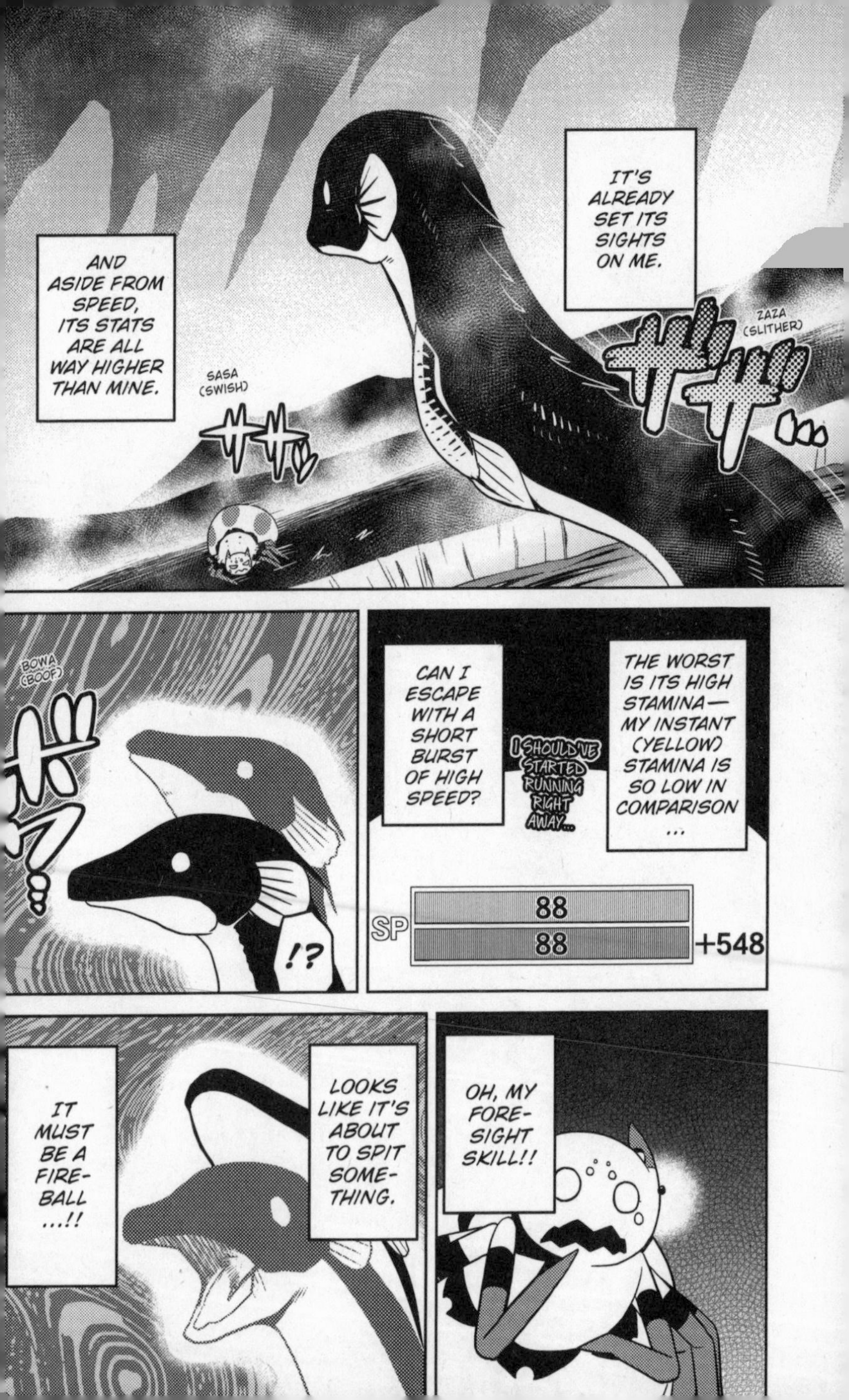
IT'S ALREADY SET ITS SIGHTS ON ME.
ZAZA (SLITHER)
SASA (SWISH)
AND ASIDE FROM SPEED, ITS STATS ARE ALL WAY HIGHER THAN MINE.
THE WORST IS ITS HIGH STAMINA— MY INSTANT (YELLOW) STAMINA IS SO LOW IN COMPARISON ...
I SHOULD'VE STARTED RUNNING RIGHT AWAY...
CAN I ESCAPE WITH A SHORT BURST OF HIGH SPEED?
SP
88
88
+548
BOWA (BOOF)
!?
OH, MY FORE-SIGHT SKILL!!
LOOKS LIKE IT'S ABOUT TO SPIT SOME-THING.
IT MUST BE A FIRE-BALL ...!!

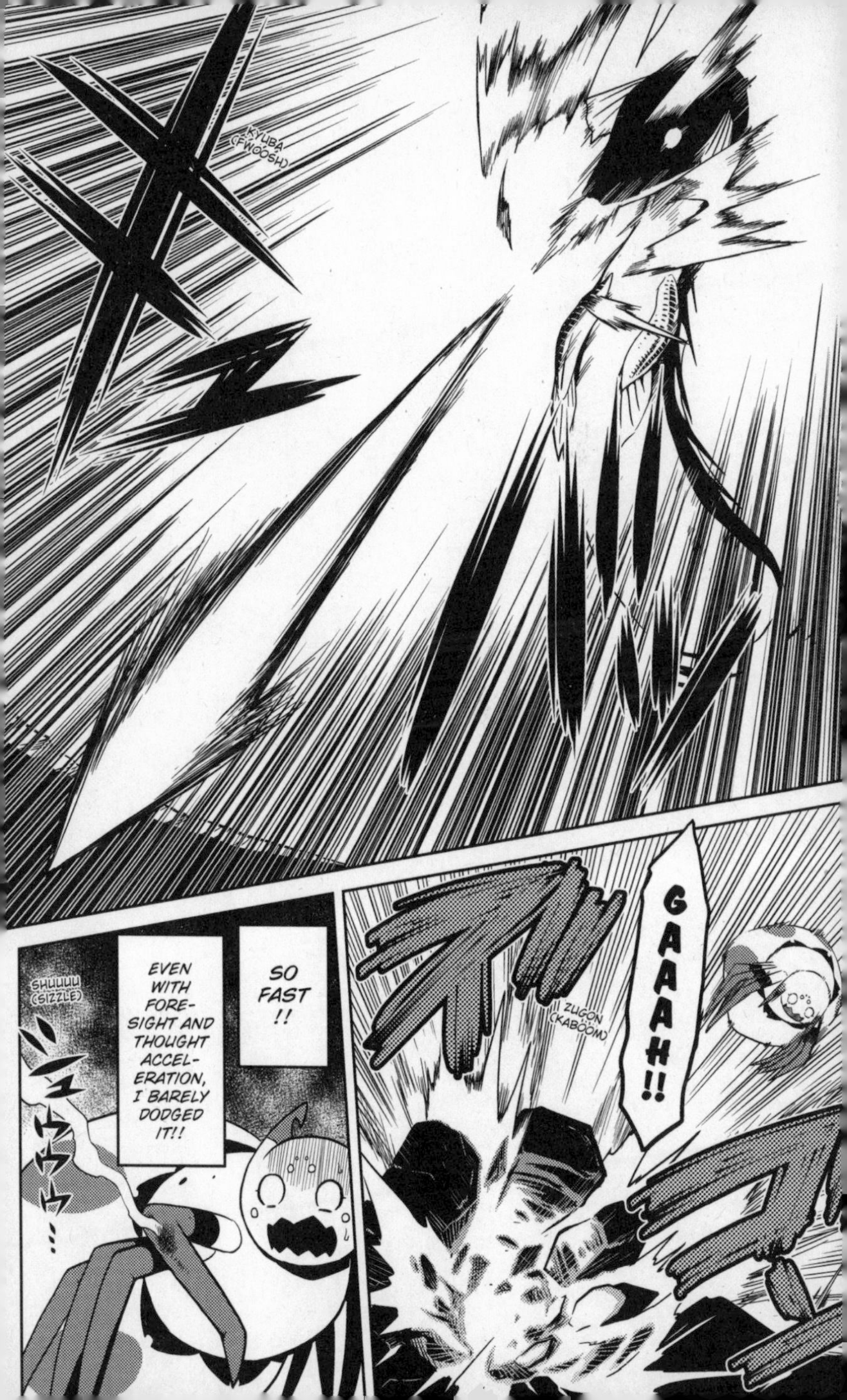
KYUBA (FWOOSH)
GAAAAH!!
ZUGON (KABOOM)
SO FAST!!
EVEN WITH FORE-SIGHT AND THOUGHT ACCEL-ERATION, I BARELY DODGED IT!!
SHUUUU (SIZZLE)

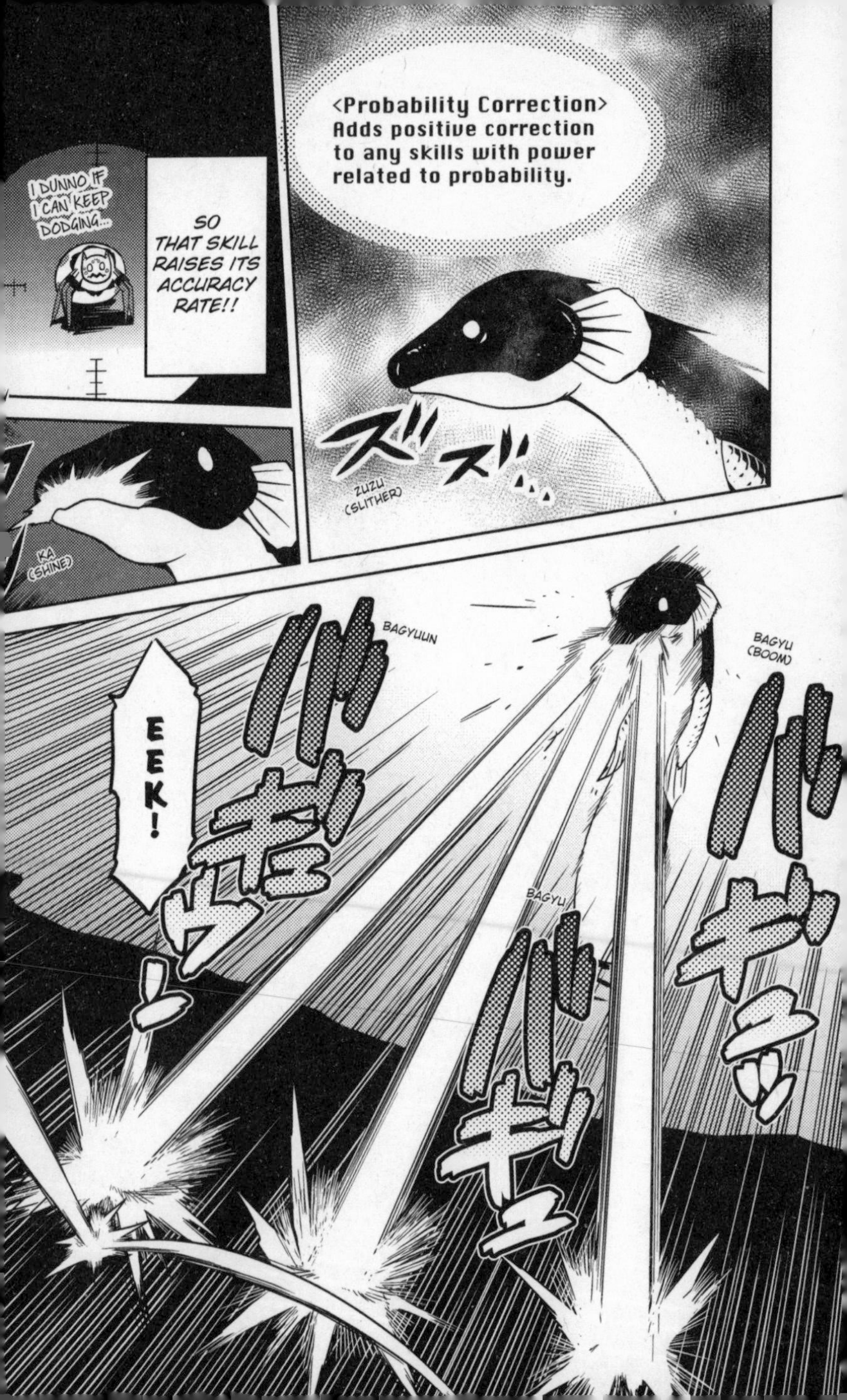
<Probability Correction> Adds positive correction to any skills with power related to probability.
ZUZU (SLITHER)
SO THAT SKILL RAISES ITS ACCURACY RATE!!
I DUNNO IF I CAN KEEP DODGING...
KA (SHINE)
BAGYU (BOOM)
BAGYU
BAGYUUN
EEK!

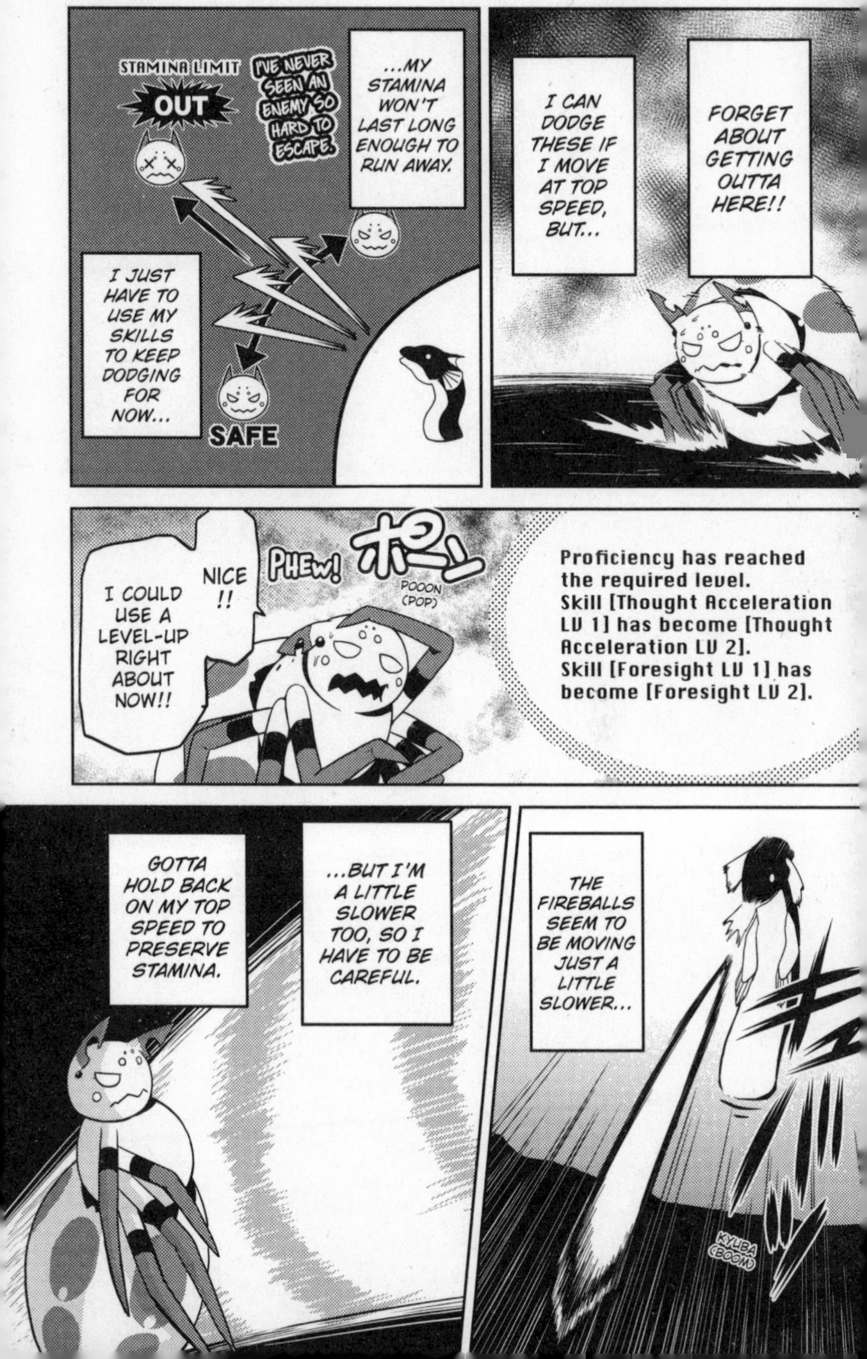
FORGET ABOUT GETTING OUTTA HERE!!
I CAN DODGE THESE IF I MOVE AT TOP SPEED, BUT...
...MY STAMINA WON'T LAST LONG ENOUGH TO RUN AWAY.
I'VE NEVER SEEN AN ENEMY SO HARD TO ESCAPE.
STAMINA LIMIT
OUT
SAFE
I JUST HAVE TO USE MY SKILLS TO KEEP DODGING FOR NOW...
Proficiency has reached the required level. Skill [Thought Acceleration LV 1] has become [Thought Acceleration LV 2]. Skill [Foresight LV 1] has become [Foresight LV 2].
ポーン
POOON (POP)
PHEW!
NICE!!
I COULD USE A LEVEL-UP RIGHT ABOUT NOW!!
THE FIREBALLS SEEM TO BE MOVING JUST A LITTLE SLOWER...
KYUBA (BOOM)
...BUT I'M A LITTLE SLOWER TOO, SO I HAVE TO BE CAREFUL.
GOTTA HOLD BACK ON MY TOP SPEED TO PRESERVE STAMINA.

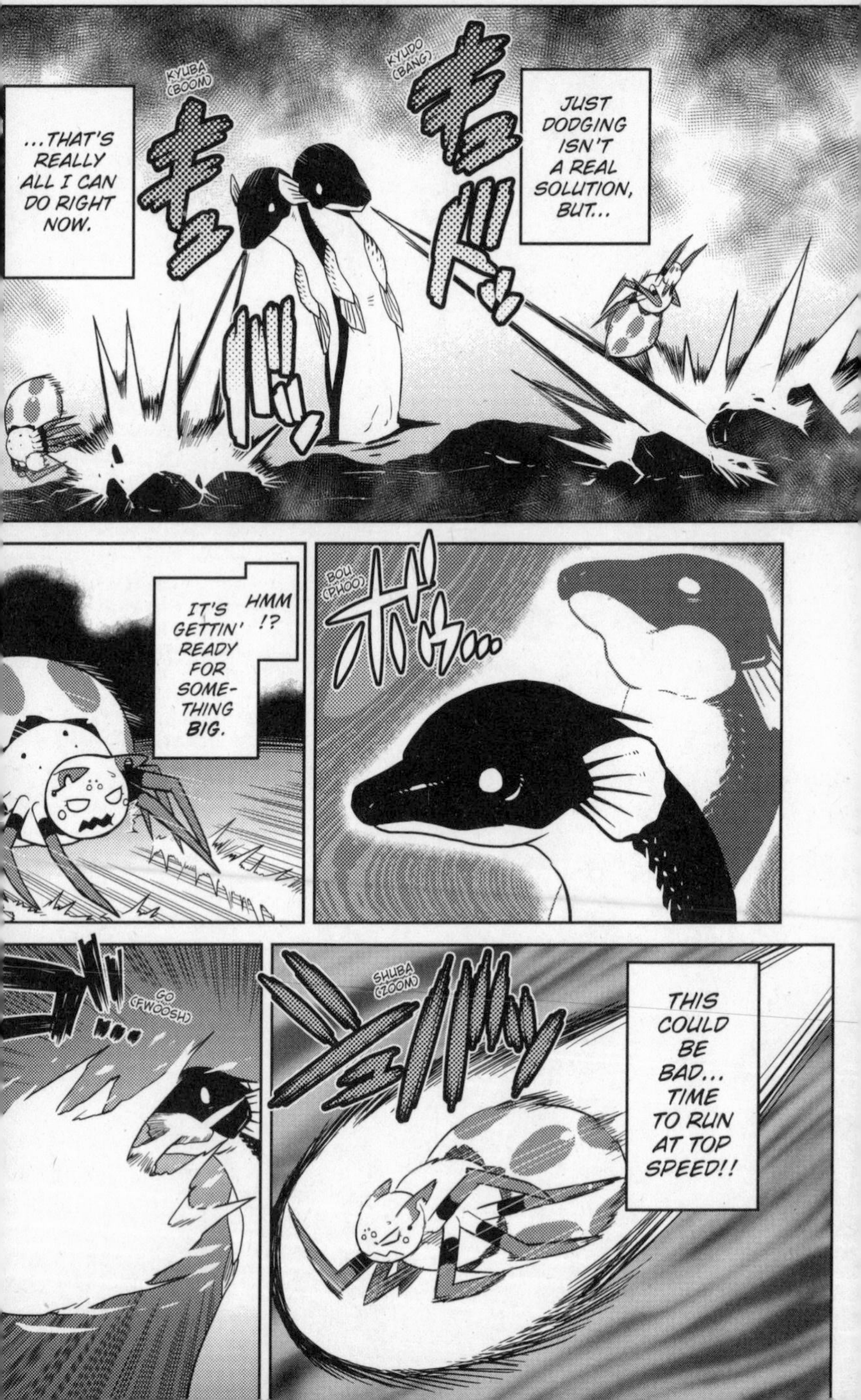
JUST DODGING ISN'T A REAL SOLUTION, BUT...
KYUDO (BANG)
KYUBA (BOOM)
...THAT'S REALLY ALL I CAN DO RIGHT NOW.
BOU (PHOO)
HMM!?
IT'S GETTIN' READY FOR SOMETHING BIG.
THIS COULD BE BAD... TIME TO RUN AT TOP SPEED!!
SHUBA (ZOOM)
GO (FWOOSH)

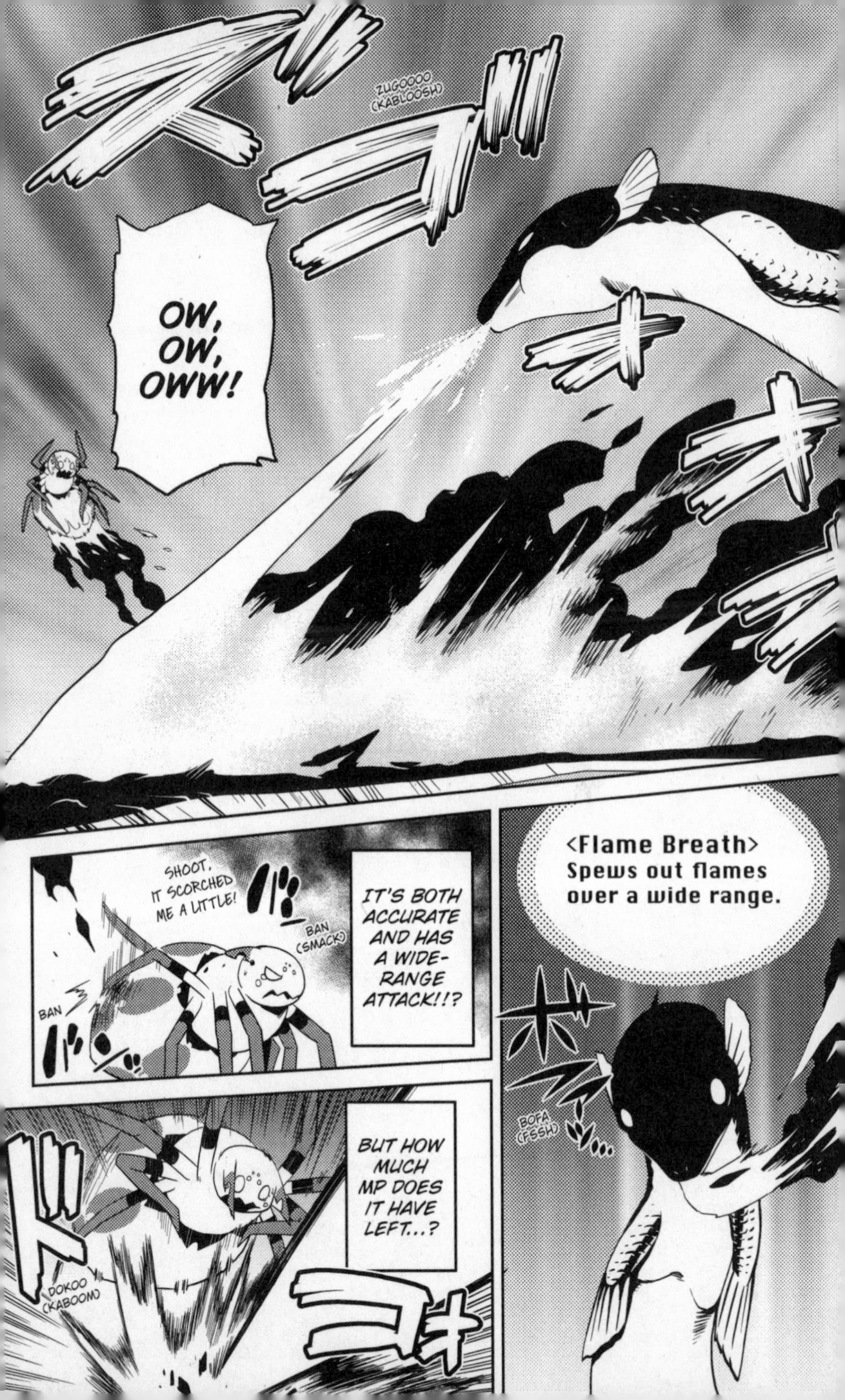
ZUGOOOO (KABLOOSH)
OW, OW, OWW!
<Flame Breath> Spews out flames over a wide range.
BOFA (FSSH)
IT'S BOTH ACCURATE AND HAS A WIDE-RANGE ATTACK!!?
SHOOT, IT SCORCHED ME A LITTLE!
BAN (SMACK)
BAN
BUT HOW MUCH MP DOES IT HAVE LEFT...?
DOKOO (KABOOM)

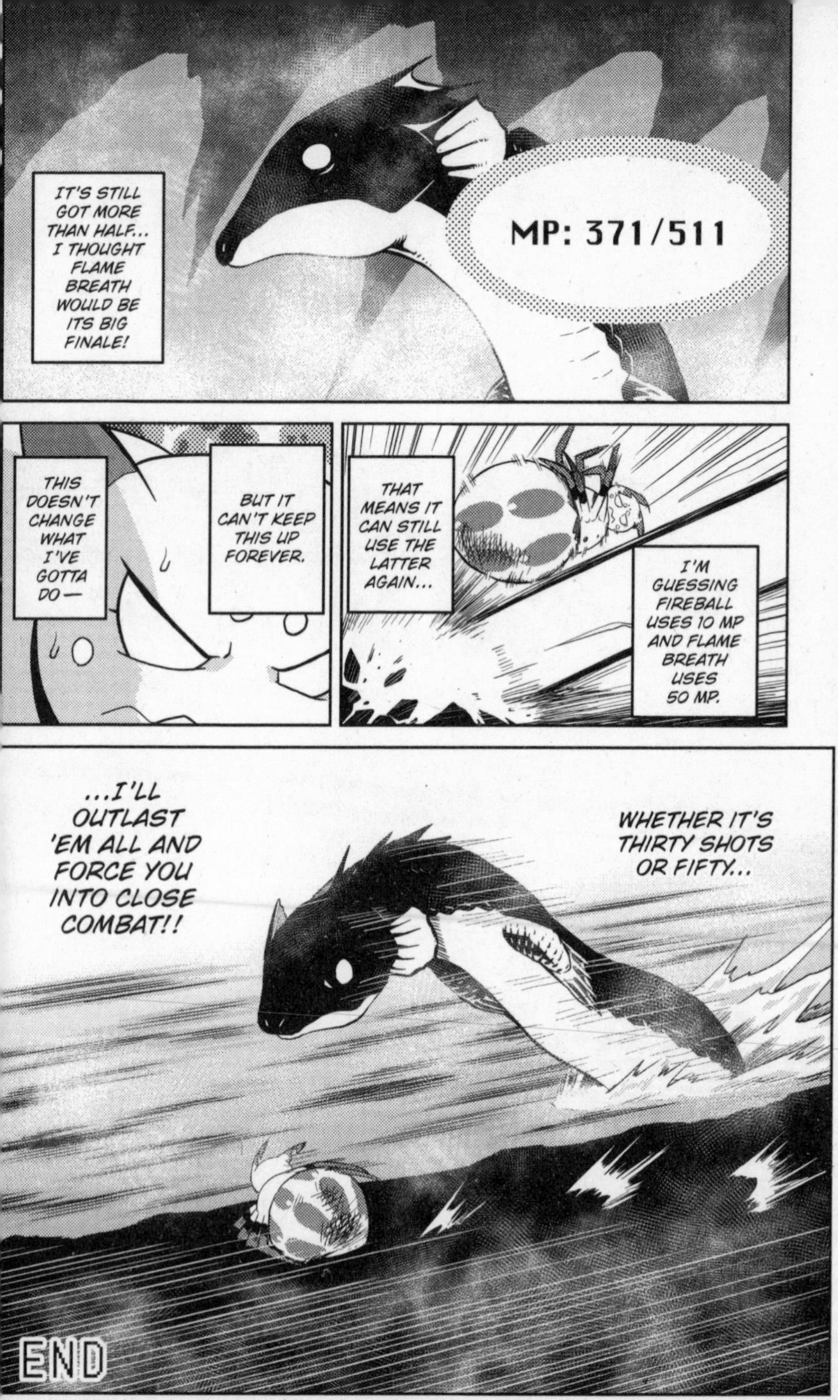
MP: 371/511
IT'S STILL GOT MORE THAN HALF... I THOUGHT FLAME BREATH WOULD BE ITS BIG FINALE!
I'M GUESSING FIREBALL USES 10 MP AND FLAME BREATH USES 50 MP.
THAT MEANS IT CAN STILL USE THE LATTER AGAIN...
BUT IT CAN'T KEEP THIS UP FOREVER.
THIS DOESN'T CHANGE WHAT I'VE GOTTA DO—
WHETHER IT'S THIRTY SHOTS OR FIFTY...
...I'LL OUTLAST 'EM ALL AND FORCE YOU INTO CLOSE COMBAT!!
END

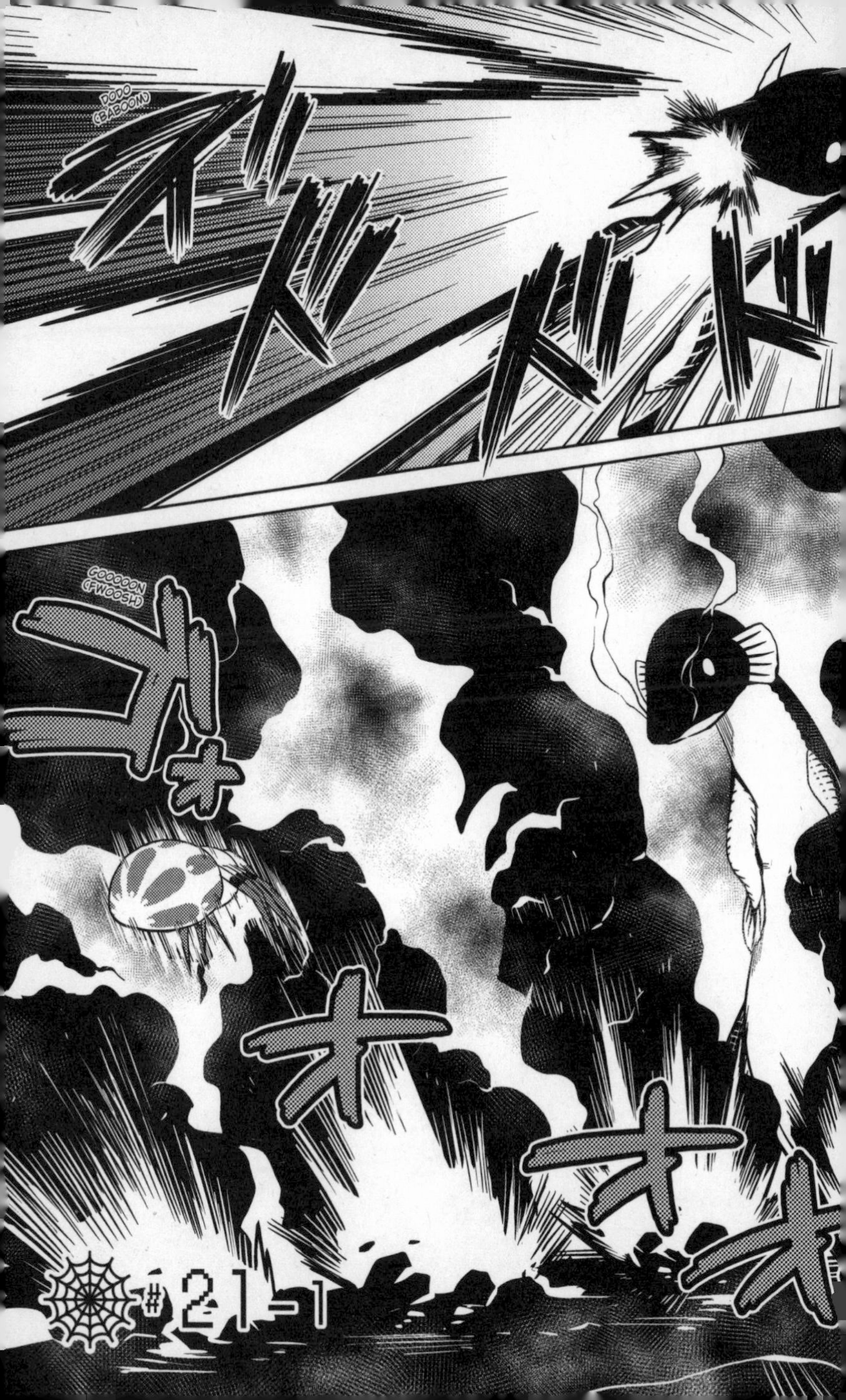
DODO (BABOOM)
GOOOOON (FWOOSH)
#21-1

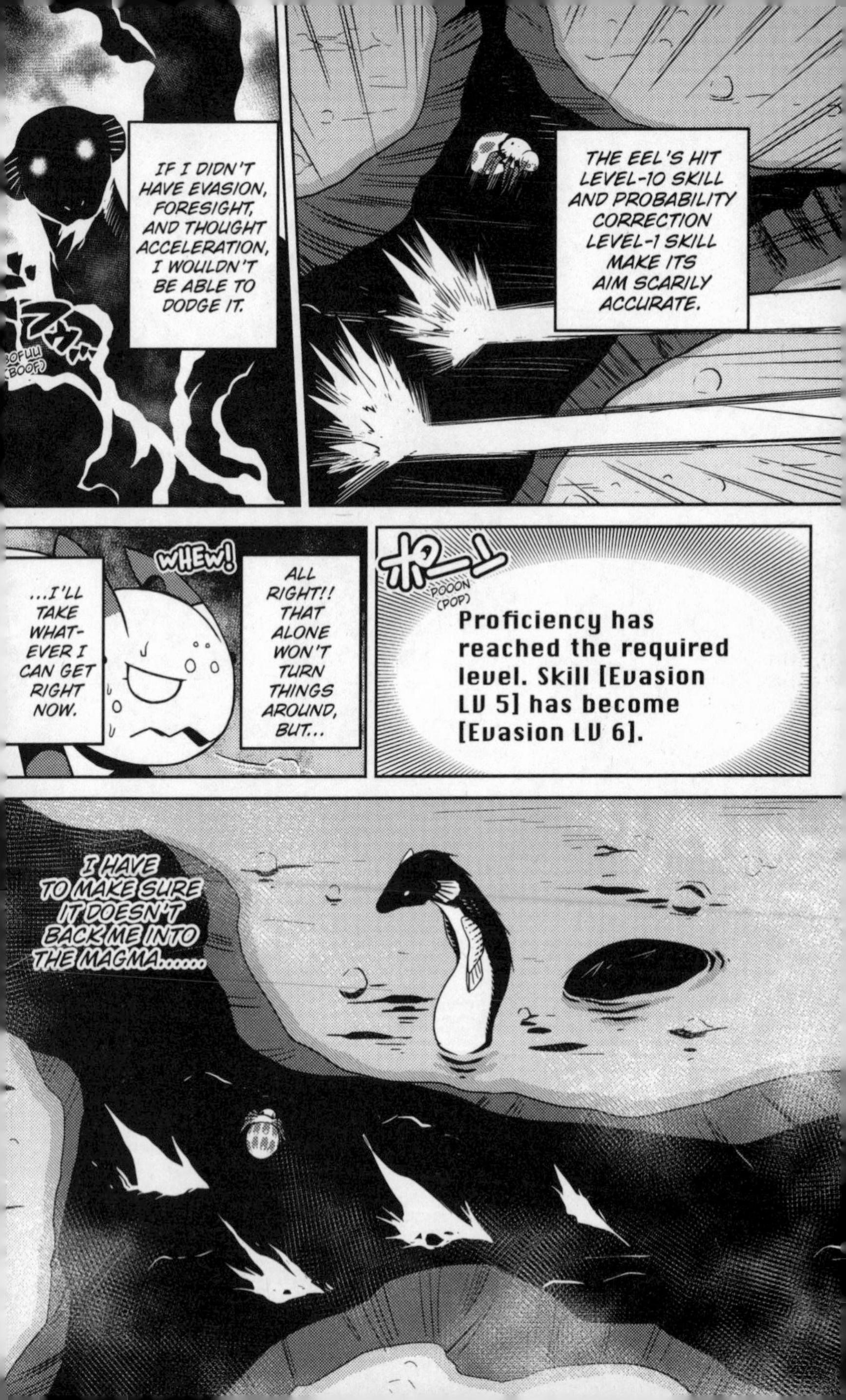
THE EEL'S HIT LEVEL-10 SKILL AND PROBABILITY CORRECTION LEVEL-1 SKILL MAKE ITS AIM SCARILY ACCURATE.
IF I DIDN'T HAVE EVASION, FORESIGHT, AND THOUGHT ACCELERATION, I WOULDN'T BE ABLE TO DODGE IT.
BOFUU (BOOF)
POOON (POP)
Proficiency has reached the required level. Skill [Evasion LV 5] has become [Evasion LV 6].
WHEW!
ALL RIGHT!! THAT ALONE WON'T TURN THINGS AROUND, BUT...
...I'LL TAKE WHAT-EVER I CAN GET RIGHT NOW.
I HAVE TO MAKE SURE IT DOESN'T BACK ME INTO THE MAGMA......

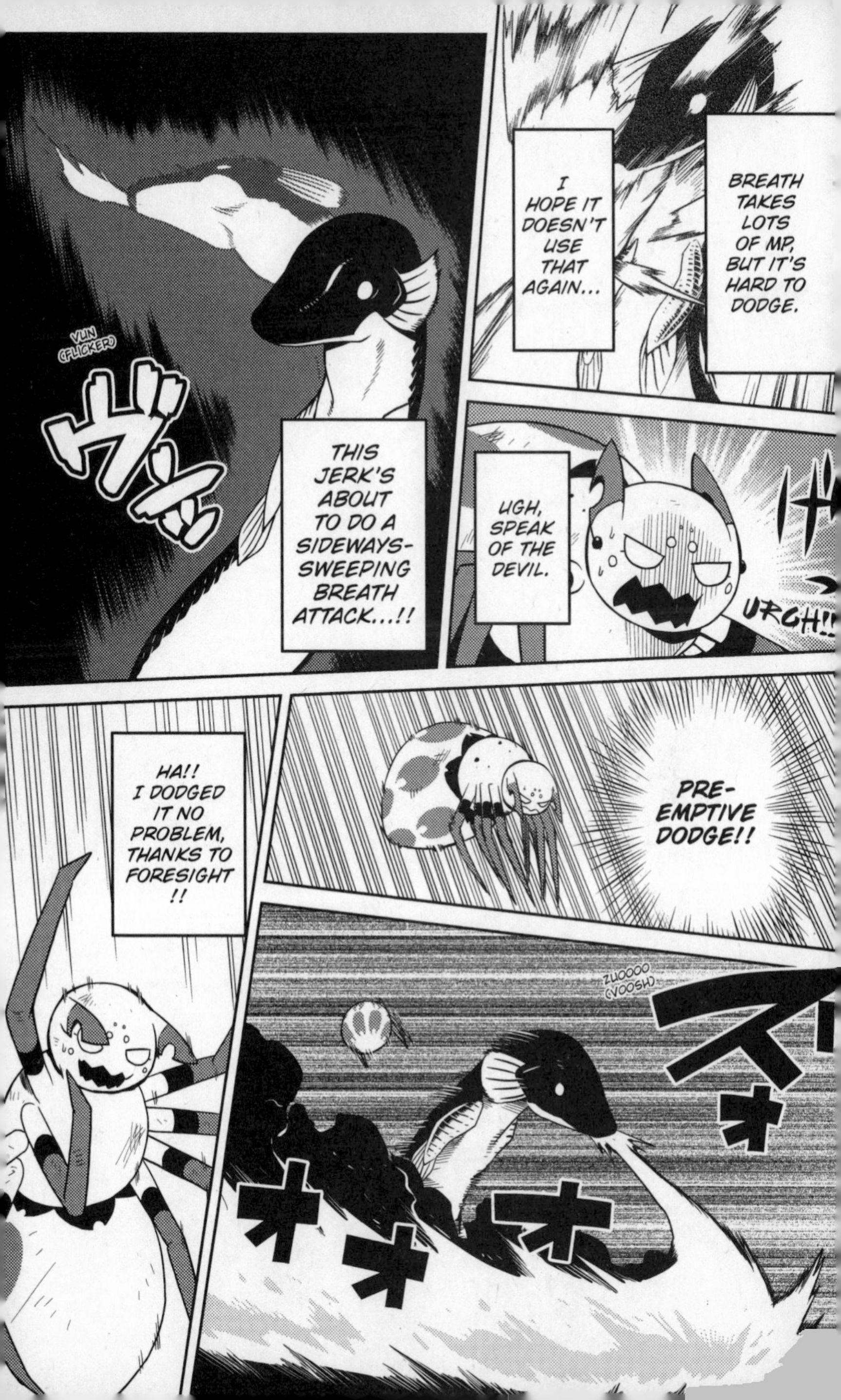

BREATH TAKES LOTS OF MP, BUT IT'S HARD TO DODGE.
I HOPE IT DOESN'T USE THAT AGAIN...
UGH, SPEAK OF THE DEVIL.
URGH!!
THIS JERK'S ABOUT TO DO A SIDEWAYS-SWEEPING BREATH ATTACK...!!
VUN (FLICKER)
PRE-EMPTIVE DODGE!!
ZUOOOO (VOOSH)
HA!! I DODGED IT NO PROBLEM, THANKS TO FORESIGHT!!

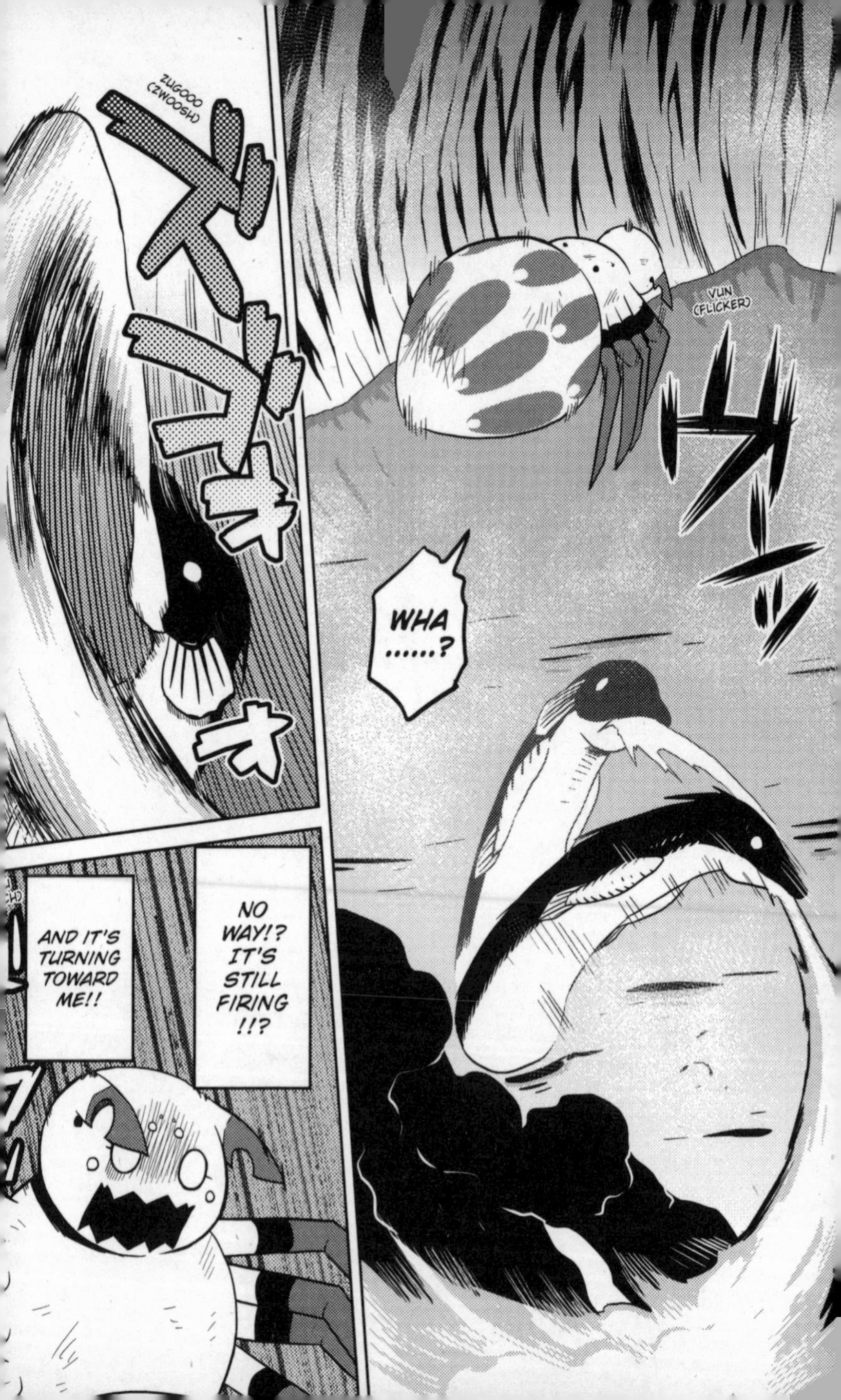
VUN (FLICKER)
WHA ......?
ZUGOOO (ZWOOSH)
NO WAY!? IT'S STILL FIRING !!?
AND IT'S TURNING TOWARD ME!!

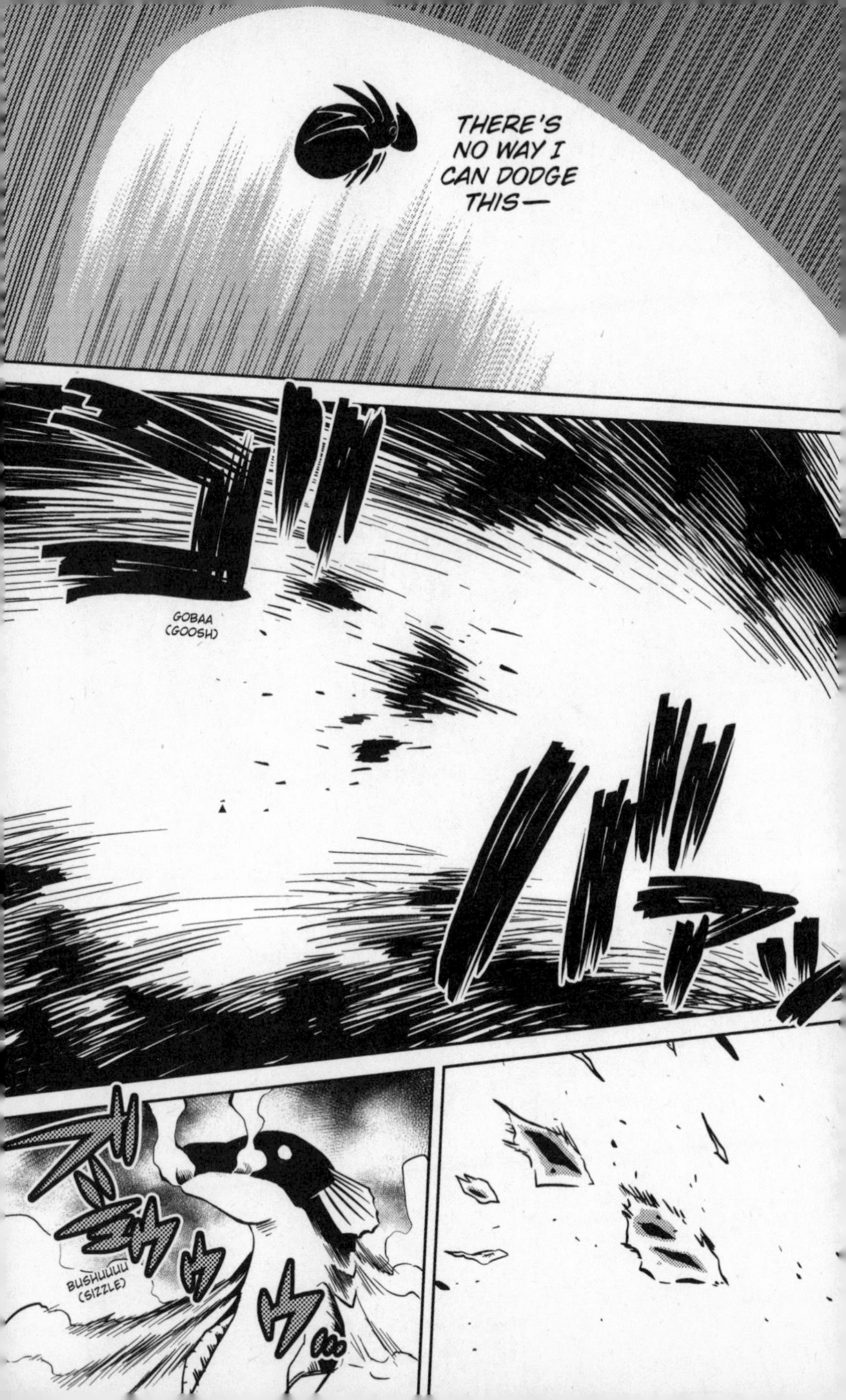
THERE'S NO WAY I CAN DODGE THIS—
GOBAA (GOOSH)
BUSHUUUU (SIZZLE)

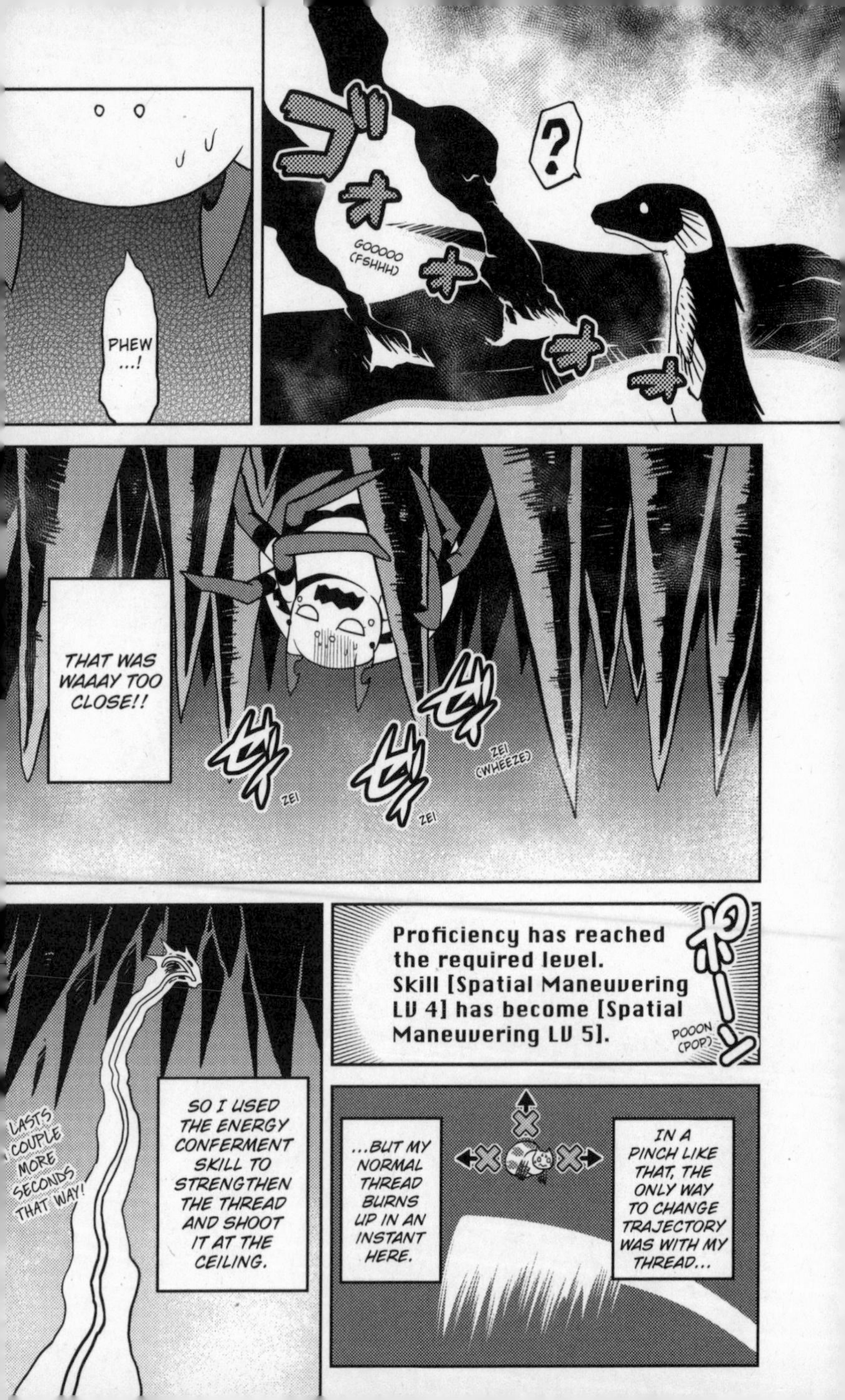
?
GOOOOO (FSHHH)
PHEW ...!
THAT WAS WAAAY TOO CLOSE!!
ZEI
ZEI
ZEI (WHEEZE)
Proficiency has reached the required level. Skill [Spatial Maneuvering LV 4] has become [Spatial Maneuvering LV 5].
POOON (POP)
IN A PINCH LIKE THAT, THE ONLY WAY TO CHANGE TRAJECTORY WAS WITH MY THREAD...
...BUT MY NORMAL THREAD BURNS UP IN AN INSTANT HERE.
SO I USED THE ENERGY CONFERMENT SKILL TO STRENGTHEN THE THREAD AND SHOOT IT AT THE CEILING.
LASTS COUPLE MORE SECONDS THAT WAY!

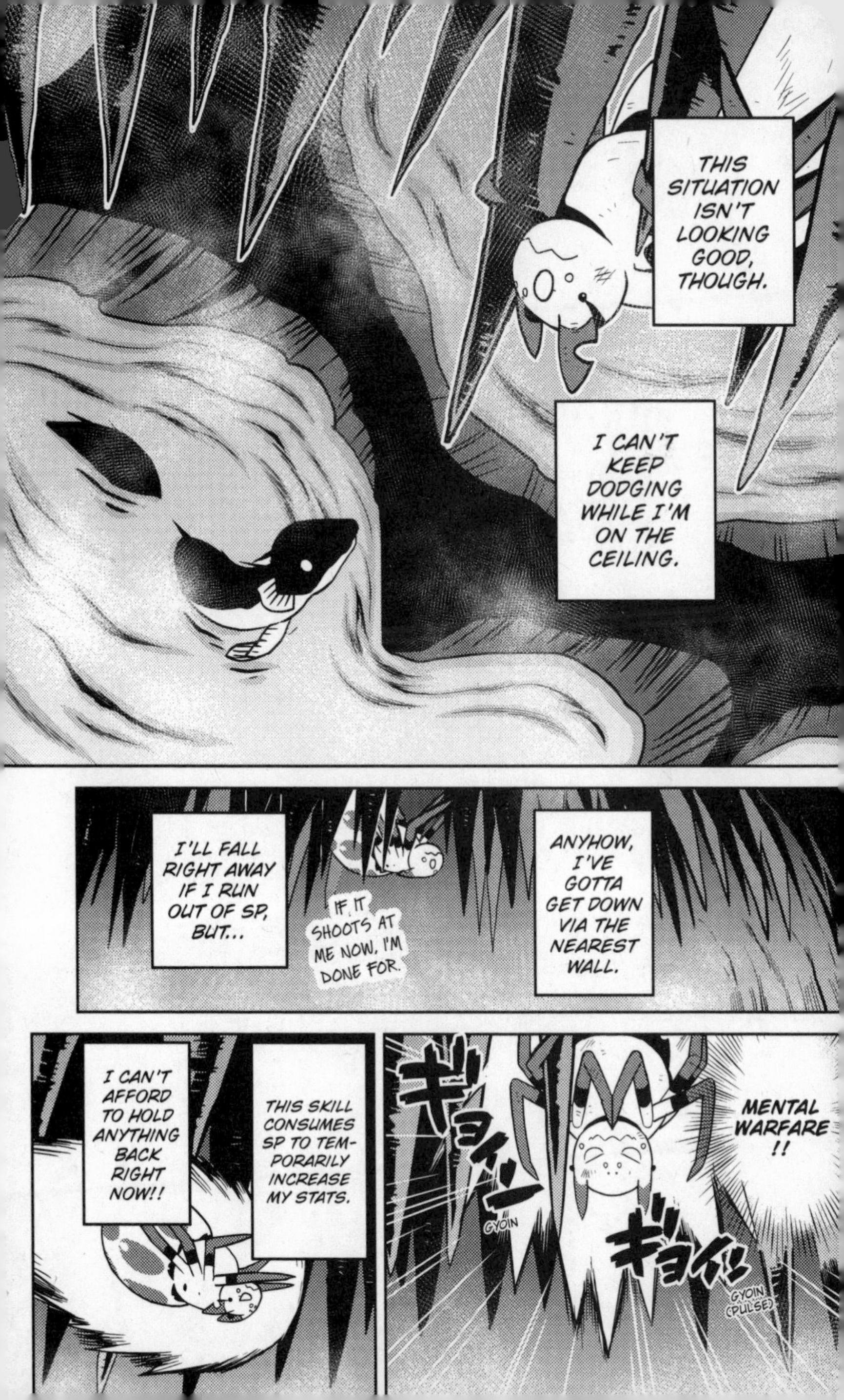
THIS SITUATION ISN'T LOOKING GOOD, THOUGH.
I CAN'T KEEP DODGING WHILE I'M ON THE CEILING.
ANYHOW, I'VE GOTTA GET DOWN VIA THE NEAREST WALL.
IF IT SHOOTS AT ME NOW, I'M DONE FOR.
I'LL FALL RIGHT AWAY IF I RUN OUT OF SP, BUT...
MENTAL WARFARE!!
ギョイン
GYOIN
ギョイン!!
GYOIN (PULSE)
THIS SKILL CONSUMES SP TO TEMPORARILY INCREASE MY STATS.
I CAN'T AFFORD TO HOLD ANYTHING BACK RIGHT NOW!!

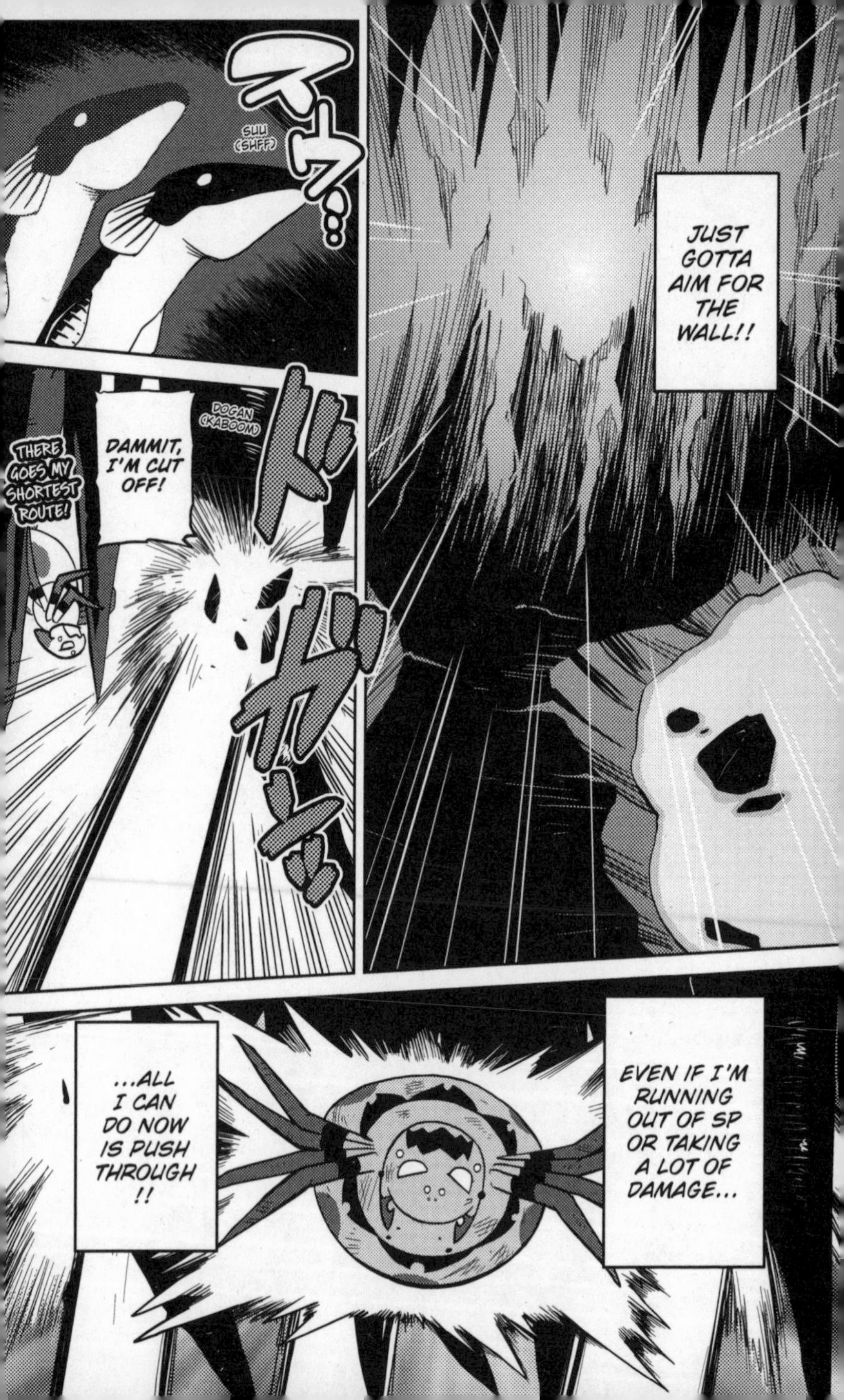
JUST GOTTA AIM FOR THE WALL!!
SUU (SHFF)
DOGAN (KABOOM)
DAMMIT, I'M CUT OFF!
THERE GOES MY SHORTEST ROUTE!
EVEN IF I'M RUNNING OUT OF SP OR TAKING A LOT OF DAMAGE...
...ALL I CAN DO NOW IS PUSH THROUGH!!

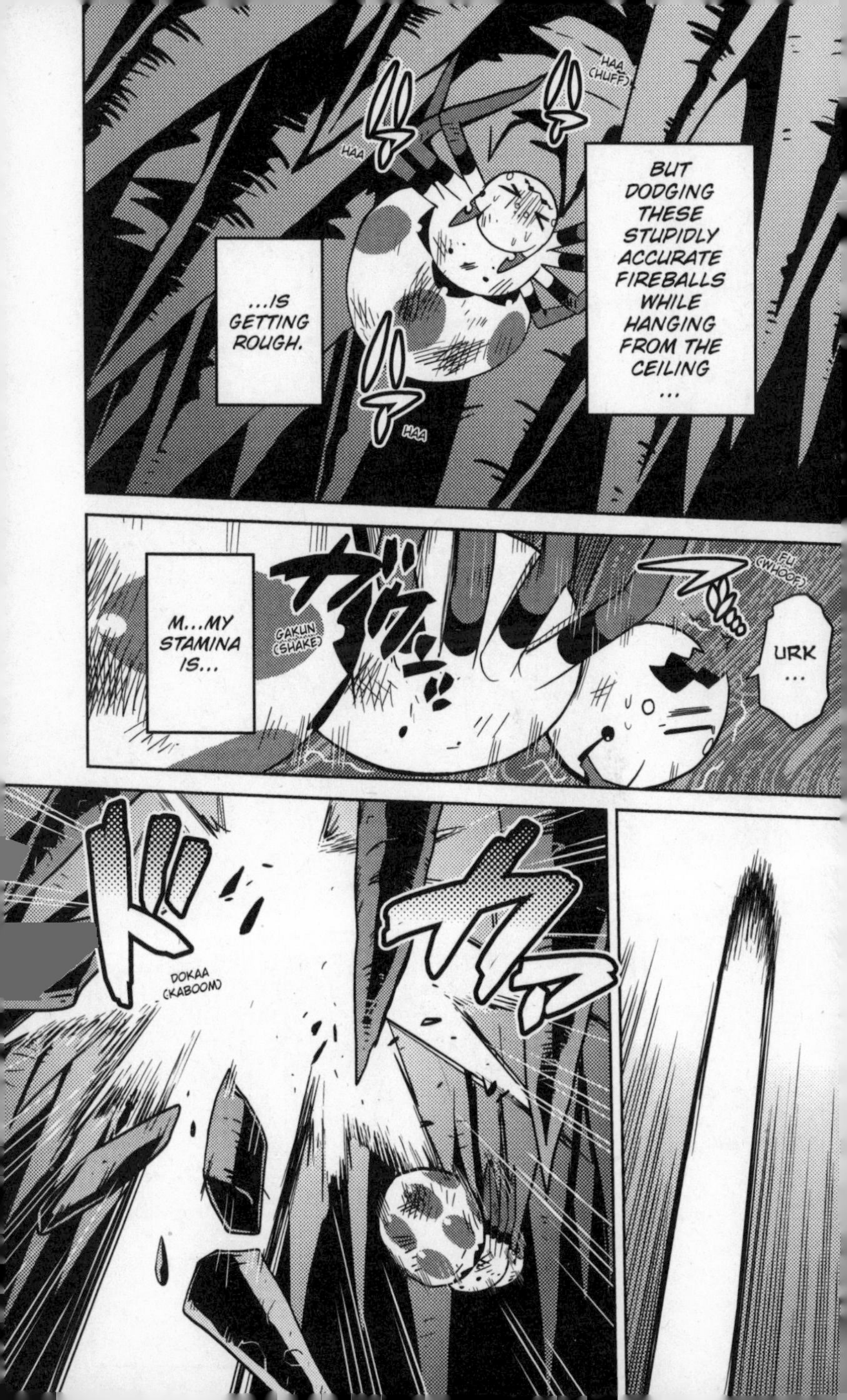
HAA (HUFF)
BUT DODGING THESE STUPIDLY ACCURATE FIREBALLS WHILE HANGING FROM THE CEILING ...
HAA
...IS GETTING ROUGH.
HAA
FU (WHOOF)
URK ...
GAKUN (SHAKE)
M...MY STAMINA IS...
DOKAA (KABOOM)

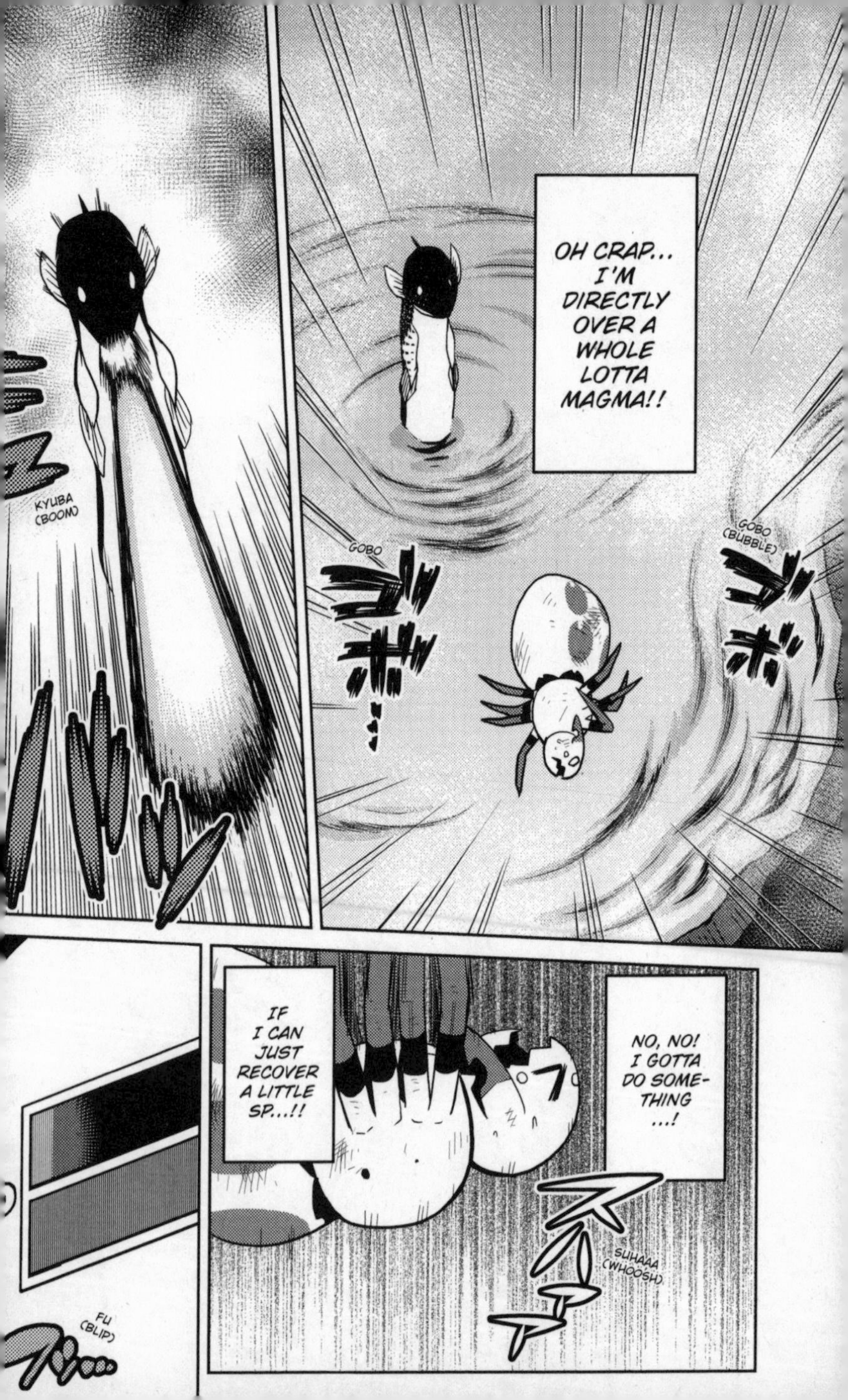
OH CRAP... I'M DIRECTLY OVER A WHOLE LOTTA MAGMA!!
GOBO (BUBBLE)
GOBO
KYUBA (BOOM)
NO, NO! I GOTTA DO SOME-THING ...!
IF I CAN JUST RECOVER A LITTLE SP...!!
SUHAAA (WHOOSH)
FU (BLIP)

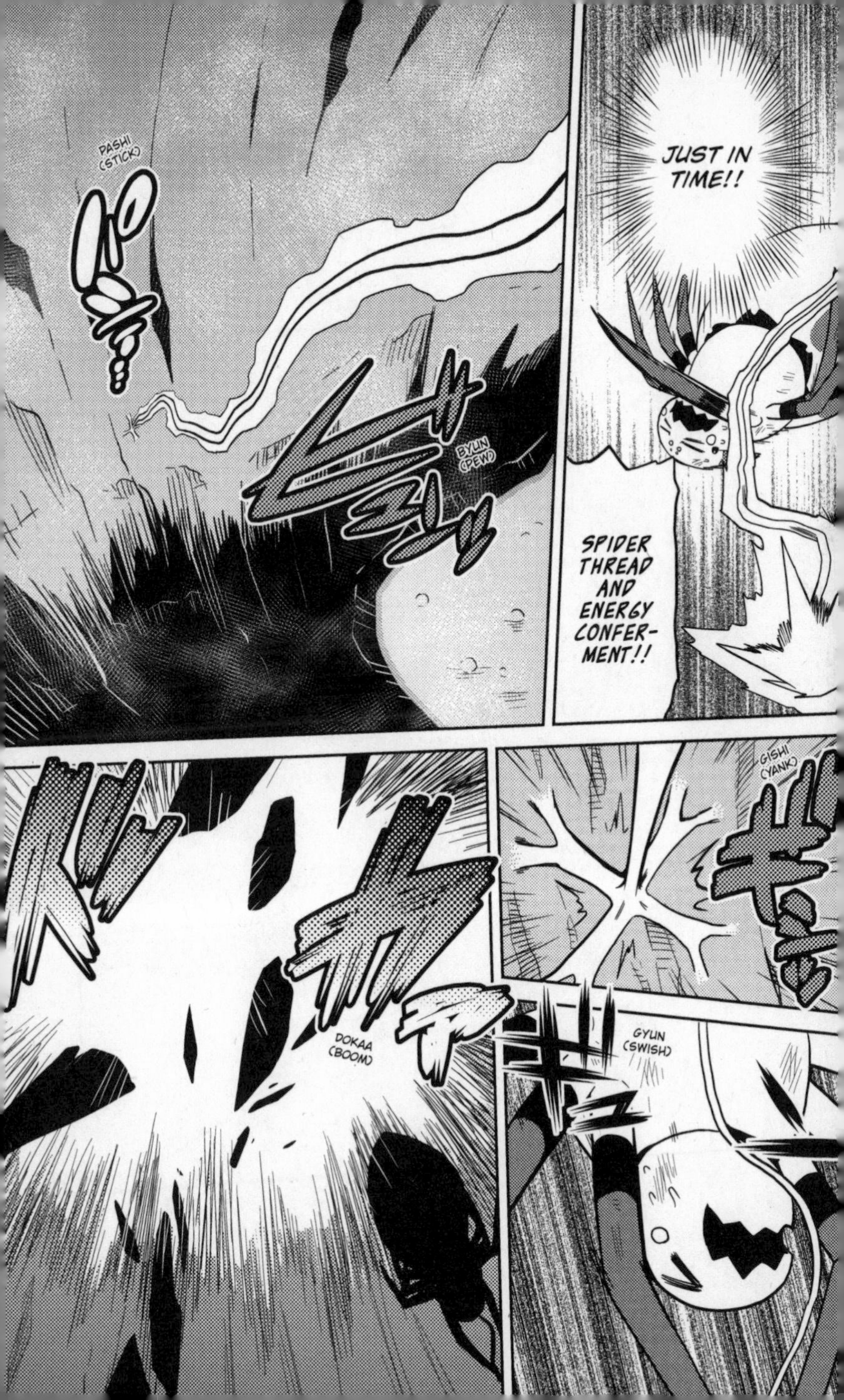
JUST IN TIME!!
SPIDER THREAD AND ENERGY CONFER-MENT!!
BYUN (PEW)
PASHI (STICK)
GISHI (YANK)
GYUN (SWISH)
DOKAA (BOOM)

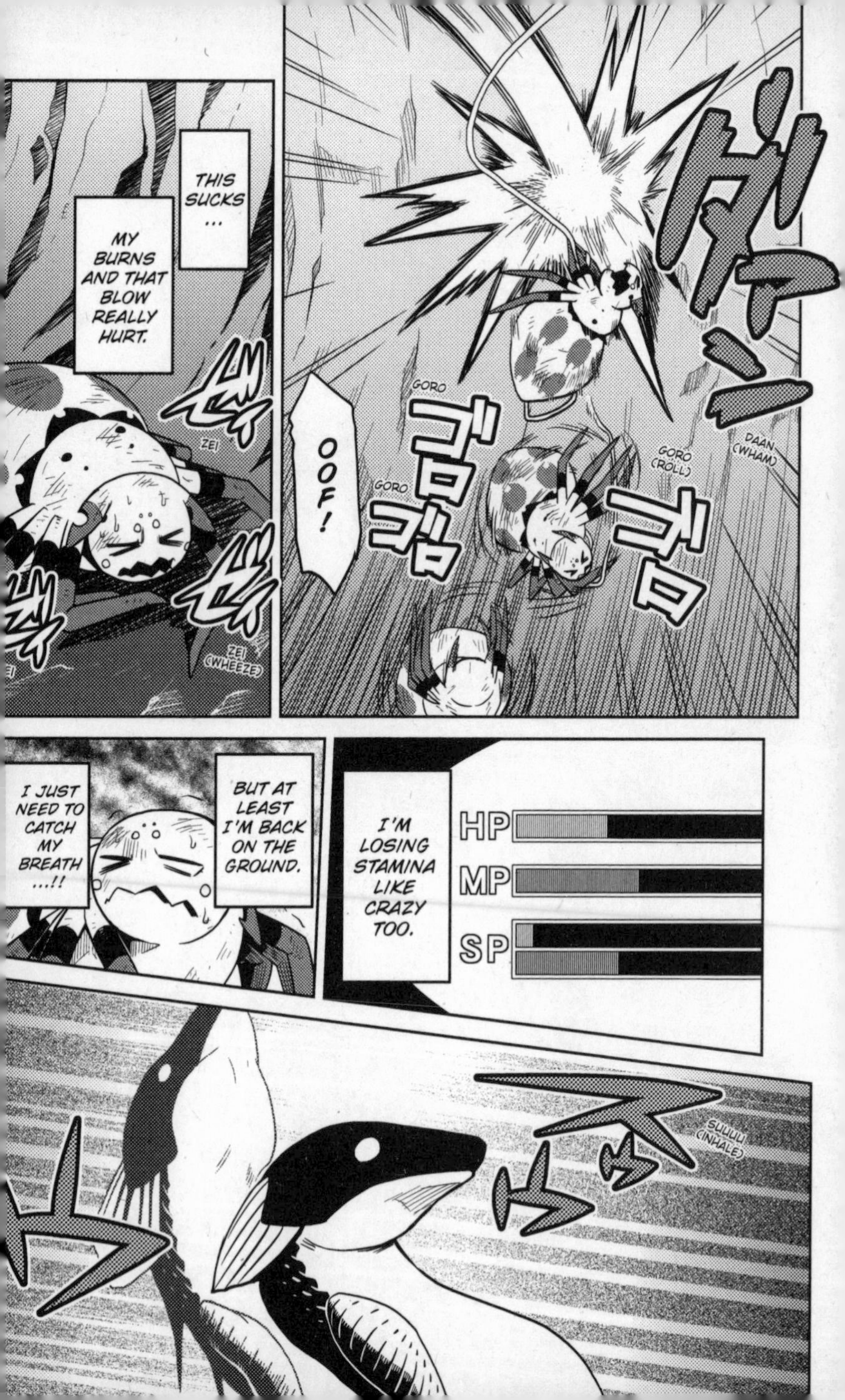
DAAN (WHAM)
GORO (ROLL)
GORO
GORO
OOF!
THIS SUCKS...
MY BURNS AND THAT BLOW REALLY HURT.
ZEI
ZEI (WHEEZE)
I'M LOSING STAMINA LIKE CRAZY TOO.
HP
MP
SP
BUT AT LEAST I'M BACK ON THE GROUND.
I JUST NEED TO CATCH MY BREATH...!!
SUUUU (INHALE)

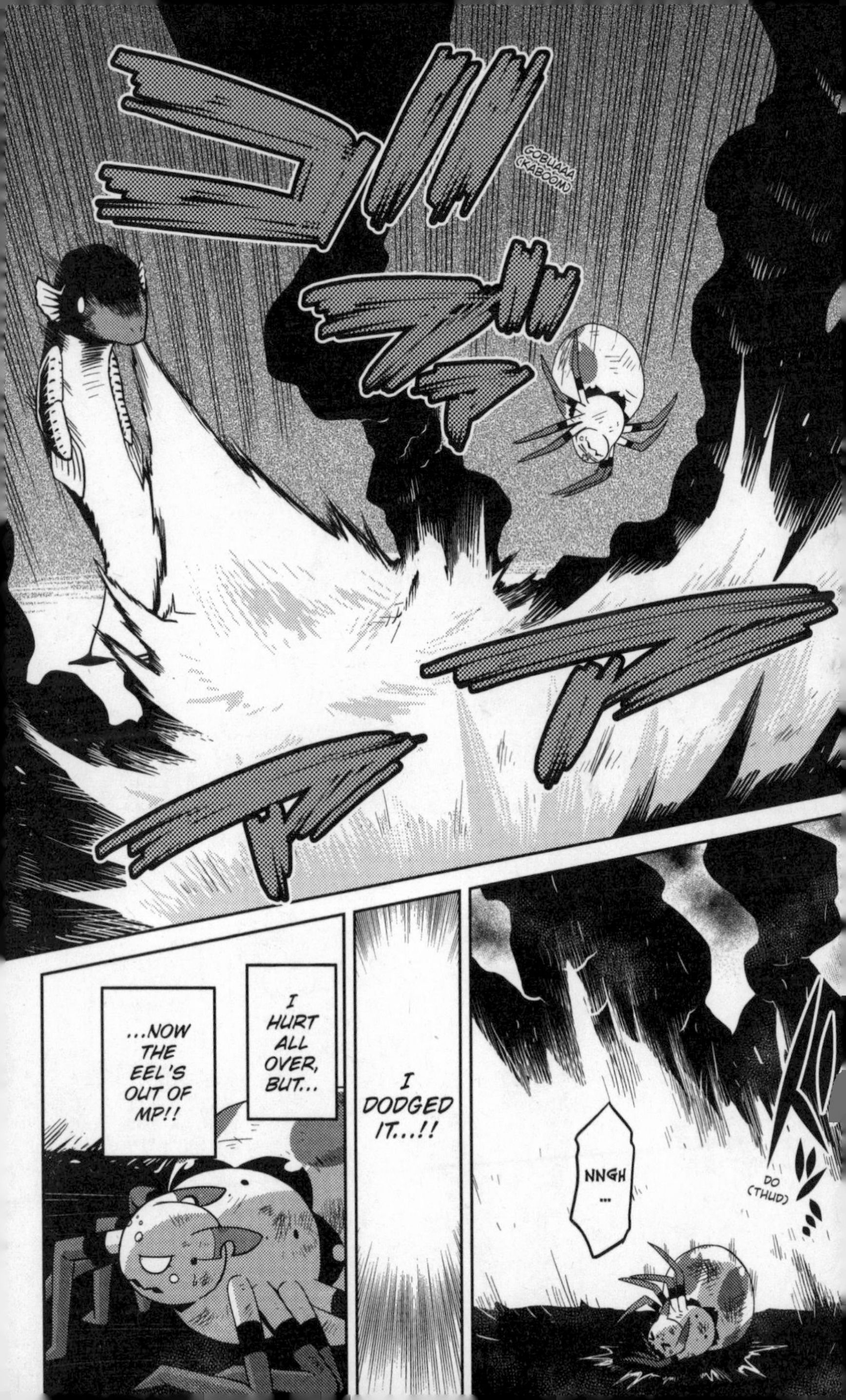
GOBUAAA
(KABOOM)
NNGH
...
DO
(THUD)
I DODGED IT...!!
I HURT ALL OVER, BUT...
...NOW THE EEL'S OUT OF MP!!

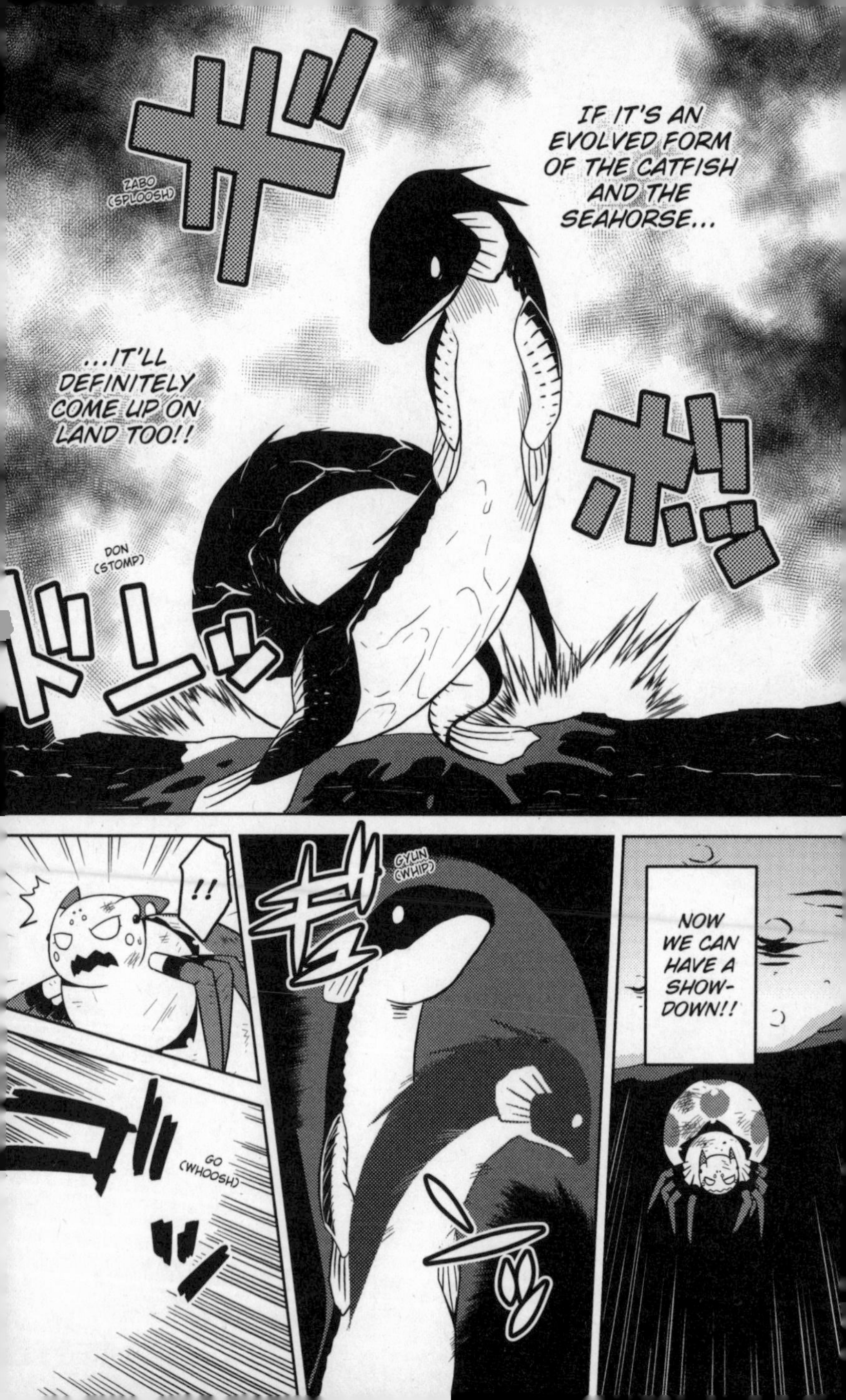
IF IT'S AN EVOLVED FORM OF THE CATFISH AND THE SEAHORSE...
ZABO (SPLOOSH)
...IT'LL DEFINITELY COME UP ON LAND TOO!!
DON (STOMP)
NOW WE CAN HAVE A SHOW-DOWN!!
GYUN (WHIP)
!!
GO (WHOOSH)

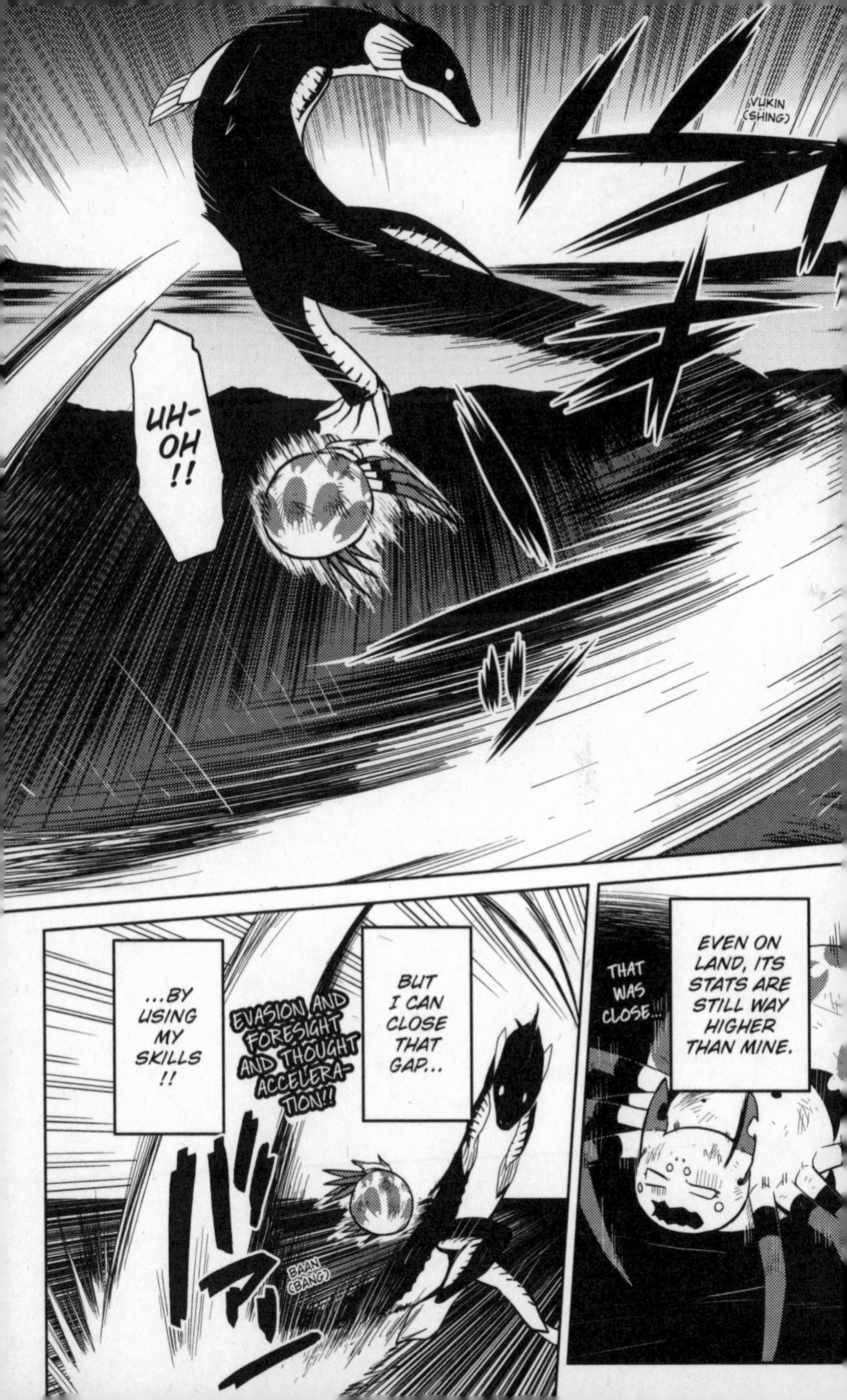
VUKIN (SHING)
UH-OH!!
EVEN ON LAND, ITS STATS ARE STILL WAY HIGHER THAN MINE.
THAT WAS CLOSE...
BUT I CAN CLOSE THAT GAP...
EVASION AND FORESIGHT AND THOUGHT ACCELERATION!!
...BY USING MY SKILLS!!
BAAN (BANG)

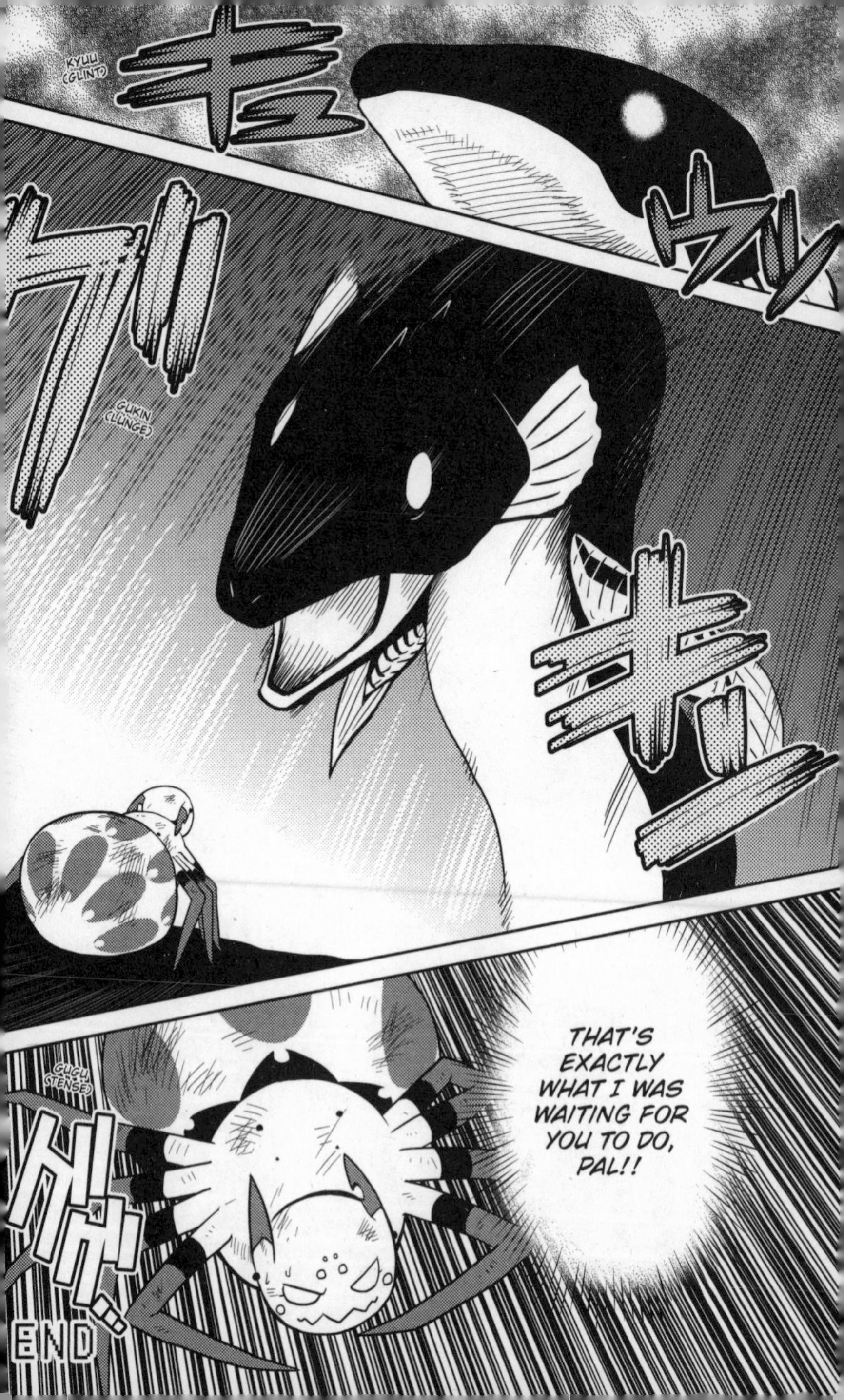
KYUU (GLINT)
GUKIN (LUNGE)
THAT'S EXACTLY WHAT I WAS WAITING FOR YOU TO DO, PAL!!
GUGU (TENSE)
END

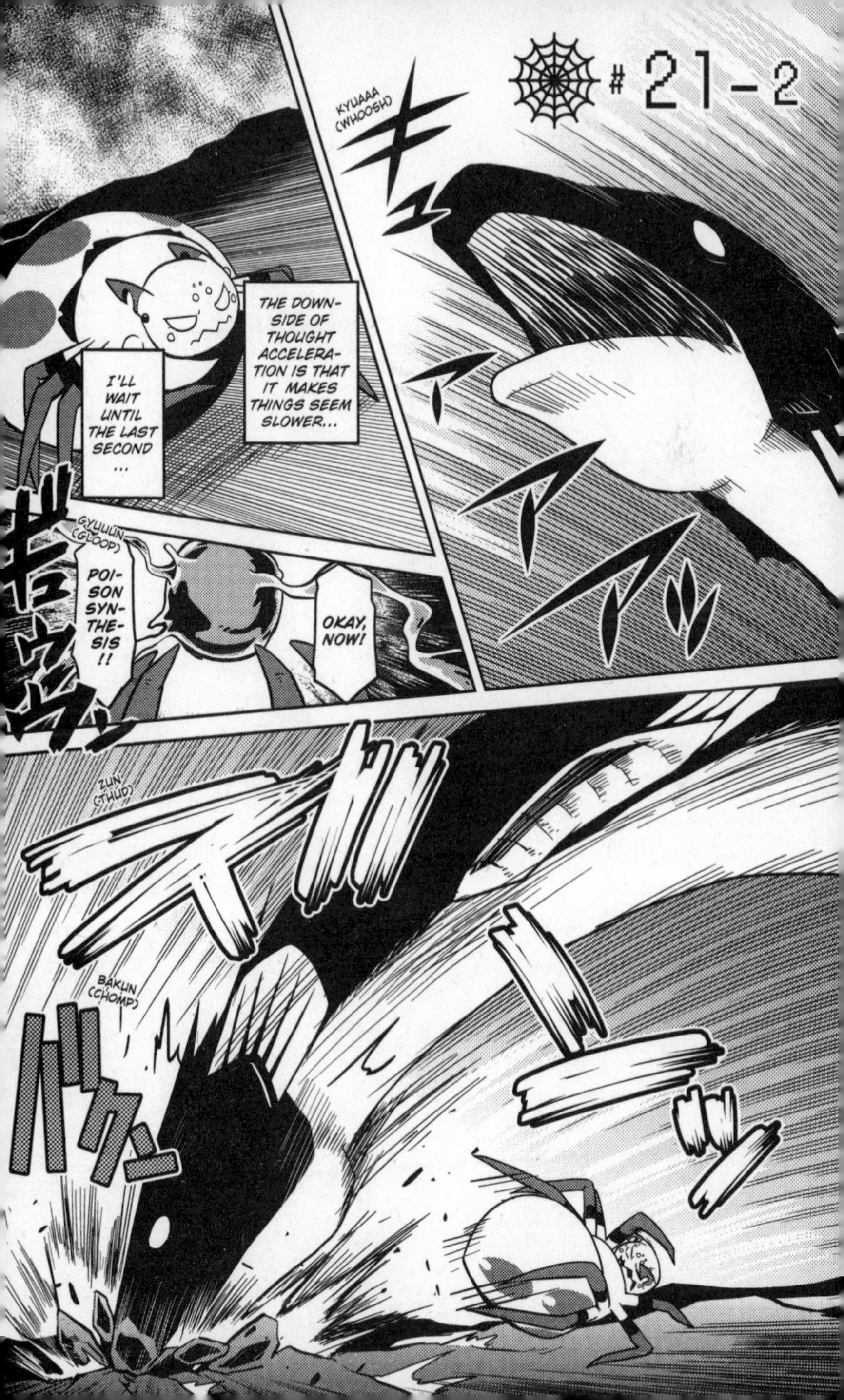
#21-2
KYUAAA (WHOOSH)
THE DOWN-SIDE OF THOUGHT ACCELERA-TION IS THAT IT MAKES THINGS SEEM SLOWER...
I'LL WAIT UNTIL THE LAST SECOND ...
OKAY, NOW!
GYUUUN (GLOOP)
POI-SON SYN-THE-SIS !!
ZUN (THUD)
BAKUN (CHOMP)

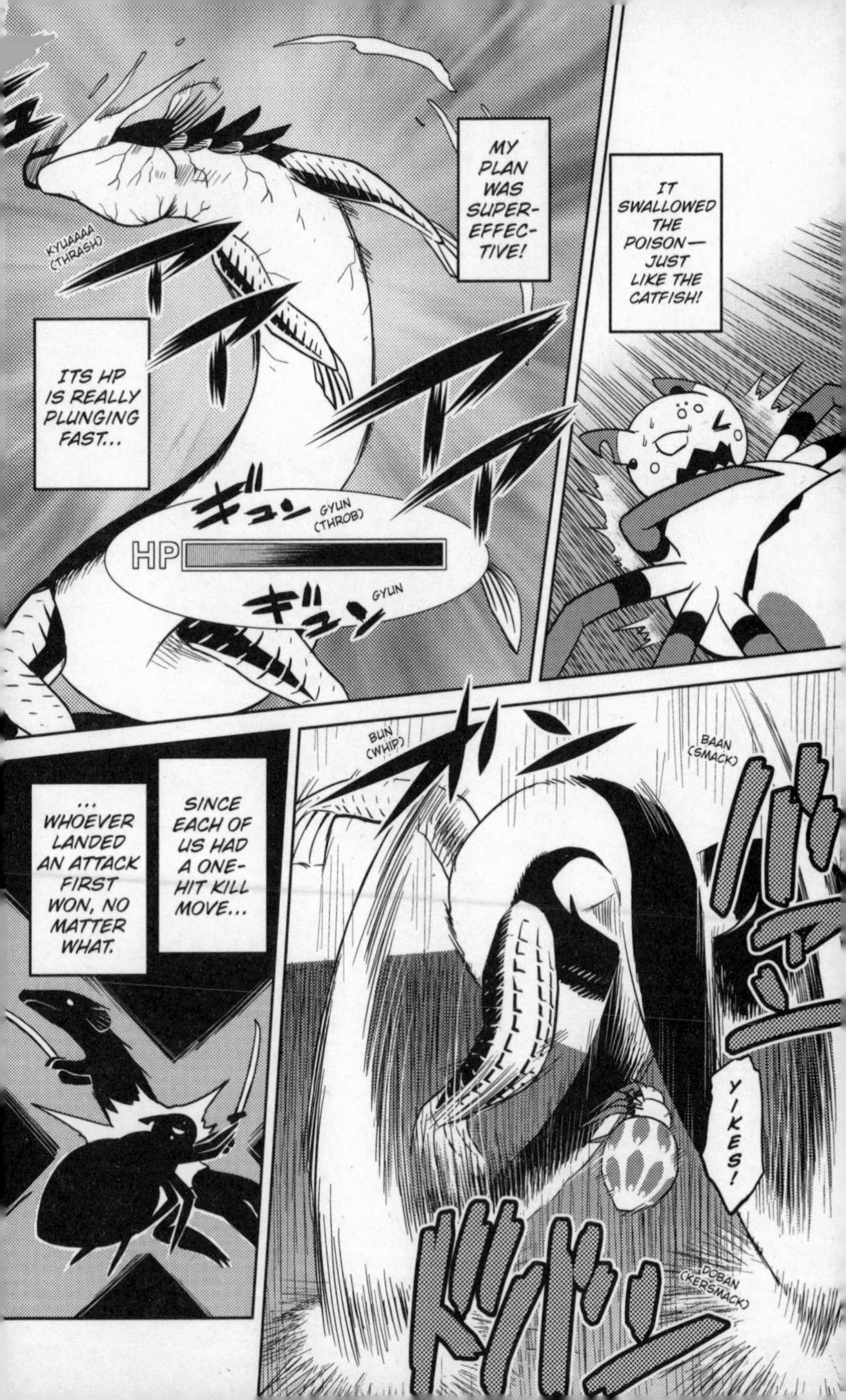
IT SWALLOWED THE POISON—JUST LIKE THE CATFISH!
MY PLAN WAS SUPER-EFFECTIVE!
KYUAAAA (THRASH)
ITS HP IS REALLY PLUNGING FAST...
GYUN (THROB)
HP
GYUN
BAAN (SMACK)
BUN (WHIP)
YIKES!
DOBAN (KERSMACK)
SINCE EACH OF US HAD A ONE-HIT KILL MOVE...
... WHOEVER LANDED AN ATTACK FIRST WON, NO MATTER WHAT.

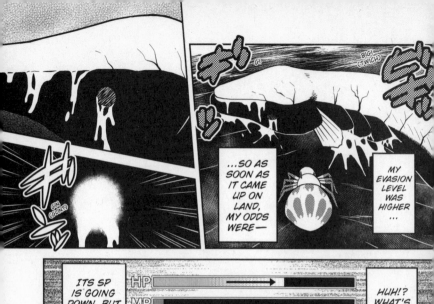

BIGI (TWICH)
GI
MY EVASION LEVEL WAS HIGHER ...
...SO AS SOON AS IT CAME UP ON LAND, MY ODDS WERE—
GIN (GLINT)
HUH!? WHAT'S THIS?
HP
MP
SP
ITS SP IS GOING DOWN, BUT ITS HP IS GOING UP!!
SUUUU (SLITHER)
<Life Exchange>
A level-3 skill for fire-wyrm-type monsters. Recovers HP by consuming SP.

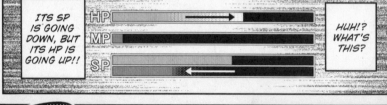

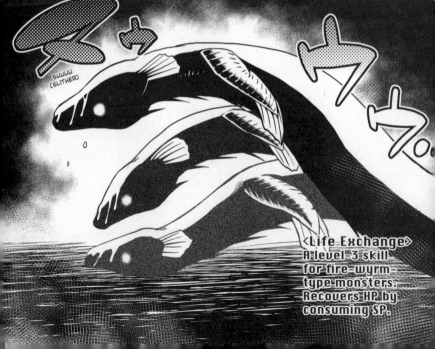

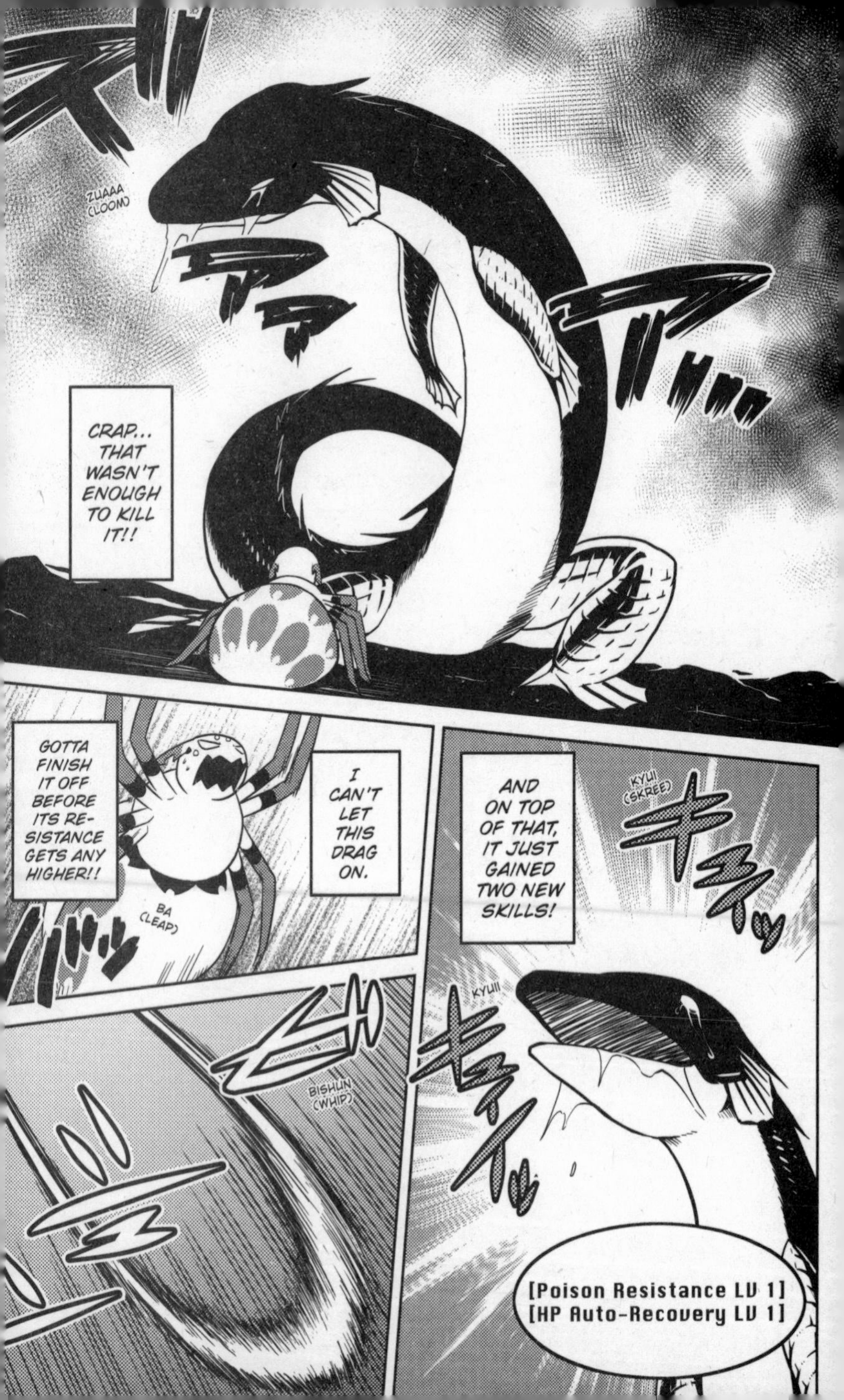
ZUAAA (LOOM)
CRAP... THAT WASN'T ENOUGH TO KILL IT!!
AND ON TOP OF THAT, IT JUST GAINED TWO NEW SKILLS!
KYUI (SKREE)
KYUII
[Poison Resistance LV 1]
[HP Auto-Recovery LV 1]
I CAN'T LET THIS DRAG ON.
GOTTA FINISH IT OFF BEFORE ITS RESISTANCE GETS ANY HIGHER!!
BA (LEAP)
BISHUN (WHIP)

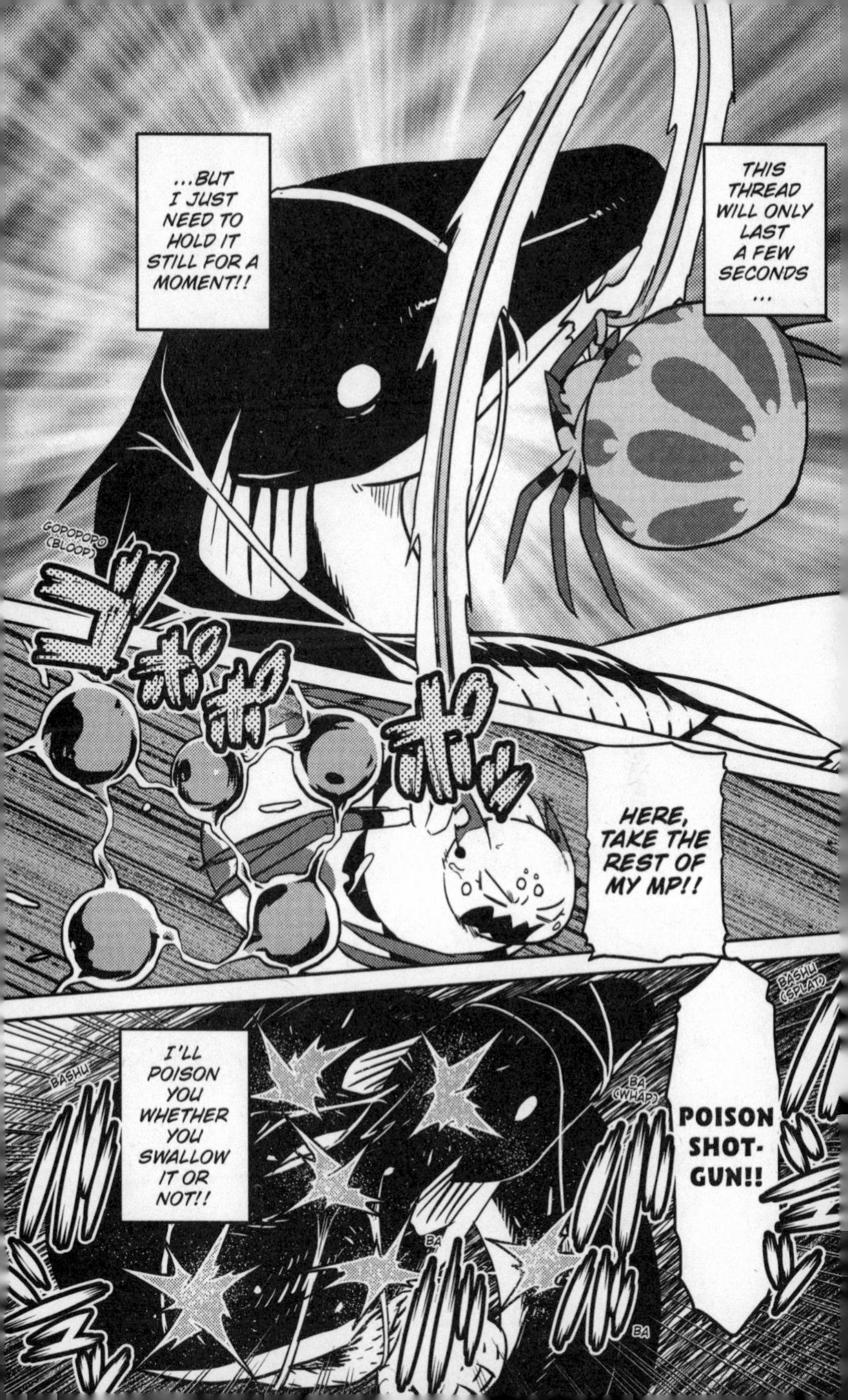
THIS THREAD WILL ONLY LAST A FEW SECONDS ...
...BUT I JUST NEED TO HOLD IT STILL FOR A MOMENT!!
GOPOPOPO (BLOOP)
HERE, TAKE THE REST OF MY MP!!
BASHU (SPLAT)
POISON SHOT-GUN!!
BA (WHAP)
I'LL POISON YOU WHETHER YOU SWALLOW IT OR NOT!!
BASHU
BA
BA

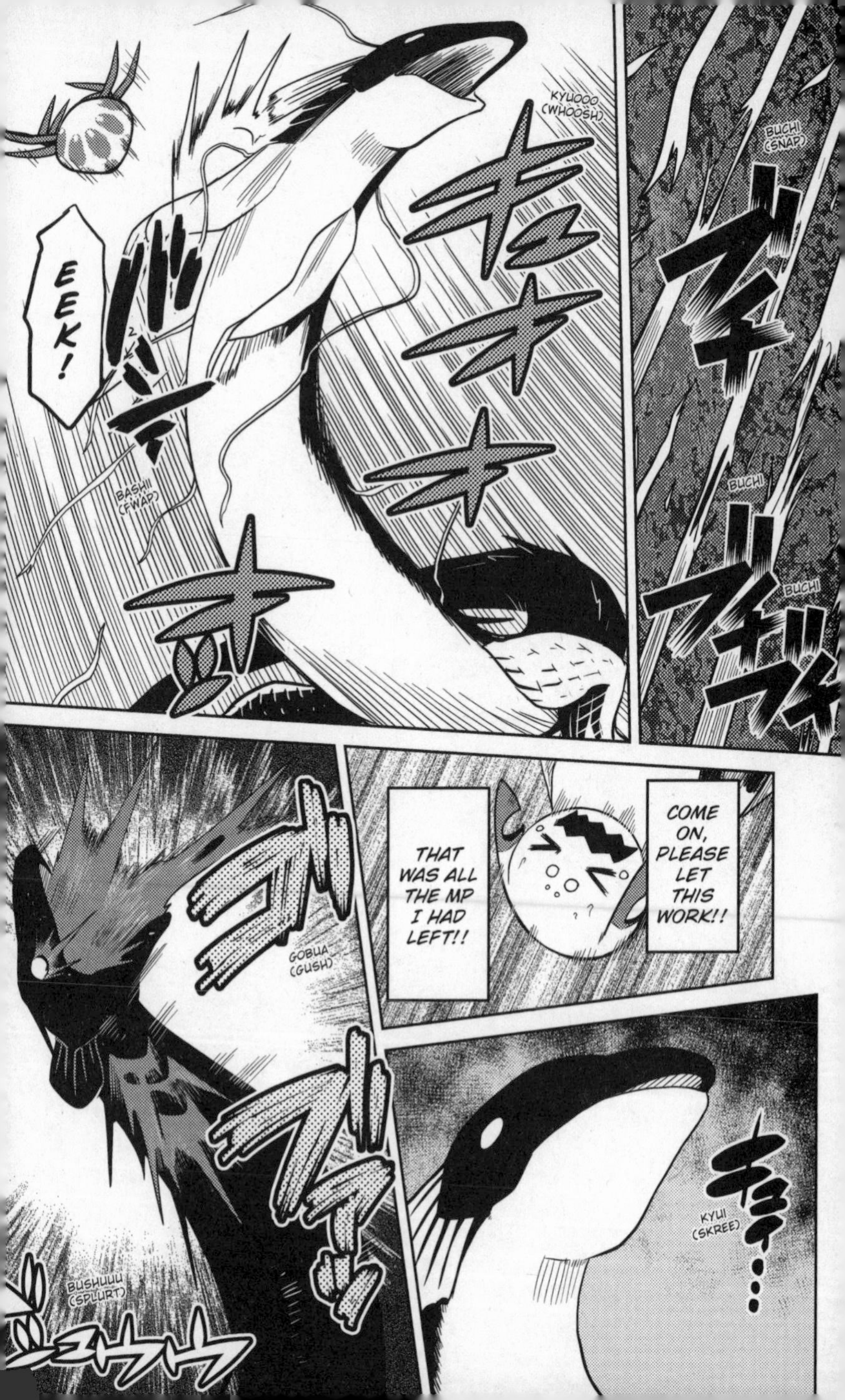
BUCHI (SNAP)
BUCHI
BUCHI
KYUOOO (WHOOSH)
EEK!
BASHII (FWAP)
COME ON, PLEASE LET THIS WORK!!
THAT WAS ALL THE MP I HAD LEFT!!
KYUI (SKREE)
GOBUA (GUSH)
BUSHUUU (SPLURT)

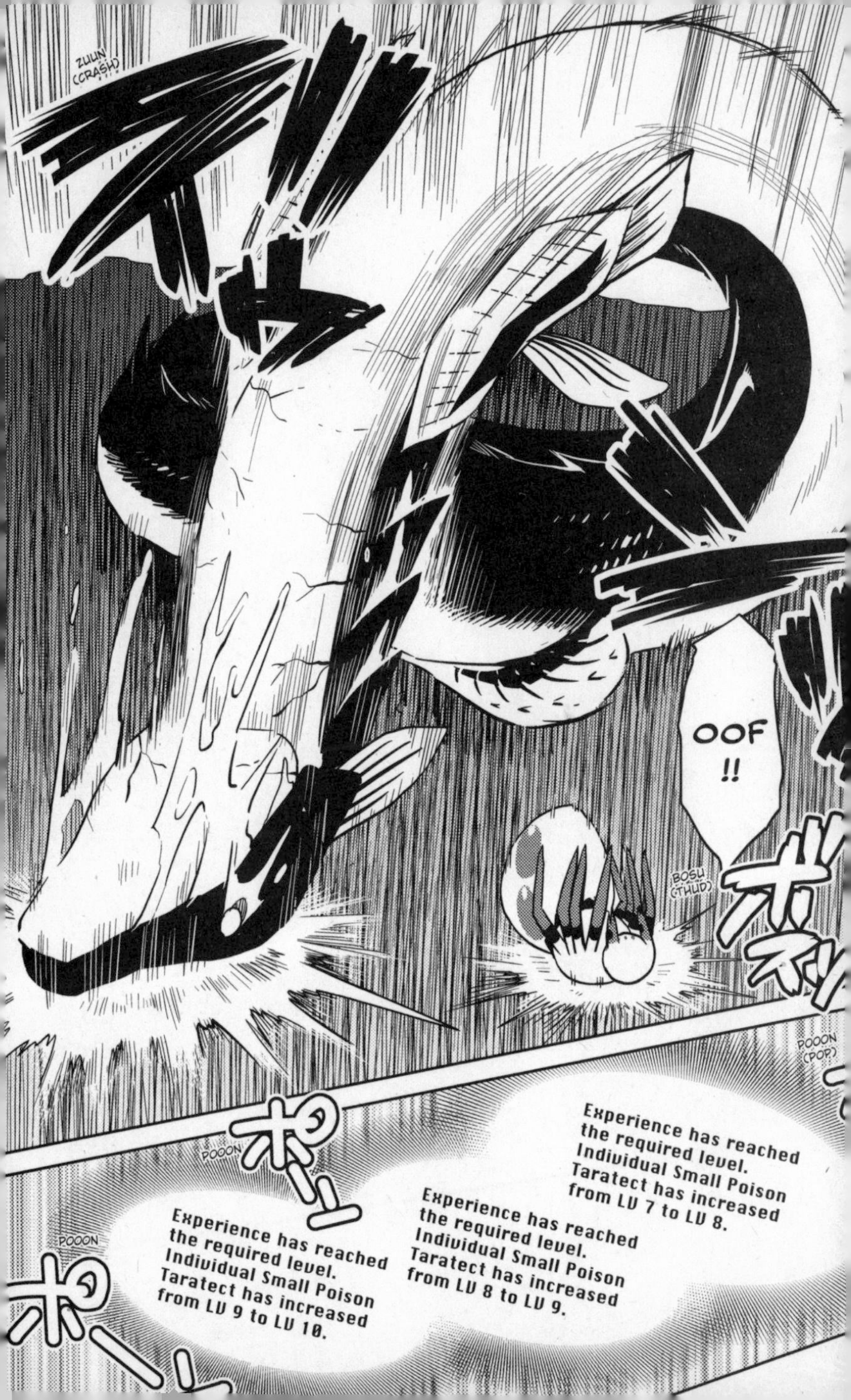

ZUUN (CRASH)
OOF !!
BOSU (THUD)
POOON (POP)
Experience has reached the required level. Individual Small Poison Taratect has increased from LV 7 to LV 8.
POOON
Experience has reached the required level. Individual Small Poison Taratect has increased from LV 8 to LV 9.
POOON
Experience has reached the required level. Individual Small Poison Taratect has increased from LV 9 to LV 10.

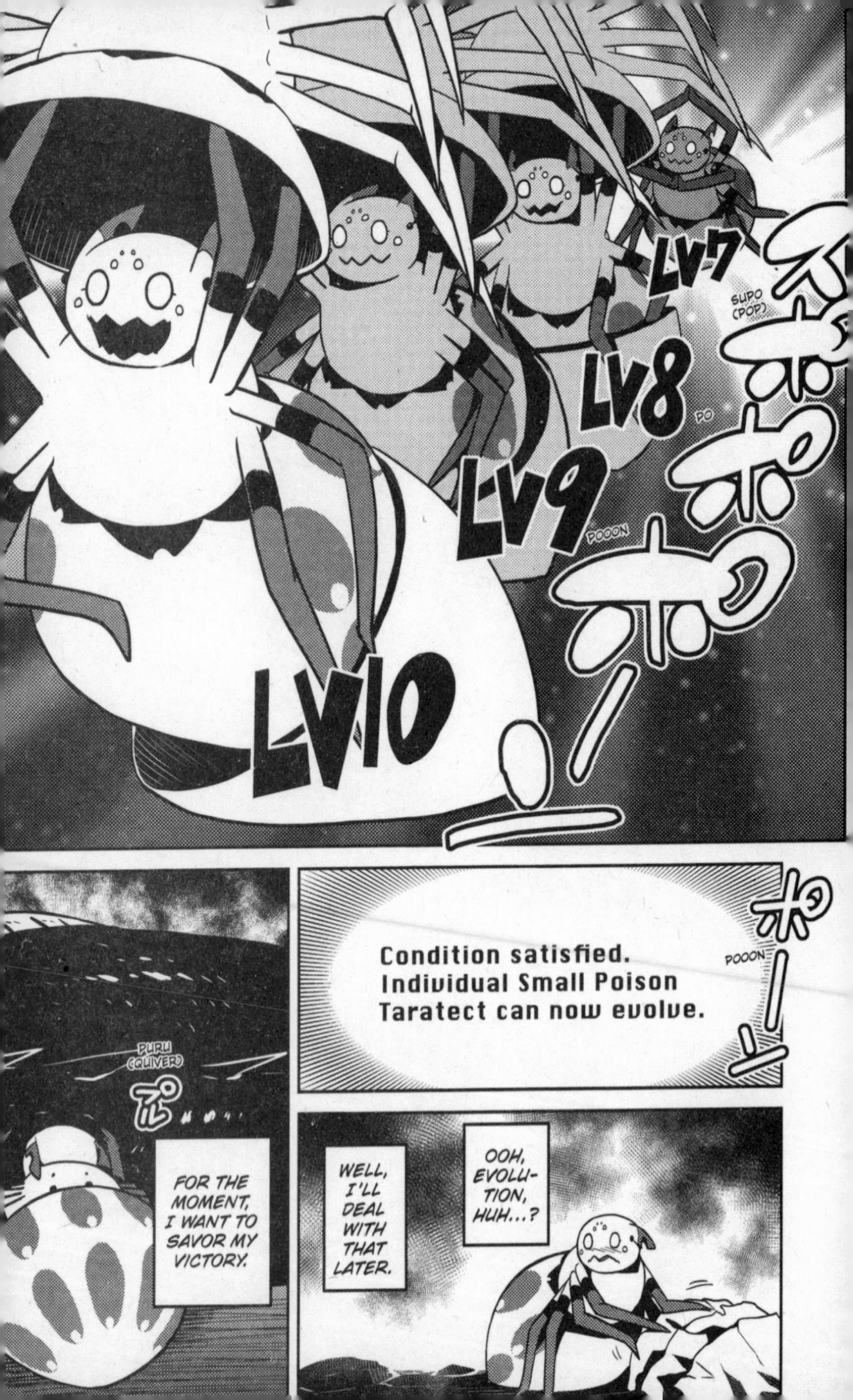
SUPO (POP)
LV7
LV8
PO
LV9
POOON
LV10
POOON
Condition satisfied. Individual Small Poison Taratect can now evolve.
OOH, EVOLUTION, HUH...?
WELL, I'LL DEAL WITH THAT LATER.
PURU (QUIVER)
FOR THE MOMENT, I WANT TO SAVOR MY VICTORY.

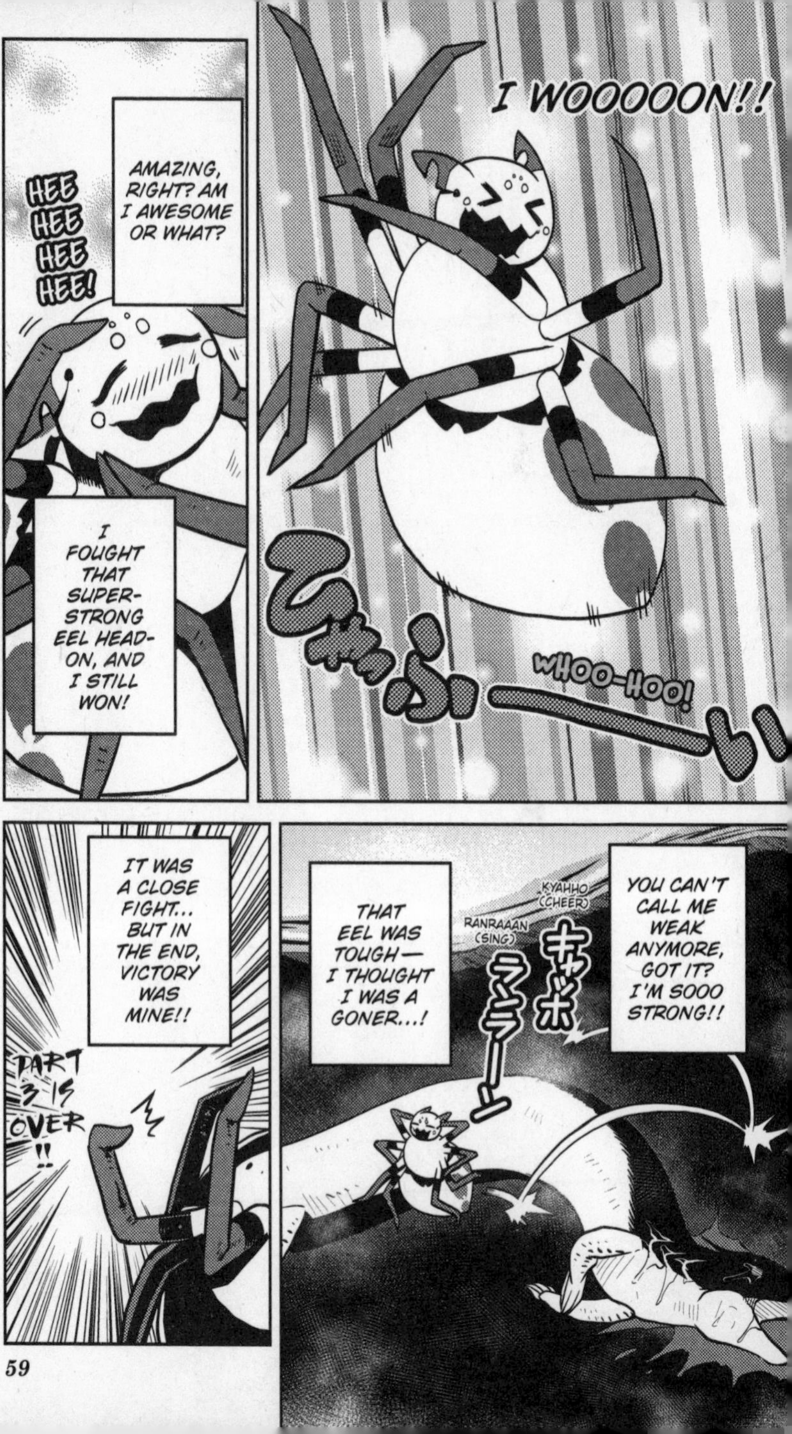
I WOOOOON!!
ひゃっふーい
WHOO-HOO!
AMAZING, RIGHT? AM I AWESOME OR WHAT?
HEE HEE HEE HEE!
I FOUGHT THAT SUPER-STRONG EEL HEAD-ON, AND I STILL WON!
YOU CAN'T CALL ME WEAK ANYMORE, GOT IT? I'M SOOO STRONG!!
KYAHHO (CHEER)
キャッホ
RANRAAAN (SING)
ランラーン
THAT EEL WAS TOUGH— I THOUGHT I WAS A GONER...!
IT WAS A CLOSE FIGHT... BUT IN THE END, VICTORY WAS MINE!!
PART 3 IS OVER!!

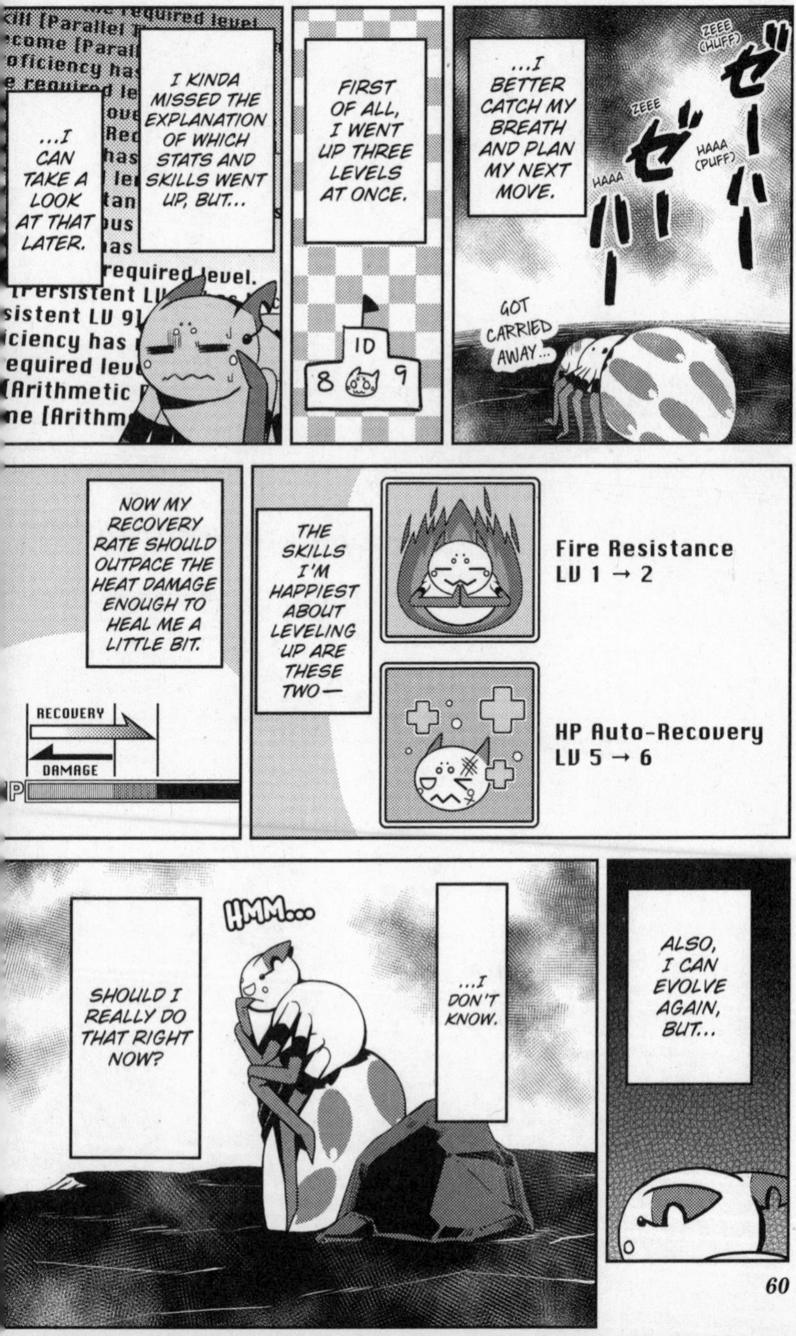
ZEEE (HUFF)
ZEEE
HAAA (PUFF)
HAAA
...I BETTER CATCH MY BREATH AND PLAN MY NEXT MOVE.
GOT CARRIED AWAY...
FIRST OF ALL, I WENT UP THREE LEVELS AT ONCE.
10
8
9
I KINDA MISSED THE EXPLANATION OF WHICH STATS AND SKILLS WENT UP, BUT...
...I CAN TAKE A LOOK AT THAT LATER.
THE SKILLS I'M HAPPIEST ABOUT LEVELING UP ARE THESE TWO—
Fire Resistance LV 1 → 2
HP Auto-Recovery LV 5 → 6
NOW MY RECOVERY RATE SHOULD OUTPACE THE HEAT DAMAGE ENOUGH TO HEAL ME A LITTLE BIT.
RECOVERY
DAMAGE
ALSO, I CAN EVOLVE AGAIN, BUT...
...I DON'T KNOW.
HMM...
SHOULD I REALLY DO THAT RIGHT NOW?

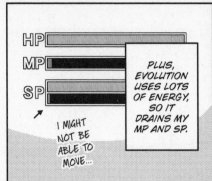

WHEN I EVOLVE, I PASS OUT AND CAN'T DEFEND MYSELF.
I CAN'T MAKE A HOME HERE, SO I'D BE TOTALLY UNPROTECTED.
PLUS, EVOLUTION USES LOTS OF ENERGY, SO IT DRAINS MY MP AND SP.
HP
MP
SP
I MIGHT NOT BE ABLE TO MOVE...
UNTIL NOW, I'VE ALWAYS HAD LOTS OF FOOD TO RESTORE ME WHEN I EVOLVE...
...BUT I DON'T THINK THIS EEL ALONE WILL BE ENOUGH TO REFILL MY SP.
UMM...
I WANT TO EVOLVE, I REALLY DO, BUT...
HMM...
POOON (POP)
There are multiple options for evolution. Please choose from the following.
Poison Taratect
Zoa Ele

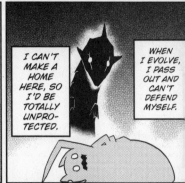

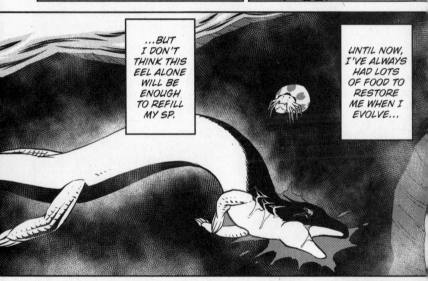

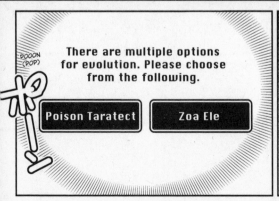

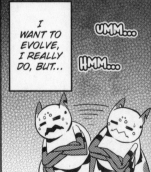

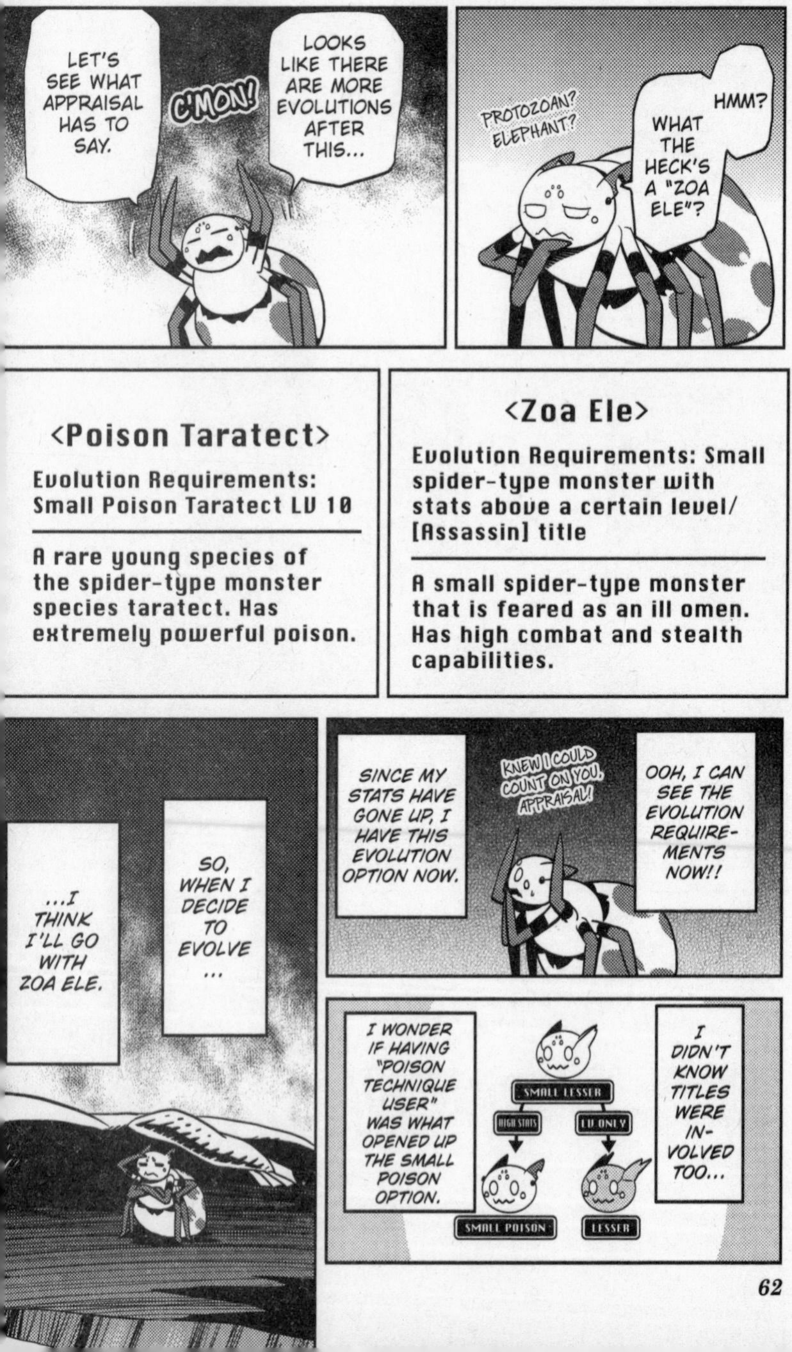
HMM?
WHAT THE HECK'S A "ZOA ELE"?
PROTOZOAN? ELEPHANT?
LOOKS LIKE THERE ARE MORE EVOLUTIONS AFTER THIS...
C'MON!
LET'S SEE WHAT APPRAISAL HAS TO SAY.
<Zoa Ele>
Evolution Requirements: Small spider-type monster with stats above a certain level/ [Assassin] title
A small spider-type monster that is feared as an ill omen. Has high combat and stealth capabilities.
<Poison Taratect>
Evolution Requirements: Small Poison Taratect LV 10
A rare young species of the spider-type monster species taratect. Has extremely powerful poison.
OOH, I CAN SEE THE EVOLUTION REQUIRE-MENTS NOW!!
KNEW I COULD COUNT ON YOU, APPRAISAL!
SINCE MY STATS HAVE GONE UP, I HAVE THIS EVOLUTION OPTION NOW.
I DIDN'T KNOW TITLES WERE IN-VOLVED TOO...
SMALL LESSER
HIGH STATS
LV ONLY
SMALL POISON
LESSER
I WONDER IF HAVING "POISON TECHNIQUE USER" WAS WHAT OPENED UP THE SMALL POISON OPTION.
SO, WHEN I DECIDE TO EVOLVE...
...I THINK I'LL GO WITH ZOA ELE.

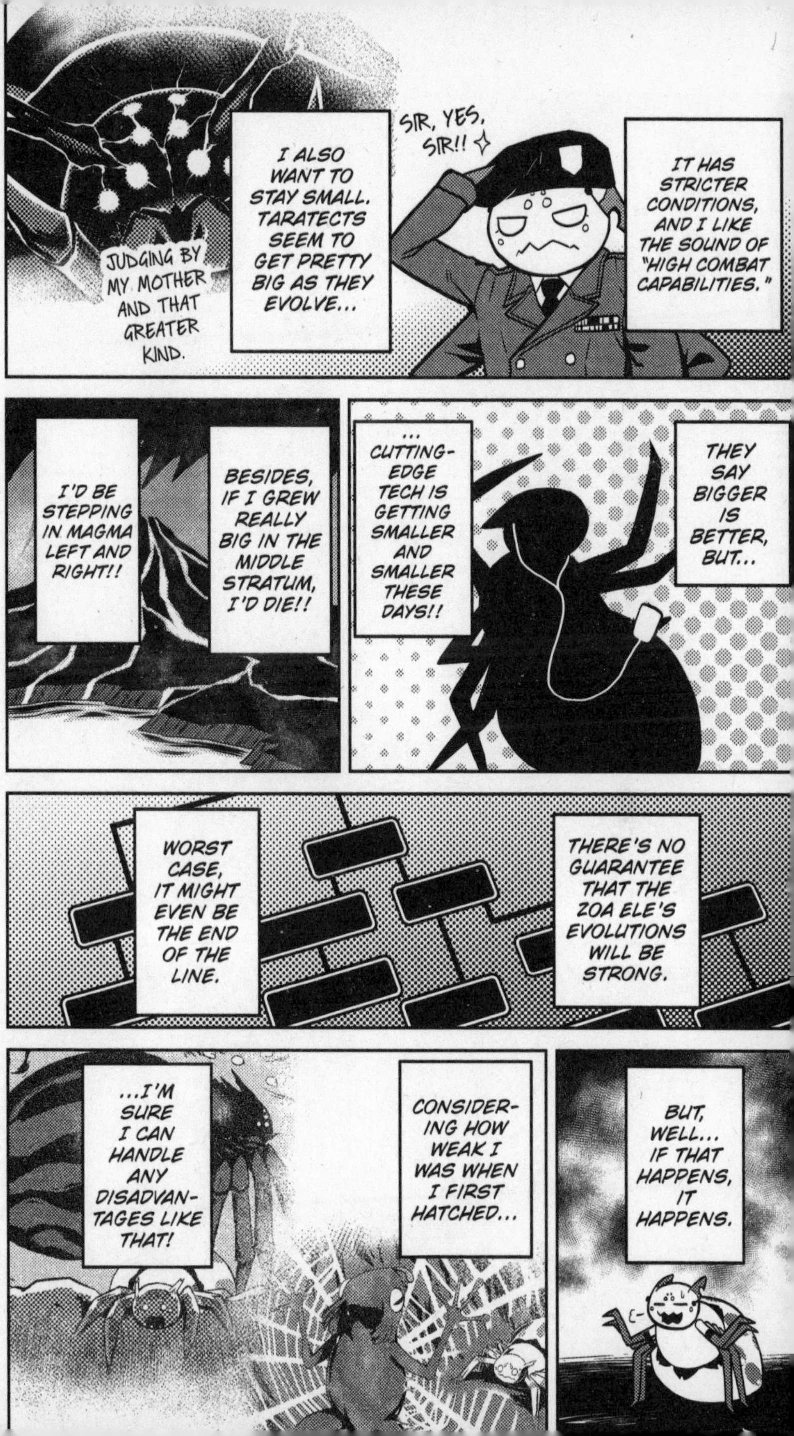
IT HAS STRICTER CONDITIONS, AND I LIKE THE SOUND OF "HIGH COMBAT CAPABILITIES."
SIR, YES, SIR!!
I ALSO WANT TO STAY SMALL. TARATECTS SEEM TO GET PRETTY BIG AS THEY EVOLVE...
JUDGING BY MY MOTHER AND THAT GREATER KIND.
THEY SAY BIGGER IS BETTER, BUT...
...CUTTING-EDGE TECH IS GETTING SMALLER AND SMALLER THESE DAYS!!
BESIDES, IF I GREW REALLY BIG IN THE MIDDLE STRATUM, I'D DIE!!
I'D BE STEPPING IN MAGMA LEFT AND RIGHT!!
THERE'S NO GUARANTEE THAT THE ZOA ELE'S EVOLUTIONS WILL BE STRONG.
WORST CASE, IT MIGHT EVEN BE THE END OF THE LINE.
BUT, WELL... IF THAT HAPPENS, IT HAPPENS.
CONSIDERING HOW WEAK I WAS WHEN I FIRST HATCHED...
...I'M SURE I CAN HANDLE ANY DISADVANTAGES LIKE THAT!

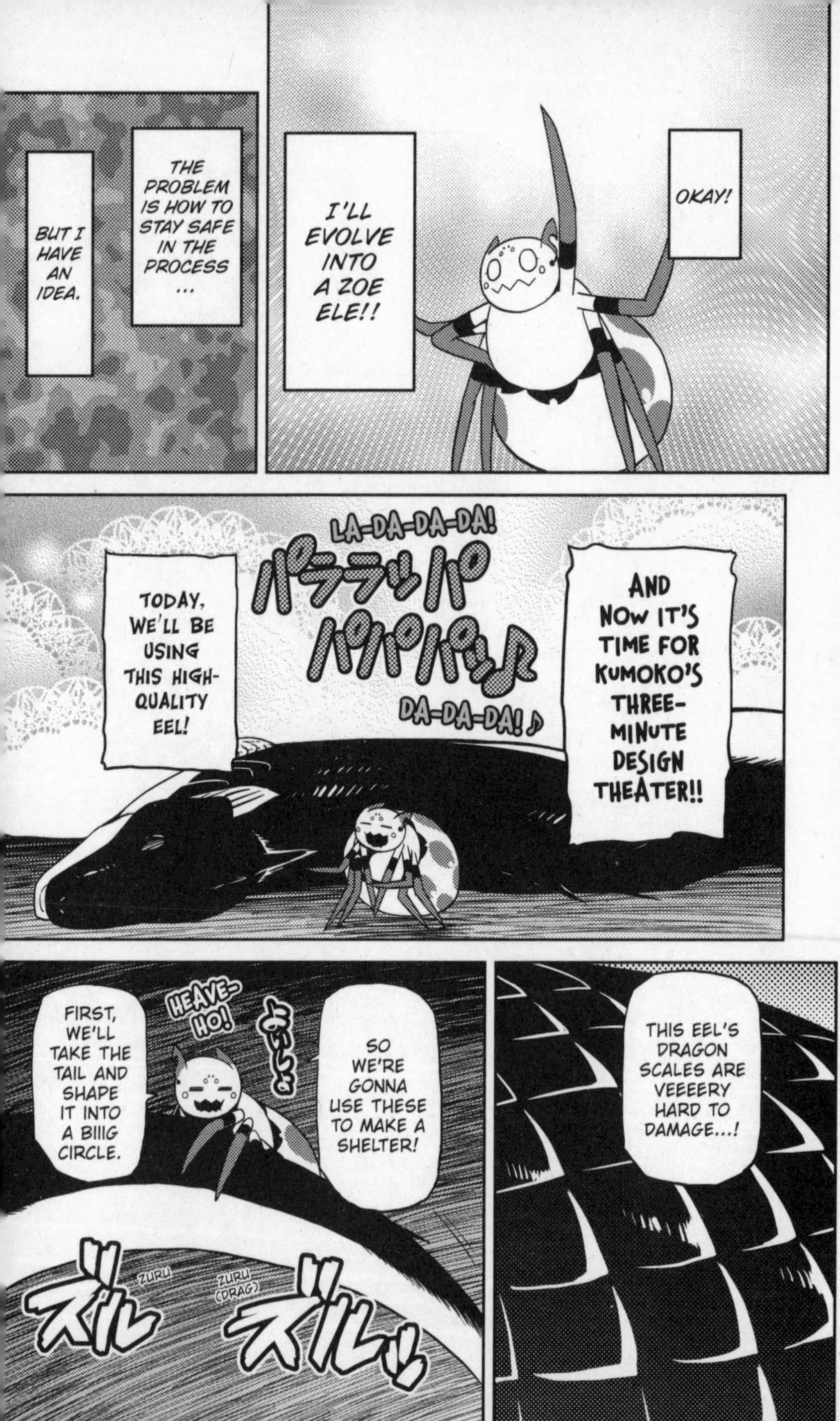
OKAY!
I'LL EVOLVE INTO A ZOE ELE!!
THE PROBLEM IS HOW TO STAY SAFE IN THE PROCESS...
BUT I HAVE AN IDEA.
AND NOW IT'S TIME FOR KUMOKO'S THREE-MINUTE DESIGN THEATER!!
LA-DA-DA-DA!
パラッパ
パパパッ♪
DA-DA-DA!♪
TODAY, WE'LL BE USING THIS HIGH-QUALITY EEL!
THIS EEL'S DRAGON SCALES ARE VEEEERY HARD TO DAMAGE...!
SO WE'RE GONNA USE THESE TO MAKE A SHELTER!
よいしょ
HEAVE-HO!
FIRST, WE'LL TAKE THE TAIL AND SHAPE IT INTO A BIIIG CIRCLE.
ズル
ズルッ
ZURU
ZURU (DRAG)

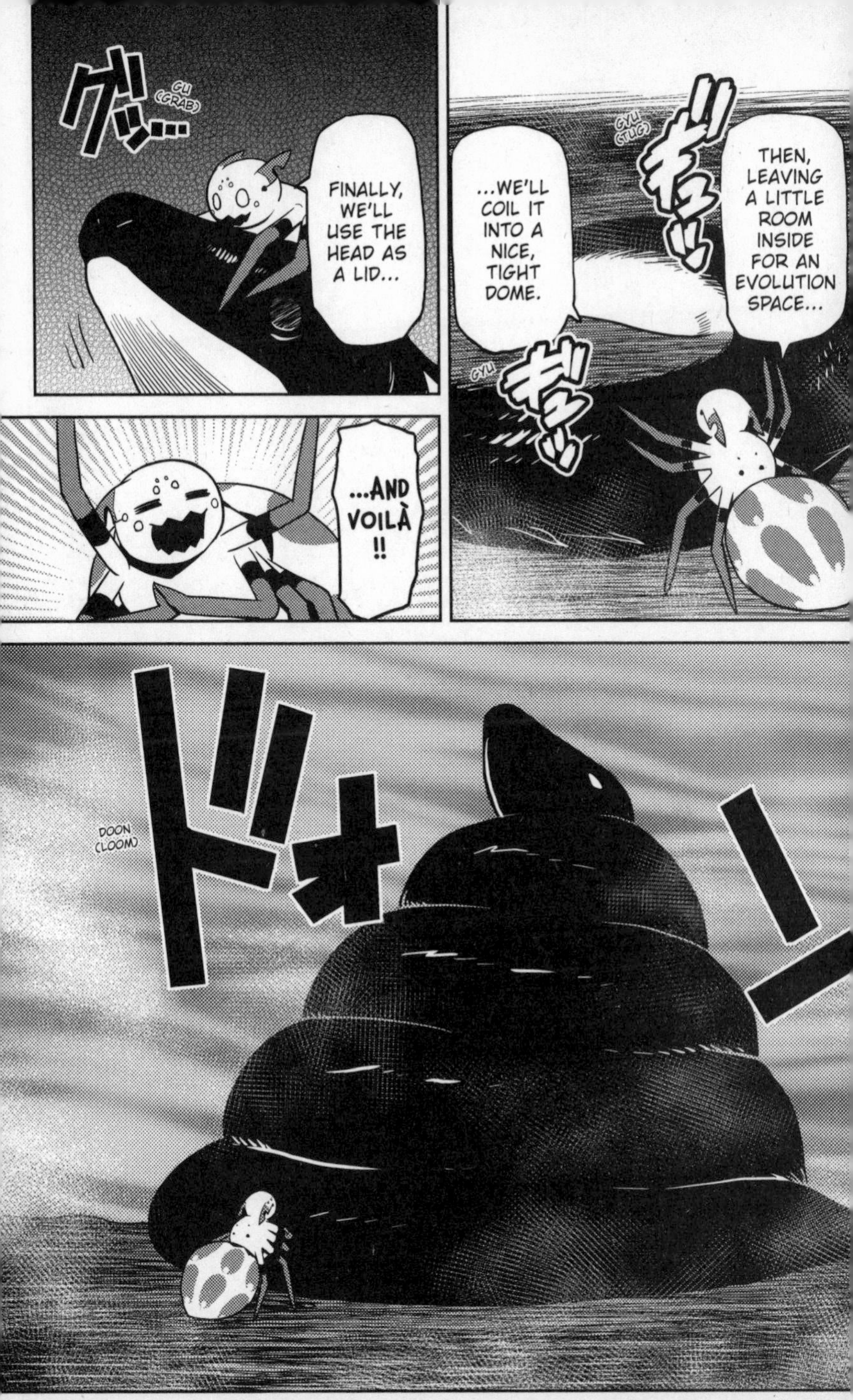
THEN, LEAVING A LITTLE ROOM INSIDE FOR AN EVOLUTION SPACE...
GYU (TUG)
...WE'LL COIL IT INTO A NICE, TIGHT DOME.
GYU
GU (GRAB)
FINALLY, WE'LL USE THE HEAD AS A LID...
...AND VOILÀ!!
DOON (LOOM)

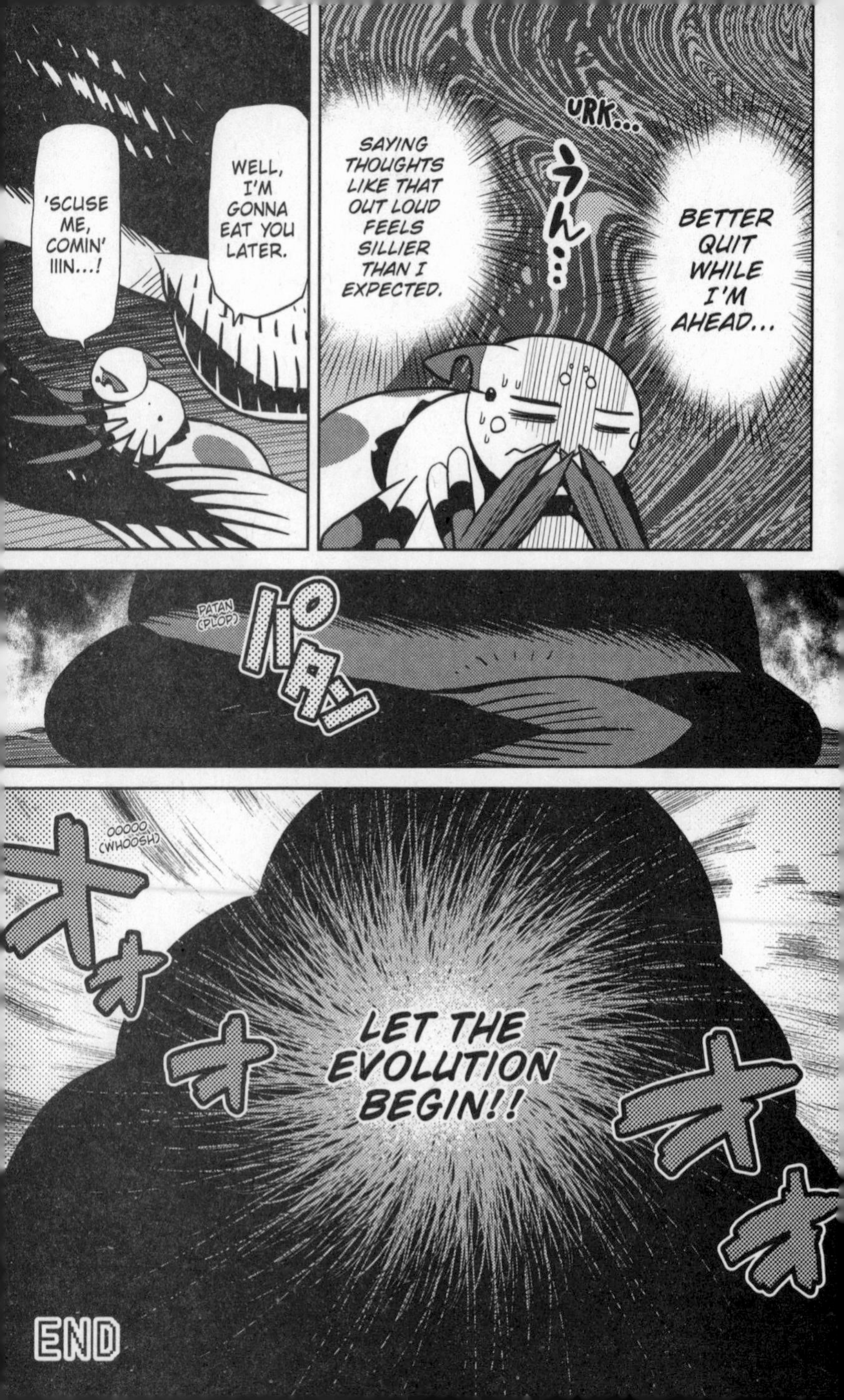
URK...
うん…
BETTER QUIT WHILE I'M AHEAD...
SAYING THOUGHTS LIKE THAT OUT LOUD FEELS SILLIER THAN I EXPECTED.
WELL, I'M GONNA EAT YOU LATER.
'SCUSE ME, COMIN' IIIN...!
PATAN (PLOP)
パタン
OOOOO (WHOOSH)
LET THE EVOLUTION BEGIN!!
END

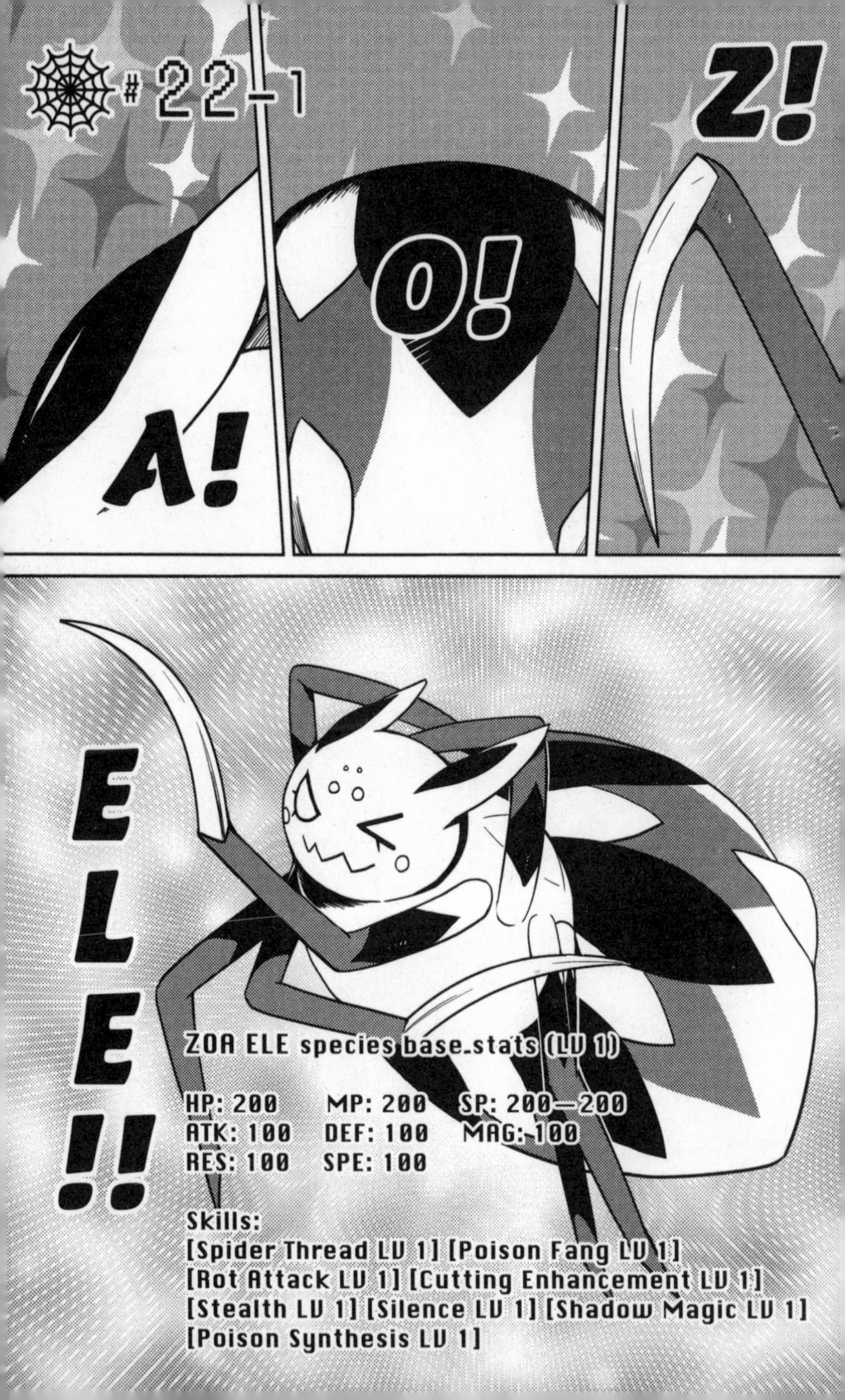
#22-1
Z!
O!
A!
ELE!!
ZOA ELE species base stats (LV 1)
HP: 200 MP: 200 SP: 200—200
ATK: 100 DEF: 100 MAG: 100
RES: 100 SPE: 100
Skills:
[Spider Thread LV 1] [Poison Fang LV 1]
[Rot Attack LV 1] [Cutting Enhancement LV 1]
[Stealth LV 1] [Silence LV 1] [Shadow Magic LV 1]
[Poison Synthesis LV 1]

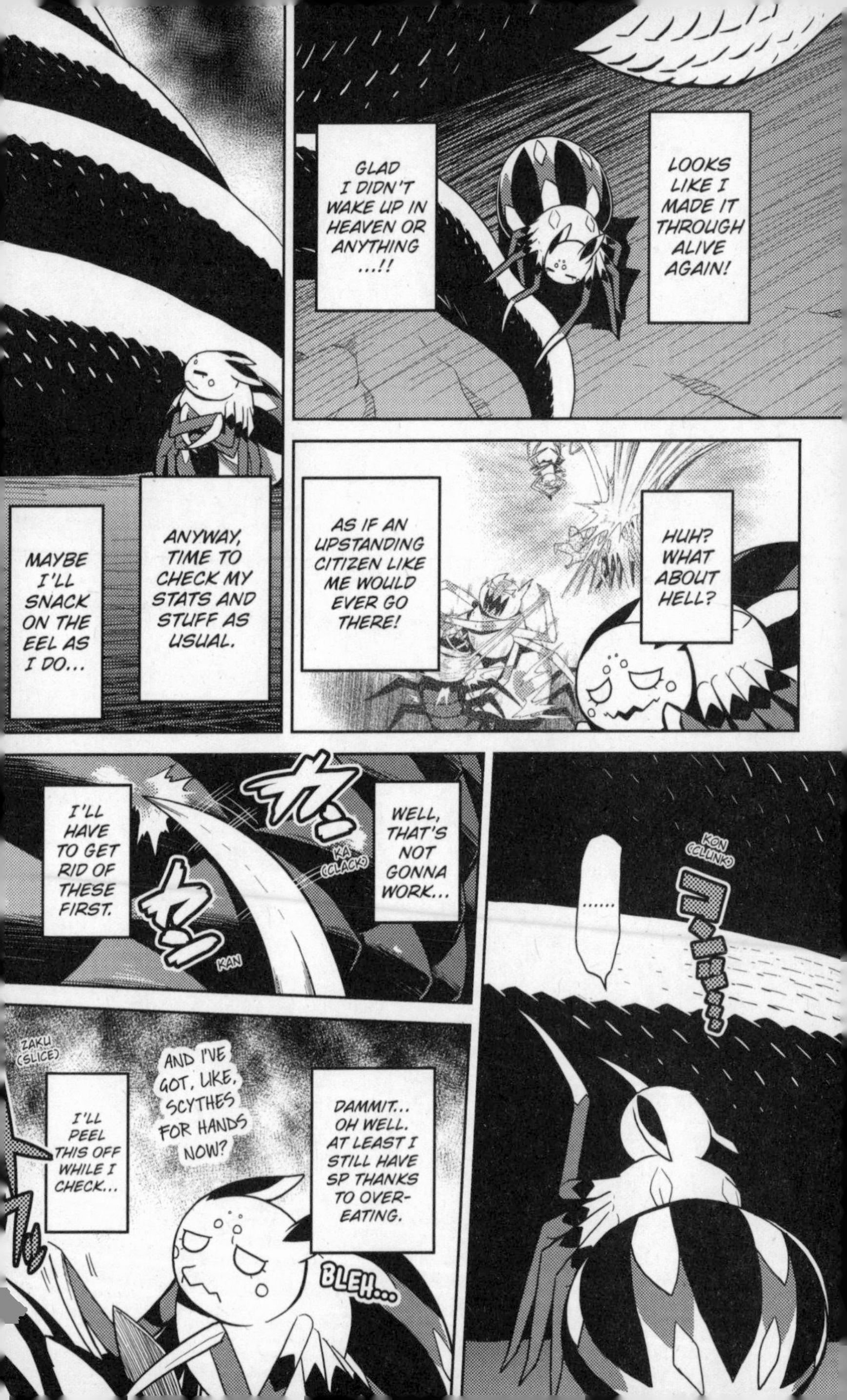
LOOKS LIKE I MADE IT THROUGH ALIVE AGAIN!
GLAD I DIDN'T WAKE UP IN HEAVEN OR ANYTHING ...!!
HUH? WHAT ABOUT HELL?
AS IF AN UPSTANDING CITIZEN LIKE ME WOULD EVER GO THERE!
ANYWAY, TIME TO CHECK MY STATS AND STUFF AS USUAL.
MAYBE I'LL SNACK ON THE EEL AS I DO...
KON (CLINK)
......
WELL, THAT'S NOT GONNA WORK...
KA (CLACK)
I'LL HAVE TO GET RID OF THESE FIRST.
KAN
DAMMIT... OH WELL. AT LEAST I STILL HAVE SP THANKS TO OVER-EATING.
AND I'VE GOT, LIKE, SCYTHES FOR HANDS NOW?
BLEH...
I'LL PEEL THIS OFF WHILE I CHECK...
ZAKU (SLICE)

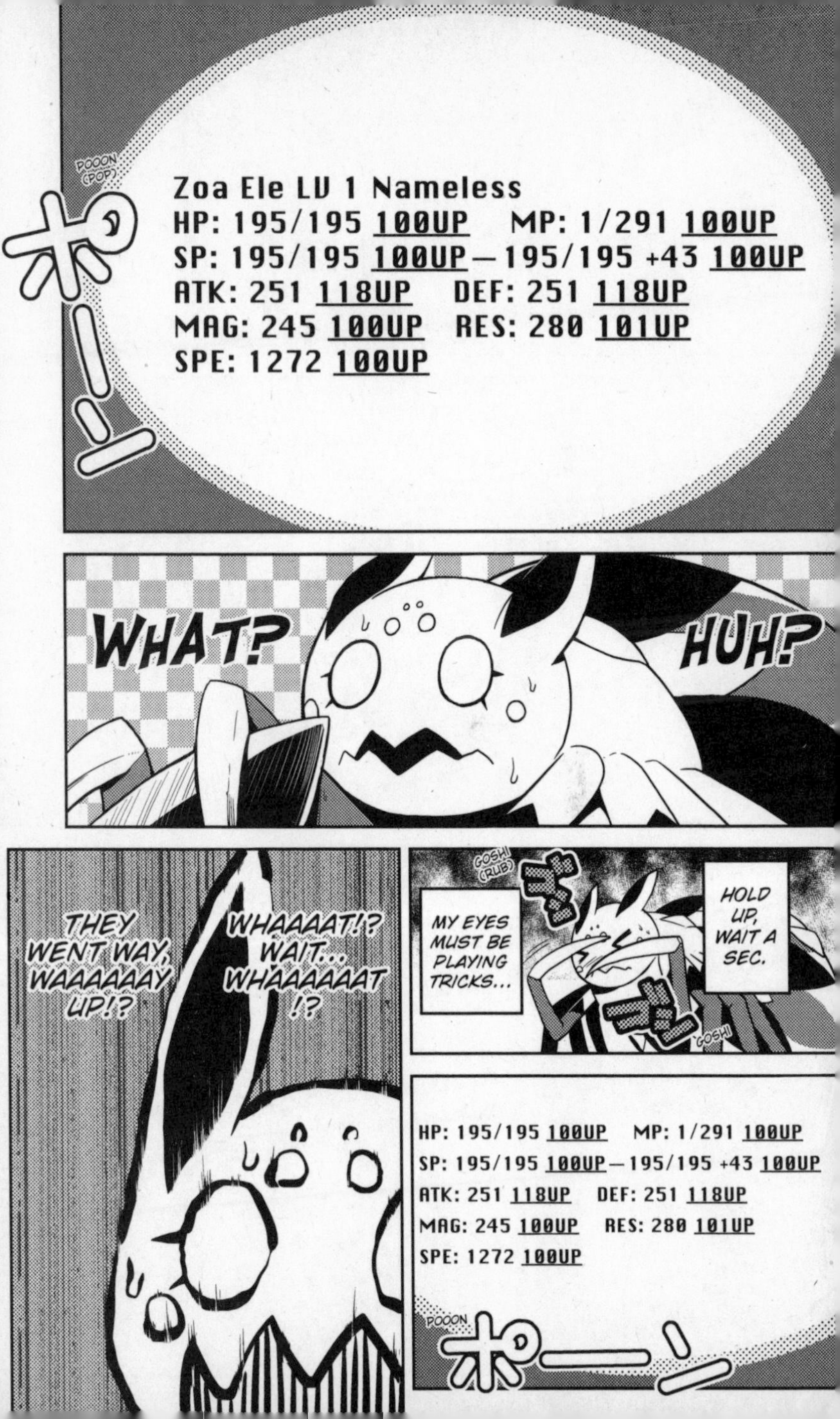
Zoa Ele LV 1 Nameless
HP: 195/195 100UP MP: 1/291 100UP
SP: 195/195 100UP—195/195 +43 100UP
ATK: 251 118UP DEF: 251 118UP
MAG: 245 100UP RES: 280 101UP
SPE: 1272 100UP
POOON (POP)
HUH?
WHAT?
HOLD UP, WAIT A SEC.
GOSHI (RUB)
MY EYES MUST BE PLAYING TRICKS...
GOSHI
HP: 195/195 100UP MP: 1/291 100UP
SP: 195/195 100UP—195/195 +43 100UP
ATK: 251 118UP DEF: 251 118UP
MAG: 245 100UP RES: 280 101UP
SPE: 1272 100UP
POOON
WHAAAAT!? WAIT... WHAAAAAAT!?
THEY WENT WAY, WAAAAAAY UP!?

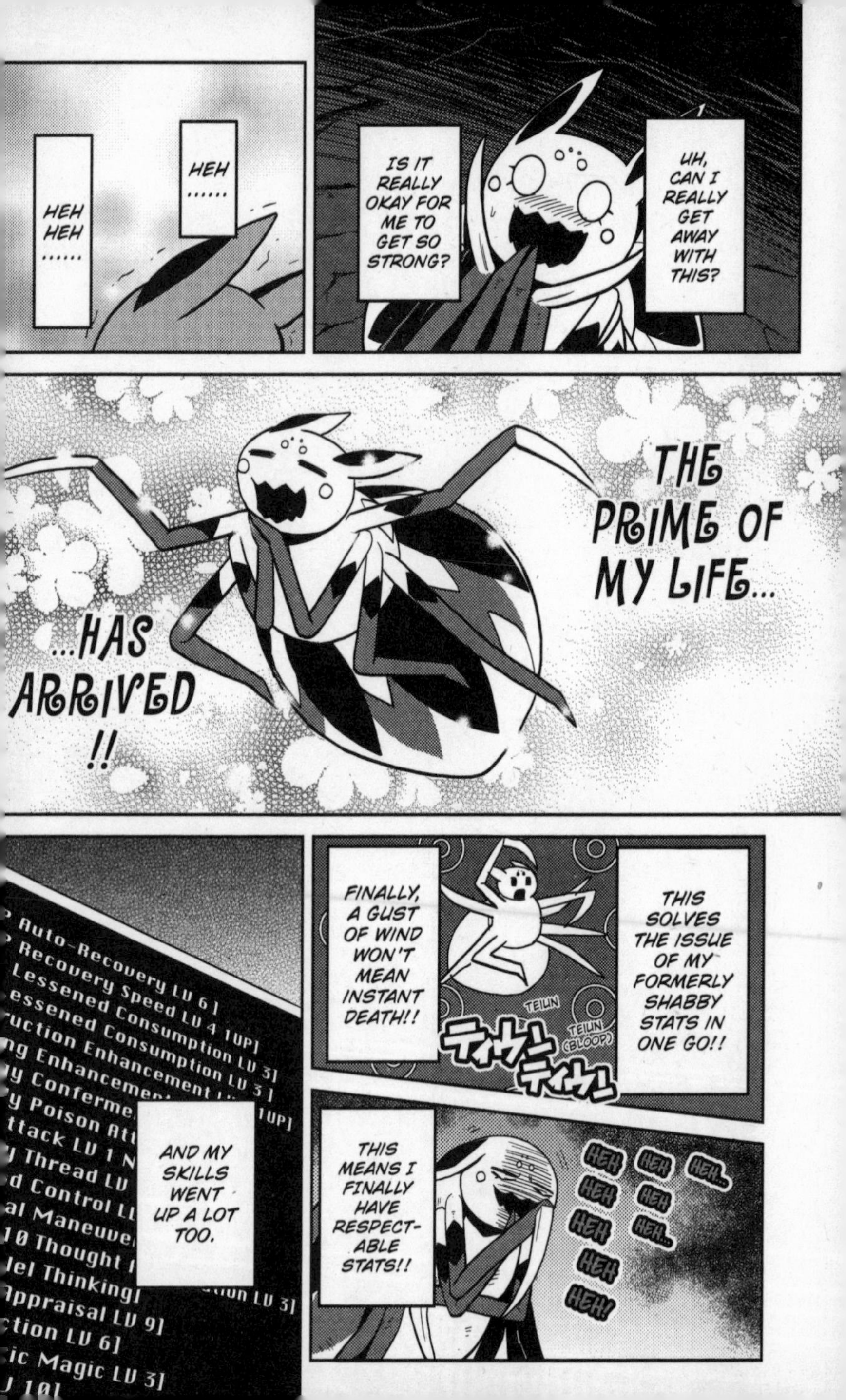
UH, CAN I REALLY GET AWAY WITH THIS?
IS IT REALLY OKAY FOR ME TO GET SO STRONG?
HEH......
HEH HEH......
THE PRIME OF MY LIFE...
...HAS ARRIVED!!
THIS SOLVES THE ISSUE OF MY FORMERLY SHABBY STATS IN ONE GO!!
FINALLY, A GUST OF WIND WON'T MEAN INSTANT DEATH!!
TEIUN TEIUN (BLOOP)
ティウン ティウン
HEH HEH HEH... HEH HEH HEH... HEH HEH HEH!
THIS MEANS I FINALLY HAVE RESPECT-ABLE STATS!!
Auto-Recovery
Recovery Speed LV 6]
Lessened Consumption LV 4 1UP]
essened Consumption LV 3]
uction Enhancement LV 3]
ng Enhancement
y Conferme 1UP]
y Poison Att
ttack LV 1 N
y Thread LV
d Control L
al Maneuve
10 Thought
lel Thinking] tion LV 3]
Appraisal LV 9]
ction LV 6]
ic Magic LV 3]
J 10]
AND MY SKILLS WENT UP A LOT TOO.

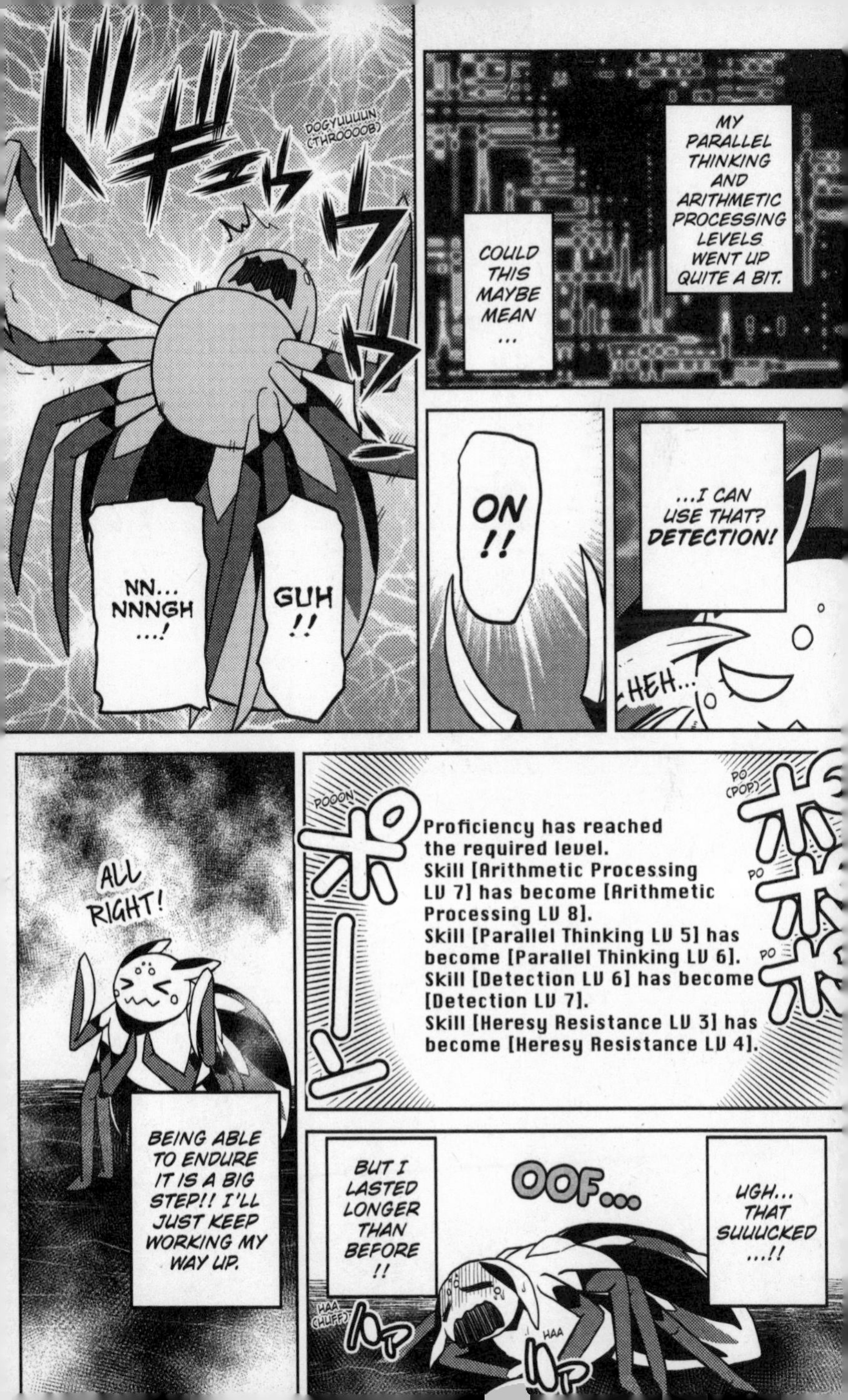
MY PARALLEL THINKING AND ARITHMETIC PROCESSING LEVELS WENT UP QUITE A BIT.
COULD THIS MAYBE MEAN ...
...I CAN USE THAT? DETECTION!
HEH...
ON !!
DOGYUUUUN (THROOOOB)
GUH !!
NN... NNNGH ...!
PO (POP)
PO
PO
POOOON
Proficiency has reached the required level.
Skill [Arithmetic Processing LV 7] has become [Arithmetic Processing LV 8].
Skill [Parallel Thinking LV 5] has become [Parallel Thinking LV 6].
Skill [Detection LV 6] has become [Detection LV 7].
Skill [Heresy Resistance LV 3] has become [Heresy Resistance LV 4].
UGH... THAT SUUUCKED ...!!
OOF...
BUT I LASTED LONGER THAN BEFORE !!
HAA (HUFF)
HAA
ALL RIGHT!
BEING ABLE TO ENDURE IT IS A BIG STEP!! I'LL JUST KEEP WORKING MY WAY UP.

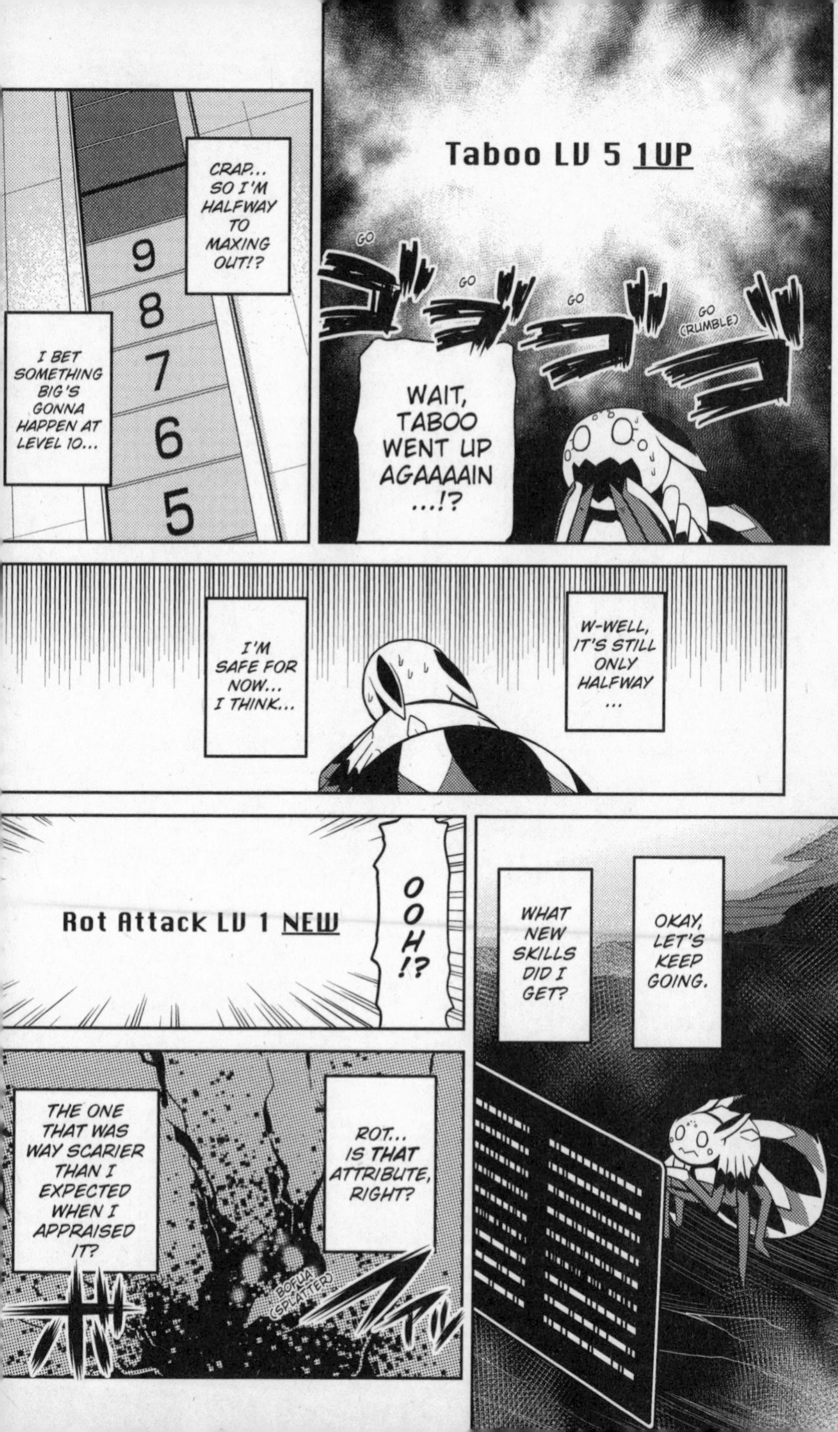
Taboo LV 5 1UP
GO
GO
GO
GO (RUMBLE)
WAIT, TABOO WENT UP AGAAAAIN ...!?
CRAP... SO I'M HALFWAY TO MAXING OUT!?
I BET SOMETHING BIG'S GONNA HAPPEN AT LEVEL 10...
9
8
7
6
5
W-WELL, IT'S STILL ONLY HALFWAY ...
I'M SAFE FOR NOW... I THINK...
OKAY, LET'S KEEP GOING.
WHAT NEW SKILLS DID I GET?
Rot Attack LV 1 NEW
OOH!?
ROT... IS THAT ATTRIBUTE, RIGHT?
THE ONE THAT WAS WAY SCARIER THAN I EXPECTED WHEN I APPRAISED IT?
BOFUA (SPLATTER)

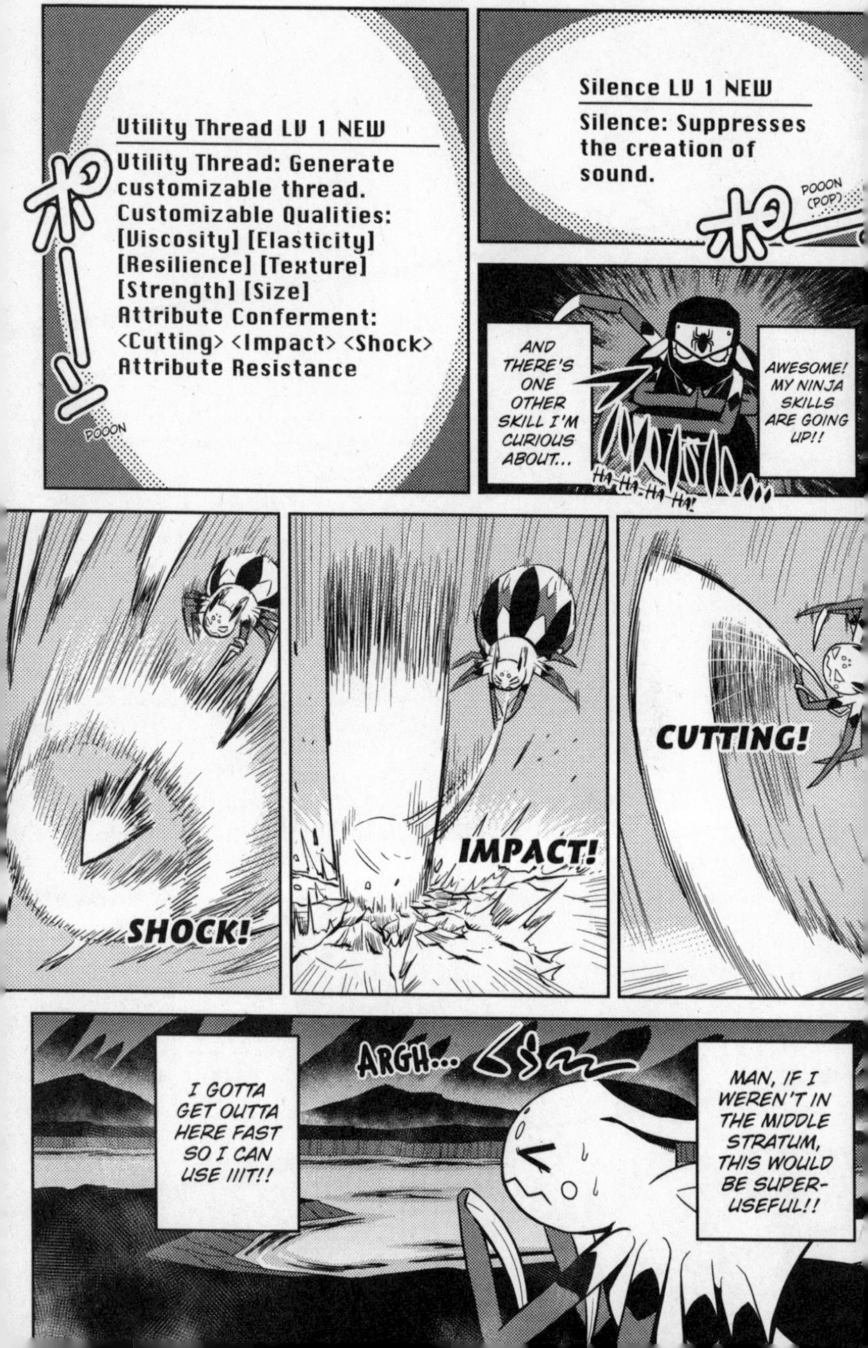

Silence LV 1 NEW
Silence: Suppresses the creation of sound.
POOON (POP)
AWESOME! MY NINJA SKILLS ARE GOING UP!!
AND THERE'S ONE OTHER SKILL I'M CURIOUS ABOUT...
HA HA HA HA!
Utility Thread LV 1 NEW
Utility Thread: Generate customizable thread.
Customizable Qualities:
[Viscosity] [Elasticity]
[Resilience] [Texture]
[Strength] [Size]
Attribute Conferment:
<Cutting> <Impact> <Shock>
Attribute Resistance
POOON
CUTTING!
IMPACT!
SHOCK!
ARGH...
MAN, IF I WEREN'T IN THE MIDDLE STRATUM, THIS WOULD BE SUPER-USEFUL!!
I GOTTA GET OUTTA HERE FAST SO I CAN USE IIIT!!

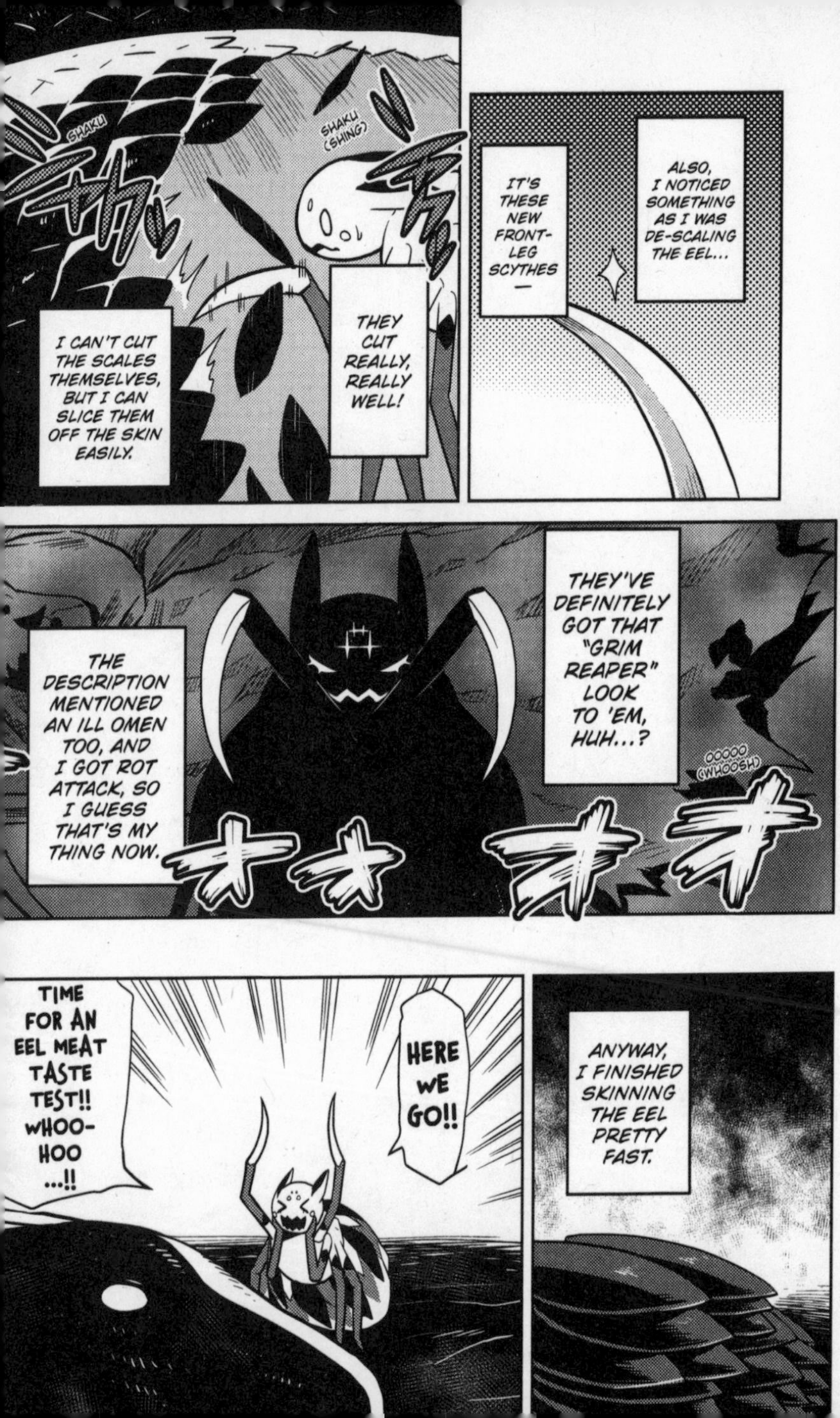
ALSO, I NOTICED SOMETHING AS I WAS DE-SCALING THE EEL...
IT'S THESE NEW FRONT-LEG SCYTHES —
SHAKU (SHING)
SHAKU
THEY CUT REALLY, REALLY WELL!
I CAN'T CUT THE SCALES THEMSELVES, BUT I CAN SLICE THEM OFF THE SKIN EASILY.
THEY'VE DEFINITELY GOT THAT "GRIM REAPER" LOOK TO 'EM, HUH...?
OOOOO (WHOOSH)
THE DESCRIPTION MENTIONED AN ILL OMEN TOO, AND I GOT ROT ATTACK, SO I GUESS THAT'S MY THING NOW.
ANYWAY, I FINISHED SKINNING THE EEL PRETTY FAST.
HERE WE GO!!
TIME FOR AN EEL MEAT TASTE TEST!! WHOO-HOO...!!

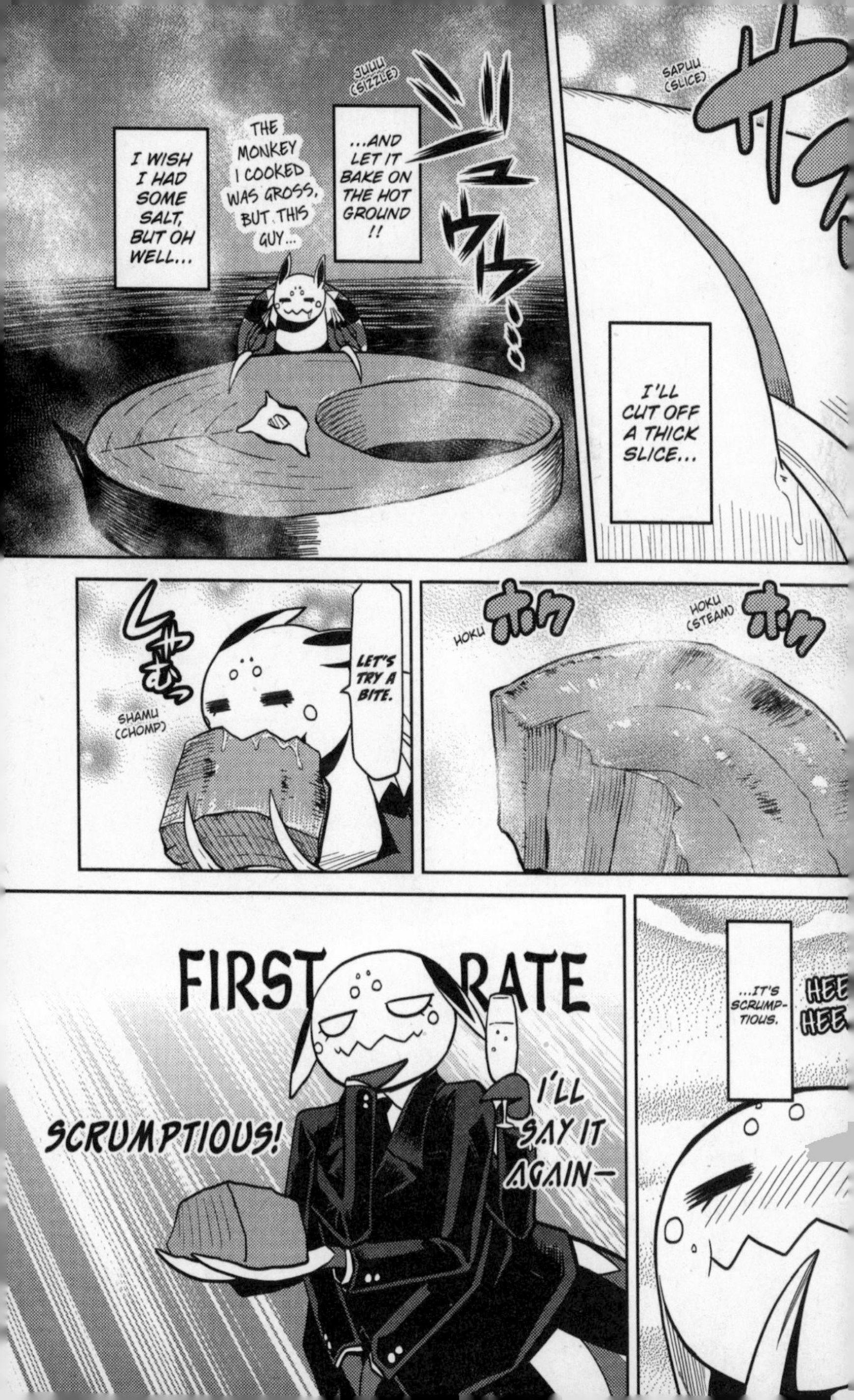
SAPUU (SLICE)
I'LL CUT OFF A THICK SLICE...
JUUU (SIZZLE)
...AND LET IT BAKE ON THE HOT GROUND !!
THE MONKEY I COOKED WAS GROSS, BUT THIS GUY...
I WISH I HAD SOME SALT, BUT OH WELL...
HOKU (STEAM)
HOKU
LET'S TRY A BITE.
SHAMU (CHOMP)
...IT'S SCRUMPTIOUS.
HEE HEE
FIRST RATE
I'LL SAY IT AGAIN—
SCRUMPTIOUS!

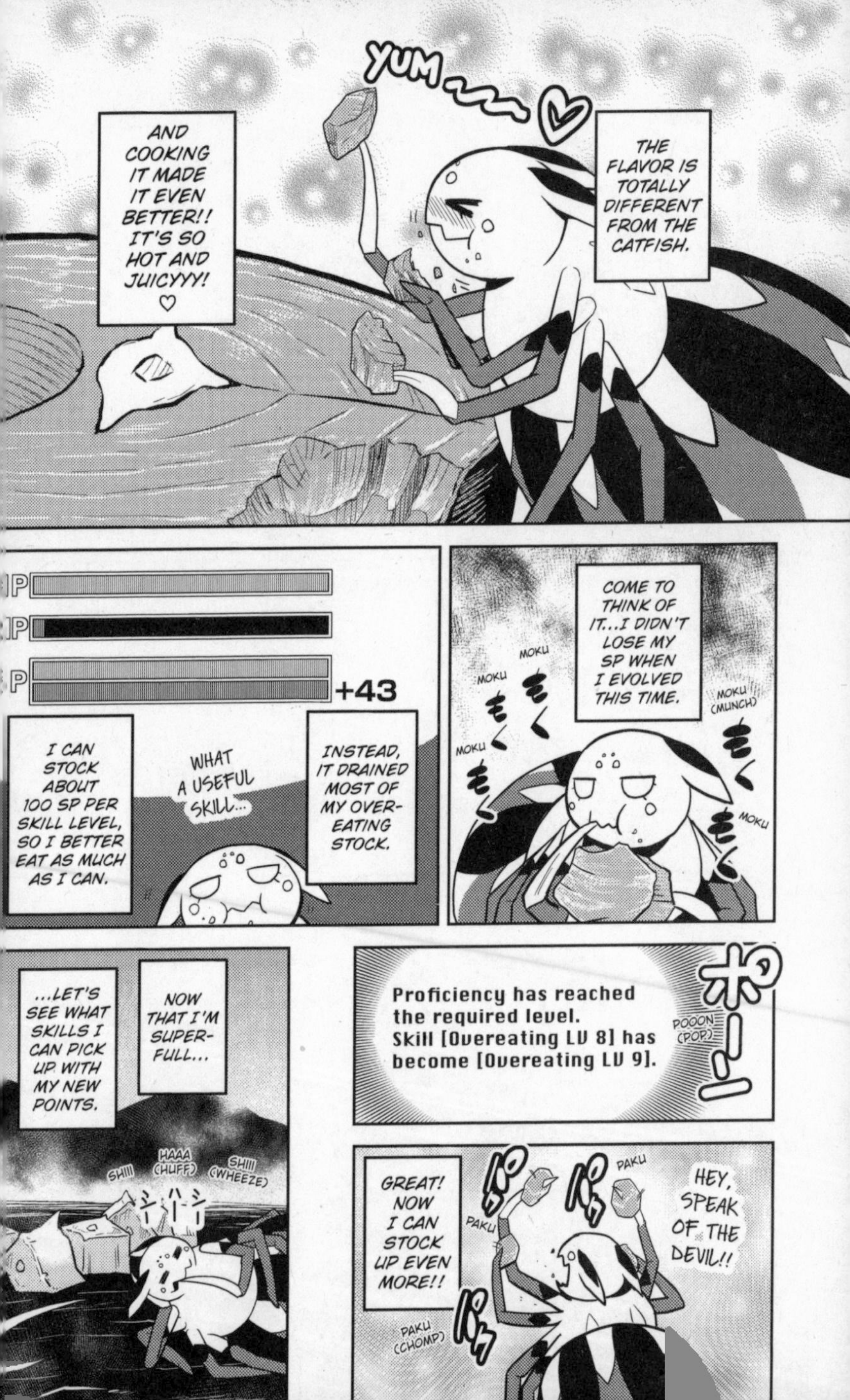
YUM ~~~ ♡
THE FLAVOR IS TOTALLY DIFFERENT FROM THE CATFISH.
AND COOKING IT MADE IT EVEN BETTER!! IT'S SO HOT AND JUICYYY! ♡
COME TO THINK OF IT...I DIDN'T LOSE MY SP WHEN I EVOLVED THIS TIME.
MOKU (MUNCH)
MOKU
MOKU
MOKU
MOKU
+43
INSTEAD, IT DRAINED MOST OF MY OVER-EATING STOCK.
WHAT A USEFUL SKILL...
I CAN STOCK ABOUT 100 SP PER SKILL LEVEL, SO I BETTER EAT AS MUCH AS I CAN.
POOON (POP)
Proficiency has reached the required level.
Skill [Overeating LV 8] has become [Overeating LV 9].
HEY, SPEAK OF THE DEVIL!!
PAKU
PAKU
GREAT! NOW I CAN STOCK UP EVEN MORE!!
PAKU (CHOMP)
NOW THAT I'M SUPER-FULL...
...LET'S SEE WHAT SKILLS I CAN PICK UP WITH MY NEW POINTS.
SHIII (WHEEZE)
HAAA (HUFF)
SHIII

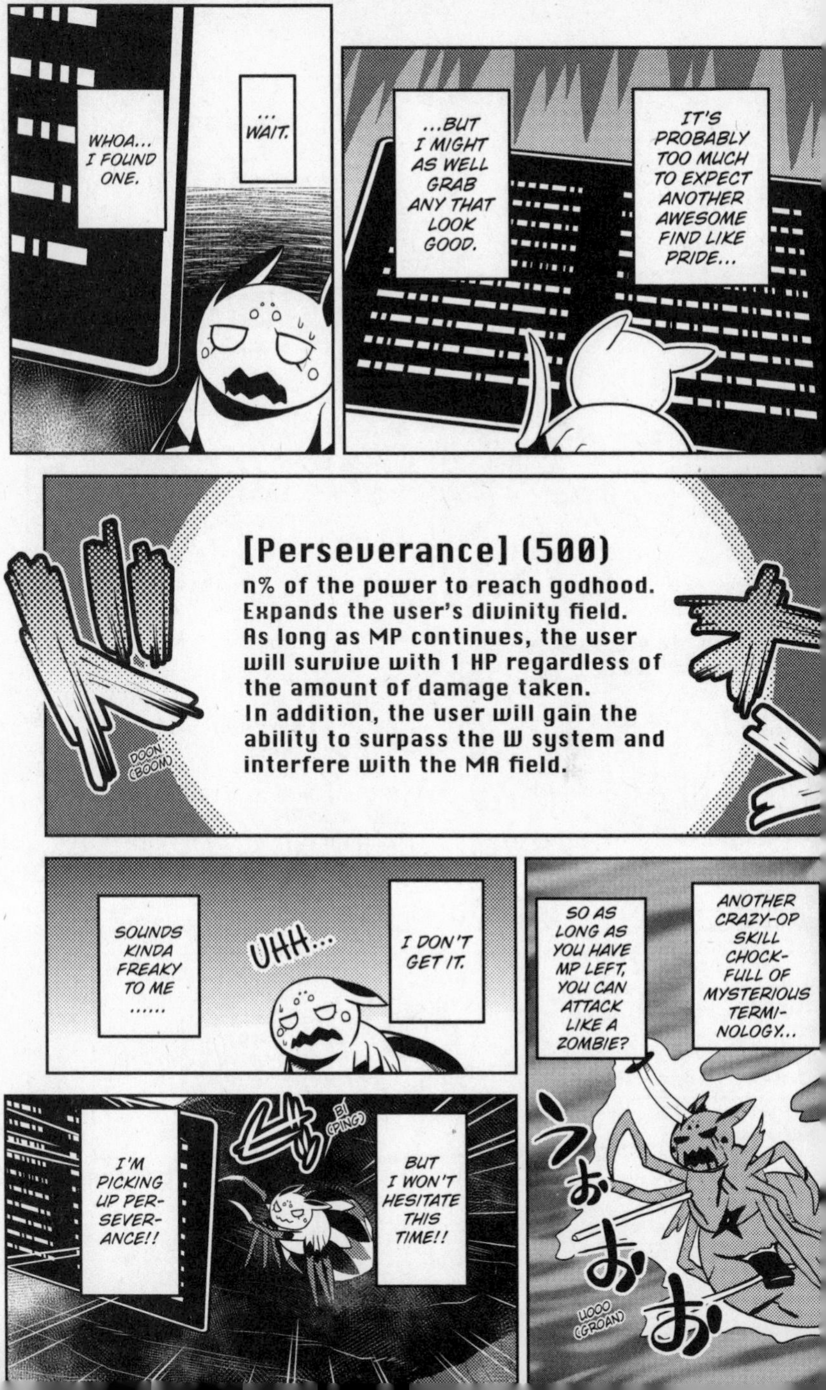
IT'S PROBABLY TOO MUCH TO EXPECT ANOTHER AWESOME FIND LIKE PRIDE...
...BUT I MIGHT AS WELL GRAB ANY THAT LOOK GOOD.
...WAIT.
WHOA... I FOUND ONE.
[Perseverance] (500)
n% of the power to reach godhood.
Expands the user's divinity field.
As long as MP continues, the user will survive with 1 HP regardless of the amount of damage taken.
In addition, the user will gain the ability to surpass the W system and interfere with the MA field.
DOON (BOOM)
ANOTHER CRAZY-OP SKILL CHOCK-FULL OF MYSTERIOUS TERMI-NOLOGY...
SO AS LONG AS YOU HAVE MP LEFT, YOU CAN ATTACK LIKE A ZOMBIE?
うぉおお
UOOO (GROAN)
I DON'T GET IT.
UHH...
SOUNDS KINDA FREAKY TO ME ......
BUT I WON'T HESITATE THIS TIME!!
BI (PING)
I'M PICKING UP PER-SEVER-ANCE!!

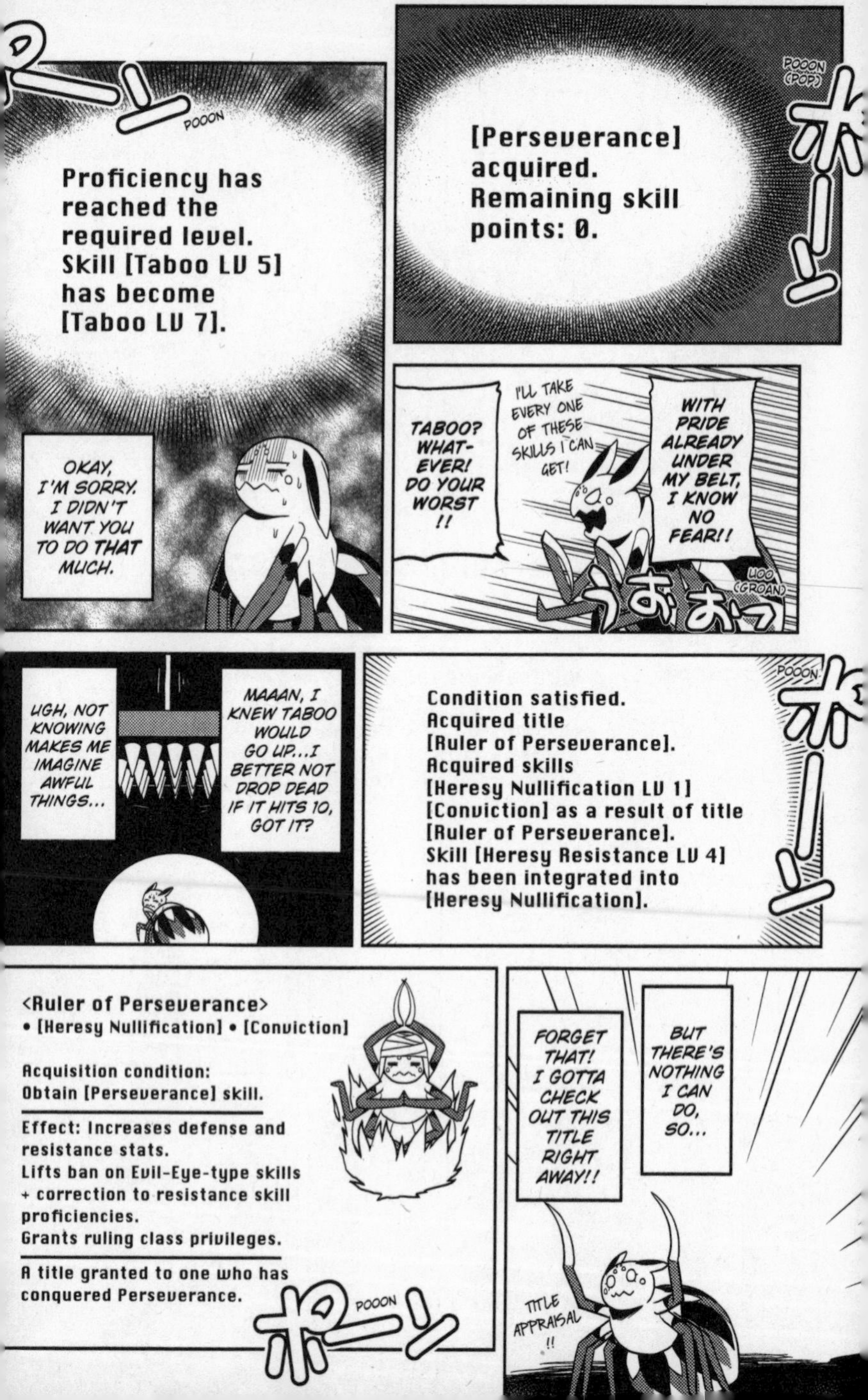
POOON (POP)
[Perseverance] acquired. Remaining skill points: 0.
WITH PRIDE ALREADY UNDER MY BELT, I KNOW NO FEAR!!
I'LL TAKE EVERY ONE OF THESE SKILLS I CAN GET!
TABOO? WHAT-EVER! DO YOUR WORST!!
UOO (GROAN)
POOON
Proficiency has reached the required level. Skill [Taboo LV 5] has become [Taboo LV 7].
OKAY, I'M SORRY. I DIDN'T WANT YOU TO DO THAT MUCH.
POOON
Condition satisfied. Acquired title [Ruler of Perseverance]. Acquired skills [Heresy Nullification LV 1] [Conviction] as a result of title [Ruler of Perseverance]. Skill [Heresy Resistance LV 4] has been integrated into [Heresy Nullification].
MAAAN, I KNEW TABOO WOULD GO UP...I BETTER NOT DROP DEAD IF IT HITS 10, GOT IT?
UGH, NOT KNOWING MAKES ME IMAGINE AWFUL THINGS...
BUT THERE'S NOTHING I CAN DO, SO...
FORGET THAT! I GOTTA CHECK OUT THIS TITLE RIGHT AWAY!!
TITLE APPRAISAL!!
<Ruler of Perseverance>
• [Heresy Nullification] • [Conviction]
Acquisition condition: Obtain [Perseverance] skill.
Effect: Increases defense and resistance stats.
Lifts ban on Evil-Eye-type skills + correction to resistance skill proficiencies.
Grants ruling class privileges.
A title granted to one who has conquered Perseverance.
POOON

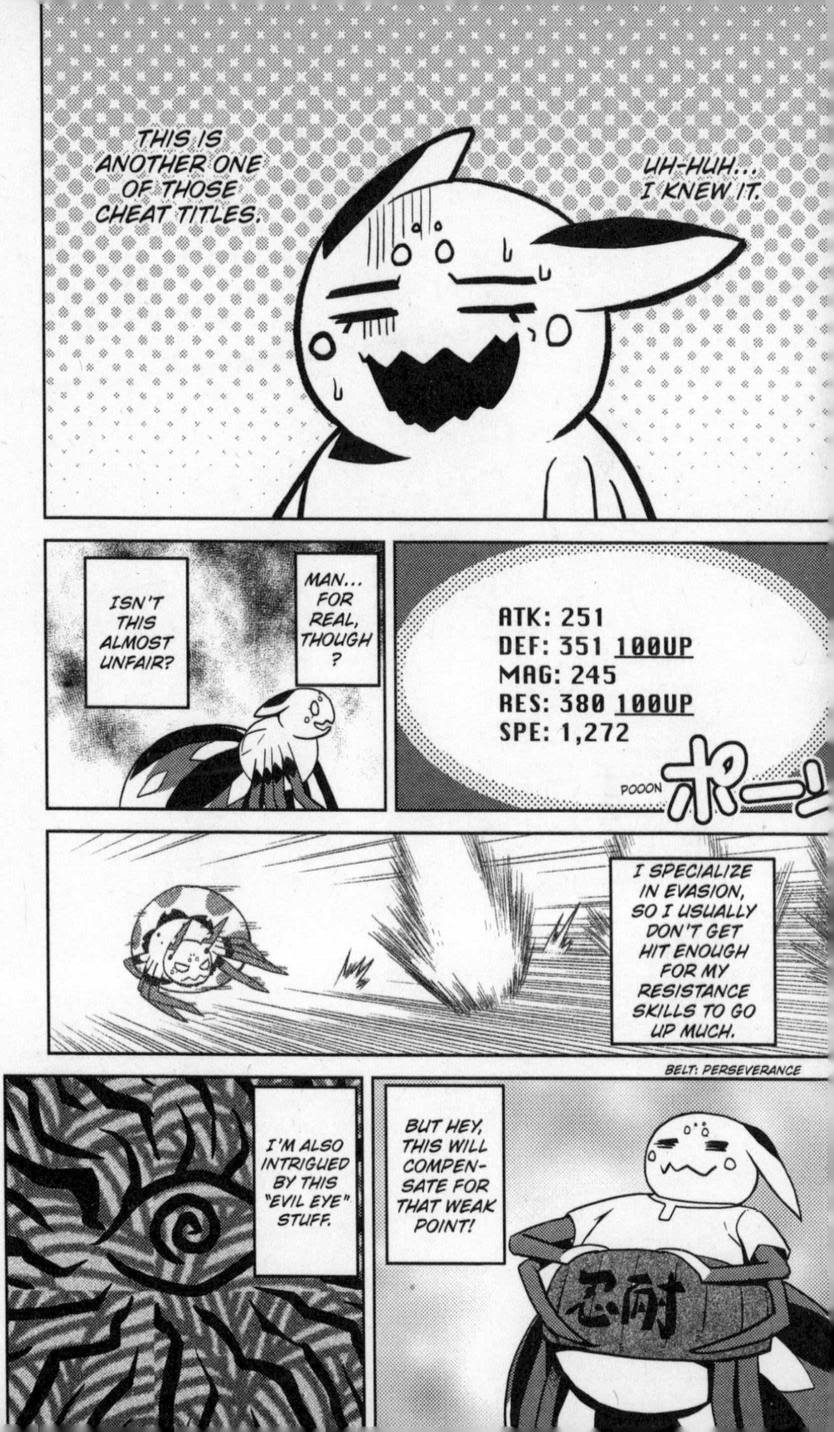
UH-HUH... I KNEW IT.
THIS IS ANOTHER ONE OF THOSE CHEAT TITLES.
ATK: 251
DEF: 351 100UP
MAG: 245
RES: 380 100UP
SPE: 1,272
POOON
ポー
MAN... FOR REAL, THOUGH?
ISN'T THIS ALMOST UNFAIR?
I SPECIALIZE IN EVASION, SO I USUALLY DON'T GET HIT ENOUGH FOR MY RESISTANCE SKILLS TO GO UP MUCH.
BELT: PERSEVERANCE
BUT HEY, THIS WILL COMPEN-SATE FOR THAT WEAK POINT!
忍耐
I'M ALSO INTRIGUED BY THIS "EVIL EYE" STUFF.

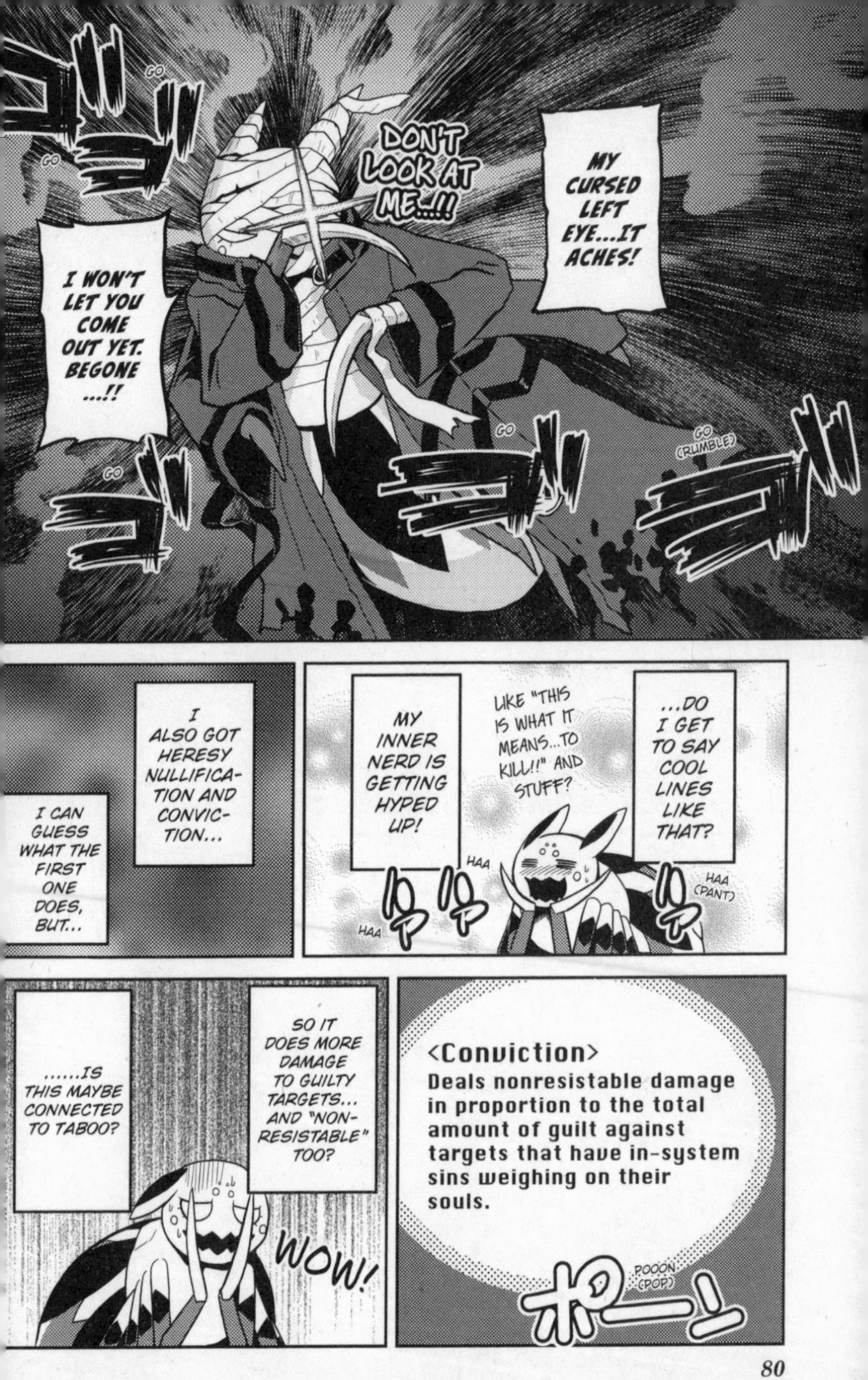
GO
GO
MY CURSED LEFT EYE...IT ACHES!
DON'T LOOK AT ME...!!
I WON'T LET YOU COME OUT YET. BEGONE ...!!
GO (RUMBLE)
GO
GO
...DO I GET TO SAY COOL LINES LIKE THAT?
LIKE "THIS IS WHAT IT MEANS...TO KILL!!" AND STUFF?
MY INNER NERD IS GETTING HYPED UP!
HAA (PANT)
HAA
HAA
I ALSO GOT HERESY NULLIFICATION AND CONVICTION...
I CAN GUESS WHAT THE FIRST ONE DOES, BUT...
<Conviction>
Deals nonresistable damage in proportion to the total amount of guilt against targets that have in-system sins weighing on their souls.
POOON (POP)
SO IT DOES MORE DAMAGE TO GUILTY TARGETS... AND "NON-RESISTABLE" TOO?
......IS THIS MAYBE CONNECTED TO TABOO?
WOW!

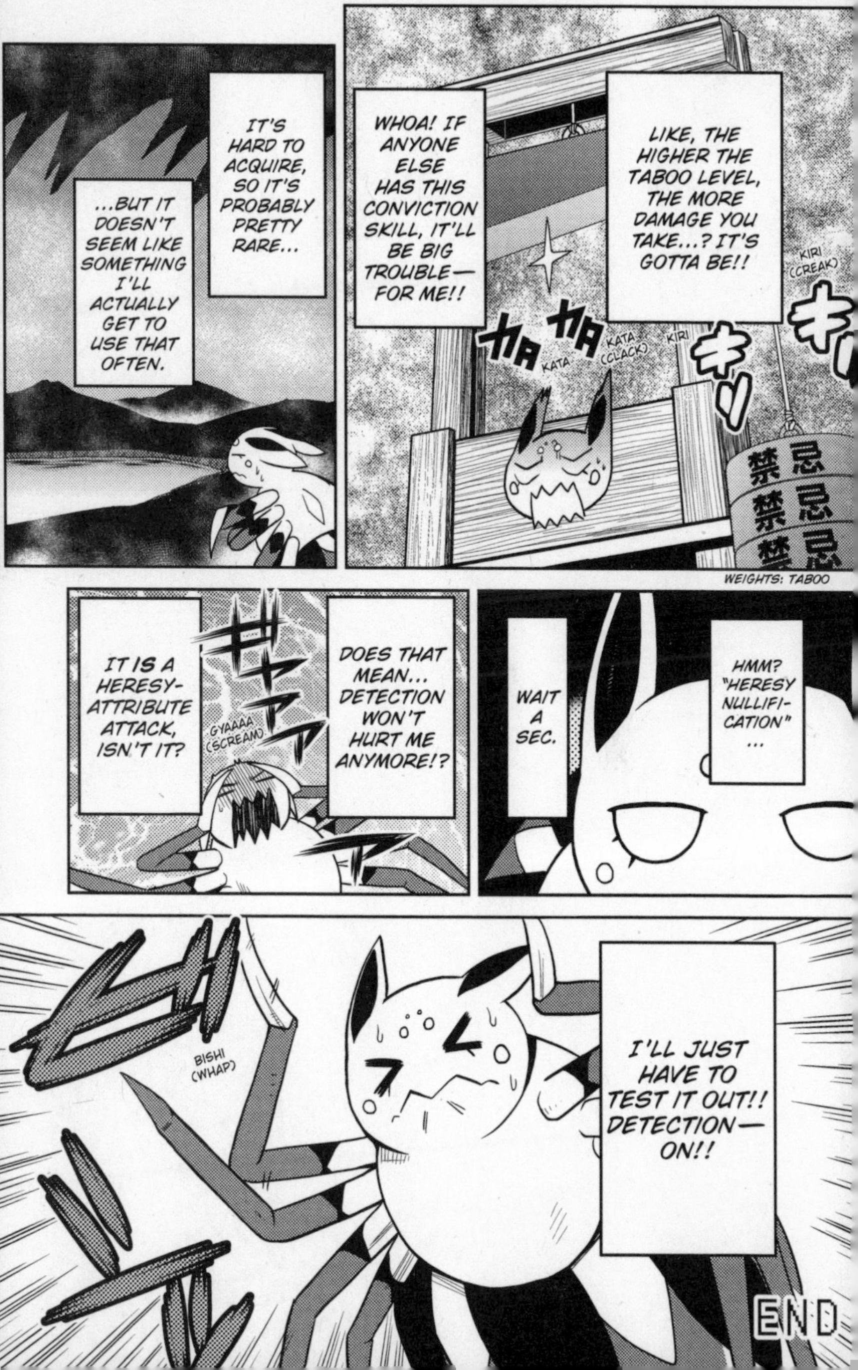
LIKE, THE HIGHER THE TABOO LEVEL, THE MORE DAMAGE YOU TAKE...? IT'S GOTTA BE!!
KIRI (CREAK)
WHOA! IF ANYONE ELSE HAS THIS CONVICTION SKILL, IT'LL BE BIG TROUBLE—FOR ME!!
KIRI
KATA (CLACK)
KATA
禁忌
禁忌
禁忌
WEIGHTS: TABOO
IT'S HARD TO ACQUIRE, SO IT'S PROBABLY PRETTY RARE...
...BUT IT DOESN'T SEEM LIKE SOMETHING I'LL ACTUALLY GET TO USE THAT OFTEN.
HMM? "HERESY NULLIFICATION"...
WAIT A SEC.
DOES THAT MEAN... DETECTION WON'T HURT ME ANYMORE!?
GYAAAA (SCREAM)
IT **IS** A HERESY-ATTRIBUTE ATTACK, ISN'T IT?
I'LL JUST HAVE TO TEST IT OUT!! DETECTION—ON!!
BISHI (WHAP)
END

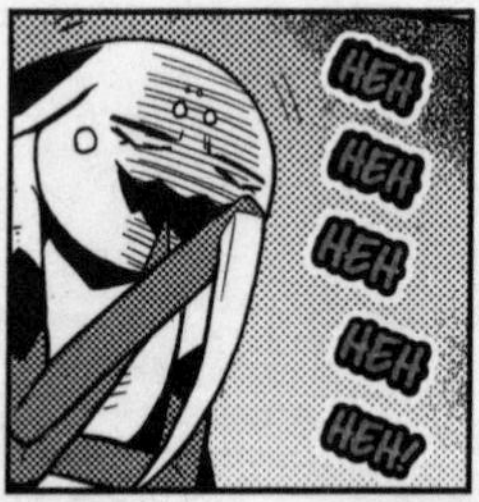
HEH HEH HEH HEH HEH!

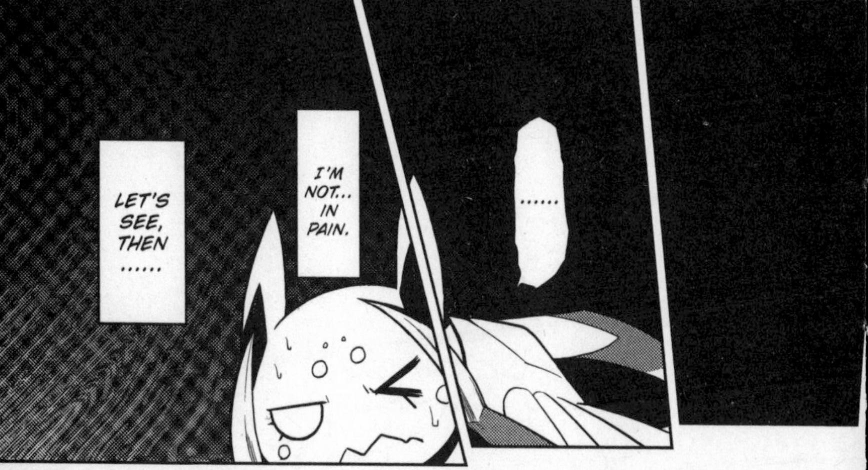
......
I'M NOT... IN PAIN.
LET'S SEE, THEN ......

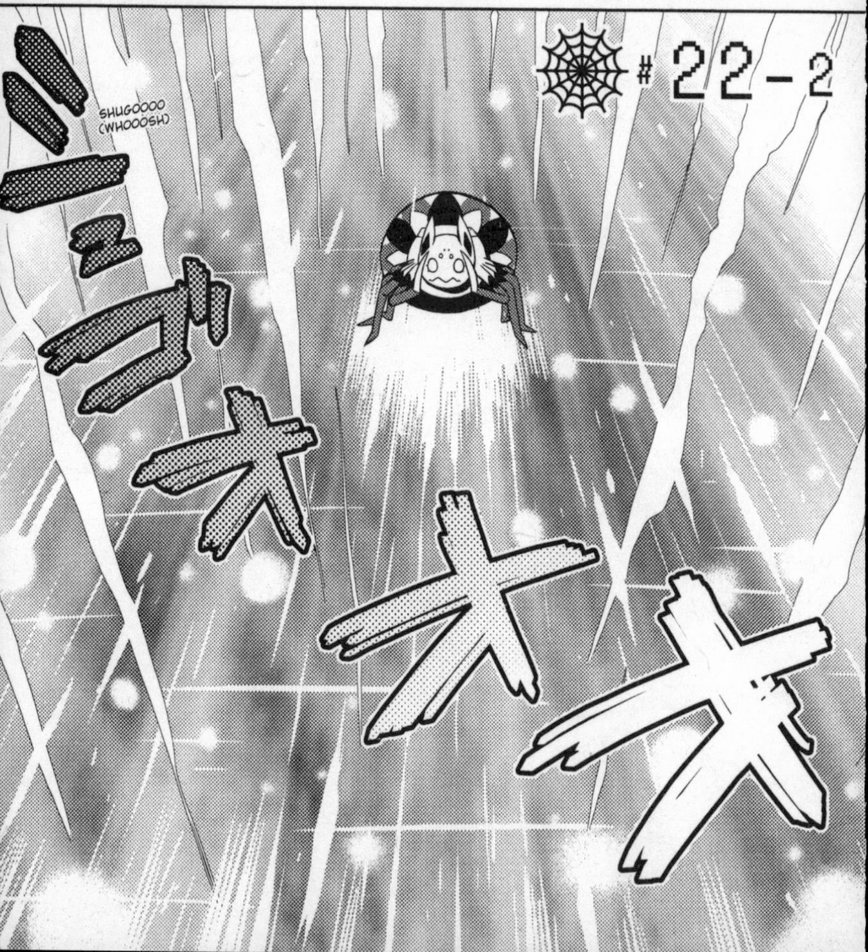
#22-2
SHUGOOOO (WHOOOSH)

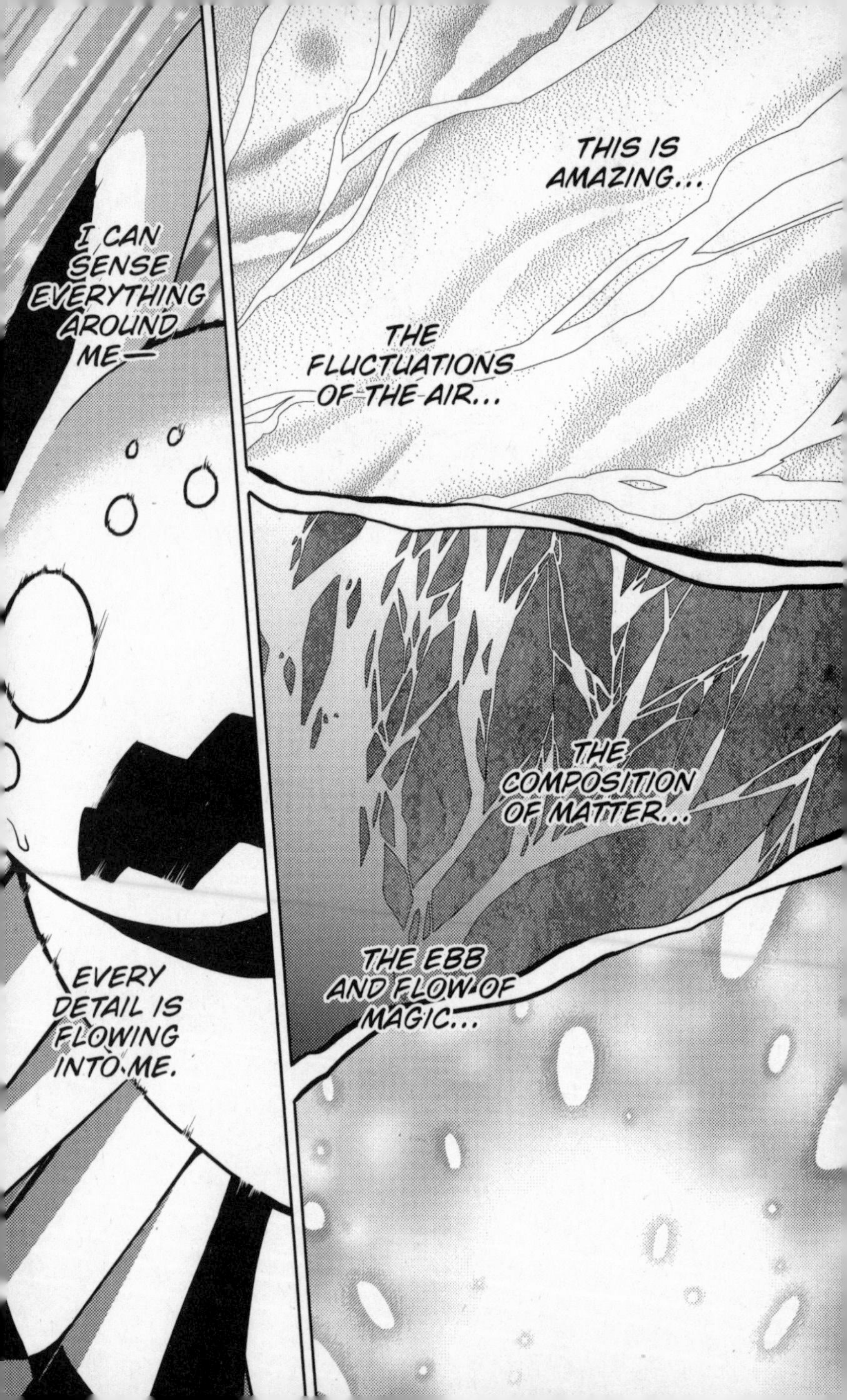
THIS IS AMAZING...
THE FLUCTUATIONS OF THE AIR...
THE COMPOSITION OF MATTER...
THE EBB AND FLOW OF MAGIC...
I CAN SENSE EVERYTHING AROUND ME—
EVERY DETAIL IS FLOWING INTO ME.

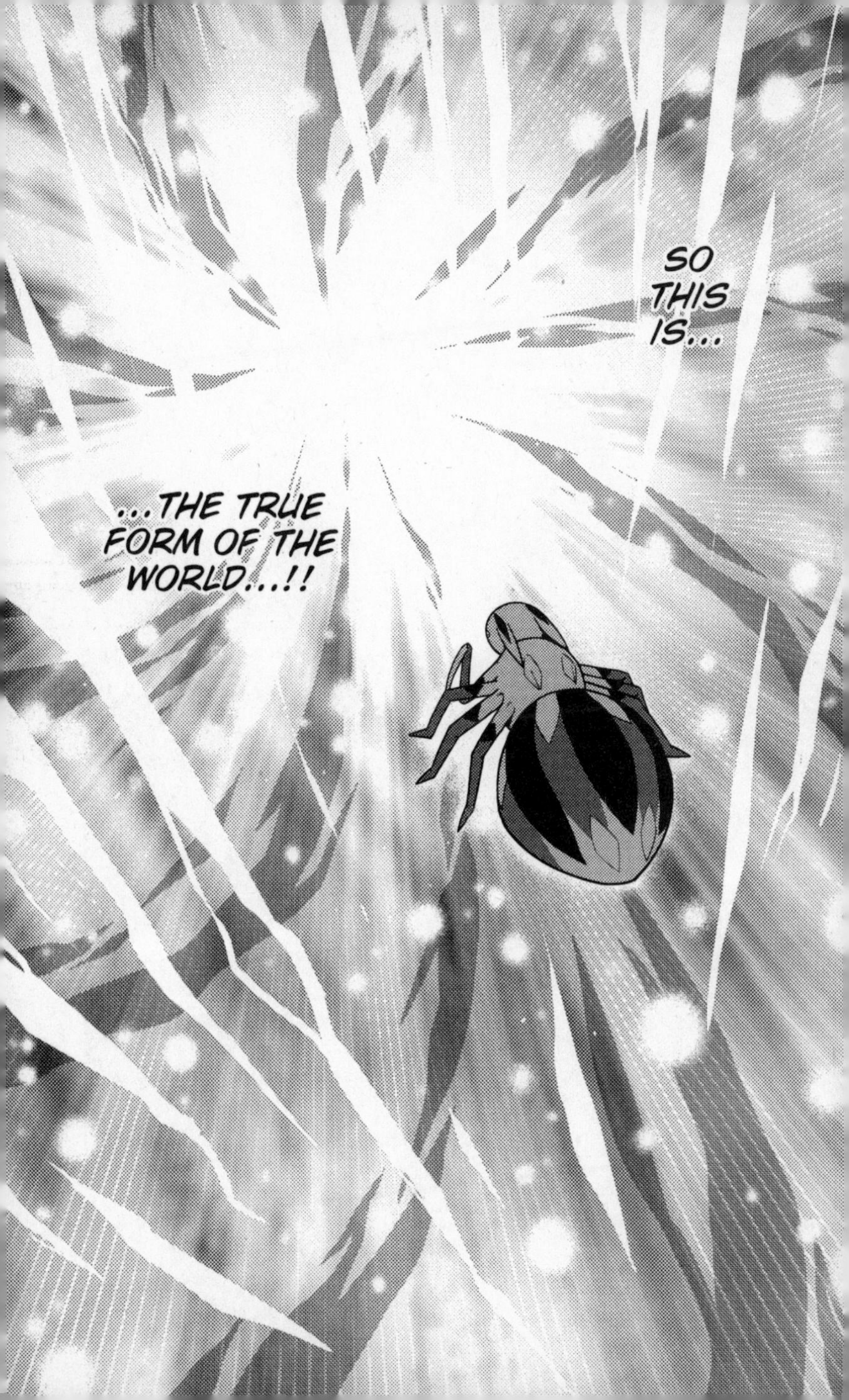
SO THIS IS...
...THE TRUE FORM OF THE WORLD...!!

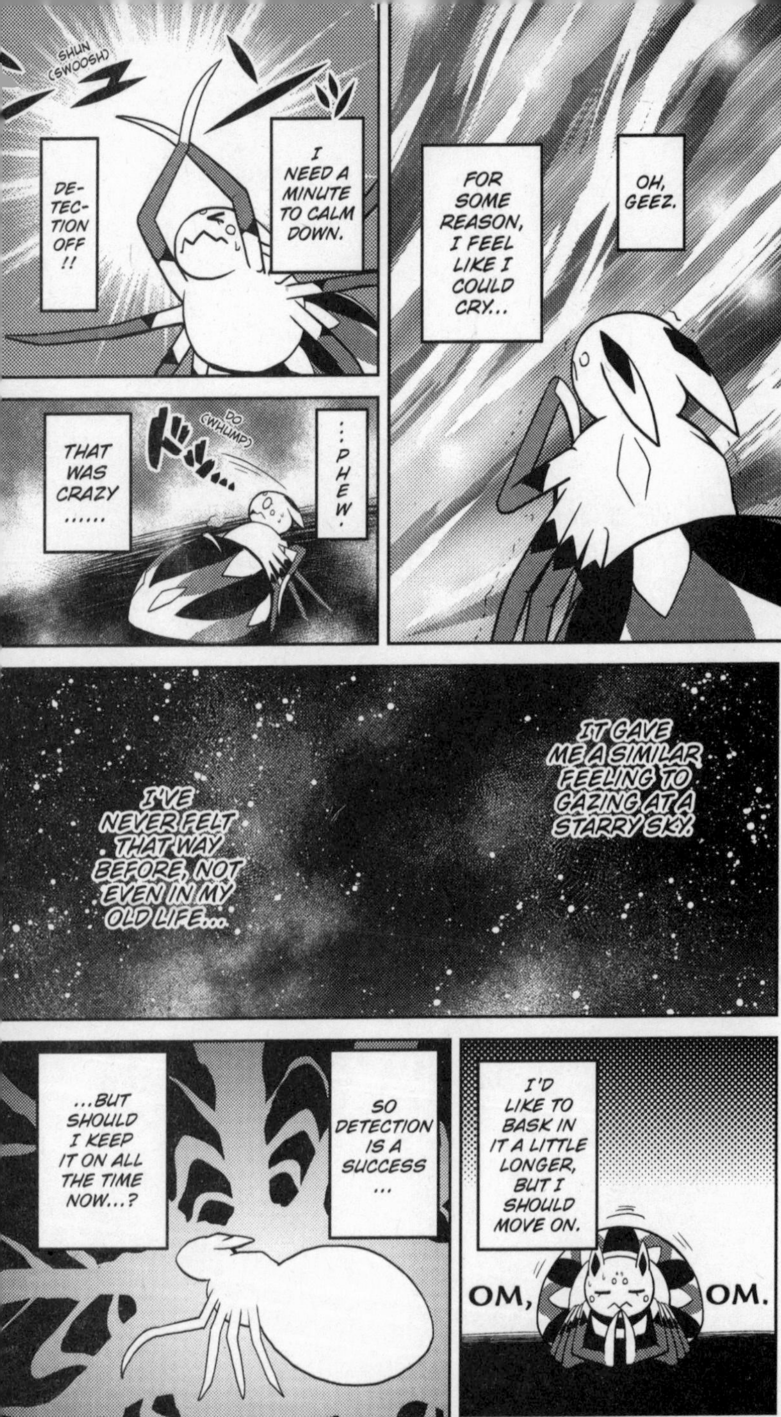
OH, GEEZ.
FOR SOME REASON, I FEEL LIKE I COULD CRY...
I NEED A MINUTE TO CALM DOWN.
SHUN (SWOOSH)
DE-TEC-TION OFF !!
...PHEW.
DO (WHUMP)
THAT WAS CRAZY......
IT GAVE ME A SIMILAR FEELING TO GAZING AT A STARRY SKY.
I'VE NEVER FELT THAT WAY BEFORE, NOT EVEN IN MY OLD LIFE...
I'D LIKE TO BASK IN IT A LITTLE LONGER, BUT I SHOULD MOVE ON.
OM, OM.
SO DETECTION IS A SUCCESS...
...BUT SHOULD I KEEP IT ON ALL THE TIME NOW...?

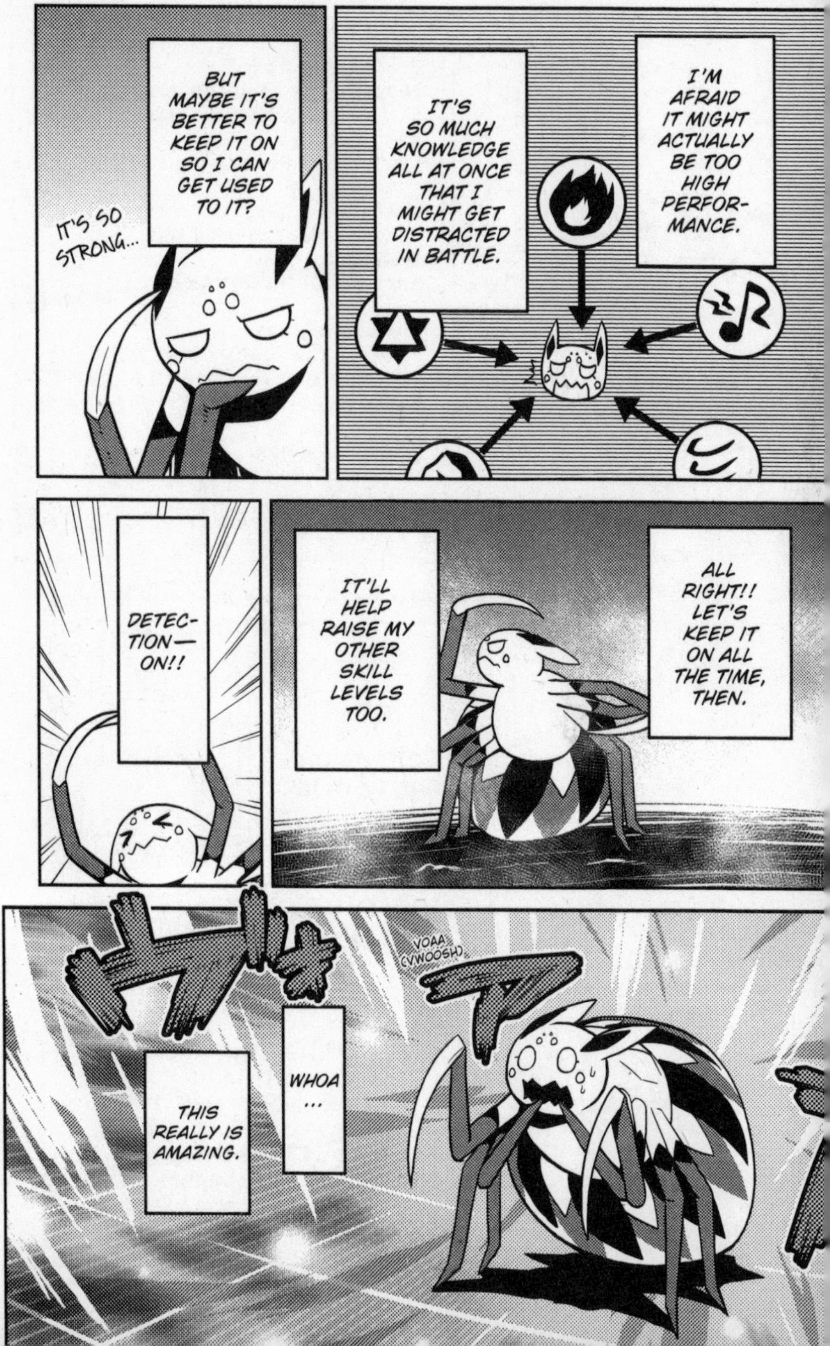
I'M AFRAID IT MIGHT ACTUALLY BE TOO HIGH PERFORMANCE.
IT'S SO MUCH KNOWLEDGE ALL AT ONCE THAT I MIGHT GET DISTRACTED IN BATTLE.
BUT MAYBE IT'S BETTER TO KEEP IT ON SO I CAN GET USED TO IT?
IT'S SO STRONG...
ALL RIGHT!! LET'S KEEP IT ON ALL THE TIME, THEN.
IT'LL HELP RAISE MY OTHER SKILL LEVELS TOO.
DETECTION—ON!!
VOAA (VWOOSH)
WHOA ...
THIS REALLY IS AMAZING.

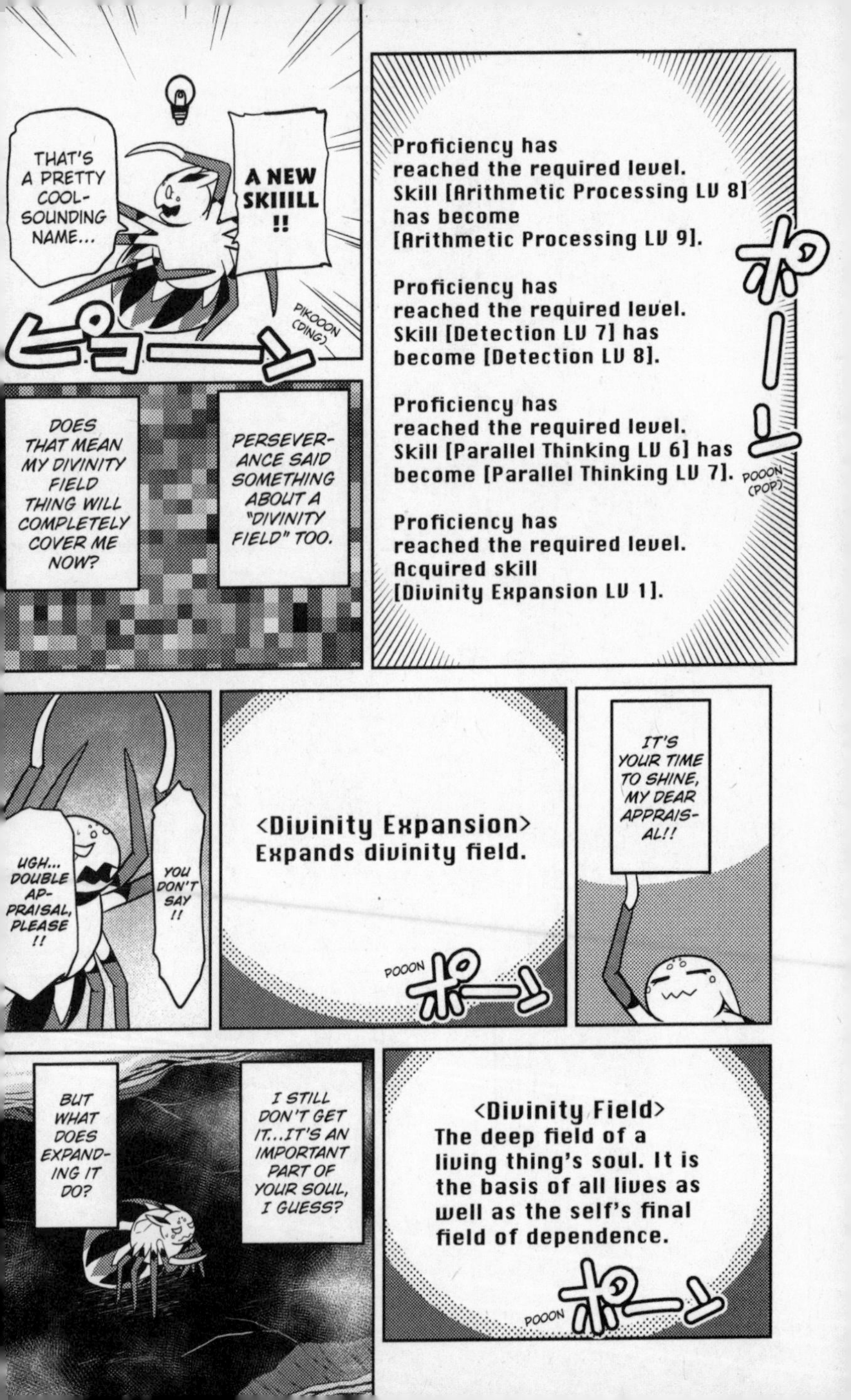
Proficiency has reached the required level. Skill [Arithmetic Processing LV 8] has become [Arithmetic Processing LV 9].
Proficiency has reached the required level. Skill [Detection LV 7] has become [Detection LV 8].
Proficiency has reached the required level. Skill [Parallel Thinking LV 6] has become [Parallel Thinking LV 7].
Proficiency has reached the required level. Acquired skill [Divinity Expansion LV 1].
POOON (POP)
A NEW SKIIIILL !!
THAT'S A PRETTY COOL-SOUNDING NAME...
PIKOOON (DING)
PERSEVERANCE SAID SOMETHING ABOUT A "DIVINITY FIELD" TOO.
DOES THAT MEAN MY DIVINITY FIELD THING WILL COMPLETELY COVER ME NOW?
IT'S YOUR TIME TO SHINE, MY DEAR APPRAISAL!!
<Divinity Expansion>
Expands divinity field.
POOON
YOU DON'T SAY!!
UGH... DOUBLE APPRAISAL, PLEASE!!
<Divinity Field>
The deep field of a living thing's soul. It is the basis of all lives as well as the self's final field of dependence.
POOON
I STILL DON'T GET IT...IT'S AN IMPORTANT PART OF YOUR SOUL, I GUESS?
BUT WHAT DOES EXPANDING IT DO?

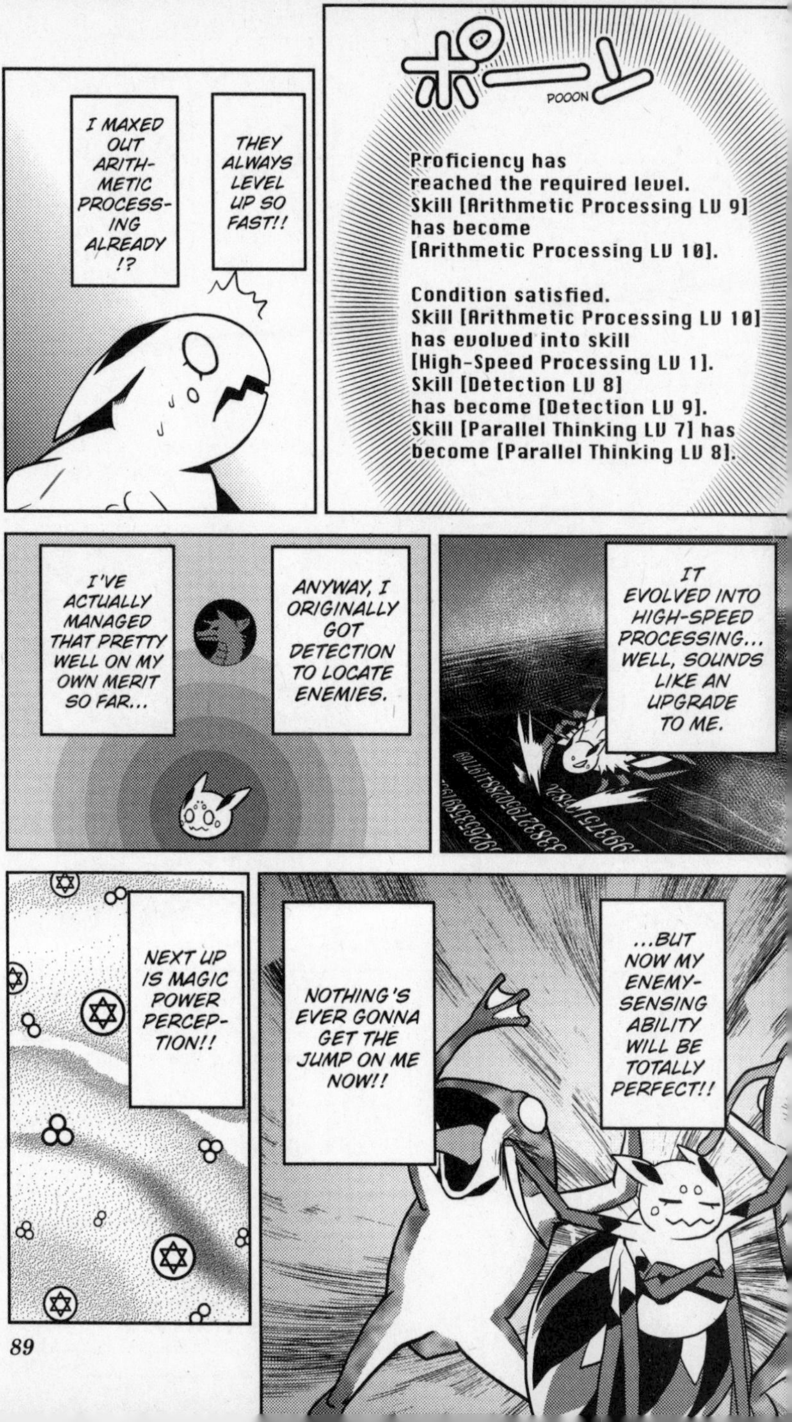
ポーン
POOON
Proficiency has reached the required level. Skill [Arithmetic Processing LV 9] has become [Arithmetic Processing LV 10].
Condition satisfied. Skill [Arithmetic Processing LV 10] has evolved into skill [High-Speed Processing LV 1]. Skill [Detection LV 8] has become [Detection LV 9]. Skill [Parallel Thinking LV 7] has become [Parallel Thinking LV 8].
THEY ALWAYS LEVEL UP SO FAST!!
I MAXED OUT ARITHMETIC PROCESSING ALREADY!?
IT EVOLVED INTO HIGH-SPEED PROCESSING... WELL, SOUNDS LIKE AN UPGRADE TO ME.
ANYWAY, I ORIGINALLY GOT DETECTION TO LOCATE ENEMIES.
I'VE ACTUALLY MANAGED THAT PRETTY WELL ON MY OWN MERIT SO FAR...
...BUT NOW MY ENEMY-SENSING ABILITY WILL BE TOTALLY PERFECT!!
NOTHING'S EVER GONNA GET THE JUMP ON ME NOW!!
NEXT UP IS MAGIC POWER PERCEPTION!!

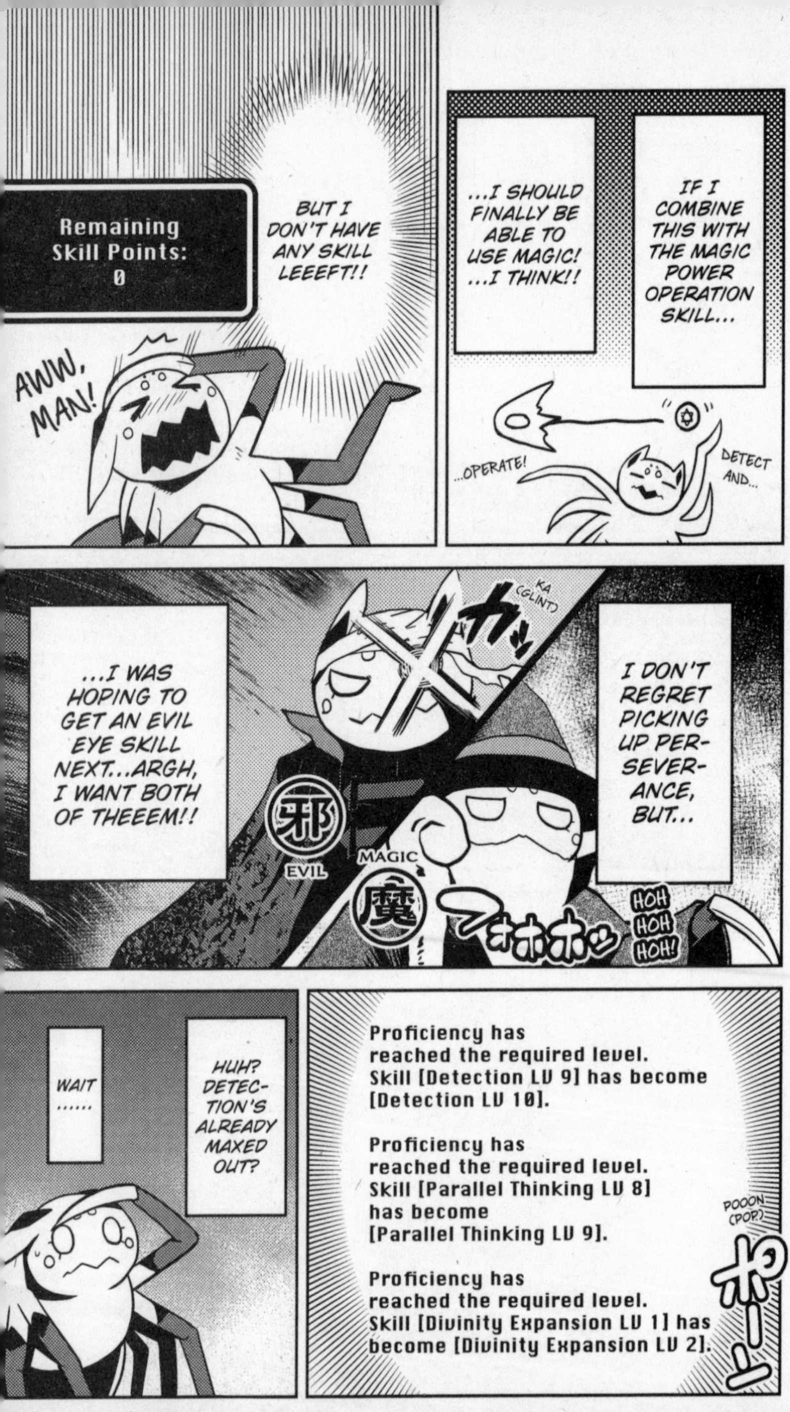
IF I COMBINE THIS WITH THE MAGIC POWER OPERATION SKILL...
...I SHOULD FINALLY BE ABLE TO USE MAGIC! ...I THINK!!
DETECT AND...
...OPERATE!
Remaining Skill Points: 0
BUT I DON'T HAVE ANY SKILL LEEEFT!!
AWW, MAN!
I DON'T REGRET PICKING UP PER-SEVER-ANCE, BUT...
KA (GLINT)
...I WAS HOPING TO GET AN EVIL EYE SKILL NEXT...ARGH, I WANT BOTH OF THEEEM!!
邪 EVIL
魔 MAGIC
HOH HOH HOH!
Proficiency has reached the required level. Skill [Detection LV 9] has become [Detection LV 10].
Proficiency has reached the required level. Skill [Parallel Thinking LV 8] has become [Parallel Thinking LV 9].
Proficiency has reached the required level. Skill [Divinity Expansion LV 1] has become [Divinity Expansion LV 2].
POOON (POP)
HUH? DETECTION'S ALREADY MAXED OUT?
WAIT......

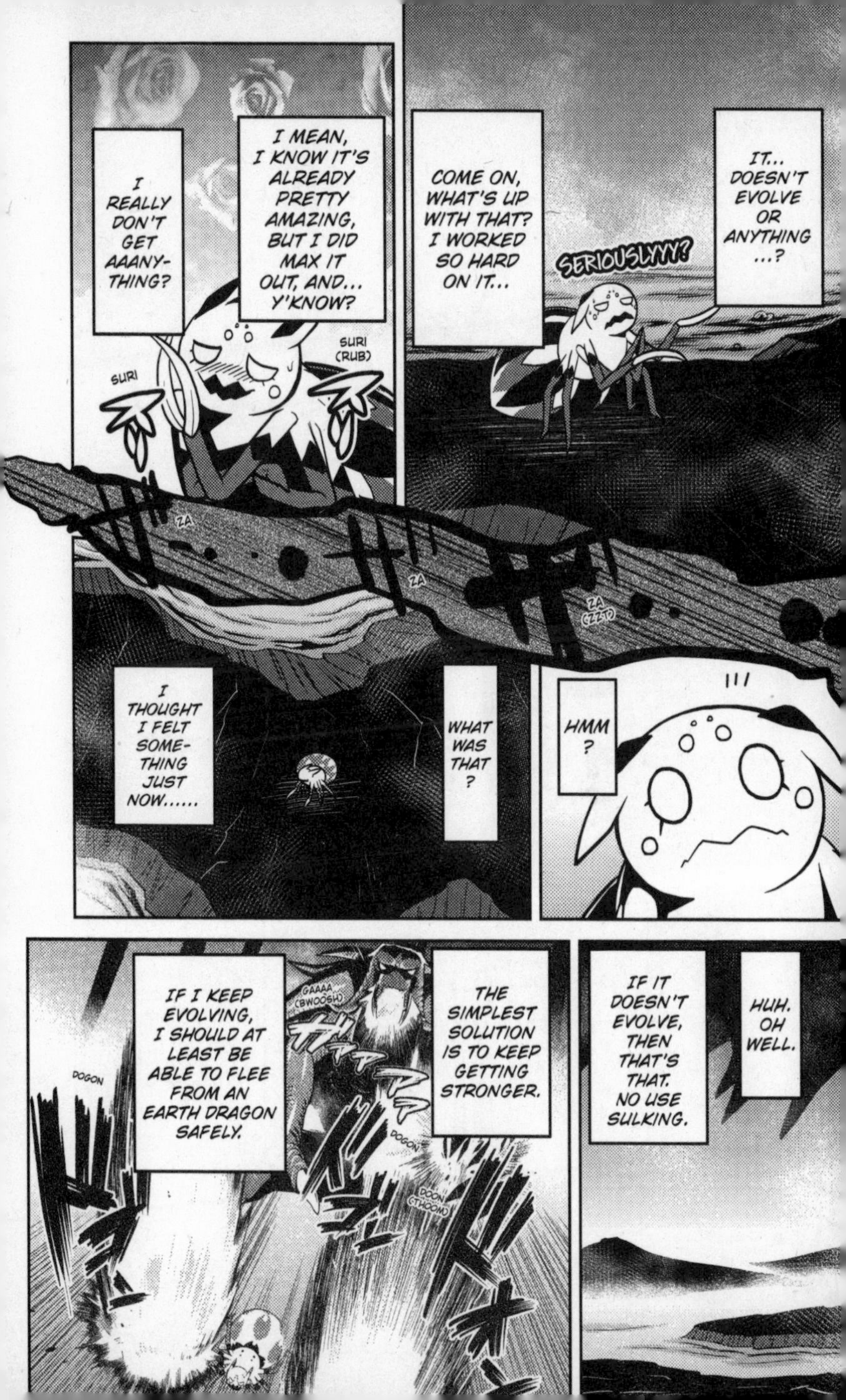
IT... DOESN'T EVOLVE OR ANYTHING ...?
SERIOUSLYYY?
COME ON, WHAT'S UP WITH THAT? I WORKED SO HARD ON IT...
I MEAN, I KNOW IT'S ALREADY PRETTY AMAZING, BUT I DID MAX IT OUT, AND... Y'KNOW?
SURI (RUB)
SURI
I REALLY DON'T GET AAANY-THING?
ZA
ZA
ZA (ZZZT)
HMM ?
WHAT WAS THAT ?
I THOUGHT I FELT SOME-THING JUST NOW......
HUH. OH WELL.
IF IT DOESN'T EVOLVE, THEN THAT'S THAT. NO USE SULKING.
THE SIMPLEST SOLUTION IS TO KEEP GETTING STRONGER.
GAAAA (BWOOSH)
IF I KEEP EVOLVING, I SHOULD AT LEAST BE ABLE TO FLEE FROM AN EARTH DRAGON SAFELY.
DOGON
DOGON
DOON (THOOM)

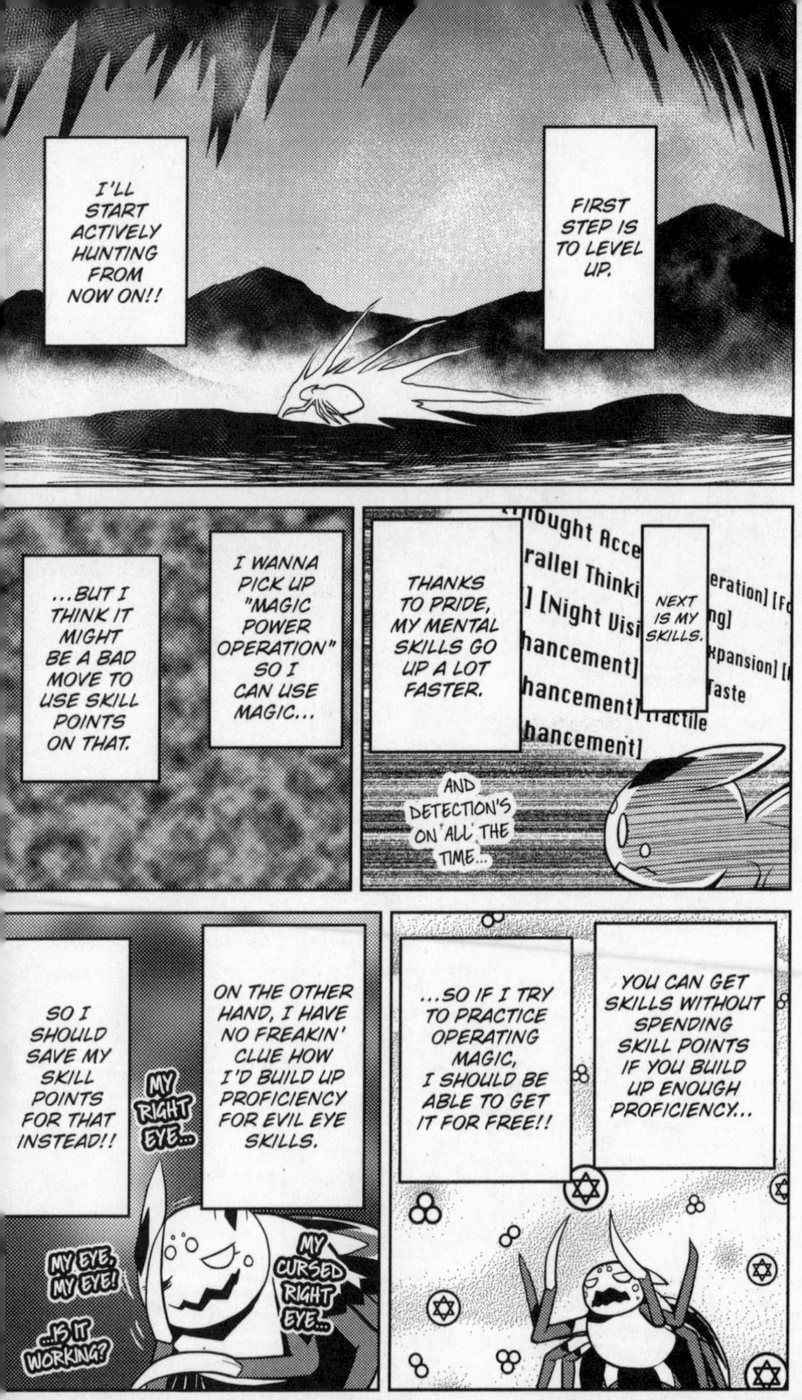
FIRST STEP IS TO LEVEL UP.
I'LL START ACTIVELY HUNTING FROM NOW ON!!
NEXT IS MY SKILLS.
THANKS TO PRIDE, MY MENTAL SKILLS GO UP A LOT FASTER.
AND DETECTION'S ON "ALL" THE TIME...
I WANNA PICK UP "MAGIC POWER OPERATION" SO I CAN USE MAGIC...
...BUT I THINK IT MIGHT BE A BAD MOVE TO USE SKILL POINTS ON THAT.
YOU CAN GET SKILLS WITHOUT SPENDING SKILL POINTS IF YOU BUILD UP ENOUGH PROFICIENCY...
...SO IF I TRY TO PRACTICE OPERATING MAGIC, I SHOULD BE ABLE TO GET IT FOR FREE!!
ON THE OTHER HAND, I HAVE NO FREAKIN' CLUE HOW I'D BUILD UP PROFICIENCY FOR EVIL EYE SKILLS.
SO I SHOULD SAVE MY SKILL POINTS FOR THAT INSTEAD!!
MY RIGHT EYE...
MY CURSED RIGHT EYE...
MY EYE, MY EYE!
...IS IT WORKING?

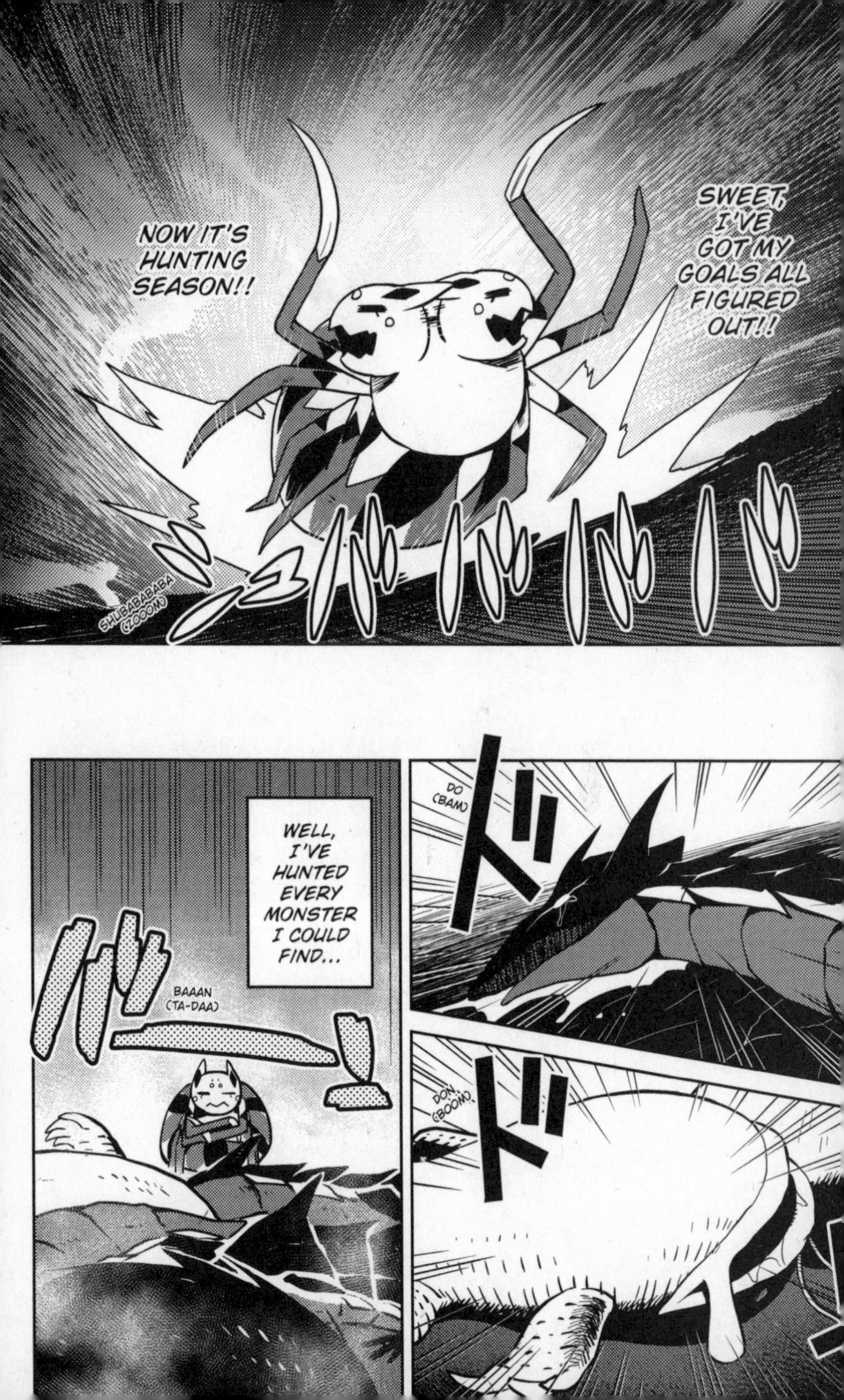
SWEET, I'VE GOT MY GOALS ALL FIGURED OUT!!
NOW IT'S HUNTING SEASON!!
SHUBABABABA (ZOOOM)
DO (BAM)
DON (BOOM)
WELL, I'VE HUNTED EVERY MONSTER I COULD FIND...
BAAAN (TA-DAA)

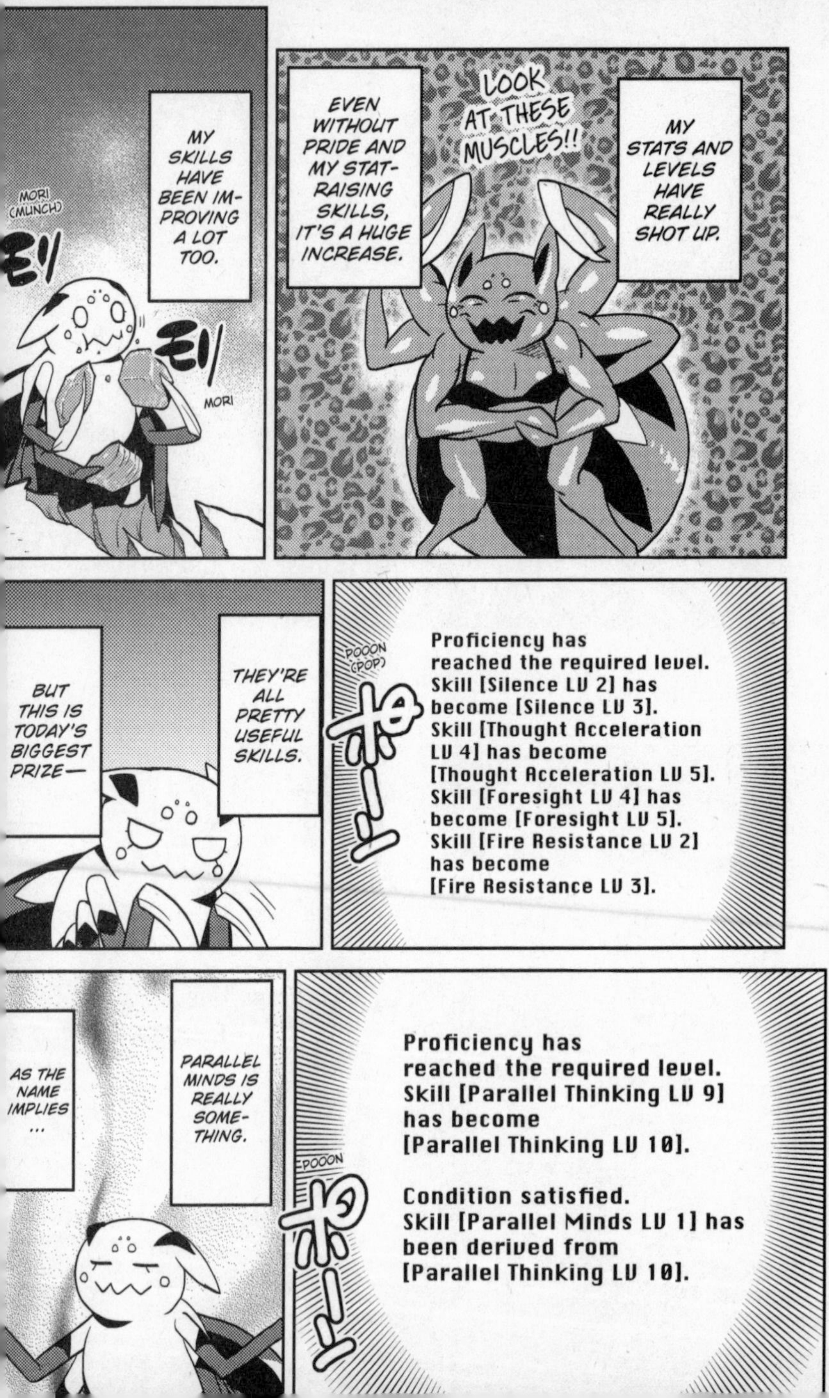
MY STATS AND LEVELS HAVE REALLY SHOT UP.
LOOK AT THESE MUSCLES!!
EVEN WITHOUT PRIDE AND MY STAT-RAISING SKILLS, IT'S A HUGE INCREASE.
MY SKILLS HAVE BEEN IM-PROVING A LOT TOO.
MORI (MUNCH)
MORI
POOON (POP)
Proficiency has reached the required level.
Skill [Silence LV 2] has become [Silence LV 3].
Skill [Thought Acceleration LV 4] has become [Thought Acceleration LV 5].
Skill [Foresight LV 4] has become [Foresight LV 5].
Skill [Fire Resistance LV 2] has become [Fire Resistance LV 3].
THEY'RE ALL PRETTY USEFUL SKILLS.
BUT THIS IS TODAY'S BIGGEST PRIZE—
Proficiency has reached the required level.
Skill [Parallel Thinking LV 9] has become [Parallel Thinking LV 10].
Condition satisfied.
Skill [Parallel Minds LV 1] has been derived from [Parallel Thinking LV 10].
POOON
PARALLEL MINDS IS REALLY SOME-THING.
AS THE NAME IMPLIES ...

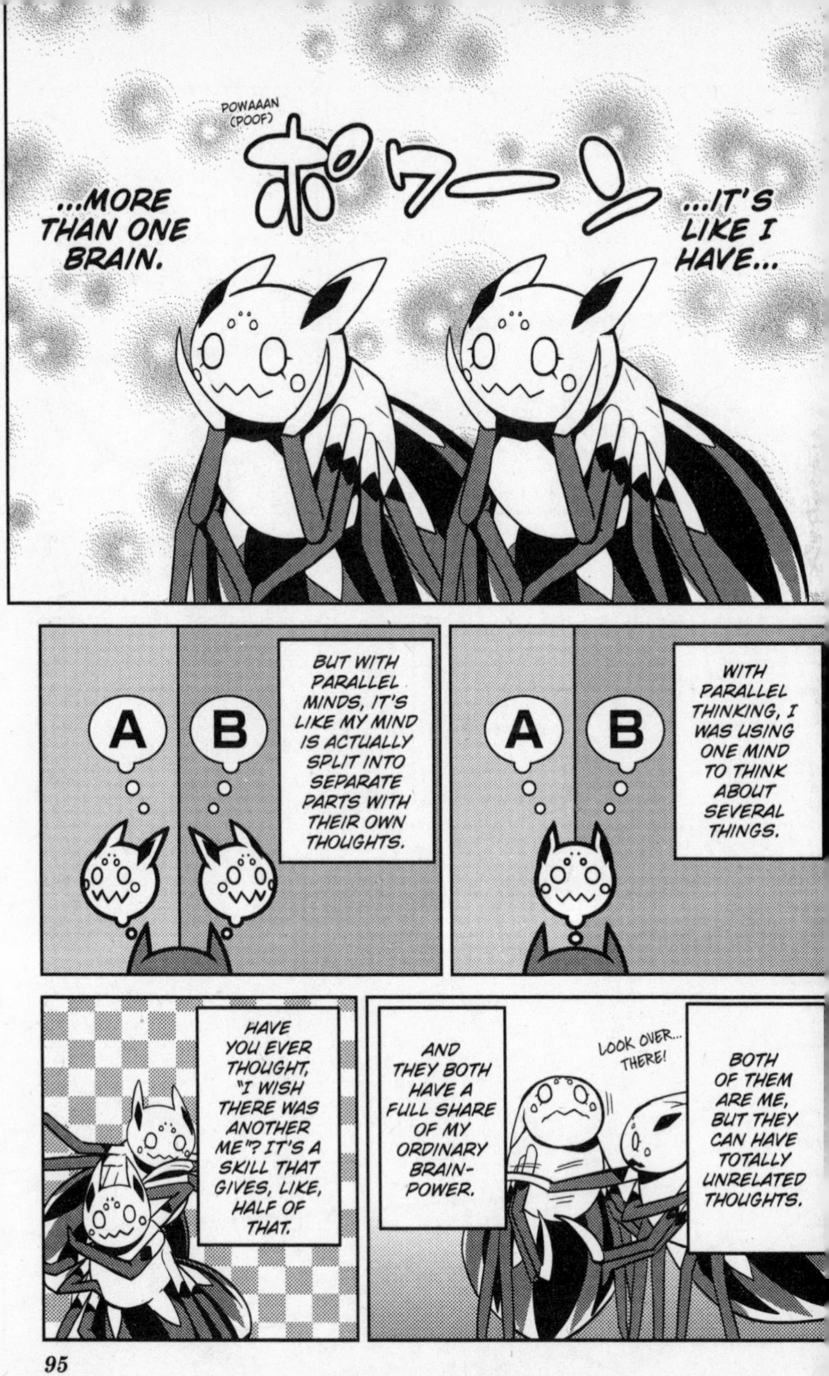
...IT'S LIKE I HAVE...
POWAAAN (POOF)
ポワーン
...MORE THAN ONE BRAIN.
WITH PARALLEL THINKING, I WAS USING ONE MIND TO THINK ABOUT SEVERAL THINGS.
A
B
BUT WITH PARALLEL MINDS, IT'S LIKE MY MIND IS ACTUALLY SPLIT INTO SEPARATE PARTS WITH THEIR OWN THOUGHTS.
A
B
BOTH OF THEM ARE ME, BUT THEY CAN HAVE TOTALLY UNRELATED THOUGHTS.
LOOK OVER... THERE!
AND THEY BOTH HAVE A FULL SHARE OF MY ORDINARY BRAIN-POWER.
HAVE YOU EVER THOUGHT, "I WISH THERE WAS ANOTHER ME"? IT'S A SKILL THAT GIVES, LIKE, HALF OF THAT.

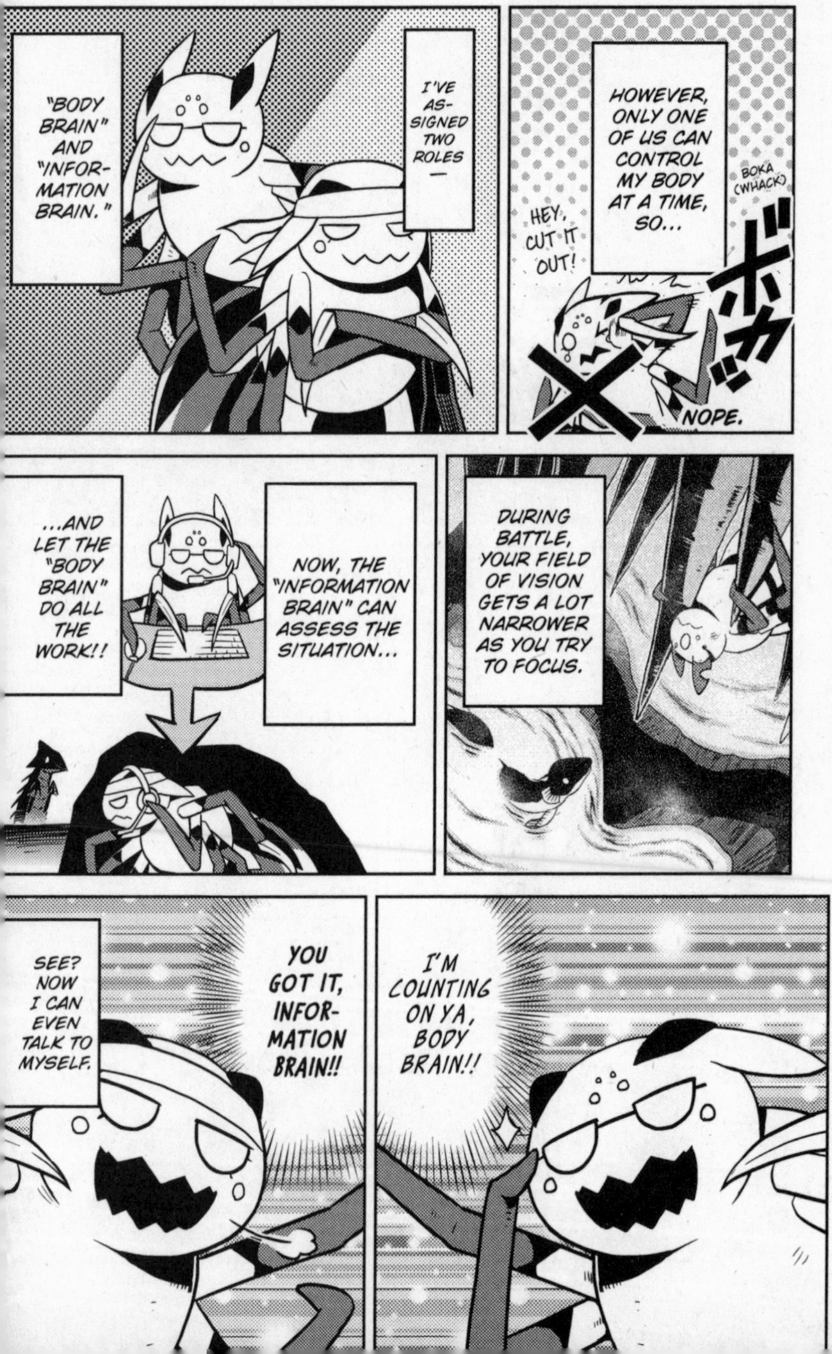
HOWEVER, ONLY ONE OF US CAN CONTROL MY BODY AT A TIME, SO...
BOKA (WHACK)
HEY, CUT IT OUT!
NOPE.
I'VE AS-SIGNED TWO ROLES—
"BODY BRAIN" AND "INFOR-MATION BRAIN."
DURING BATTLE, YOUR FIELD OF VISION GETS A LOT NARROWER AS YOU TRY TO FOCUS.
NOW, THE "INFORMATION BRAIN" CAN ASSESS THE SITUATION...
...AND LET THE "BODY BRAIN" DO ALL THE WORK!!
I'M COUNTING ON YA, BODY BRAIN!!
YOU GOT IT, INFOR-MATION BRAIN!!
SEE? NOW I CAN EVEN TALK TO MYSELF.

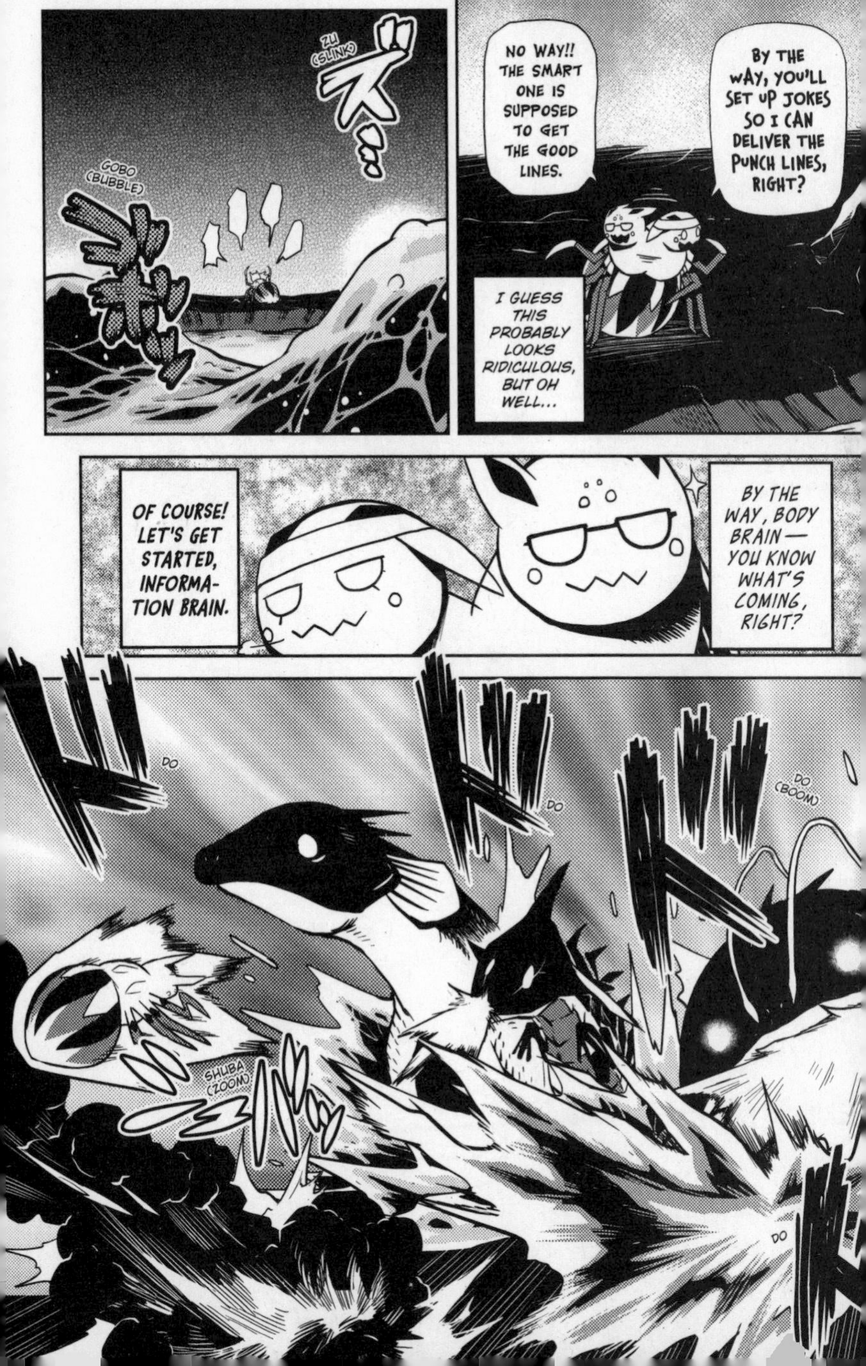

BY THE WAY, YOU'LL SET UP JOKES SO I CAN DELIVER THE PUNCH LINES, RIGHT?
NO WAY!! THE SMART ONE IS SUPPOSED TO GET THE GOOD LINES.
I GUESS THIS PROBABLY LOOKS RIDICULOUS, BUT OH WELL...
ZU (SLINK)
GOBO (BUBBLE)
BY THE WAY, BODY BRAIN—YOU KNOW WHAT'S COMING, RIGHT?
OF COURSE! LET'S GET STARTED, INFORMATION BRAIN.
DO (BOOM)
DO
DO
SHUBA (ZOOM)
DO

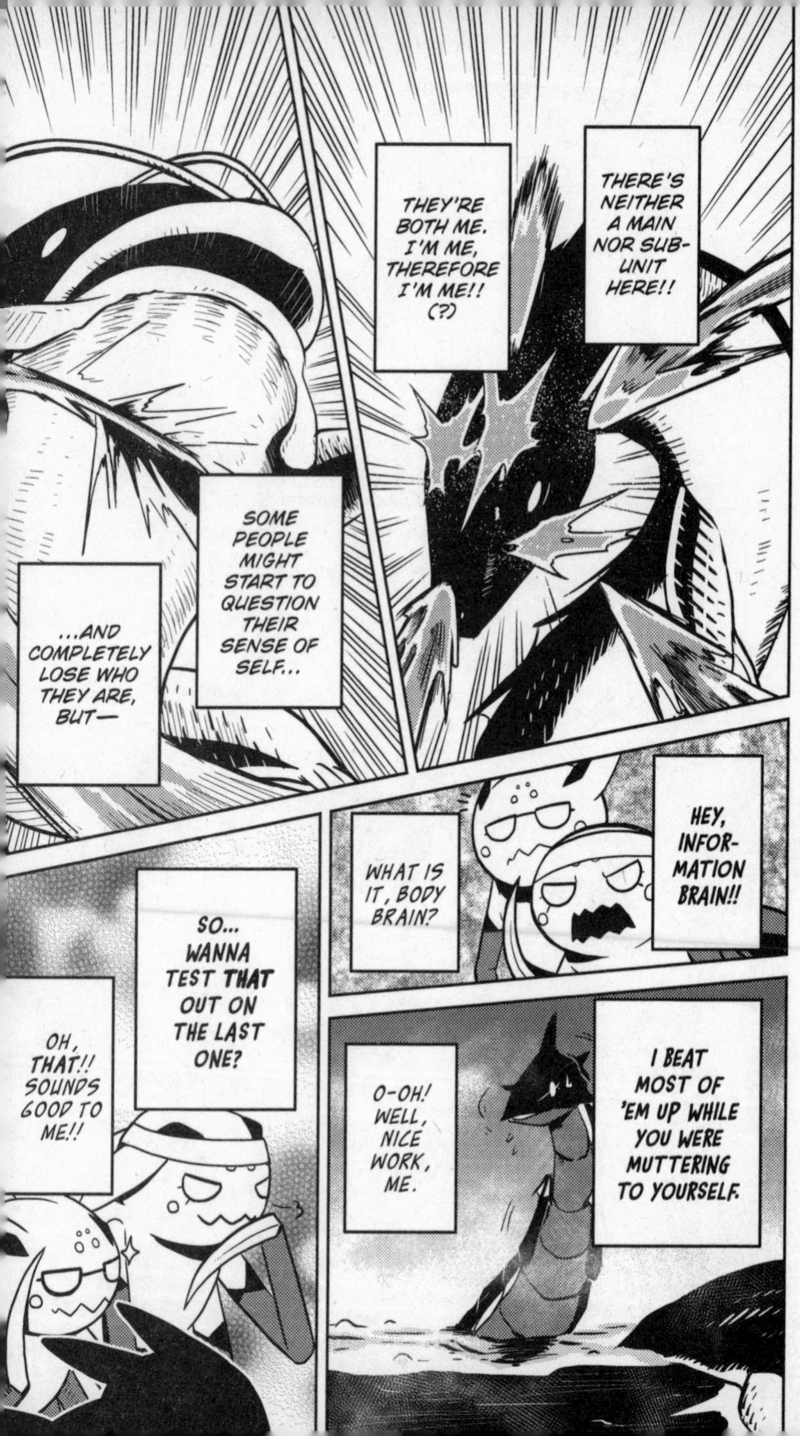
THERE'S NEITHER A MAIN NOR SUB-UNIT HERE!!
THEY'RE BOTH ME. I'M ME, THEREFORE I'M ME!! (?)
SOME PEOPLE MIGHT START TO QUESTION THEIR SENSE OF SELF...
...AND COMPLETELY LOSE WHO THEY ARE, BUT—
HEY, INFORMATION BRAIN!!
WHAT IS IT, BODY BRAIN?
I BEAT MOST OF 'EM UP WHILE YOU WERE MUTTERING TO YOURSELF.
O-OH! WELL, NICE WORK, ME.
SO... WANNA TEST THAT OUT ON THE LAST ONE?
OH, THAT!! SOUNDS GOOD TO ME!!

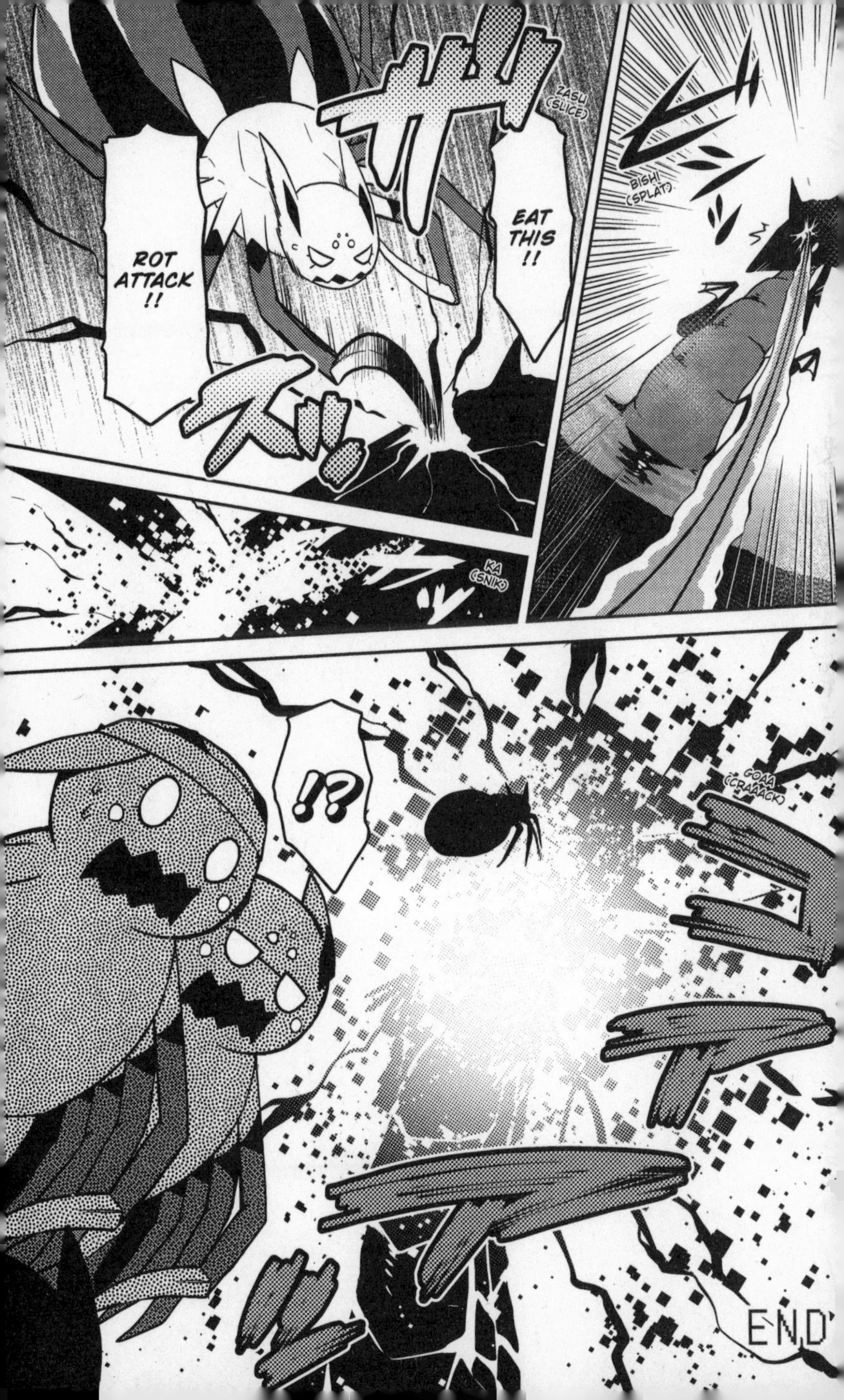
BISH! (SPLAT)
ZASU (SLICE)
EAT THIS !!
ROT ATTACK !!
KA (SNIK)
GOAA (CRAAACK)
!?
END

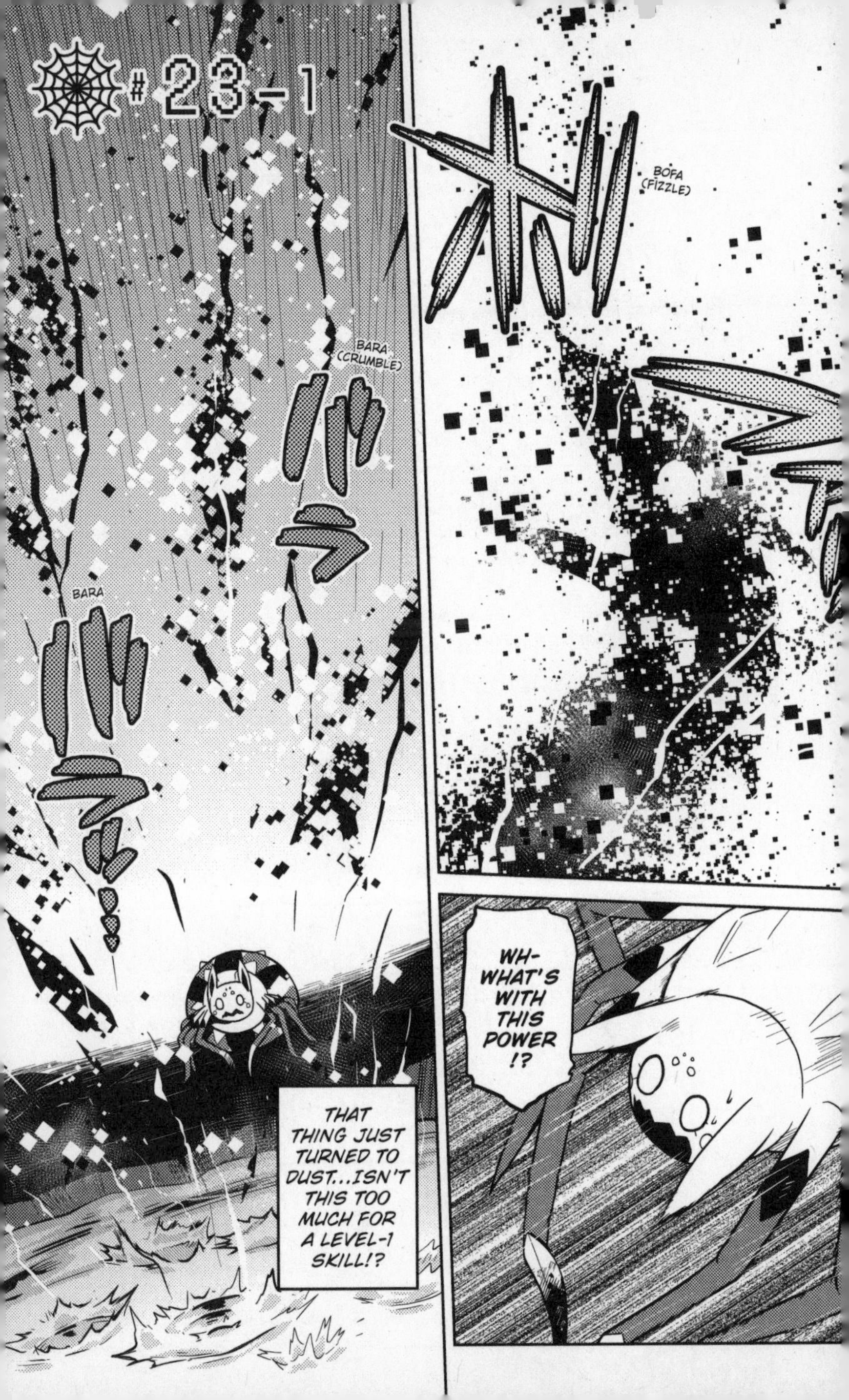
BOFA (FIZZLE)
WH-WHAT'S WITH THIS POWER !?
#23-1
BARA (CRUMBLE)
BARA
THAT THING JUST TURNED TO DUST...ISN'T THIS TOO MUCH FOR A LEVEL-1 SKILL!?

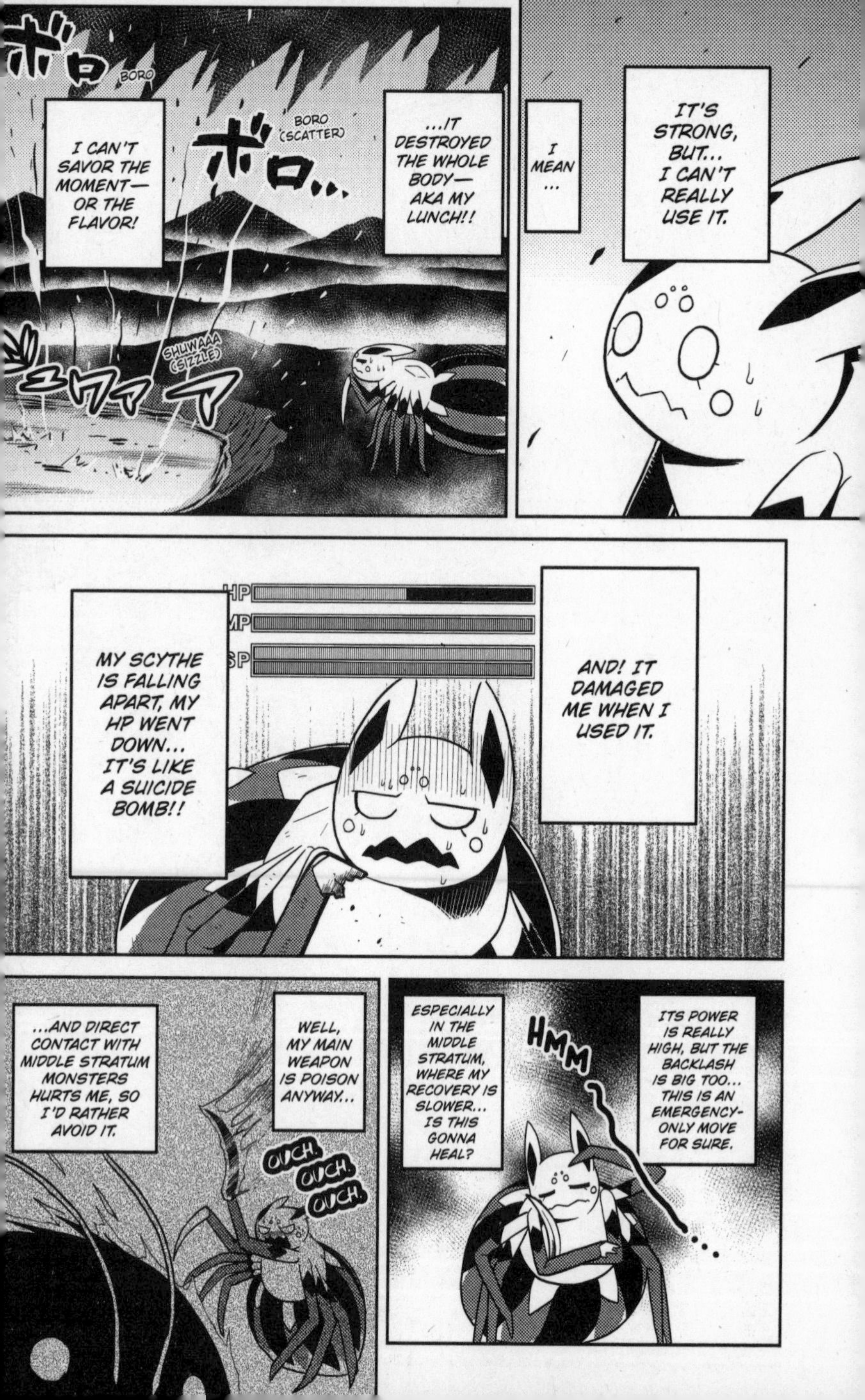
IT'S STRONG, BUT... I CAN'T REALLY USE IT.
I MEAN...
...IT DESTROYED THE WHOLE BODY—AKA MY LUNCH!!
BORO (SCATTER)
BORO
I CAN'T SAVOR THE MOMENT—OR THE FLAVOR!
SHUWAAA (SIZZLE)
AND! IT DAMAGED ME WHEN I USED IT.
HP
MP
SP
MY SCYTHE IS FALLING APART, MY HP WENT DOWN... IT'S LIKE A SUICIDE BOMB!!
ITS POWER IS REALLY HIGH, BUT THE BACKLASH IS BIG TOO... THIS IS AN EMERGENCY-ONLY MOVE FOR SURE.
HMM
ESPECIALLY IN THE MIDDLE STRATUM, WHERE MY RECOVERY IS SLOWER... IS THIS GONNA HEAL?
...
WELL, MY MAIN WEAPON IS POISON ANYWAY...
...AND DIRECT CONTACT WITH MIDDLE STRATUM MONSTERS HURTS ME, SO I'D RATHER AVOID IT.
OUCH. OUCH. OUCH.

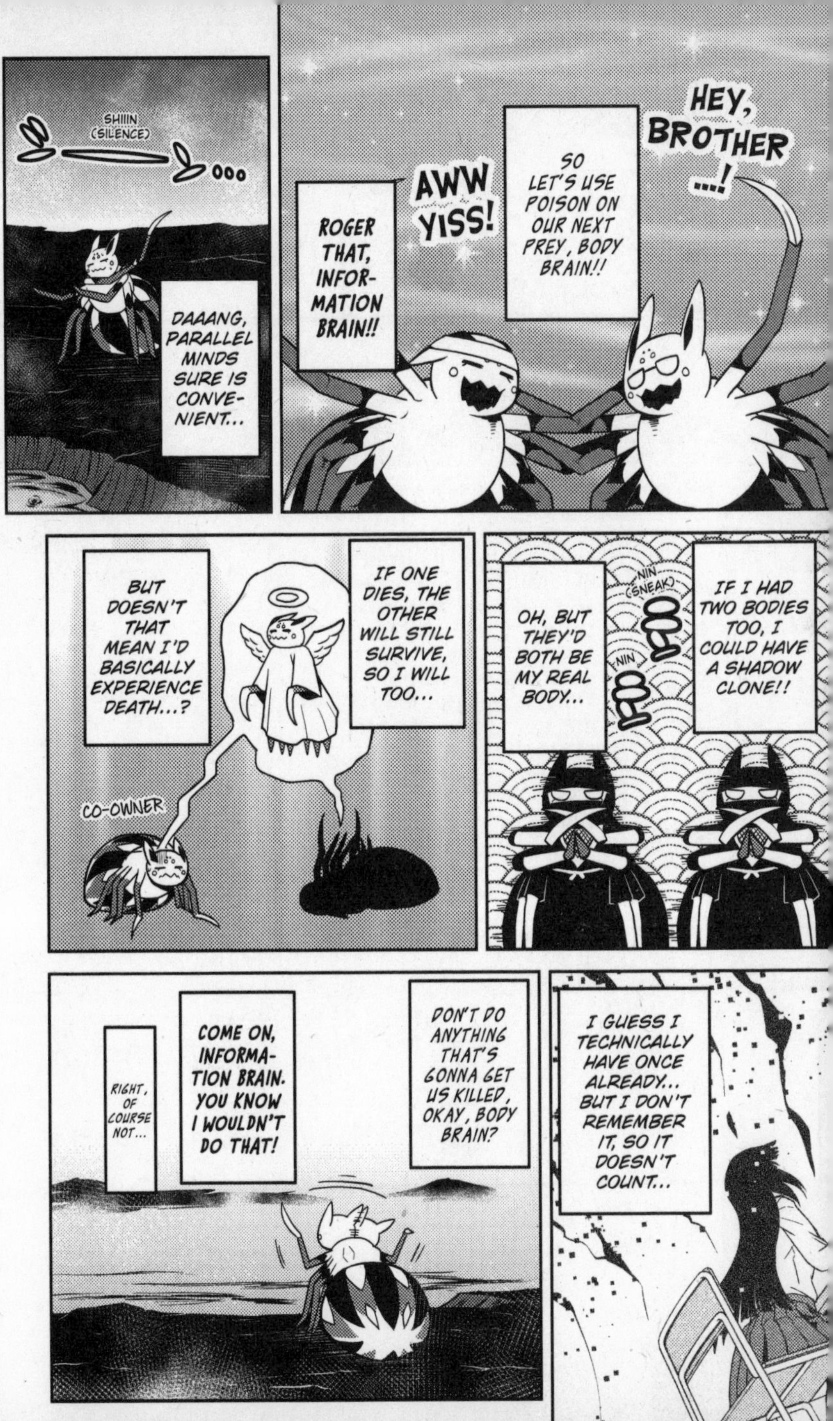
HEY, BROTHER...!
SO LET'S USE POISON ON OUR NEXT PREY, BODY BRAIN!!
AWW YISS!
ROGER THAT, INFORMATION BRAIN!!
SHIIIN (SILENCE)
DAAANG, PARALLEL MINDS SURE IS CONVENIENT...
IF I HAD TWO BODIES TOO, I COULD HAVE A SHADOW CLONE!!
NIN (SNEAK)
NIN
OH, BUT THEY'D BOTH BE MY REAL BODY...
IF ONE DIES, THE OTHER WILL STILL SURVIVE, SO I WILL TOO...
BUT DOESN'T THAT MEAN I'D BASICALLY EXPERIENCE DEATH...?
CO-OWNER
I GUESS I TECHNICALLY HAVE ONCE ALREADY... BUT I DON'T REMEMBER IT, SO IT DOESN'T COUNT...
DON'T DO ANYTHING THAT'S GONNA GET US KILLED, OKAY, BODY BRAIN?
COME ON, INFORMATION BRAIN. YOU KNOW I WOULDN'T DO THAT!
RIGHT, OF COURSE NOT...

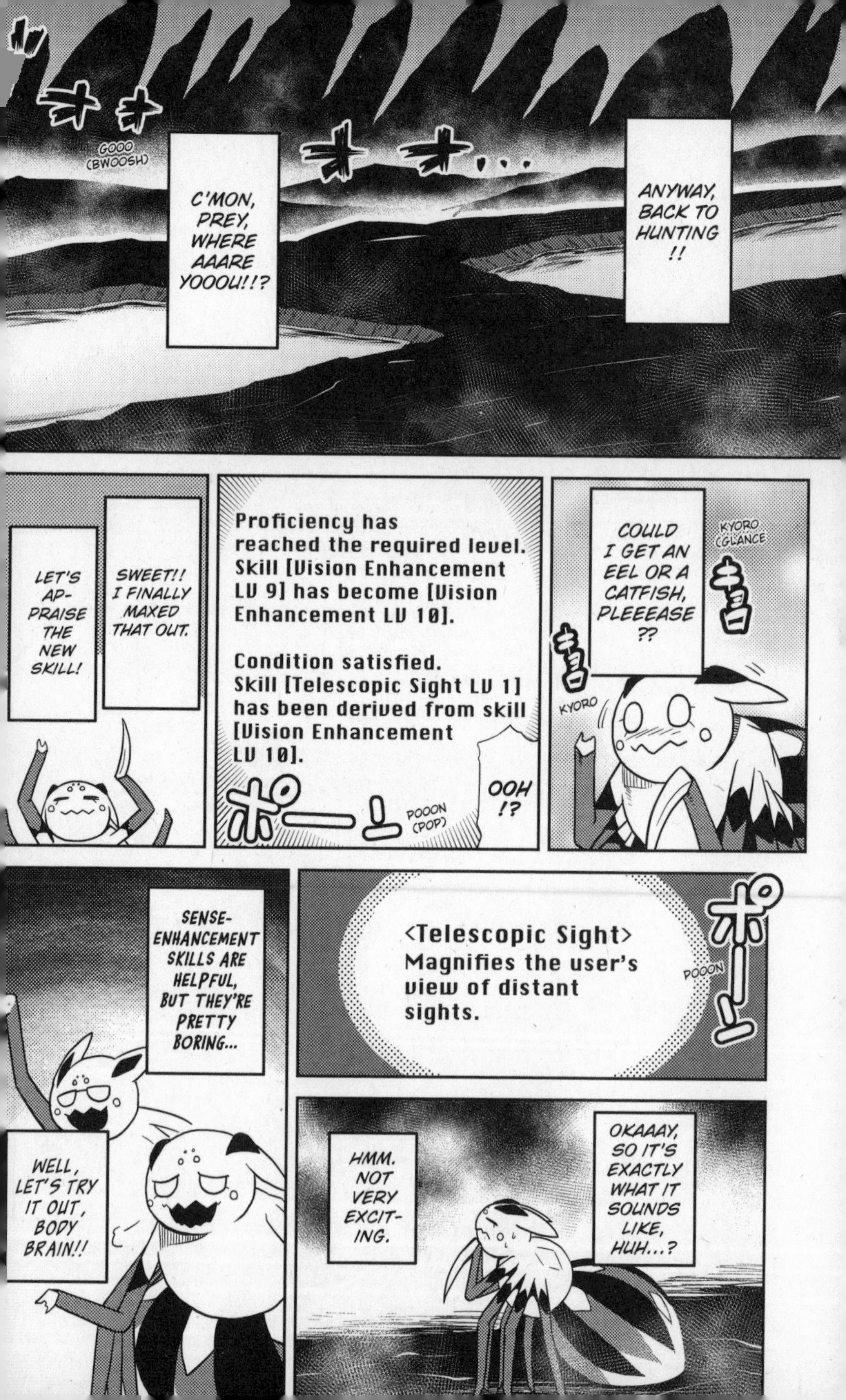
ANYWAY, BACK TO HUNTING !!
C'MON, PREY, WHERE AAARE YOOOU!!?
GOOO (BWOOSH)
COULD I GET AN EEL OR A CATFISH, PLEEEASE ??
KYORO (GLANCE)
KYORO
Proficiency has reached the required level. Skill [Vision Enhancement LV 9] has become [Vision Enhancement LV 10].
Condition satisfied. Skill [Telescopic Sight LV 1] has been derived from skill [Vision Enhancement LV 10].
OOH !?
POOON (POP)
SWEET!! I FINALLY MAXED THAT OUT.
LET'S AP- PRAISE THE NEW SKILL!
<Telescopic Sight> Magnifies the user's view of distant sights.
POOON
OKAAAY, SO IT'S EXACTLY WHAT IT SOUNDS LIKE, HUH...?
HMM. NOT VERY EXCIT- ING.
SENSE- ENHANCEMENT SKILLS ARE HELPFUL, BUT THEY'RE PRETTY BORING...
WELL, LET'S TRY IT OUT, BODY BRAIN!!

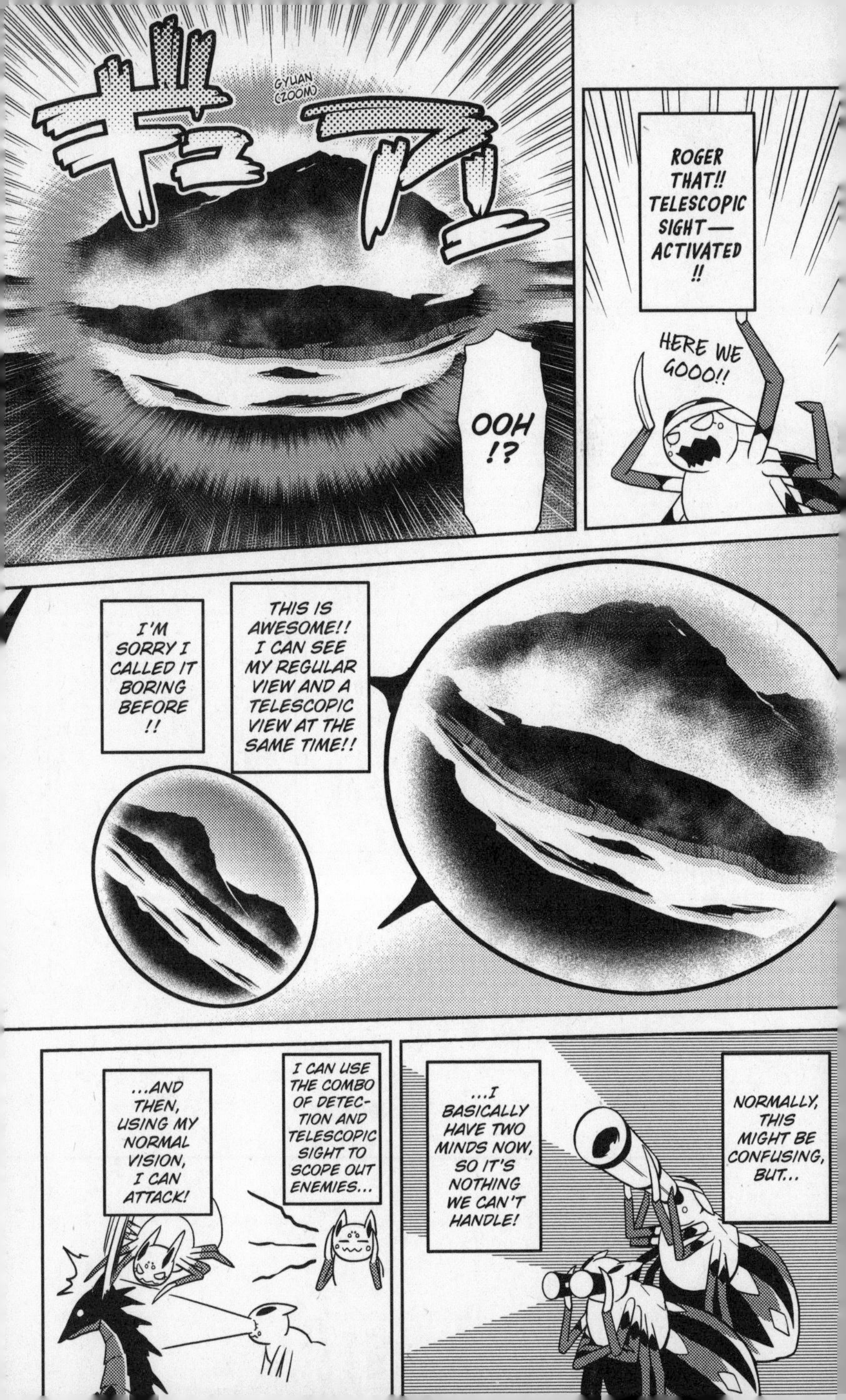
ROGER THAT!! TELESCOPIC SIGHT—ACTIVATED!!
HERE WE GOOO!!
GYUAN (ZOOM)
OOH!?
THIS IS AWESOME!! I CAN SEE MY REGULAR VIEW AND A TELESCOPIC VIEW AT THE SAME TIME!!
I'M SORRY I CALLED IT BORING BEFORE!!
NORMALLY, THIS MIGHT BE CONFUSING, BUT...
...I BASICALLY HAVE TWO MINDS NOW, SO IT'S NOTHING WE CAN'T HANDLE!
I CAN USE THE COMBO OF DETECTION AND TELESCOPIC SIGHT TO SCOPE OUT ENEMIES...
...AND THEN, USING MY NORMAL VISION, I CAN ATTACK!

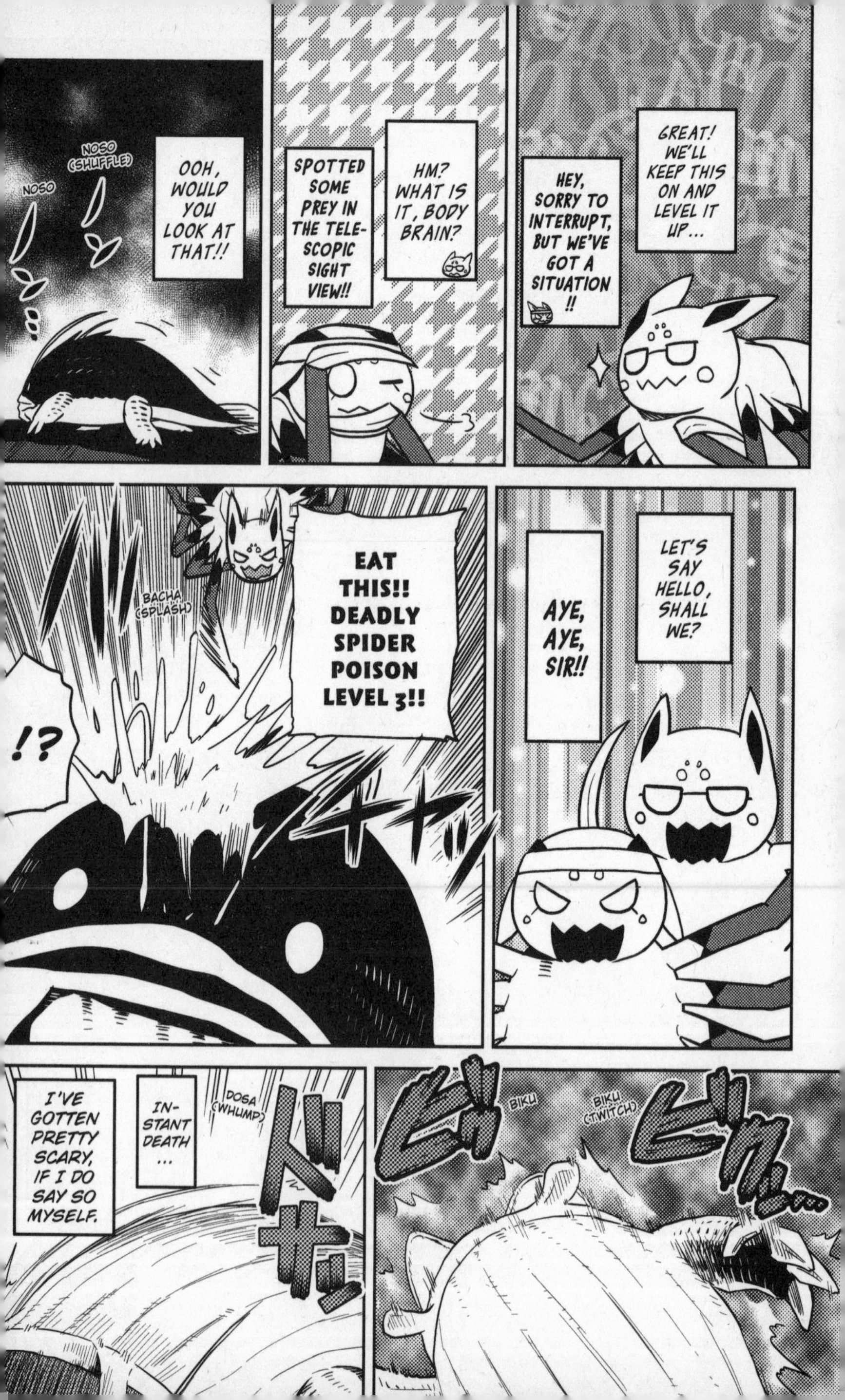
GREAT! WE'LL KEEP THIS ON AND LEVEL IT UP...
HEY, SORRY TO INTERRUPT, BUT WE'VE GOT A SITUATION!!
HM? WHAT IS IT, BODY BRAIN?
SPOTTED SOME PREY IN THE TELE-SCOPIC SIGHT VIEW!!
OOH, WOULD YOU LOOK AT THAT!!
NOSO (SHUFFLE)
NOSO
LET'S SAY HELLO, SHALL WE?
AYE, AYE, SIR!!
EAT THIS!! DEADLY SPIDER POISON LEVEL 3!!
BACHA (SPLASH)
!?
BIKU (TWITCH)
BIKU
DOSA (WHUMP)
IN-STANT DEATH...
I'VE GOTTEN PRETTY SCARY, IF I DO SAY SO MYSELF.

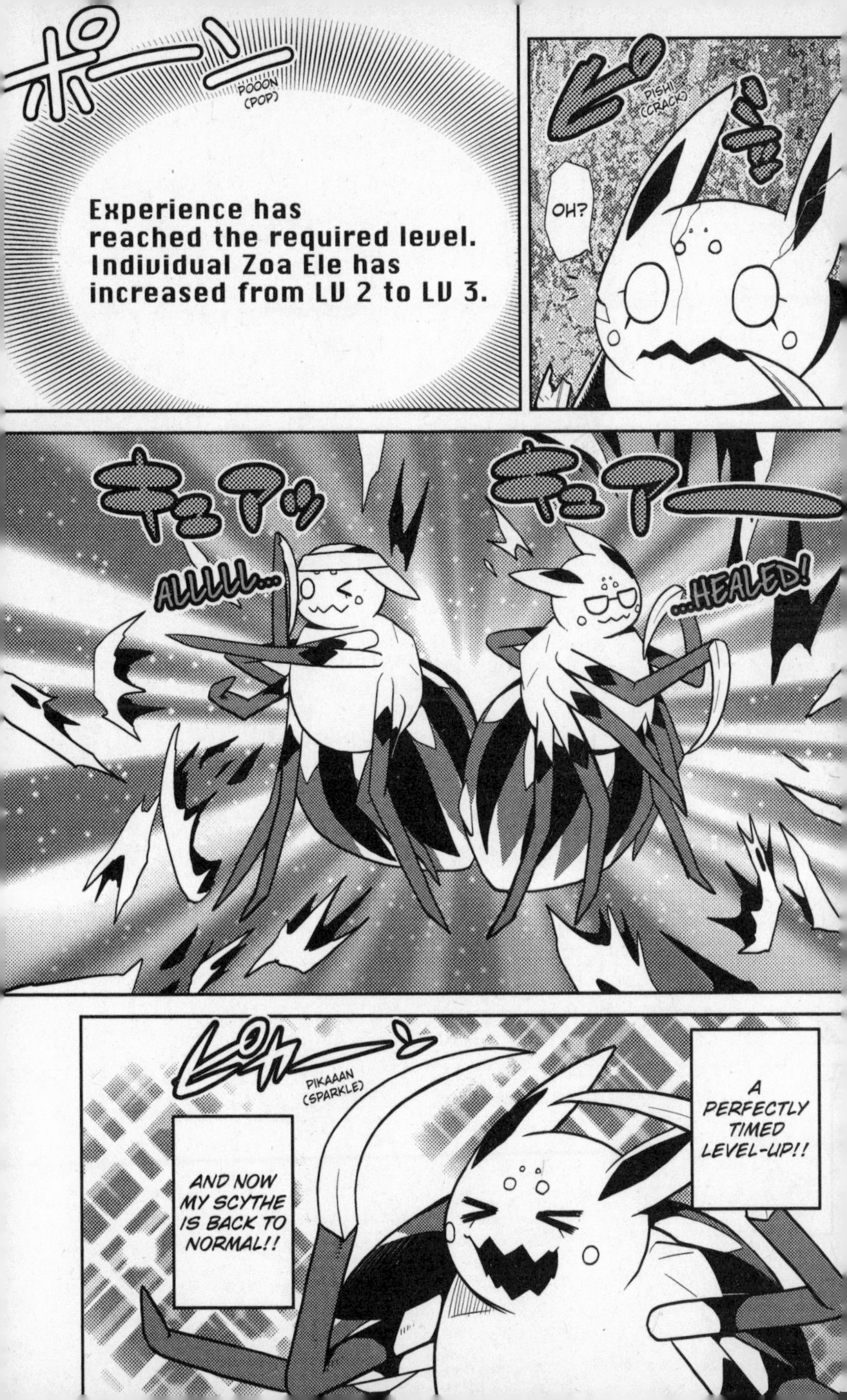
ピシッ
PISHI (CRACK)
OH?
ポーン
POOON (POP)
Experience has reached the required level. Individual Zoa Ele has increased from LV 2 to LV 3.
キュアー
キュアッ
ALLLLL...
...HEALED!
A PERFECTLY TIMED LEVEL-UP!!
ピカーン
PIKAAAN (SPARKLE)
AND NOW MY SCYTHE IS BACK TO NORMAL!!

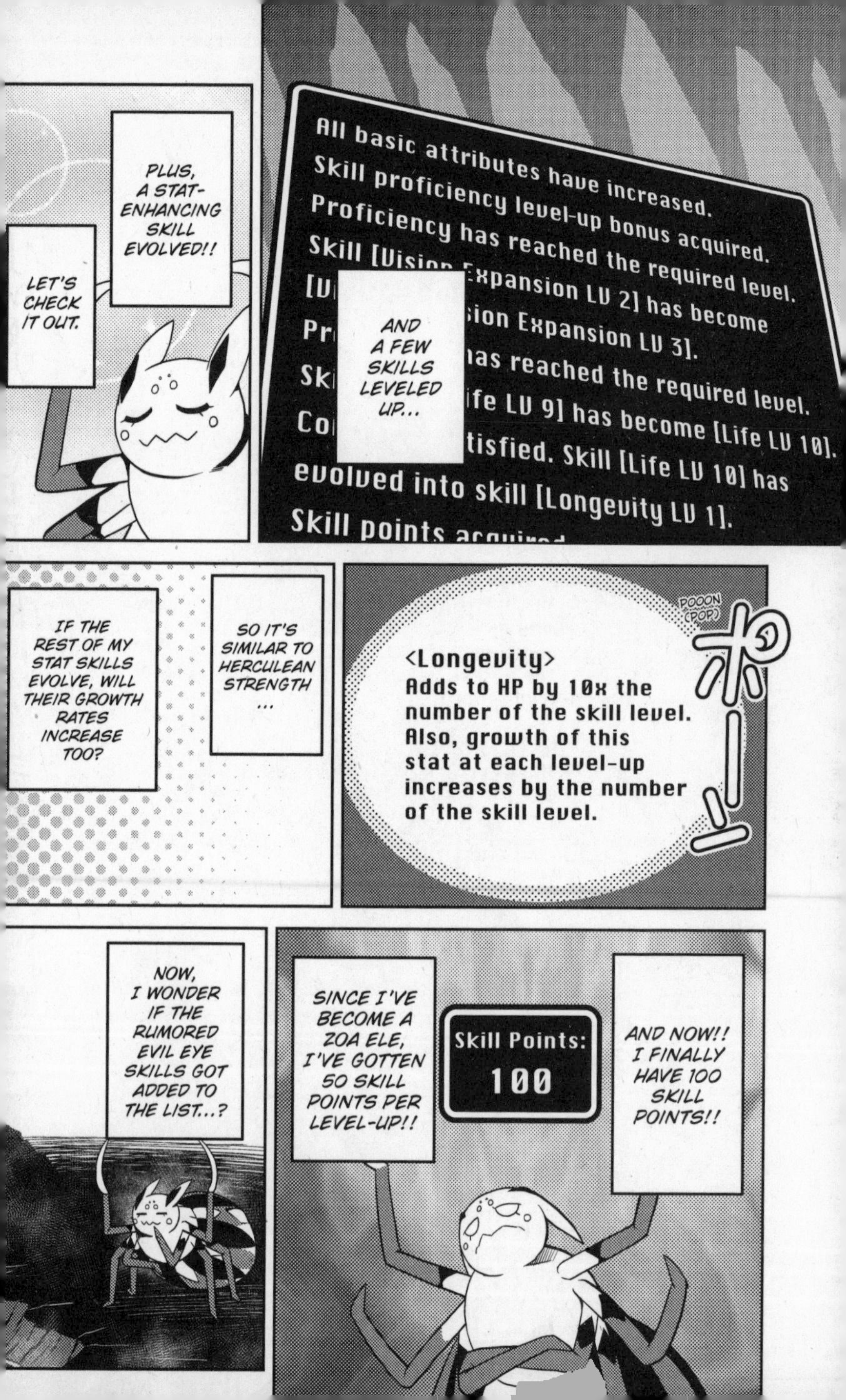
All basic attributes have increased.
Skill proficiency level-up bonus acquired.
Proficiency has reached the required level.
Skill [Visio Expansion LV 2] has become
[Vi sion Expansion LV 3].
Pr as reached the required level.
Sk ife LV 9] has become [Life LV 10].
Co tisfied. Skill [Life LV 10] has
evolved into skill [Longevity LV 1].
Skill points
AND A FEW SKILLS LEVELED UP...
PLUS, A STAT-ENHANCING SKILL EVOLVED!!
LET'S CHECK IT OUT.
POOON (POP)
<Longevity>
Adds to HP by 10x the number of the skill level. Also, growth of this stat at each level-up increases by the number of the skill level.
SO IT'S SIMILAR TO HERCULEAN STRENGTH...
IF THE REST OF MY STAT SKILLS EVOLVE, WILL THEIR GROWTH RATES INCREASE TOO?
AND NOW!! I FINALLY HAVE 100 SKILL POINTS!!
Skill Points: 100
SINCE I'VE BECOME A ZOA ELE, I'VE GOTTEN 50 SKILL POINTS PER LEVEL-UP!!
NOW, I WONDER IF THE RUMORED EVIL EYE SKILLS GOT ADDED TO THE LIST...?

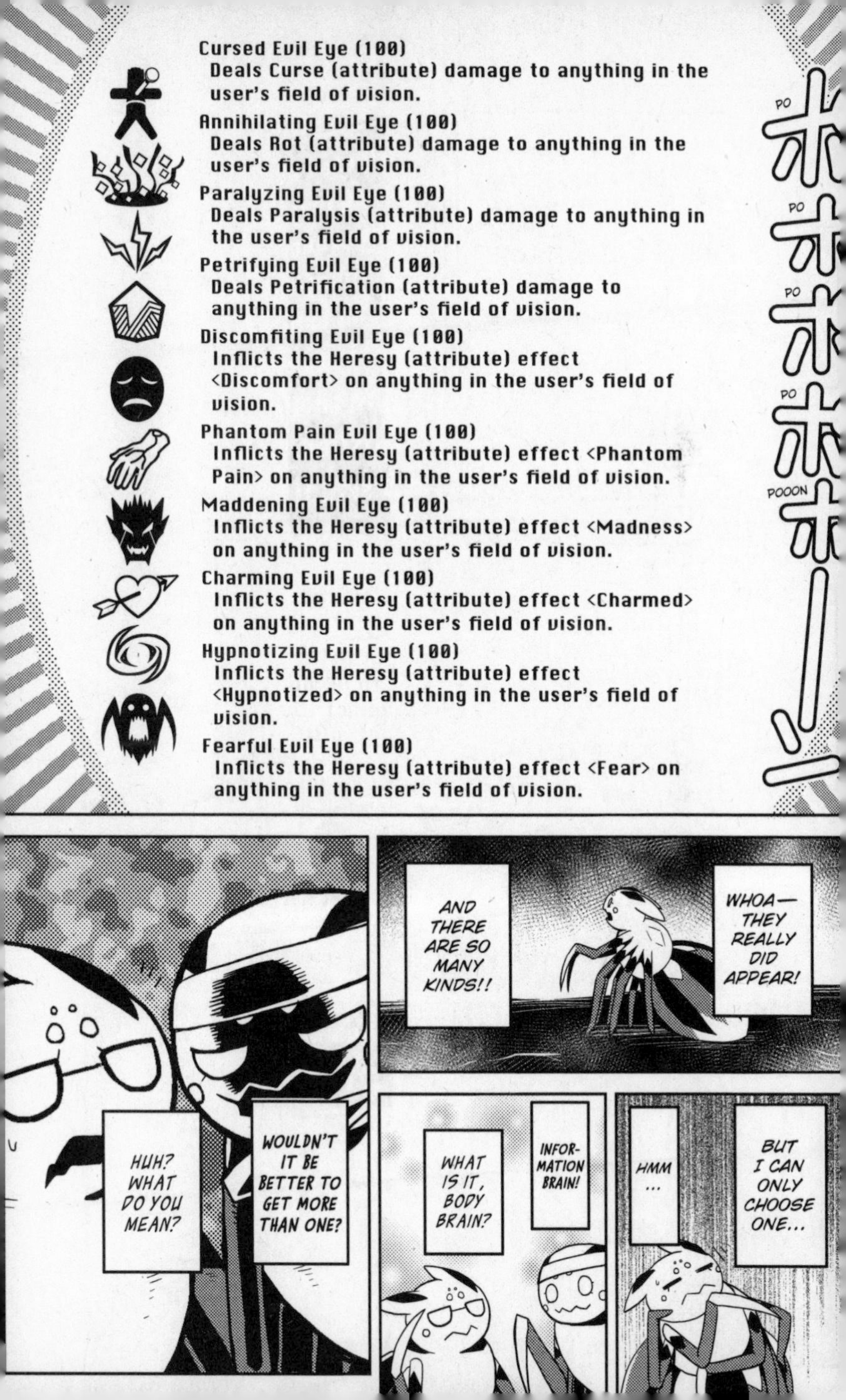
ホホホホホー
PO PO PO PO POOON
Cursed Evil Eye (100)
Deals Curse (attribute) damage to anything in the user's field of vision.
Annihilating Evil Eye (100)
Deals Rot (attribute) damage to anything in the user's field of vision.
Paralyzing Evil Eye (100)
Deals Paralysis (attribute) damage to anything in the user's field of vision.
Petrifying Evil Eye (100)
Deals Petrification (attribute) damage to anything in the user's field of vision.
Discomfiting Evil Eye (100)
Inflicts the Heresy (attribute) effect <Discomfort> on anything in the user's field of vision.
Phantom Pain Evil Eye (100)
Inflicts the Heresy (attribute) effect <Phantom Pain> on anything in the user's field of vision.
Maddening Evil Eye (100)
Inflicts the Heresy (attribute) effect <Madness> on anything in the user's field of vision.
Charming Evil Eye (100)
Inflicts the Heresy (attribute) effect <Charmed> on anything in the user's field of vision.
Hypnotizing Evil Eye (100)
Inflicts the Heresy (attribute) effect <Hypnotized> on anything in the user's field of vision.
Fearful Evil Eye (100)
Inflicts the Heresy (attribute) effect <Fear> on anything in the user's field of vision.
WHOA— THEY REALLY DID APPEAR!
AND THERE ARE SO MANY KINDS!!
BUT I CAN ONLY CHOOSE ONE...
HMM ...
INFORMATION BRAIN!
WHAT IS IT, BODY BRAIN?
WOULDN'T IT BE BETTER TO GET MORE THAN ONE?
HUH? WHAT DO YOU MEAN?

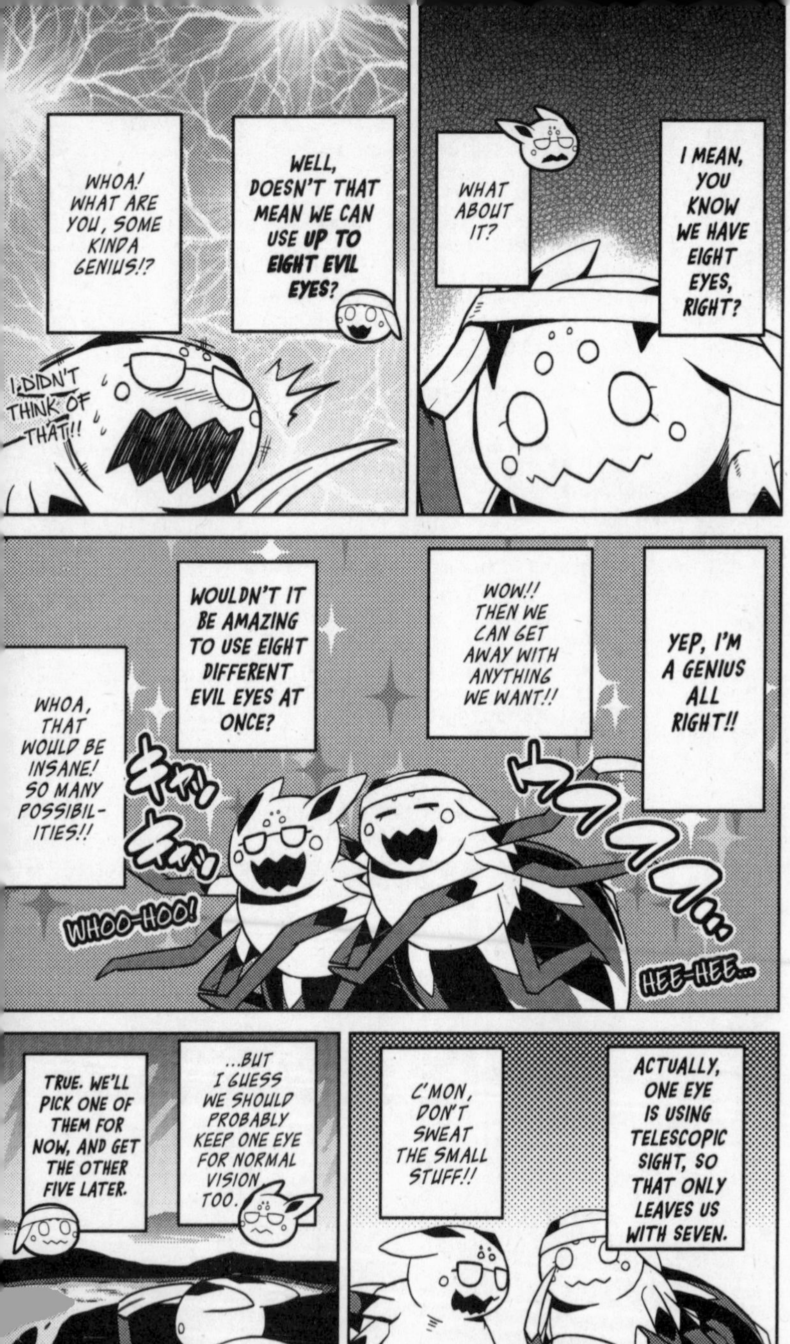
I MEAN, YOU KNOW WE HAVE EIGHT EYES, RIGHT?
WHAT ABOUT IT?
WELL, DOESN'T THAT MEAN WE CAN USE UP TO EIGHT EVIL EYES?
WHOA! WHAT ARE YOU, SOME KINDA GENIUS!?
I DIDN'T THINK OF THAT!!
YEP, I'M A GENIUS ALL RIGHT!!
WOW!! THEN WE CAN GET AWAY WITH ANYTHING WE WANT!!
HEE-HEE...
WOULDN'T IT BE AMAZING TO USE EIGHT DIFFERENT EVIL EYES AT ONCE?
WHOA, THAT WOULD BE INSANE! SO MANY POSSIBILITIES!!
WHOO-HOO!
ACTUALLY, ONE EYE IS USING TELESCOPIC SIGHT, SO THAT ONLY LEAVES US WITH SEVEN.
C'MON, DON'T SWEAT THE SMALL STUFF!!
...BUT I GUESS WE SHOULD PROBABLY KEEP ONE EYE FOR NORMAL VISION TOO.
TRUE. WE'LL PICK ONE OF THEM FOR NOW, AND GET THE OTHER FIVE LATER.

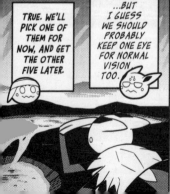

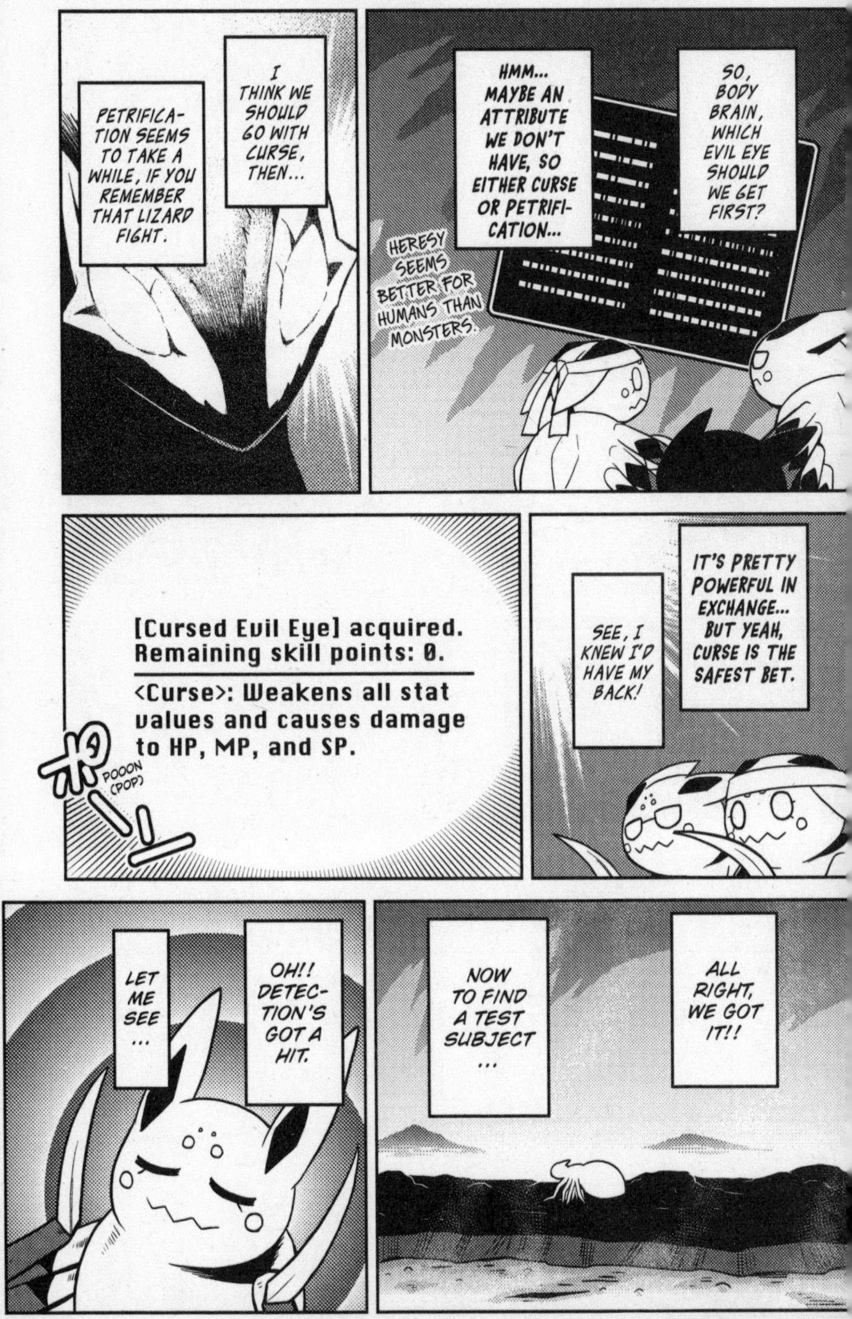
SO, BODY BRAIN, WHICH EVIL EYE SHOULD WE GET FIRST?
HMM... MAYBE AN ATTRIBUTE WE DON'T HAVE, SO EITHER CURSE OR PETRIFICATION...
HERESY SEEMS BETTER FOR HUMANS THAN MONSTERS.
I THINK WE SHOULD GO WITH CURSE, THEN...
PETRIFICATION SEEMS TO TAKE A WHILE, IF YOU REMEMBER THAT LIZARD FIGHT.
IT'S PRETTY POWERFUL IN EXCHANGE... BUT YEAH, CURSE IS THE SAFEST BET.
SEE, I KNEW I'D HAVE MY BACK!
[Cursed Evil Eye] acquired.
Remaining skill points: 0.
<Curse>: Weakens all stat values and causes damage to HP, MP, and SP.
POOON (POP)
ALL RIGHT, WE GOT IT!!
NOW TO FIND A TEST SUBJECT...
OH!! DETECTION'S GOT A HIT.
LET ME SEE...

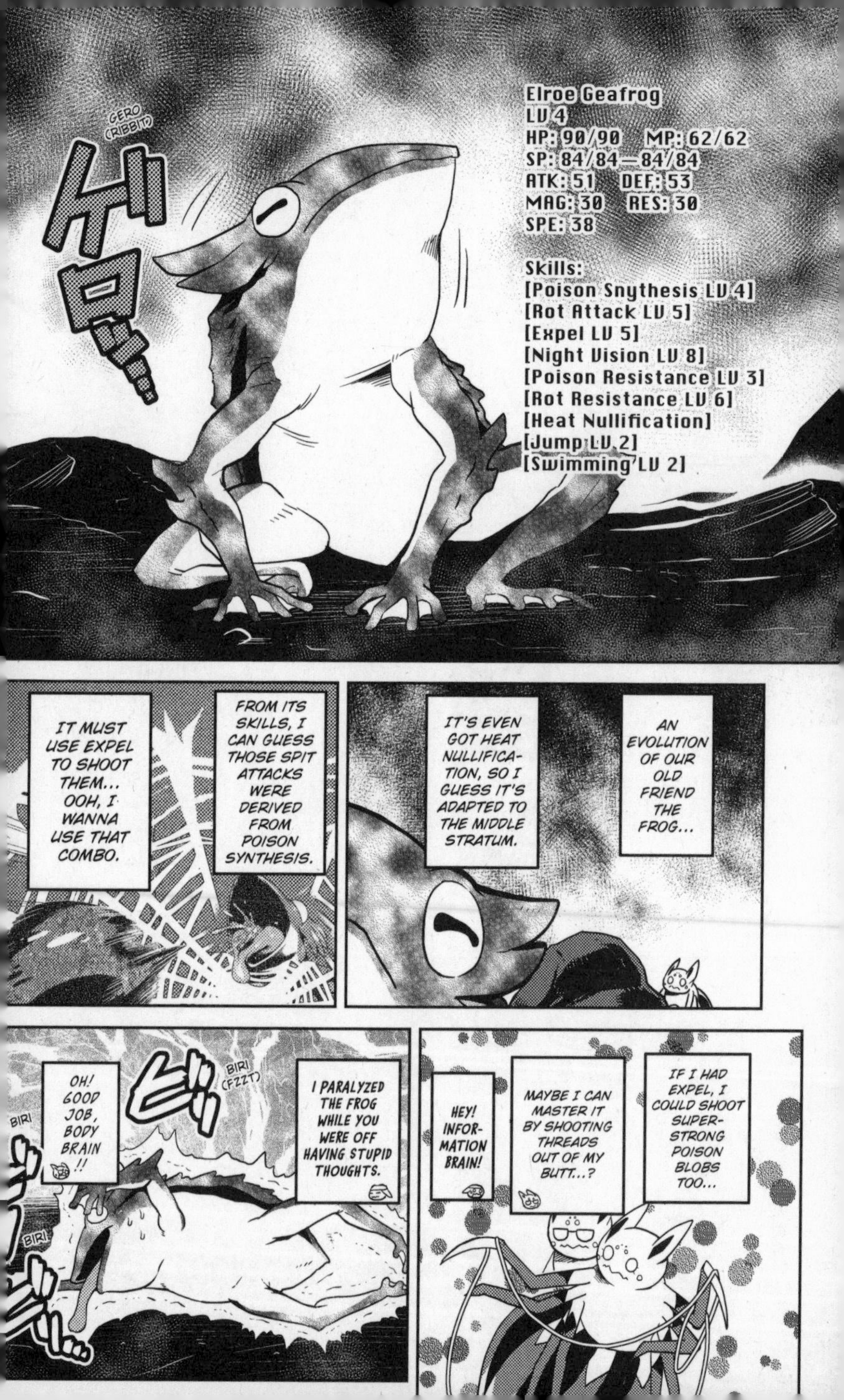
Elroe Geafrog
LV 4
HP: 90/90 MP: 62/62
SP: 84/84—84/84
ATK: 51 DEF: 53
MAG: 30 RES: 30
SPE: 38
Skills:
[Poison Snythesis LV 4]
[Rot Attack LV 5]
[Expel LV 5]
[Night Vision LV 8]
[Poison Resistance LV 3]
[Rot Resistance LV 6]
[Heat Nullification]
[Jump LV 2]
[Swimming LV 2]
GERO (RIBBIT)
AN EVOLUTION OF OUR OLD FRIEND THE FROG...
IT'S EVEN GOT HEAT NULLIFICA-TION, SO I GUESS IT'S ADAPTED TO THE MIDDLE STRATUM.
FROM ITS SKILLS, I CAN GUESS THOSE SPIT ATTACKS WERE DERIVED FROM POISON SYNTHESIS.
IT MUST USE EXPEL TO SHOOT THEM... OOH, I WANNA USE THAT COMBO.
IF I HAD EXPEL, I COULD SHOOT SUPER-STRONG POISON BLOBS TOO...
MAYBE I CAN MASTER IT BY SHOOTING THREADS OUT OF MY BUTT...?
HEY! INFOR-MATION BRAIN!
I PARALYZED THE FROG WHILE YOU WERE OFF HAVING STUPID THOUGHTS.
BIRI (FZZT)
OH! GOOD JOB, BODY BRAIN!!
BIRI
BIRI

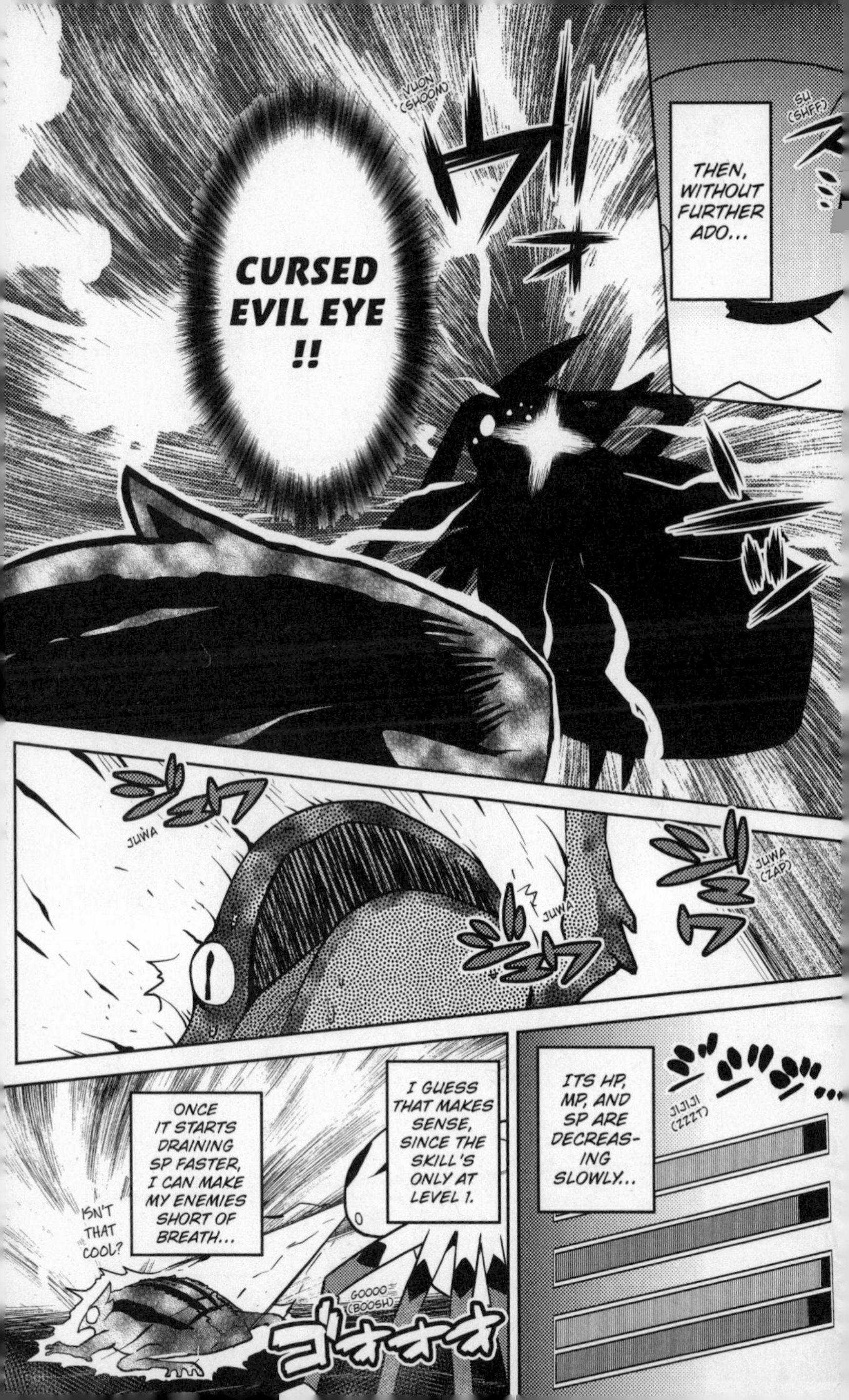
SU (SHFF)
THEN, WITHOUT FURTHER ADO...
VUON (SHOOM)
CURSED EVIL EYE !!
JUWA (ZAP)
JUWA
JUWA
JIJIJI (ZZZT)
ITS HP, MP, AND SP ARE DECREAS-ING SLOWLY...
I GUESS THAT MAKES SENSE, SINCE THE SKILL'S ONLY AT LEVEL 1.
ONCE IT STARTS DRAINING SP FASTER, I CAN MAKE MY ENEMIES SHORT OF BREATH...
ISN'T THAT COOL?
GOOOO (BOOSH)

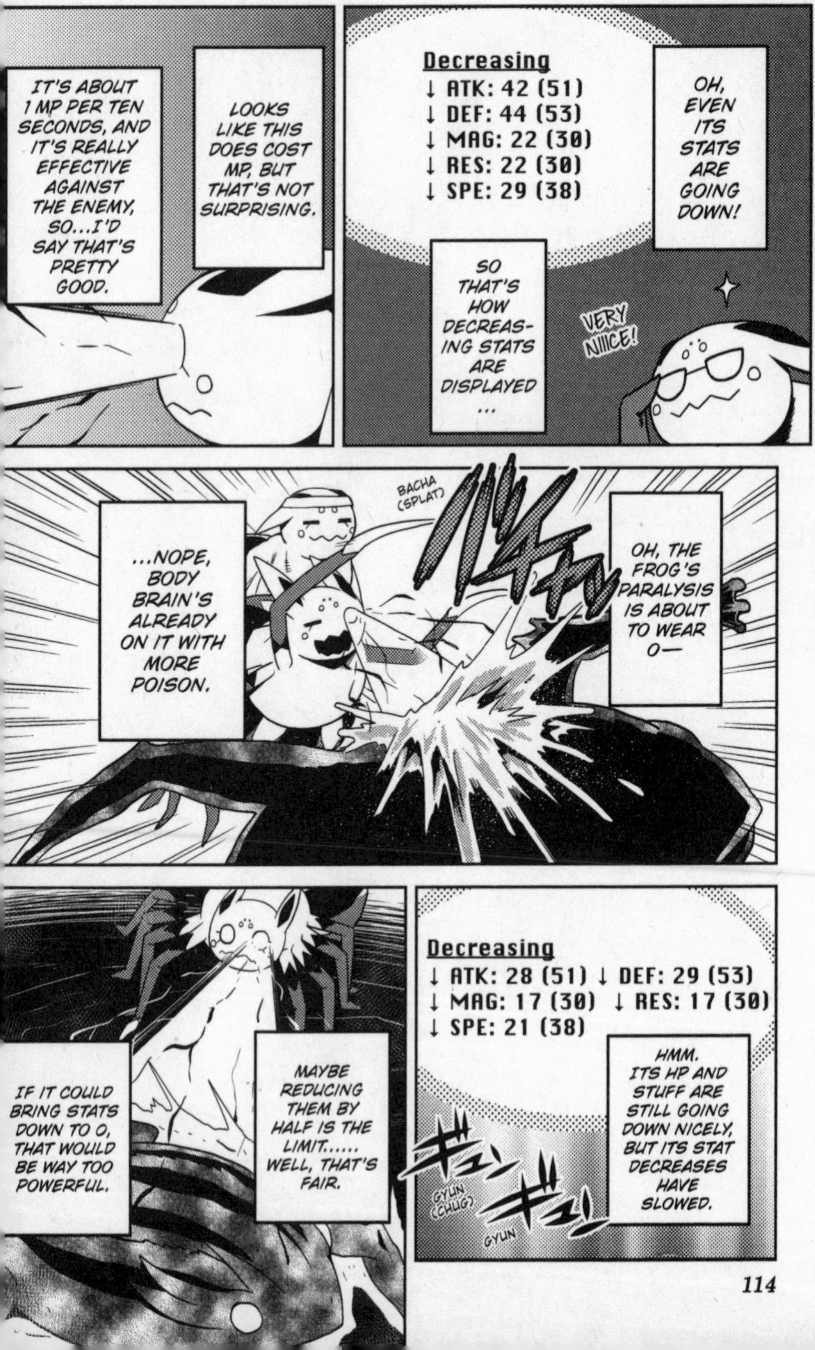
OH, EVEN ITS STATS ARE GOING DOWN!
Decreasing
↓ ATK: 42 (51)
↓ DEF: 44 (53)
↓ MAG: 22 (30)
↓ RES: 22 (30)
↓ SPE: 29 (38)
VERY NIIICE!
SO THAT'S HOW DECREASING STATS ARE DISPLAYED...
LOOKS LIKE THIS DOES COST MP, BUT THAT'S NOT SURPRISING.
IT'S ABOUT 1 MP PER TEN SECONDS, AND IT'S REALLY EFFECTIVE AGAINST THE ENEMY, SO...I'D SAY THAT'S PRETTY GOOD.
OH, THE FROG'S PARALYSIS IS ABOUT TO WEAR O—
BACHA (SPLAT)
...NOPE, BODY BRAIN'S ALREADY ON IT WITH MORE POISON.
Decreasing
↓ ATK: 28 (51) ↓ DEF: 29 (53)
↓ MAG: 17 (30) ↓ RES: 17 (30)
↓ SPE: 21 (38)
HMM. ITS HP AND STUFF ARE STILL GOING DOWN NICELY, BUT ITS STAT DECREASES HAVE SLOWED.
GYUN (CHUG)
GYUN
MAYBE REDUCING THEM BY HALF IS THE LIMIT...... WELL, THAT'S FAIR.
IF IT COULD BRING STATS DOWN TO 0, THAT WOULD BE WAY TOO POWERFUL.

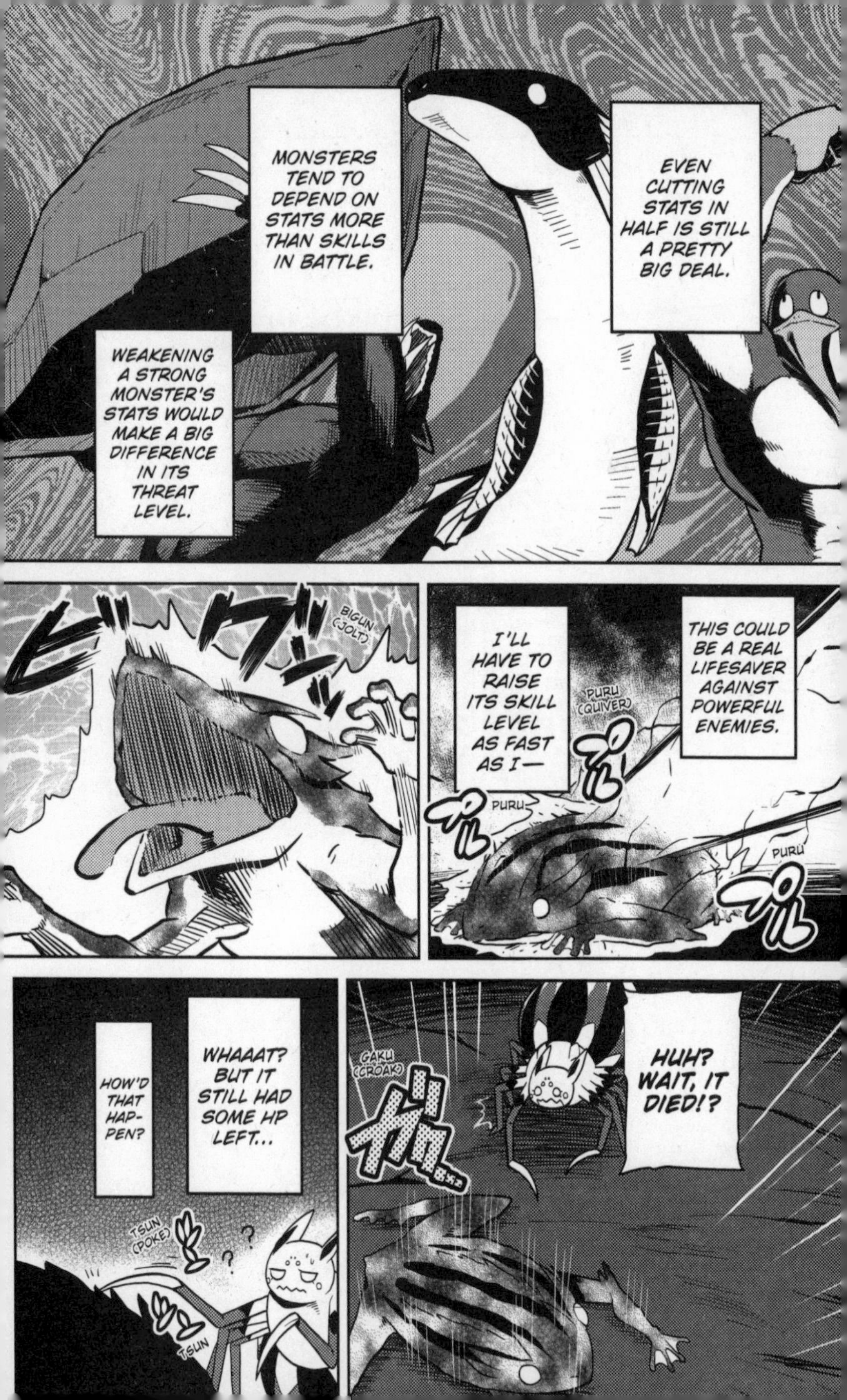
EVEN CUTTING STATS IN HALF IS STILL A PRETTY BIG DEAL.
MONSTERS TEND TO DEPEND ON STATS MORE THAN SKILLS IN BATTLE.
WEAKENING A STRONG MONSTER'S STATS WOULD MAKE A BIG DIFFERENCE IN ITS THREAT LEVEL.
THIS COULD BE A REAL LIFESAVER AGAINST POWERFUL ENEMIES.
I'LL HAVE TO RAISE ITS SKILL LEVEL AS FAST AS I—
PURU (QUIVER)
PURU
PURU
BIGUN (JOLT)
HUH? WAIT, IT DIED!?
GAKU (CROAK)
WHAAAT? BUT IT STILL HAD SOME HP LEFT...
HOW'D THAT HAP-PEN?
TSUN (POKE)
TSUN

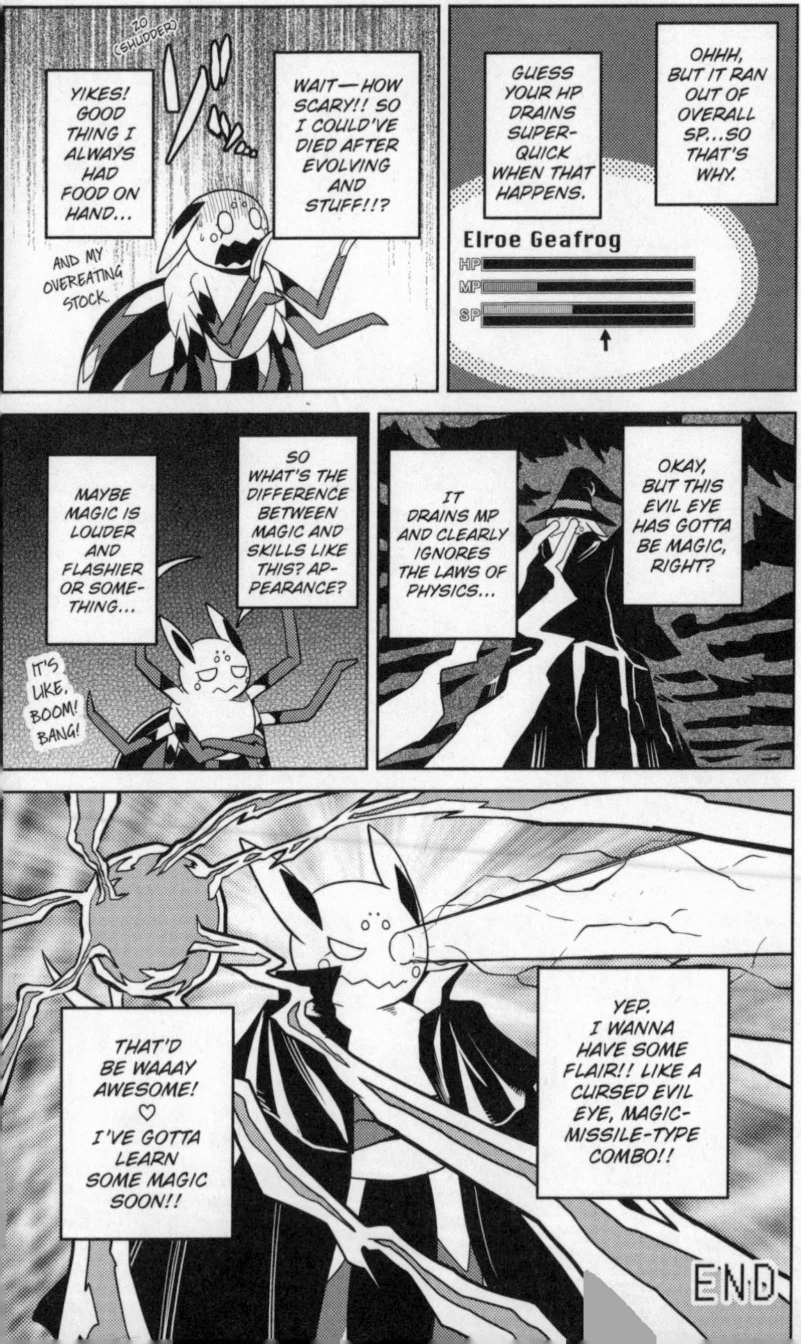
OHHH, BUT IT RAN OUT OF OVERALL SP...SO THAT'S WHY.
GUESS YOUR HP DRAINS SUPER-QUICK WHEN THAT HAPPENS.
Elroe Geafrog
HP
MP
SP
ZO (SHUDDER)
WAIT—HOW SCARY!! SO I COULD'VE DIED AFTER EVOLVING AND STUFF!!?
YIKES! GOOD THING I ALWAYS HAD FOOD ON HAND...
AND MY OVEREATING STOCK.
OKAY, BUT THIS EVIL EYE HAS GOTTA BE MAGIC, RIGHT?
IT DRAINS MP AND CLEARLY IGNORES THE LAWS OF PHYSICS...
SO WHAT'S THE DIFFERENCE BETWEEN MAGIC AND SKILLS LIKE THIS? APPEARANCE?
MAYBE MAGIC IS LOUDER AND FLASHIER OR SOMETHING...
IT'S LIKE, BOOM! BANG!
YEP. I WANNA HAVE SOME FLAIR!! LIKE A CURSED EVIL EYE, MAGIC-MISSILE-TYPE COMBO!!
THAT'D BE WAAAY AWESOME! ♡ I'VE GOTTA LEARN SOME MAGIC SOON!!
END

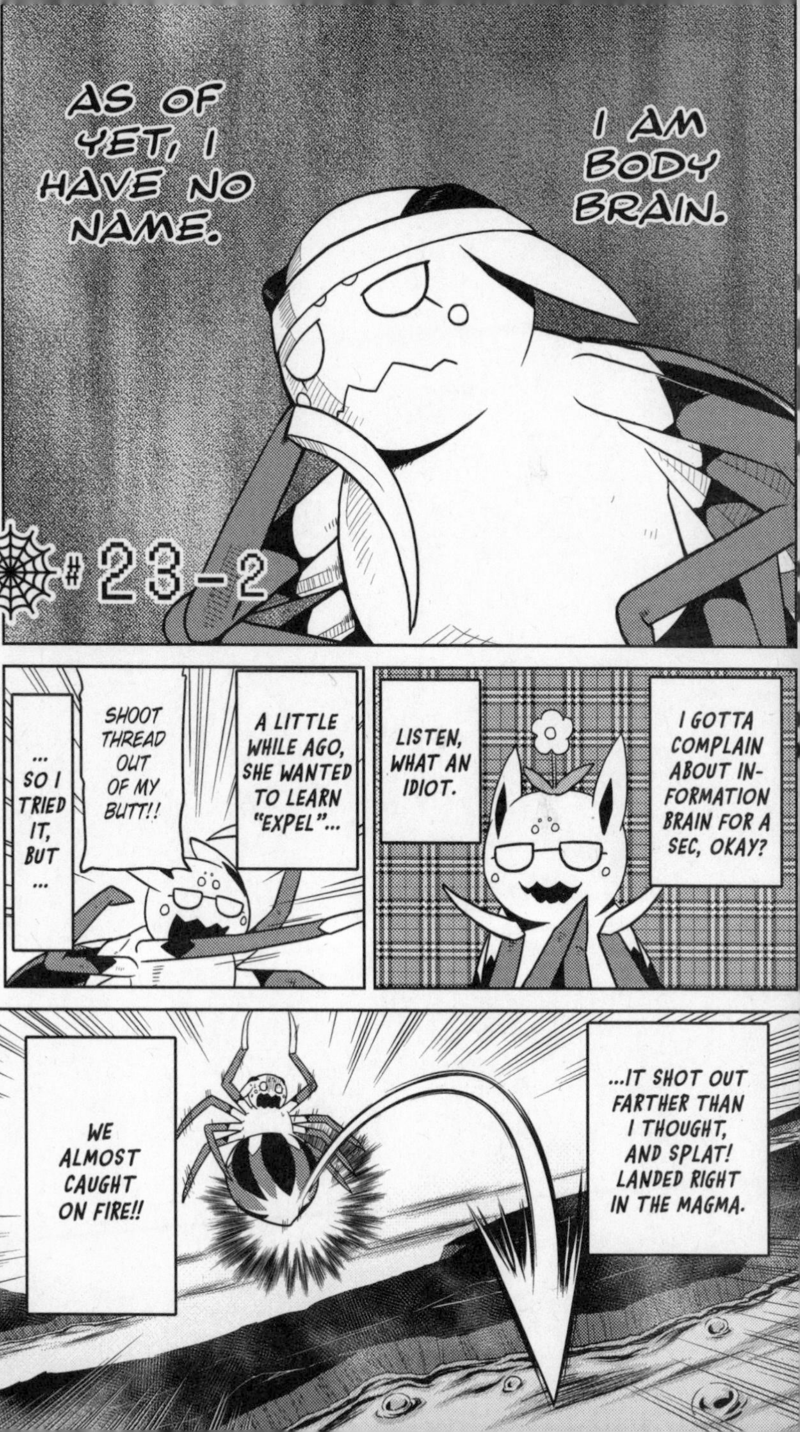
I AM BODY BRAIN.
AS OF YET, I HAVE NO NAME.
#23-2
I GOTTA COMPLAIN ABOUT IN-FORMATION BRAIN FOR A SEC, OKAY?
LISTEN, WHAT AN IDIOT.
A LITTLE WHILE AGO, SHE WANTED TO LEARN "EXPEL"...
SHOOT THREAD OUT OF MY BUTT!!
... SO I TRIED IT, BUT ...
...IT SHOT OUT FARTHER THAN I THOUGHT, AND SPLAT! LANDED RIGHT IN THE MAGMA.
WE ALMOST CAUGHT ON FIRE!!

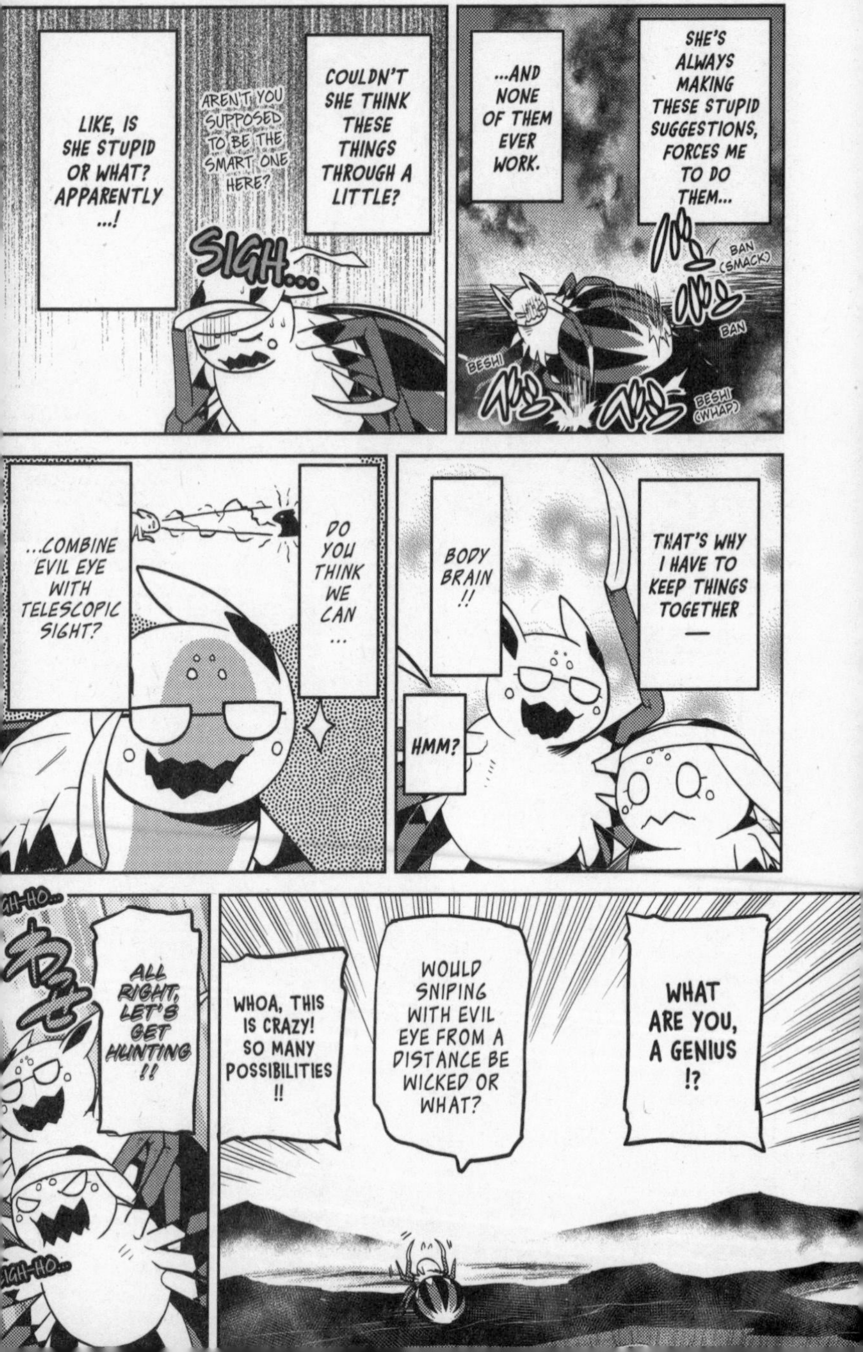
SHE'S ALWAYS MAKING THESE STUPID SUGGESTIONS, FORCES ME TO DO THEM...
...AND NONE OF THEM EVER WORK.
BAN (SMACK)
BAN
BESHI (WHAP)
BESHI
COULDN'T SHE THINK THESE THINGS THROUGH A LITTLE?
AREN'T YOU SUPPOSED TO BE THE SMART ONE HERE?
LIKE, IS SHE STUPID OR WHAT? APPARENTLY ...!
SIGH...
THAT'S WHY I HAVE TO KEEP THINGS TOGETHER —
BODY BRAIN !!
HMM?
DO YOU THINK WE CAN ...
...COMBINE EVIL EYE WITH TELESCOPIC SIGHT?
WHAT ARE YOU, A GENIUS !?
WOULD SNIPING WITH EVIL EYE FROM A DISTANCE BE WICKED OR WHAT?
WHOA, THIS IS CRAZY! SO MANY POSSIBILITIES !!
ALL RIGHT, LET'S GET HUNTING !!

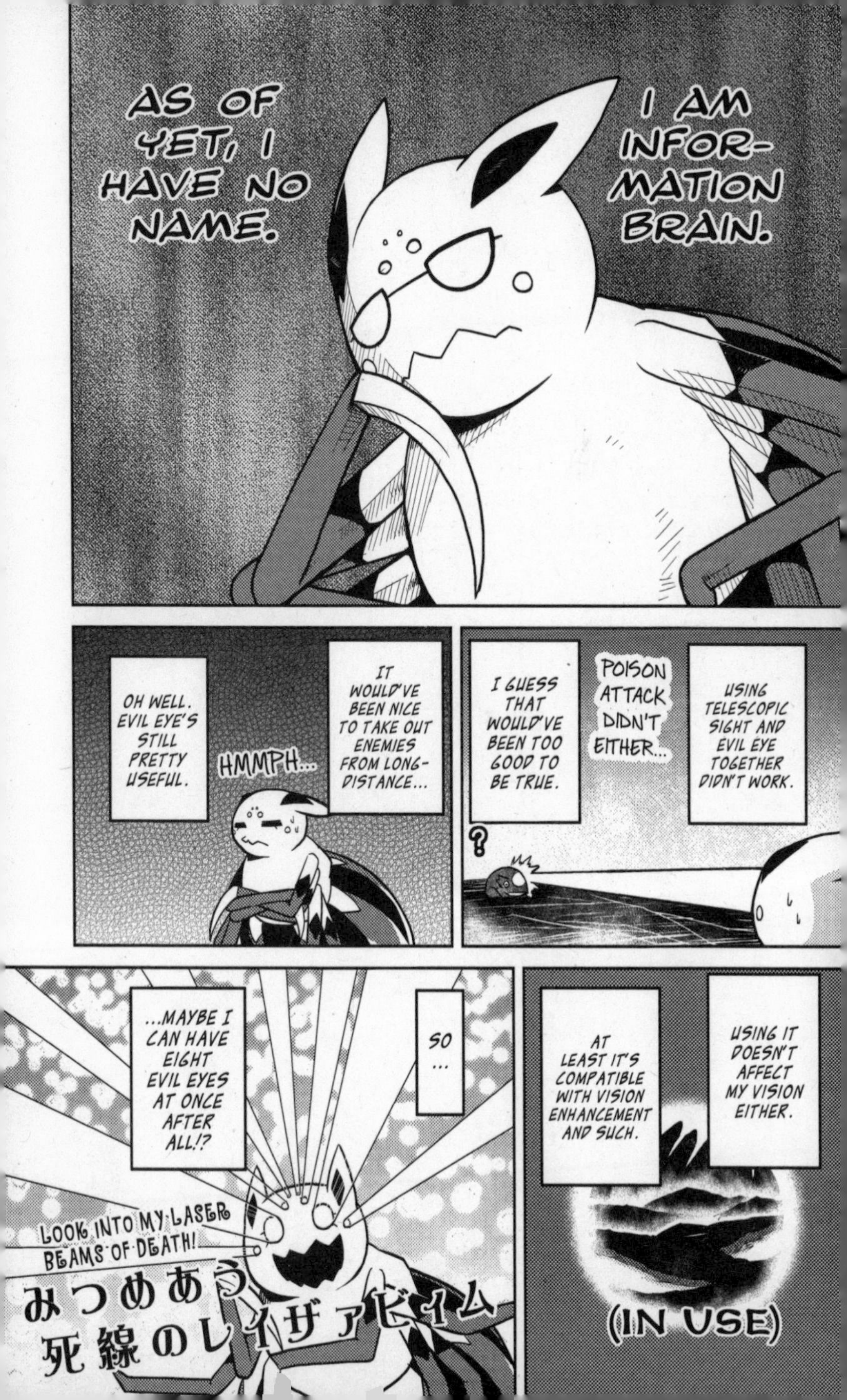
I AM INFORMATION BRAIN.
AS OF YET, I HAVE NO NAME.
USING TELESCOPIC SIGHT AND EVIL EYE TOGETHER DIDN'T WORK.
POISON ATTACK DIDN'T EITHER...
I GUESS THAT WOULD'VE BEEN TOO GOOD TO BE TRUE.
?
IT WOULD'VE BEEN NICE TO TAKE OUT ENEMIES FROM LONG-DISTANCE...
HMMPH...
OH WELL. EVIL EYE'S STILL PRETTY USEFUL.
USING IT DOESN'T AFFECT MY VISION EITHER.
AT LEAST IT'S COMPATIBLE WITH VISION ENHANCEMENT AND SUCH.
(IN USE)
SO...
...MAYBE I CAN HAVE EIGHT EVIL EYES AT ONCE AFTER ALL!?
LOOK INTO MY LASER BEAMS OF DEATH!
みつめあう
死線のレイザァビイム

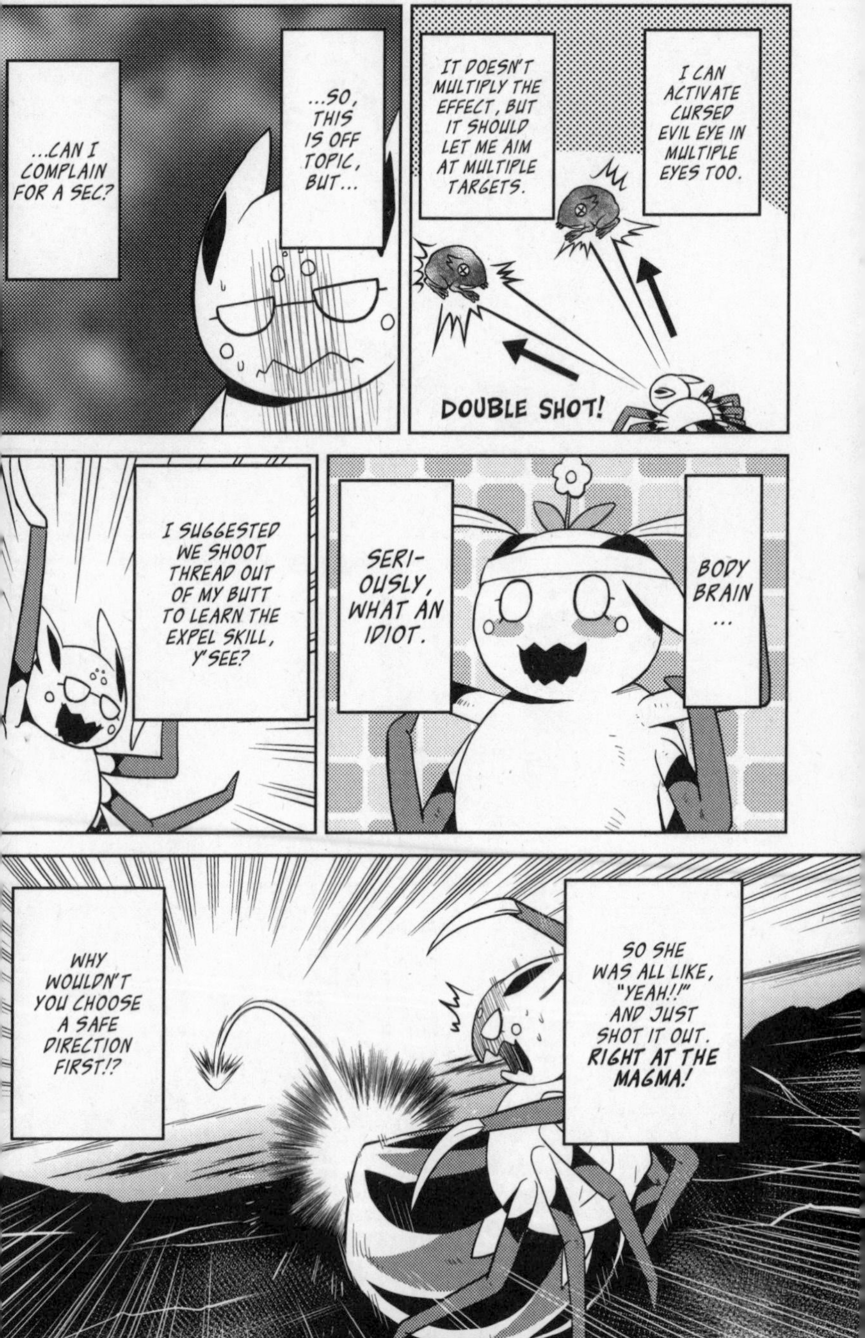
I CAN ACTIVATE CURSED EVIL EYE IN MULTIPLE EYES TOO.
IT DOESN'T MULTIPLY THE EFFECT, BUT IT SHOULD LET ME AIM AT MULTIPLE TARGETS.
DOUBLE SHOT!
...SO, THIS IS OFF TOPIC, BUT...
...CAN I COMPLAIN FOR A SEC?
BODY BRAIN...
SERI-OUSLY, WHAT AN IDIOT.
I SUGGESTED WE SHOOT THREAD OUT OF MY BUTT TO LEARN THE EXPEL SKILL, Y'SEE?
SO SHE WAS ALL LIKE, "YEAH!!" AND JUST SHOT IT OUT. RIGHT AT THE MAGMA!
WHY WOULDN'T YOU CHOOSE A SAFE DIRECTION FIRST!?

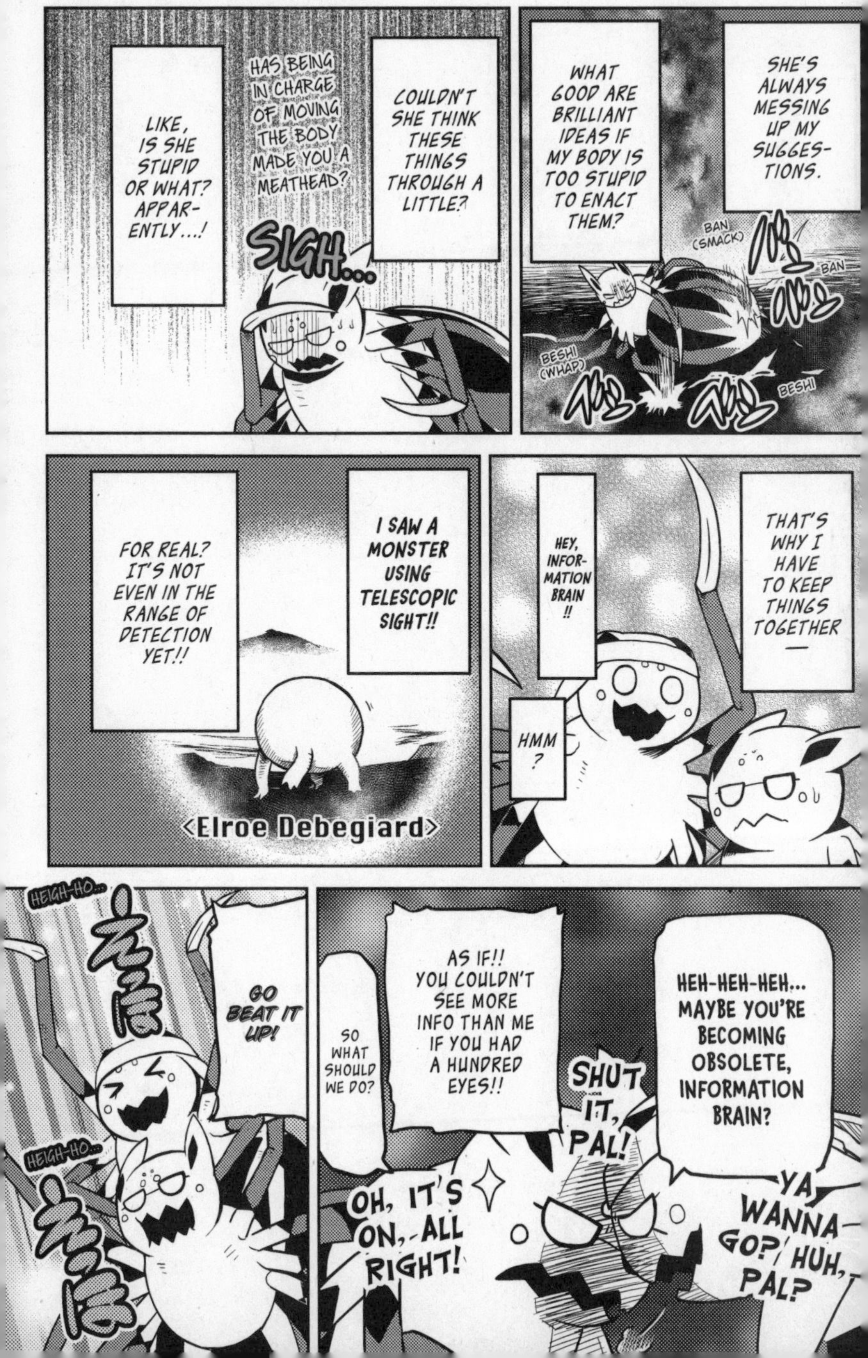
SHE'S ALWAYS MESSING UP MY SUGGES-TIONS.
WHAT GOOD ARE BRILLIANT IDEAS IF MY BODY IS TOO STUPID TO ENACT THEM?
BAN (SMACK)
BAN
BESHI (WHAP)
BESHI
COULDN'T SHE THINK THESE THINGS THROUGH A LITTLE?
HAS BEING IN CHARGE OF MOVING THE BODY MADE YOU A MEATHEAD?
LIKE, IS SHE STUPID OR WHAT? APPAR-ENTLY...!
SIGH...
THAT'S WHY I HAVE TO KEEP THINGS TOGETHER —
HEY, INFOR-MATION BRAIN !!
HMM ?
I SAW A MONSTER USING TELESCOPIC SIGHT!!
FOR REAL? IT'S NOT EVEN IN THE RANGE OF DETECTION YET!!
<Elroe Debegiard>
HEH-HEH-HEH... MAYBE YOU'RE BECOMING OBSOLETE, INFORMATION BRAIN?
YA WANNA GO? HUH, PAL?
SHUT IT, PAL!
AS IF!! YOU COULDN'T SEE MORE INFO THAN ME IF YOU HAD A HUNDRED EYES!!
OH, IT'S ON, ALL RIGHT!
SO WHAT SHOULD WE DO?
GO BEAT IT UP!
HEIGH-HO...
HEIGH-HO...

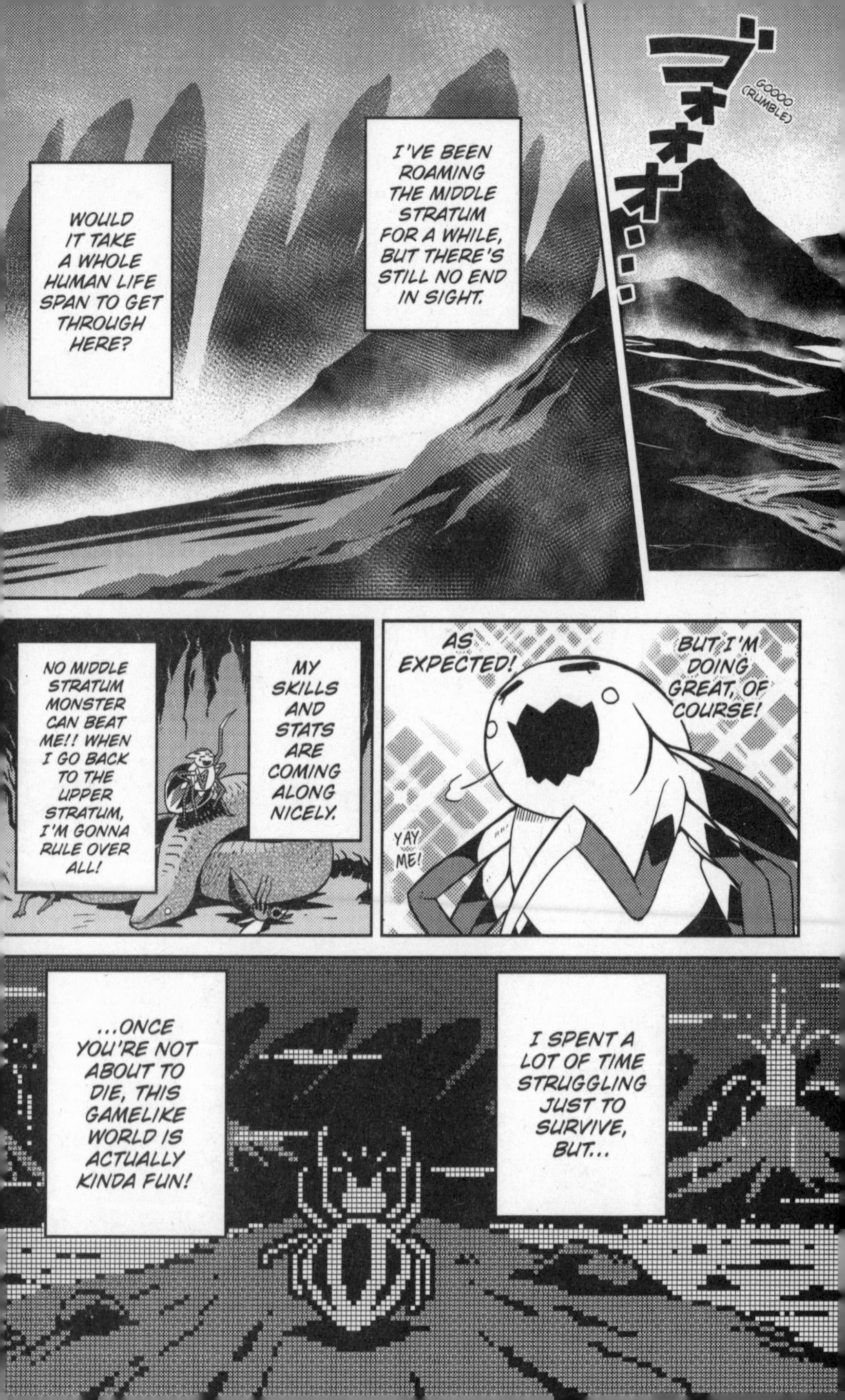
GOOOO (RUMBLE)
I'VE BEEN ROAMING THE MIDDLE STRATUM FOR A WHILE, BUT THERE'S STILL NO END IN SIGHT.
WOULD IT TAKE A WHOLE HUMAN LIFE SPAN TO GET THROUGH HERE?
BUT I'M DOING GREAT, OF COURSE!
AS EXPECTED!
YAY ME!
MY SKILLS AND STATS ARE COMING ALONG NICELY.
NO MIDDLE STRATUM MONSTER CAN BEAT ME!! WHEN I GO BACK TO THE UPPER STRATUM, I'M GONNA RULE OVER ALL!
I SPENT A LOT OF TIME STRUGGLING JUST TO SURVIVE, BUT...
...ONCE YOU'RE NOT ABOUT TO DIE, THIS GAMELIKE WORLD IS ACTUALLY KINDA FUN!

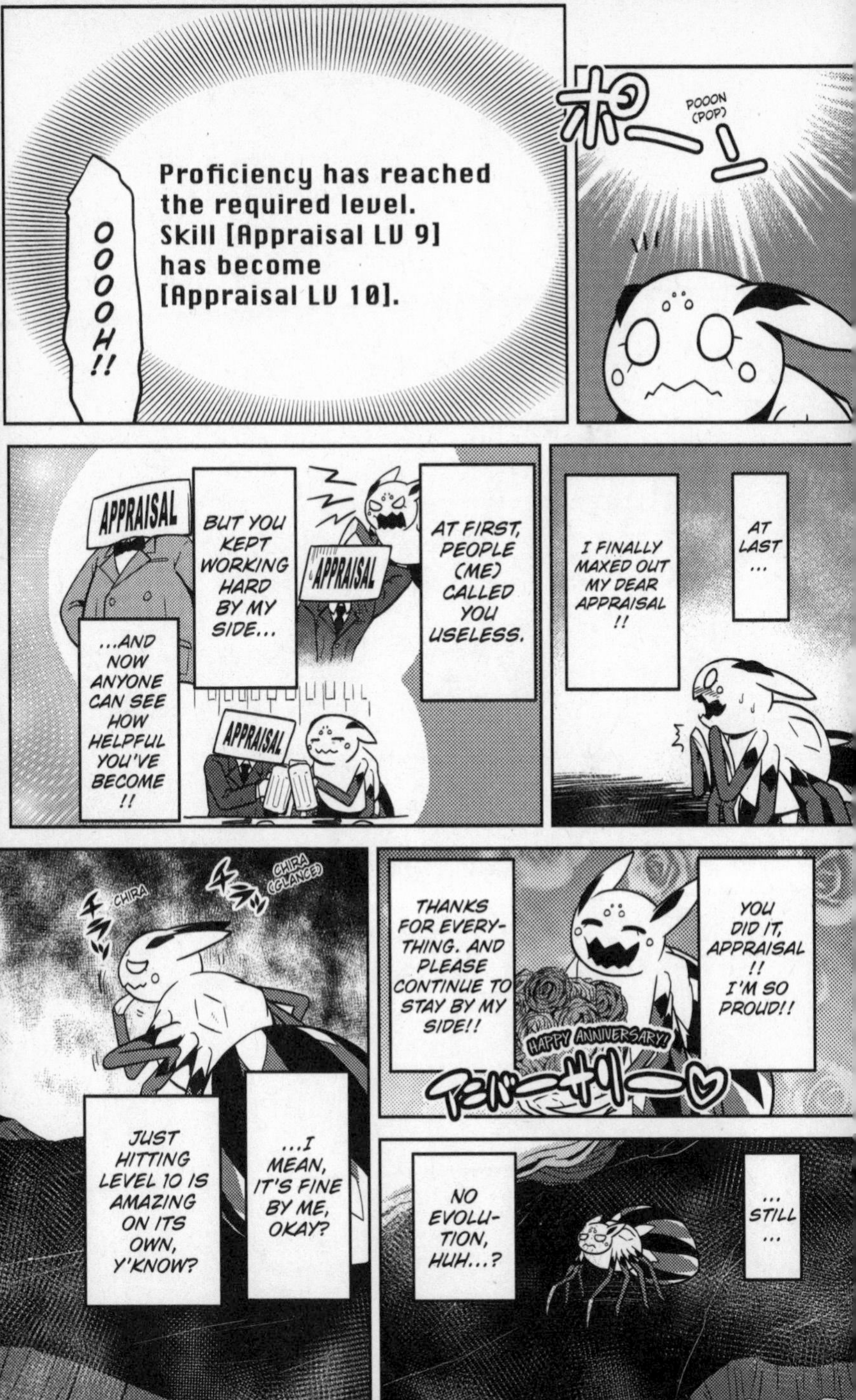
POOON (POP)
Proficiency has reached the required level. Skill [Appraisal LV 9] has become [Appraisal LV 10].
OOOOOH!!
AT LAST...
I FINALLY MAXED OUT MY DEAR APPRAISAL!!
AT FIRST, PEOPLE (ME) CALLED YOU USELESS.
APPRAISAL
APPRAISAL
BUT YOU KEPT WORKING HARD BY MY SIDE...
APPRAISAL
...AND NOW ANYONE CAN SEE HOW HELPFUL YOU'VE BECOME!!
YOU DID IT, APPRAISAL!! I'M SO PROUD!!
THANKS FOR EVERYTHING. AND PLEASE CONTINUE TO STAY BY MY SIDE!!
HAPPY ANNIVERSARY!
...STILL...
NO EVOLUTION, HUH...?
CHIRA (GLANCE)
CHIRA
...I MEAN, IT'S FINE BY ME, OKAY?
JUST HITTING LEVEL 10 IS AMAZING ON ITS OWN, Y'KNOW?

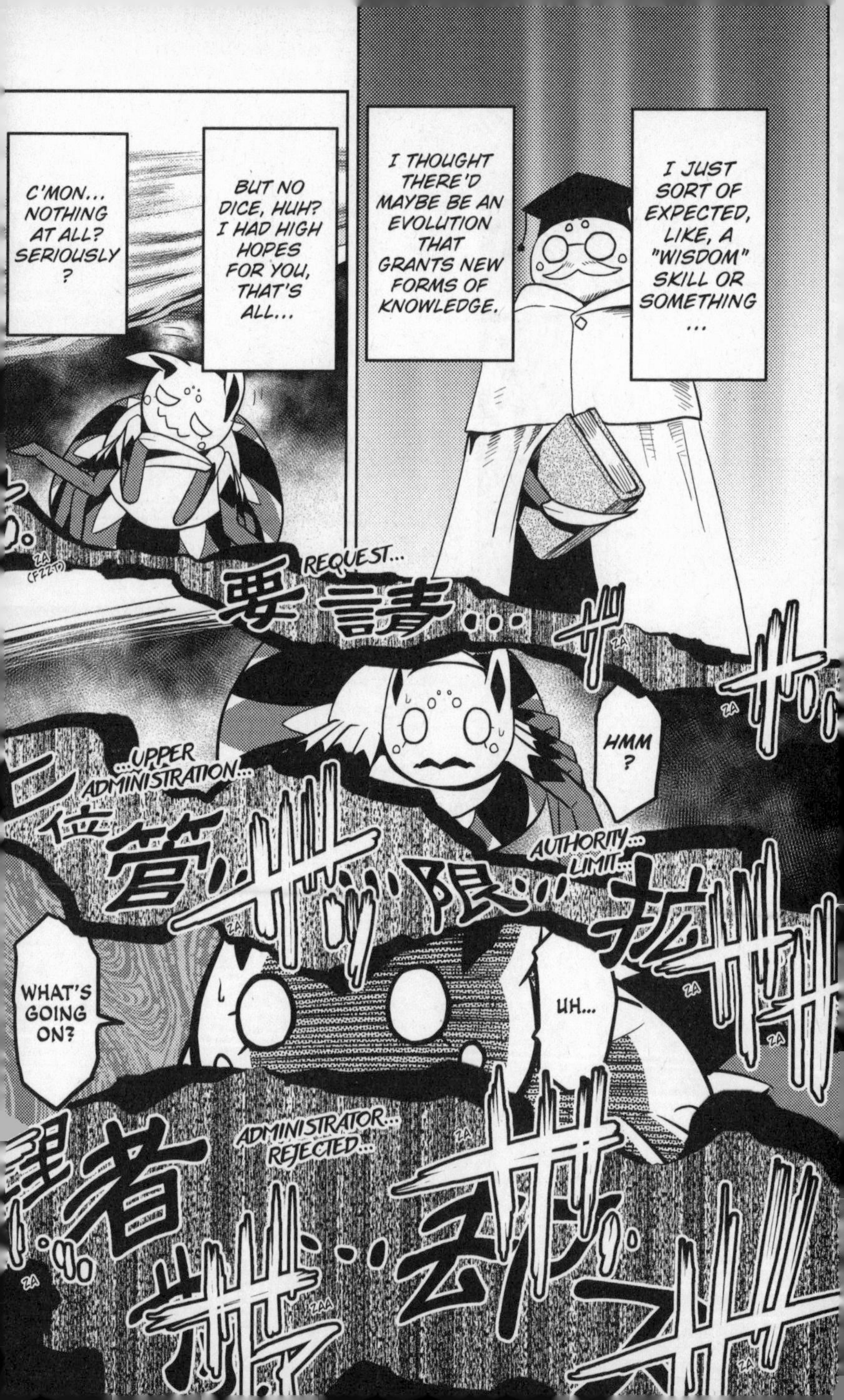

I JUST SORT OF EXPECTED, LIKE, A "WISDOM" SKILL OR SOMETHING...
I THOUGHT THERE'D MAYBE BE AN EVOLUTION THAT GRANTS NEW FORMS OF KNOWLEDGE.
BUT NO DICE, HUH? I HAD HIGH HOPES FOR YOU, THAT'S ALL...
C'MON... NOTHING AT ALL? SERIOUSLY?
ZA (FZZT)
REQUEST...
要請...
ZA
ZA
HMM?
...UPPER ADMINISTRATION...
上位管...
AUTHORITY... LIMIT...
限...
ZA
ZA
ZA
UH...
WHAT'S GOING ON?
ADMINISTRATOR... REJECTED...
理者...
ZA
ZA
ZAA
ZA

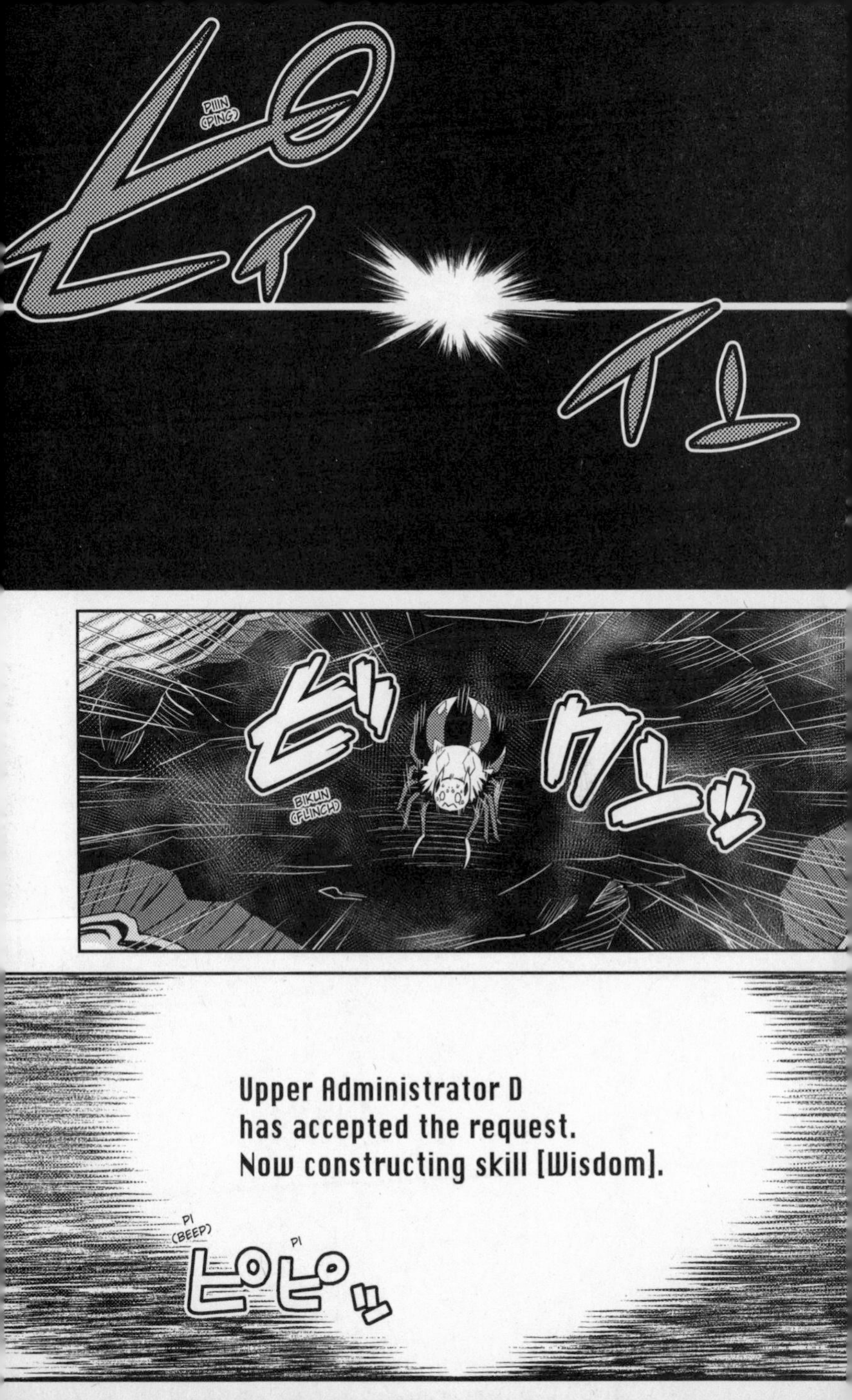
PIIIN (PING)
BIKUN (FLINCH)
Upper Administrator D has accepted the request. Now constructing skill [Wisdom].
PI (BEEP)
PI

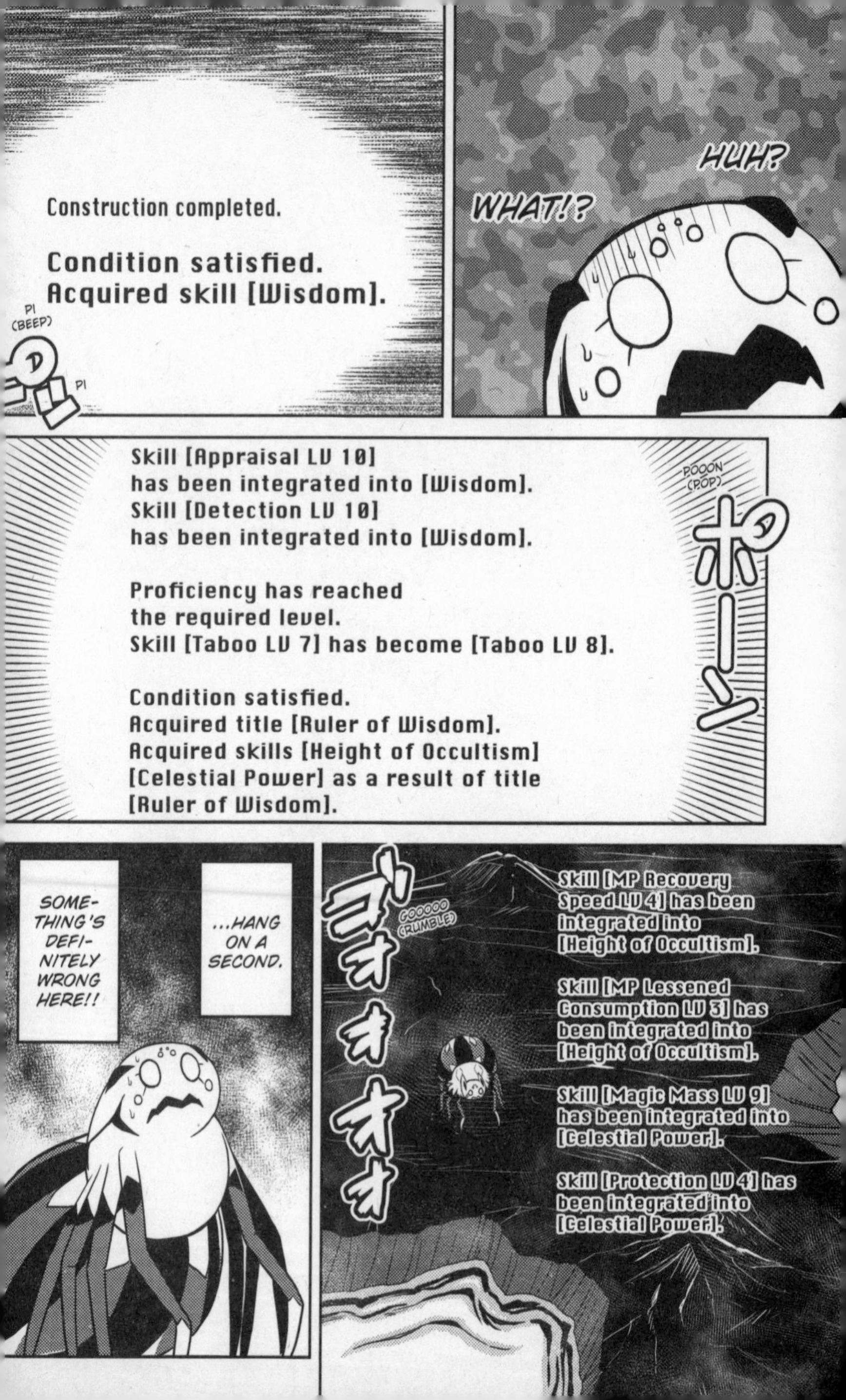
HUH?
WHAT!?
Construction completed.
Condition satisfied.
Acquired skill [Wisdom].
PI (BEEP)
PI
POOON (POP)
ポーン
Skill [Appraisal LV 10] has been integrated into [Wisdom].
Skill [Detection LV 10] has been integrated into [Wisdom].
Proficiency has reached the required level.
Skill [Taboo LV 7] has become [Taboo LV 8].
Condition satisfied.
Acquired title [Ruler of Wisdom].
Acquired skills [Height of Occultism] [Celestial Power] as a result of title [Ruler of Wisdom].
Skill [MP Recovery Speed LV 4] has been integrated into [Height of Occultism].
Skill [MP Lessened Consumption LV 3] has been integrated into [Height of Occultism].
Skill [Magic Mass LV 9] has been integrated into [Celestial Power].
Skill [Protection LV 4] has been integrated into [Celestial Power].
GOOOOO (RUMBLE)
...HANG ON A SECOND.
SOME-THING'S DEFI-NITELY WRONG HERE!!

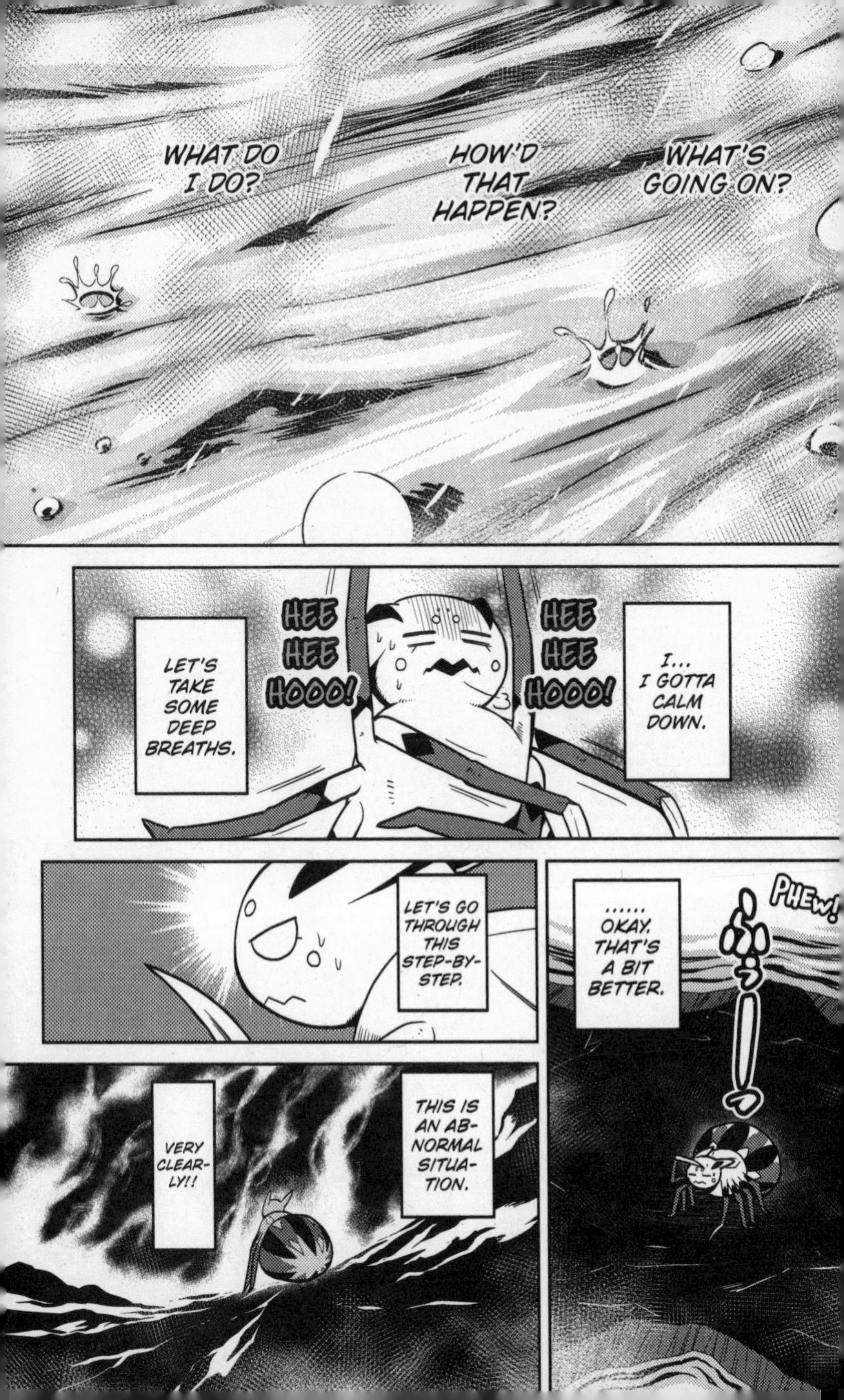
WHAT'S GOING ON?
HOW'D THAT HAPPEN?
WHAT DO I DO?
I... I GOTTA CALM DOWN.
HEE HEE HOOO!
HEE HEE HOOO!
LET'S TAKE SOME DEEP BREATHS.
PHEW!
...... OKAY. THAT'S A BIT BETTER.
LET'S GO THROUGH THIS STEP-BY-STEP.
THIS IS AN ABNORMAL SITUATION.
VERY CLEARLY!!

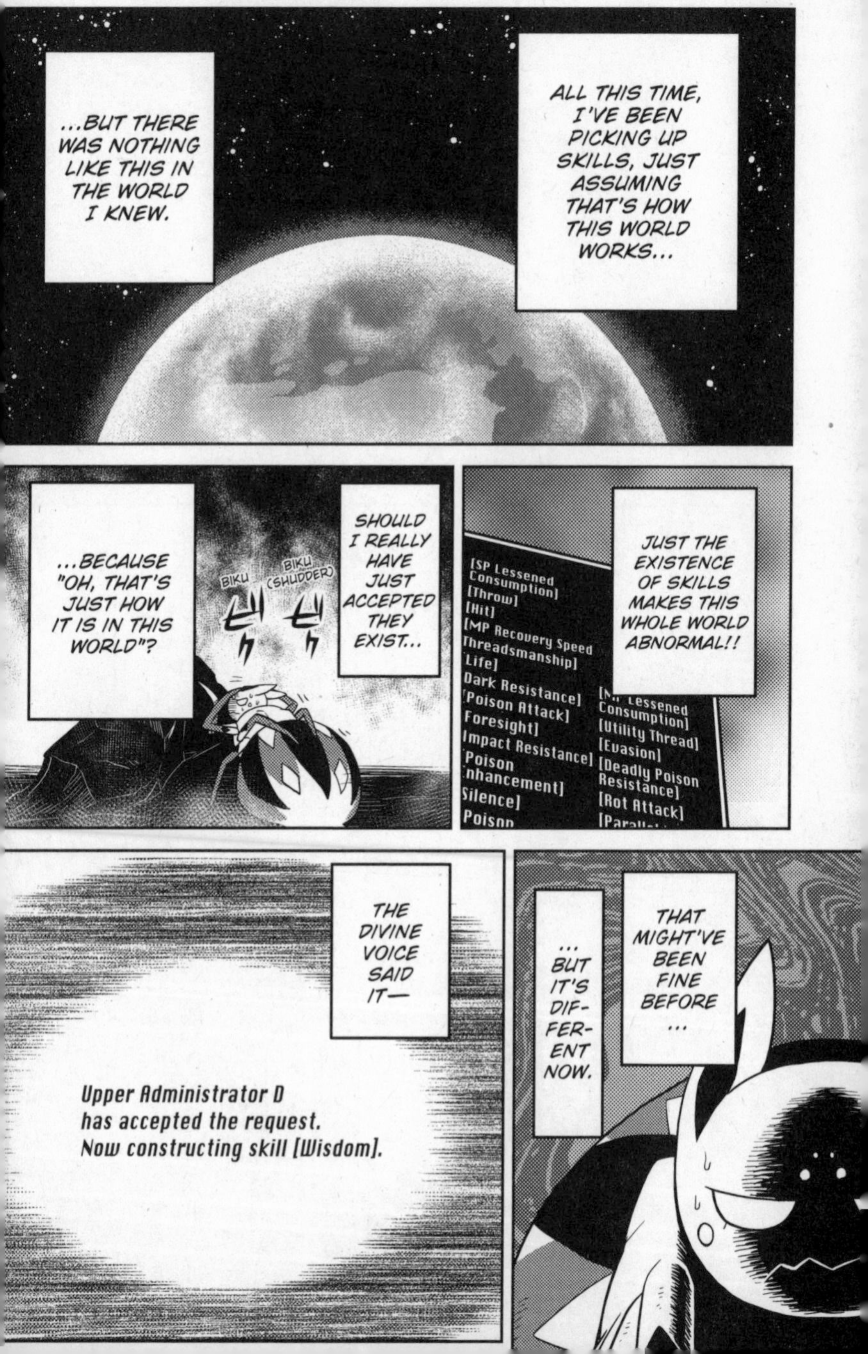
ALL THIS TIME, I'VE BEEN PICKING UP SKILLS, JUST ASSUMING THAT'S HOW THIS WORLD WORKS...
...BUT THERE WAS NOTHING LIKE THIS IN THE WORLD I KNEW.
JUST THE EXISTENCE OF SKILLS MAKES THIS WHOLE WORLD ABNORMAL!!
[SP Lessened Consumption]
[Throw]
[Hit]
[MP Recovery Speed
Threadsmanship]
Life]
Dark Resistance]
[Poison Attack]
Foresight]
Impact Resistance]
Poison
nhancement]
Silence]
Lessened Consumption]
[Utility Thread]
[Evasion]
[Deadly Poison Resistance]
[Rot Attack]
SHOULD I REALLY HAVE JUST ACCEPTED THEY EXIST...
BIKU BIKU (SHUDDER)
...BECAUSE "OH, THAT'S JUST HOW IT IS IN THIS WORLD"?
THAT MIGHT'VE BEEN FINE BEFORE...
...BUT IT'S DIF-FER-ENT NOW.
THE DIVINE VOICE SAID IT—
Upper Administrator D has accepted the request. Now constructing skill [Wisdom].

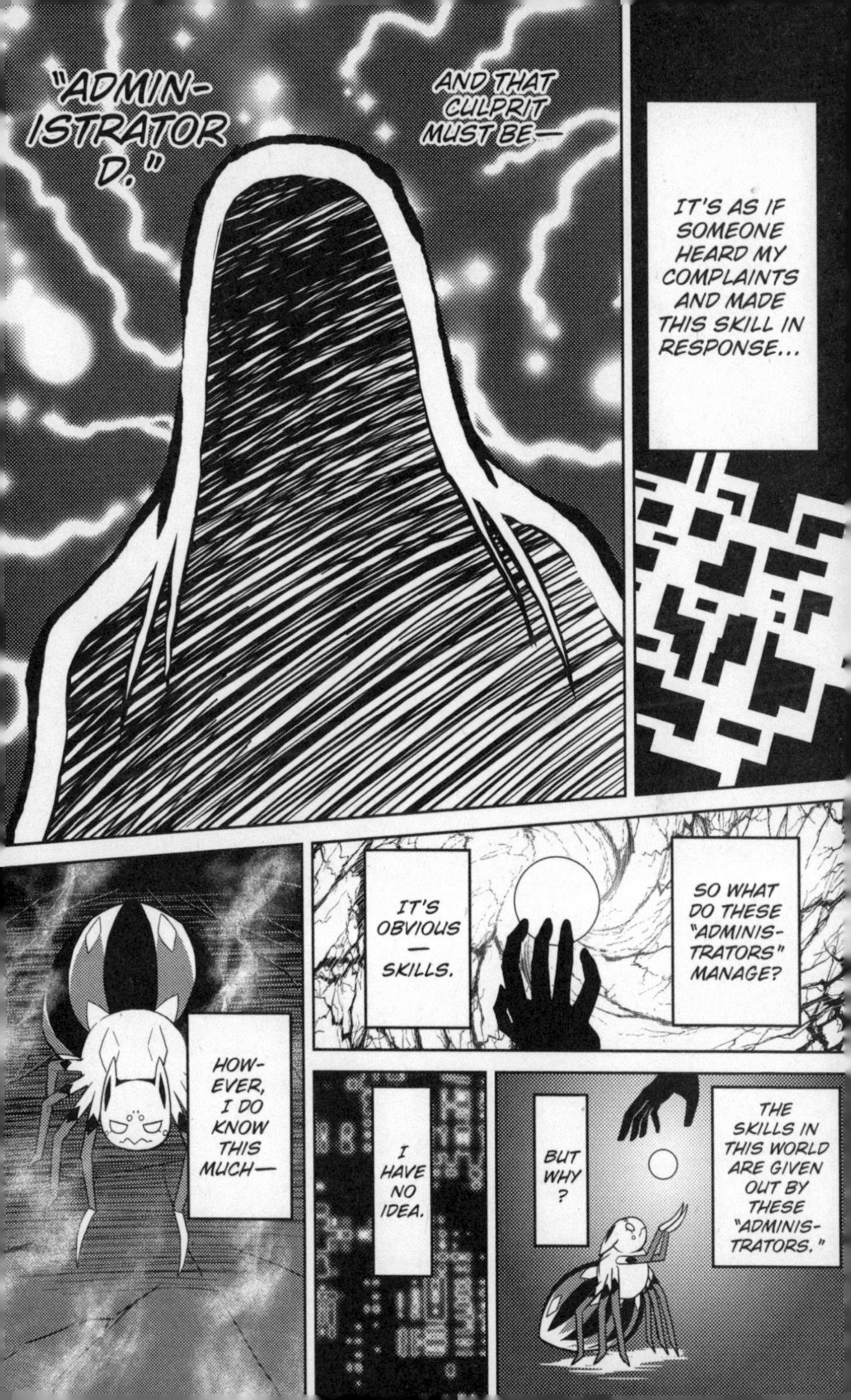
IT'S AS IF SOMEONE HEARD MY COMPLAINTS AND MADE THIS SKILL IN RESPONSE...
AND THAT CULPRIT MUST BE—
"ADMIN-ISTRATOR D."
SO WHAT DO THESE "ADMINIS-TRATORS" MANAGE?
IT'S OBVIOUS—SKILLS.
THE SKILLS IN THIS WORLD ARE GIVEN OUT BY THESE "ADMINIS-TRATORS."
BUT WHY?
I HAVE NO IDEA.
HOW-EVER, I DO KNOW THIS MUCH—

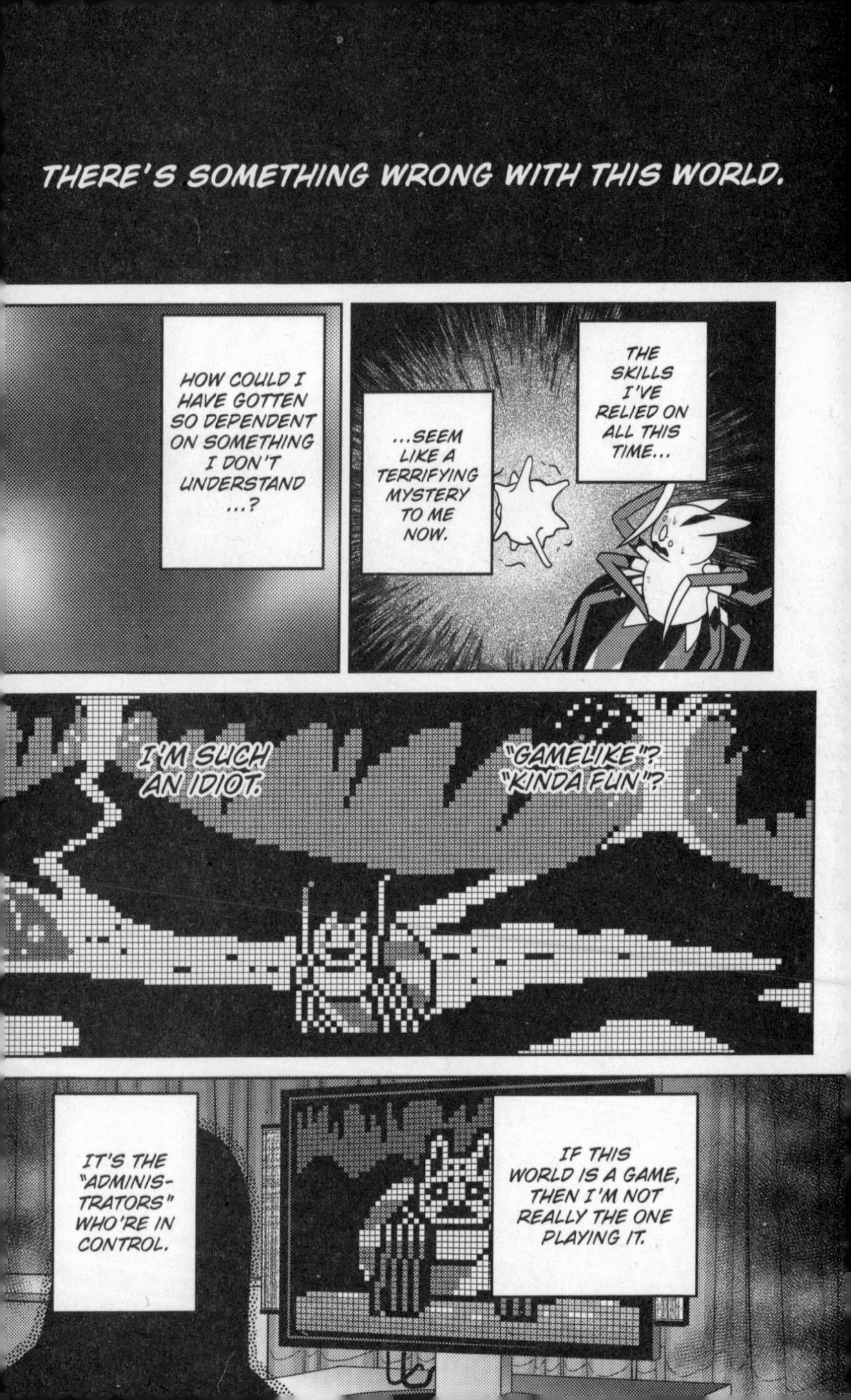
THERE'S SOMETHING WRONG WITH THIS WORLD.
THE SKILLS I'VE RELIED ON ALL THIS TIME...
...SEEM LIKE A TERRIFYING MYSTERY TO ME NOW.
HOW COULD I HAVE GOTTEN SO DEPENDENT ON SOMETHING I DON'T UNDERSTAND ...?
"GAMELIKE"? "KINDA FUN"?
I'M SUCH AN IDIOT.
IF THIS WORLD IS A GAME, THEN I'M NOT REALLY THE ONE PLAYING IT.
IT'S THE "ADMINIS-TRATORS" WHO'RE IN CONTROL.

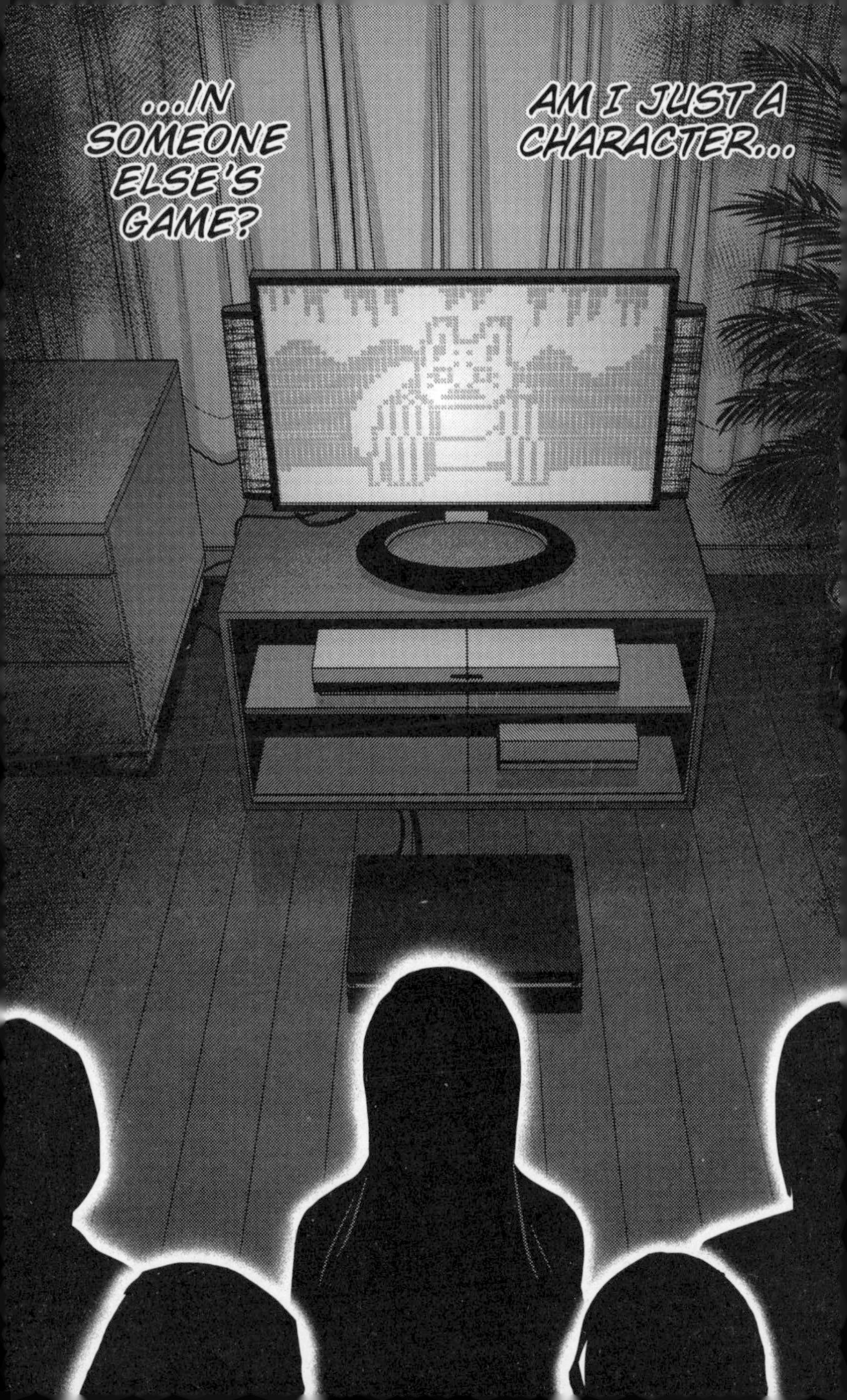
AM I JUST A CHARACTER...
...IN SOMEONE ELSE'S GAME?

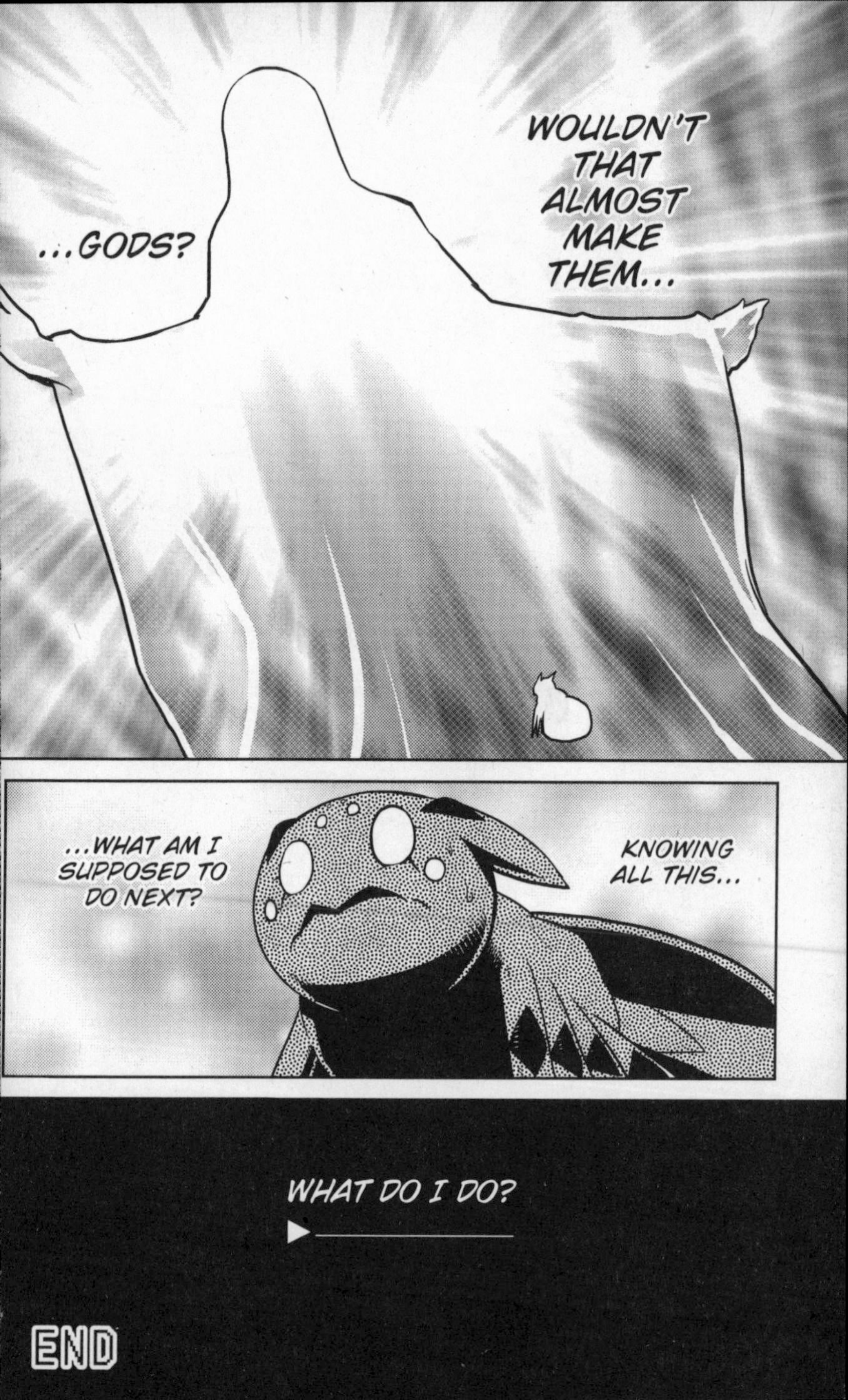
WOULDN'T THAT ALMOST MAKE THEM...
...GODS?
KNOWING ALL THIS...
...WHAT AM I SUPPOSED TO DO NEXT?
WHAT DO I DO?
END

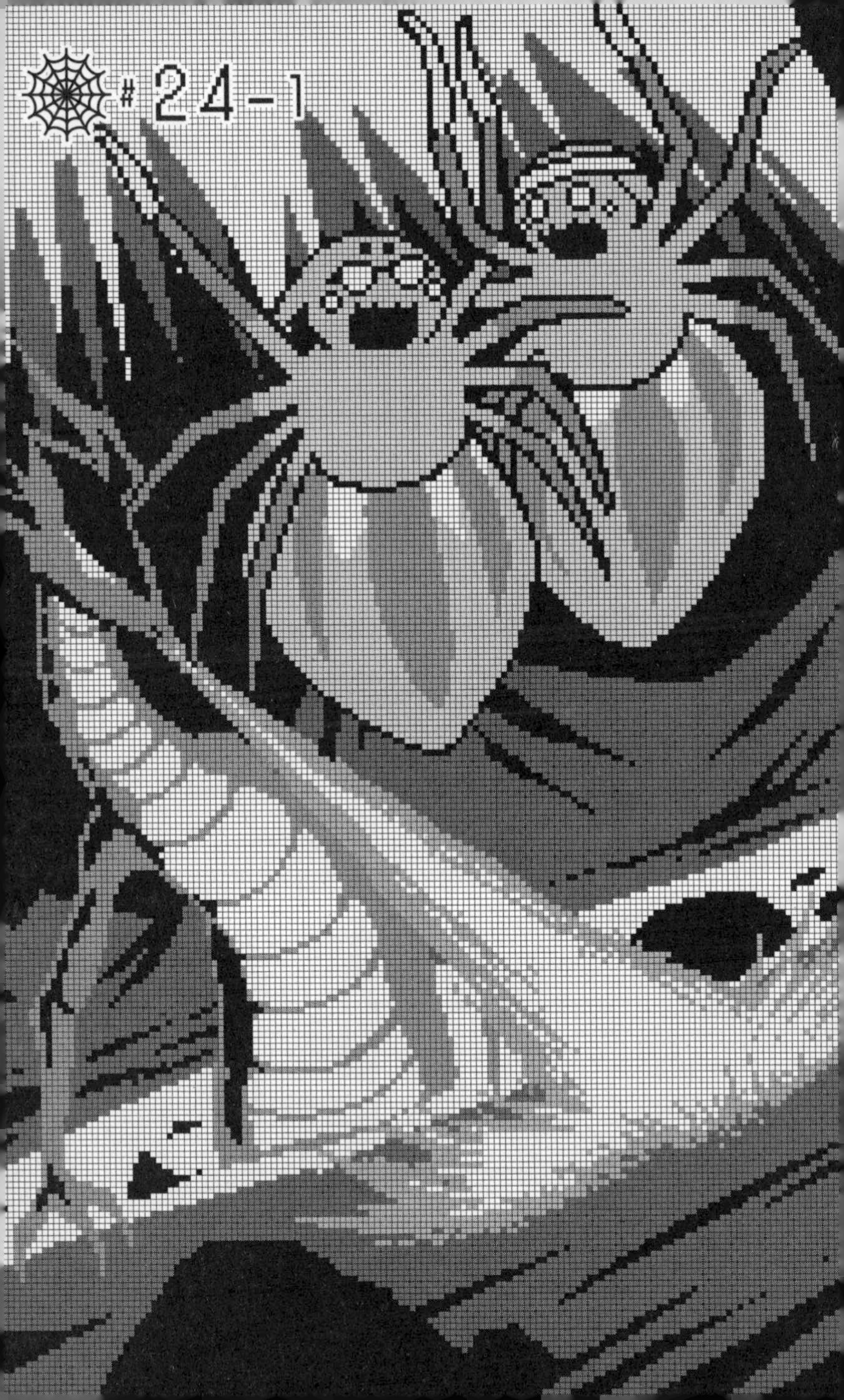
#24-1

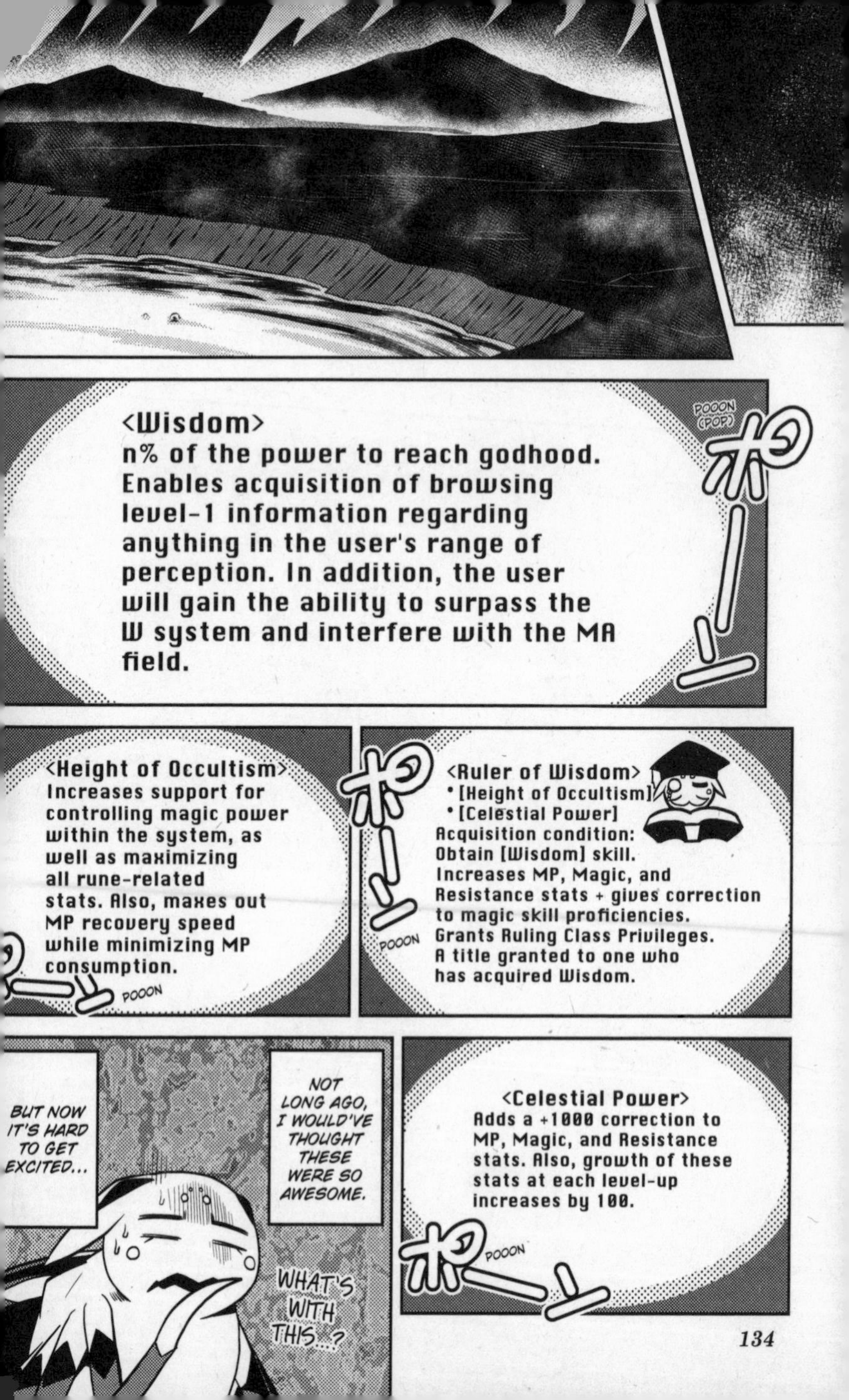

<Wisdom>
n% of the power to reach godhood. Enables acquisition of browsing level-1 information regarding anything in the user's range of perception. In addition, the user will gain the ability to surpass the W system and interfere with the MA field.
POOON (POP)
<Ruler of Wisdom>
• [Height of Occultism]
• [Celestial Power]
Acquisition condition: Obtain [Wisdom] skill.
Increases MP, Magic, and Resistance stats + gives correction to magic skill proficiencies.
Grants Ruling Class Privileges.
A title granted to one who has acquired Wisdom.
POOON
<Height of Occultism>
Increases support for controlling magic power within the system, as well as maximizing all rune-related stats. Also, maxes out MP recovery speed while minimizing MP consumption.
POOON
<Celestial Power>
Adds a +1000 correction to MP, Magic, and Resistance stats. Also, growth of these stats at each level-up increases by 100.
POOON
NOT LONG AGO, I WOULD'VE THOUGHT THESE WERE SO AWESOME.
BUT NOW IT'S HARD TO GET EXCITED...
WHAT'S WITH THIS...?

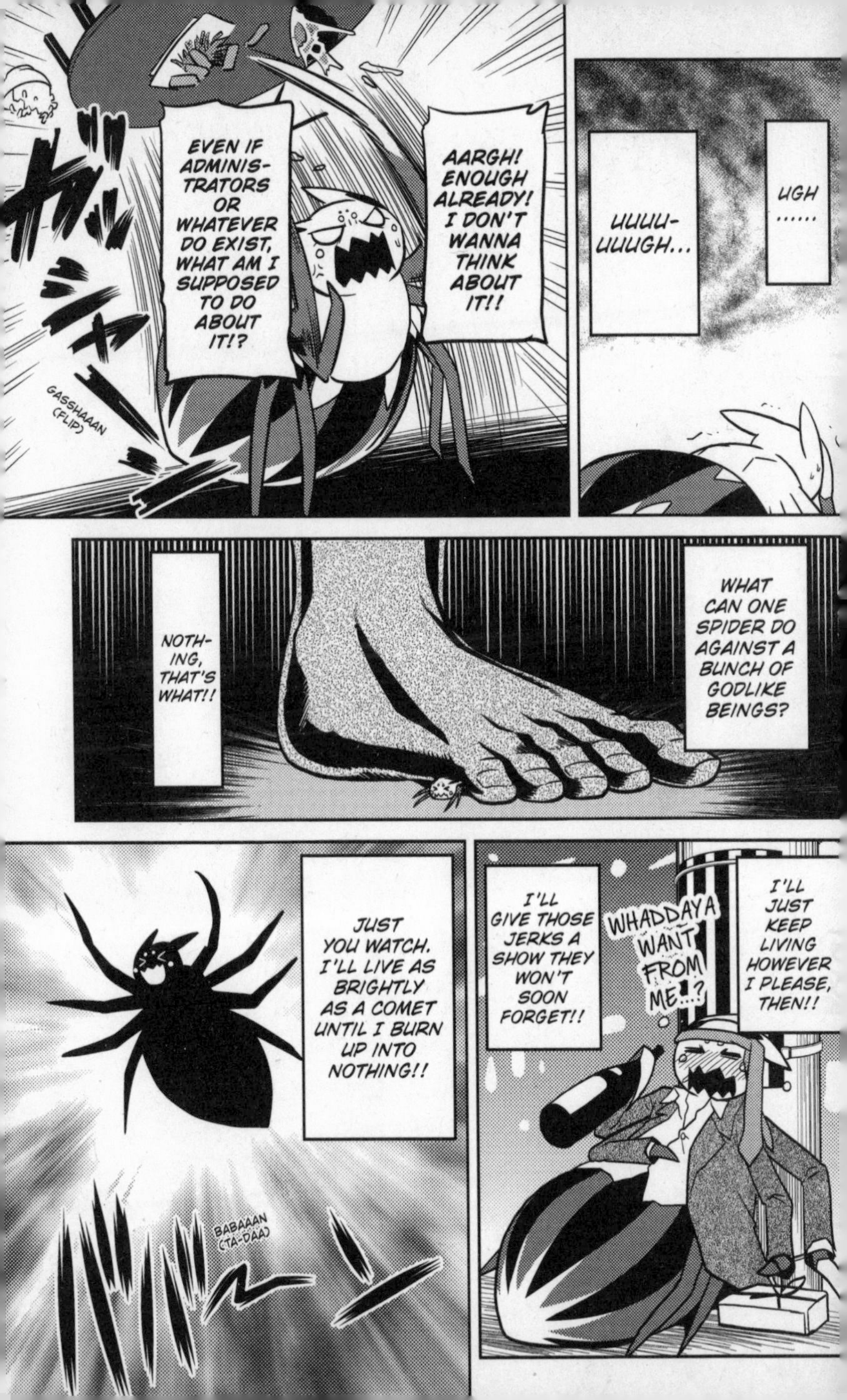
UGH ......
UUUU-UUUGH...
AARGH! ENOUGH ALREADY! I DON'T WANNA THINK ABOUT IT!!
EVEN IF ADMINIS-TRATORS OR WHATEVER DO EXIST, WHAT AM I SUPPOSED TO DO ABOUT IT!?
GASSHAAAN (FLIP)
WHAT CAN ONE SPIDER DO AGAINST A BUNCH OF GODLIKE BEINGS?
NOTH-ING, THAT'S WHAT!!
I'LL JUST KEEP LIVING HOWEVER I PLEASE, THEN!!
WHADDAYA WANT FROM ME...?
I'LL GIVE THOSE JERKS A SHOW THEY WON'T SOON FORGET!!
JUST YOU WATCH. I'LL LIVE AS BRIGHTLY AS A COMET UNTIL I BURN UP INTO NOTHING!!
BABAAAN (TA-DAA)

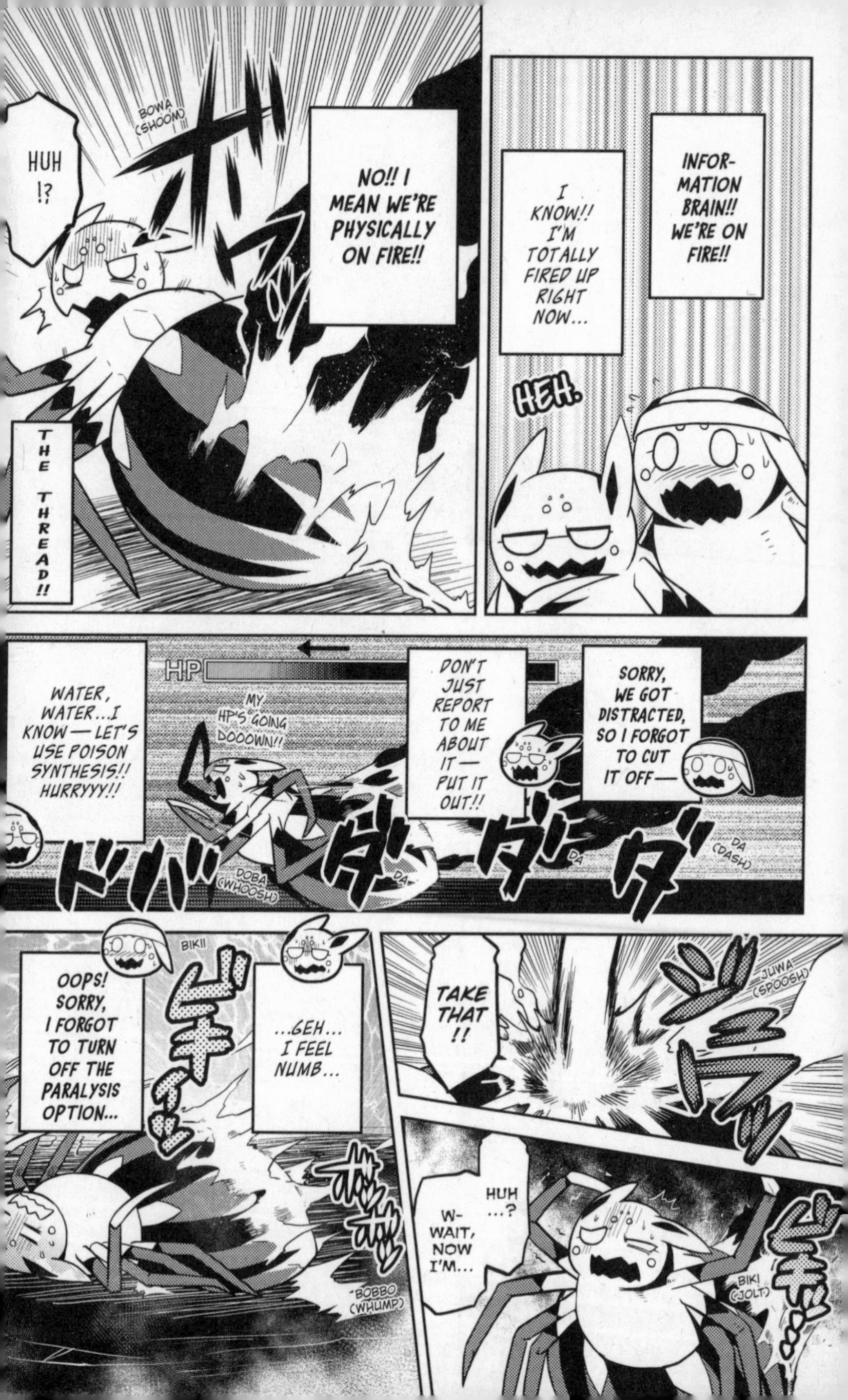
INFORMATION BRAIN!! WE'RE ON FIRE!!
I KNOW!! I'M TOTALLY FIRED UP RIGHT NOW...
HEH.
NO!! I MEAN WE'RE PHYSICALLY ON FIRE!!
BOWA (SHOOM)
HUH !?
THE THREAD!!
SORRY, WE GOT DISTRACTED, SO I FORGOT TO CUT IT OFF—
DON'T JUST REPORT TO ME ABOUT IT—PUT IT OUT!!
HP
MY HP'S GOING DOOOWN!!
WATER, WATER...I KNOW—LET'S USE POISON SYNTHESIS!! HURRYYY!!
DA (DASH)
DA
DA
DOBA (WHOOSH)
JUWA (SPOOSH)
TAKE THAT!!
HUH ...?
W-WAIT, NOW I'M...
BIKI (JOLT)
...GEH... I FEEL NUMB...
BIKII
OOPS! SORRY, I FORGOT TO TURN OFF THE PARALYSIS OPTION...
BOBBO (WHUMP)

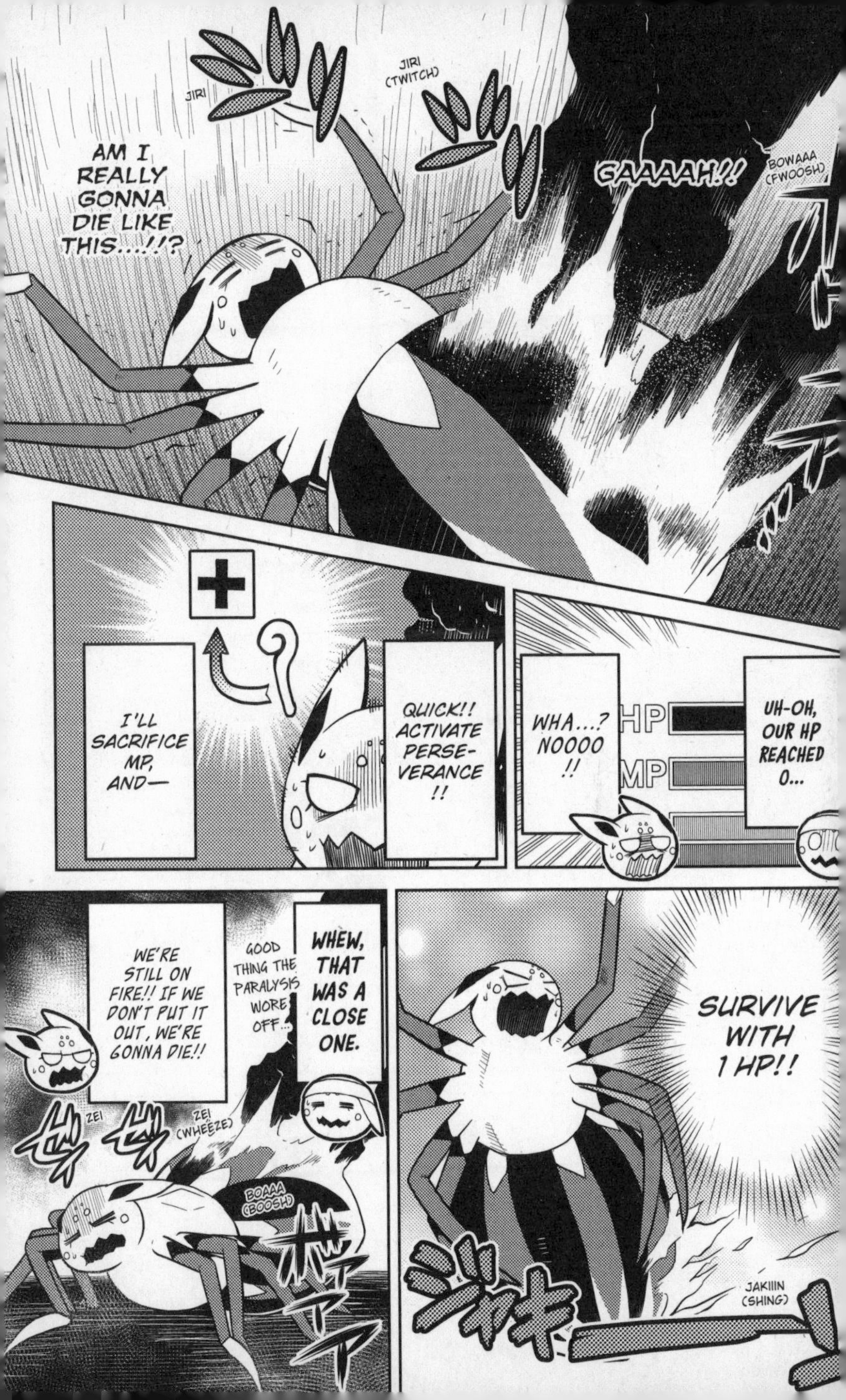
GAAAAH!!
BOWAAA (FWOOSH)
JIRI (TWITCH)
JIRI
AM I REALLY GONNA DIE LIKE THIS...!!?
UH-OH, OUR HP REACHED 0...
HP
MP
WHA...? NOOOO!!
QUICK!! ACTIVATE PERSE-VERANCE!!
I'LL SACRIFICE MP, AND—
SURVIVE WITH 1 HP!!
JAKIIIN (SHING)
WHEW, THAT WAS A CLOSE ONE.
GOOD THING THE PARALYSIS WORE OFF...
WE'RE STILL ON FIRE!! IF WE DON'T PUT IT OUT, WE'RE GONNA DIE!!
ZEI (WHEEZE)
ZEI
BOAAA (BOOSH)

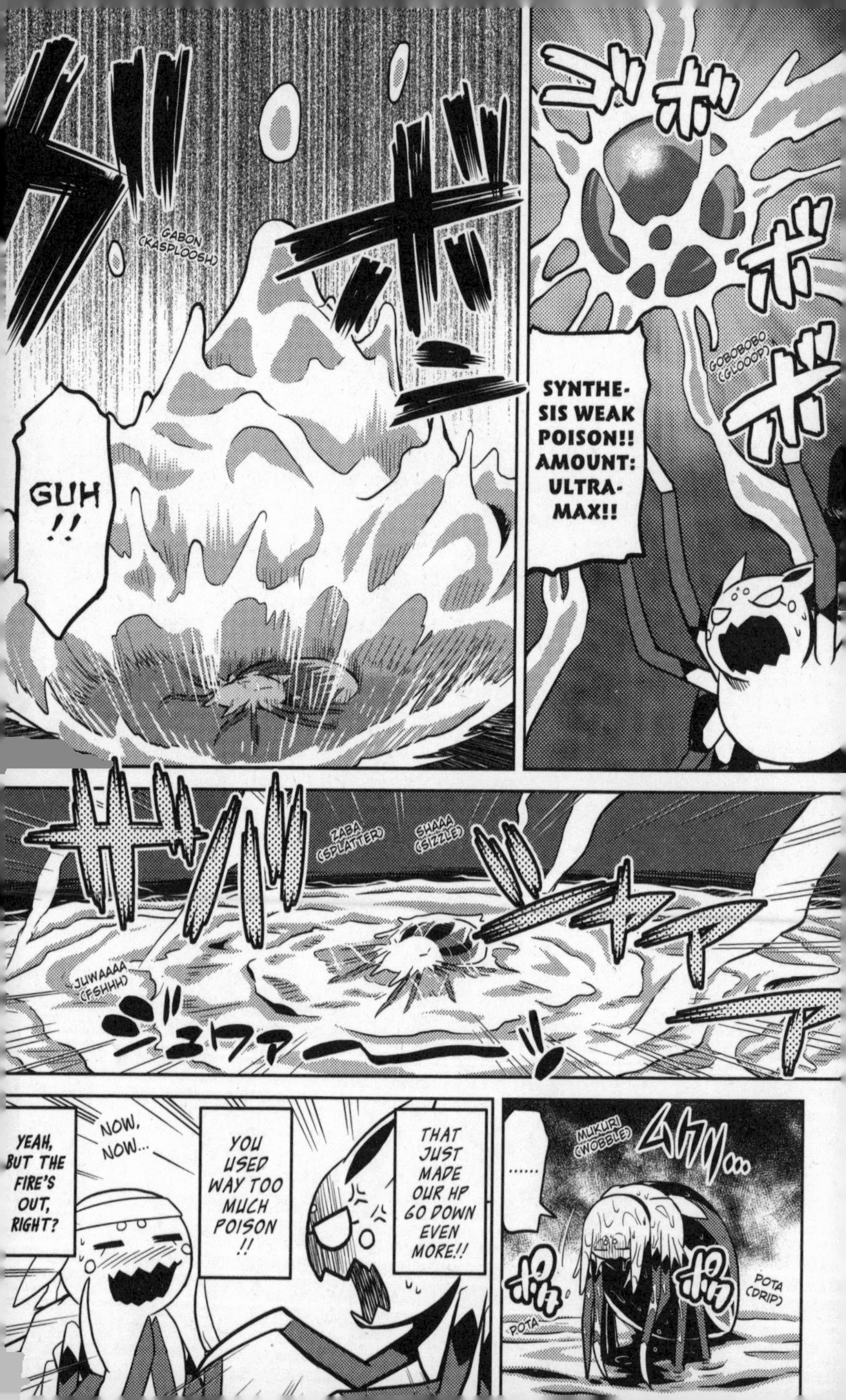

GOBOBOBO (GLOOOP)
SYNTHESIS WEAK POISON!! AMOUNT: ULTRA-MAX!!
GABON (KASPLOOSH)
GUH !!
ZABA (SPLATTER)
SHAAA (SIZZLE)
JUWAAAA (FSHHH)
......
MUKURI (WOBBLE)
POTA (DRIP)
POTA
THAT JUST MADE OUR HP GO DOWN EVEN MORE!!
YOU USED WAY TOO MUCH POISON !!
NOW, NOW...
YEAH, BUT THE FIRE'S OUT, RIGHT?

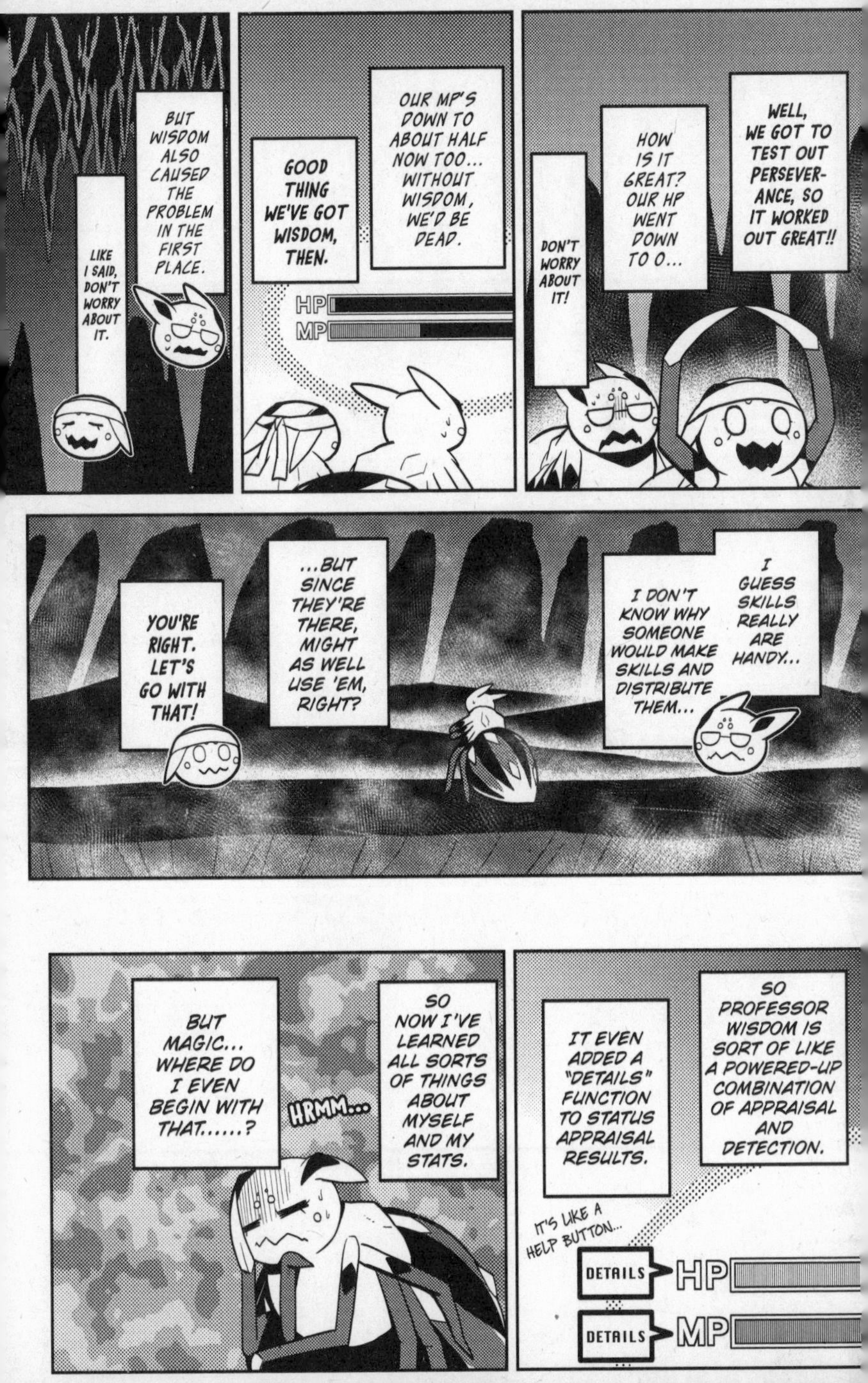
WELL, WE GOT TO TEST OUT PERSEVER-ANCE, SO IT WORKED OUT GREAT!!
HOW IS IT GREAT? OUR HP WENT DOWN TO 0...
DON'T WORRY ABOUT IT!
OUR MP'S DOWN TO ABOUT HALF NOW TOO... WITHOUT WISDOM, WE'D BE DEAD.
GOOD THING WE'VE GOT WISDOM, THEN.
HP
MP
BUT WISDOM ALSO CAUSED THE PROBLEM IN THE FIRST PLACE.
LIKE I SAID, DON'T WORRY ABOUT IT.
I GUESS SKILLS REALLY ARE HANDY...
I DON'T KNOW WHY SOMEONE WOULD MAKE SKILLS AND DISTRIBUTE THEM...
...BUT SINCE THEY'RE THERE, MIGHT AS WELL USE 'EM, RIGHT?
YOU'RE RIGHT. LET'S GO WITH THAT!
SO PROFESSOR WISDOM IS SORT OF LIKE A POWERED-UP COMBINATION OF APPRAISAL AND DETECTION.
IT EVEN ADDED A "DETAILS" FUNCTION TO STATUS APPRAISAL RESULTS.
IT'S LIKE A HELP BUTTON...
DETAILS
HP
DETAILS
MP
SO NOW I'VE LEARNED ALL SORTS OF THINGS ABOUT MYSELF AND MY STATS.
HRMM...
BUT MAGIC... WHERE DO I EVEN BEGIN WITH THAT......?

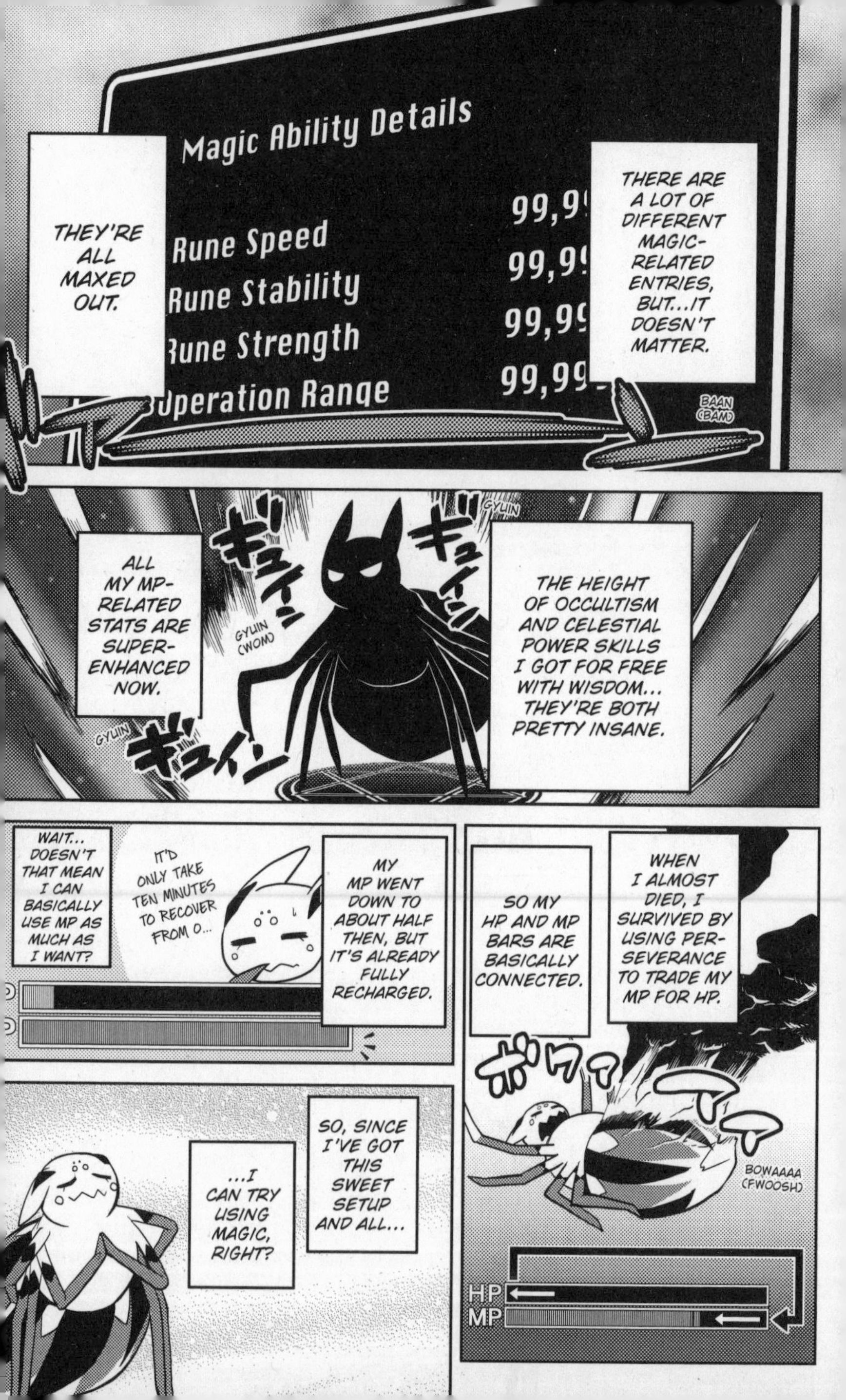

THERE ARE A LOT OF DIFFERENT MAGIC-RELATED ENTRIES, BUT...IT DOESN'T MATTER.
Magic Ability Details
Rune Speed
Rune Stability
Rune Strength
Operation Range
THEY'RE ALL MAXED OUT.
BAAN (BAM)
THE HEIGHT OF OCCULTISM AND CELESTIAL POWER SKILLS I GOT FOR FREE WITH WISDOM... THEY'RE BOTH PRETTY INSANE.
GYUIN
GYUIN (WOM)
ALL MY MP-RELATED STATS ARE SUPER-ENHANCED NOW.
GYUIN
WHEN I ALMOST DIED, I SURVIVED BY USING PERSEVERANCE TO TRADE MY MP FOR HP.
SO MY HP AND MP BARS ARE BASICALLY CONNECTED.
BOWAAAA (FWOOSH)
HP
MP
MY MP WENT DOWN TO ABOUT HALF THEN, BUT IT'S ALREADY FULLY RECHARGED.
IT'D ONLY TAKE TEN MINUTES TO RECOVER FROM 0...
WAIT... DOESN'T THAT MEAN I CAN BASICALLY USE MP AS MUCH AS I WANT?
SO, SINCE I'VE GOT THIS SWEET SETUP AND ALL...
...I CAN TRY USING MAGIC, RIGHT?

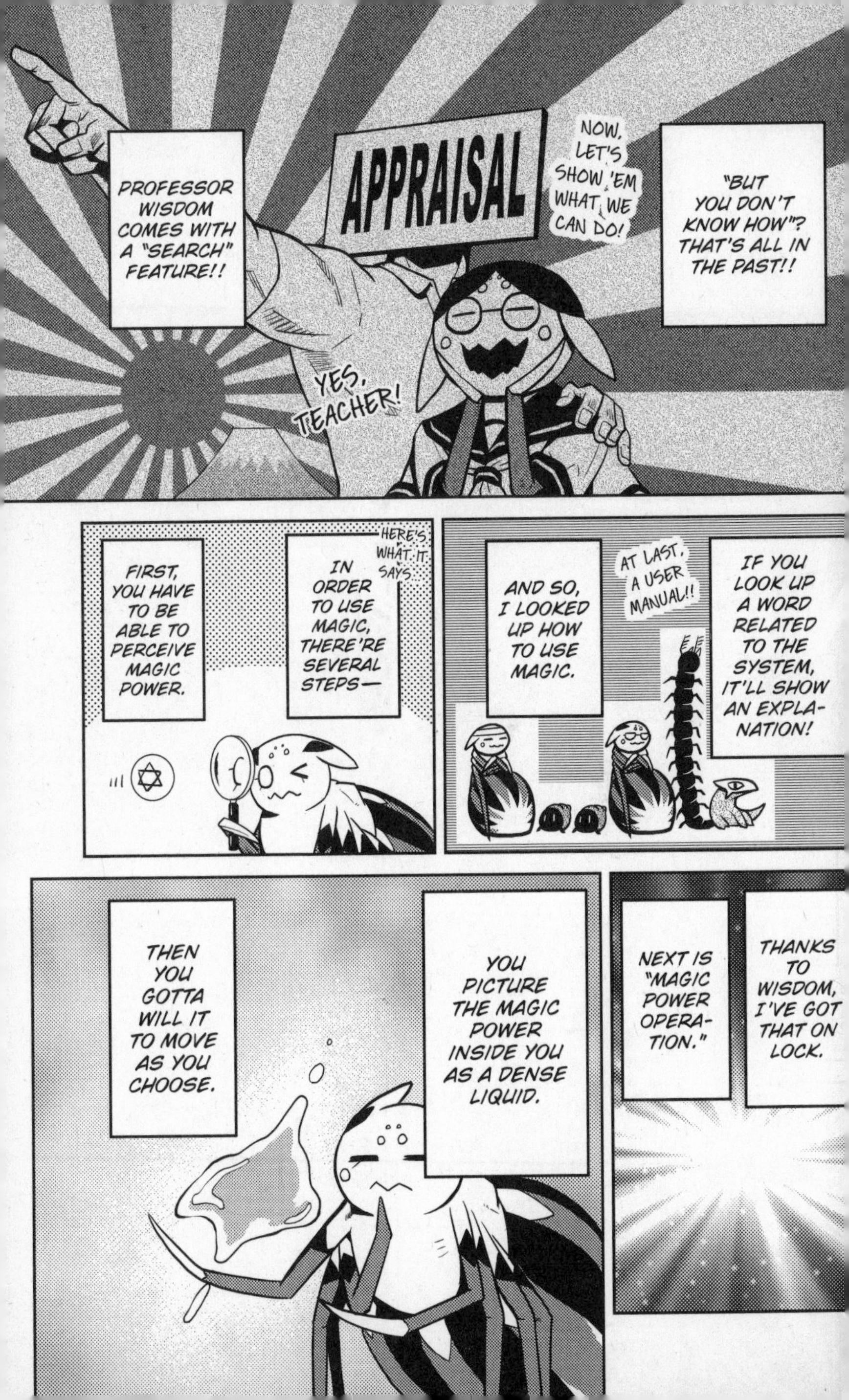
"BUT YOU DON'T KNOW HOW"? THAT'S ALL IN THE PAST!!
NOW, LET'S SHOW 'EM WHAT WE CAN DO!
APPRAISAL
PROFESSOR WISDOM COMES WITH A "SEARCH" FEATURE!!
YES, TEACHER!
IF YOU LOOK UP A WORD RELATED TO THE SYSTEM, IT'LL SHOW AN EXPLANATION!
AT LAST, A USER MANUAL!!
AND SO, I LOOKED UP HOW TO USE MAGIC.
HERE'S WHAT IT SAYS.
IN ORDER TO USE MAGIC, THERE'RE SEVERAL STEPS—
FIRST, YOU HAVE TO BE ABLE TO PERCEIVE MAGIC POWER.
THANKS TO WISDOM, I'VE GOT THAT ON LOCK.
NEXT IS "MAGIC POWER OPERATION."
YOU PICTURE THE MAGIC POWER INSIDE YOU AS A DENSE LIQUID.
THEN YOU GOTTA WILL IT TO MOVE AS YOU CHOOSE.

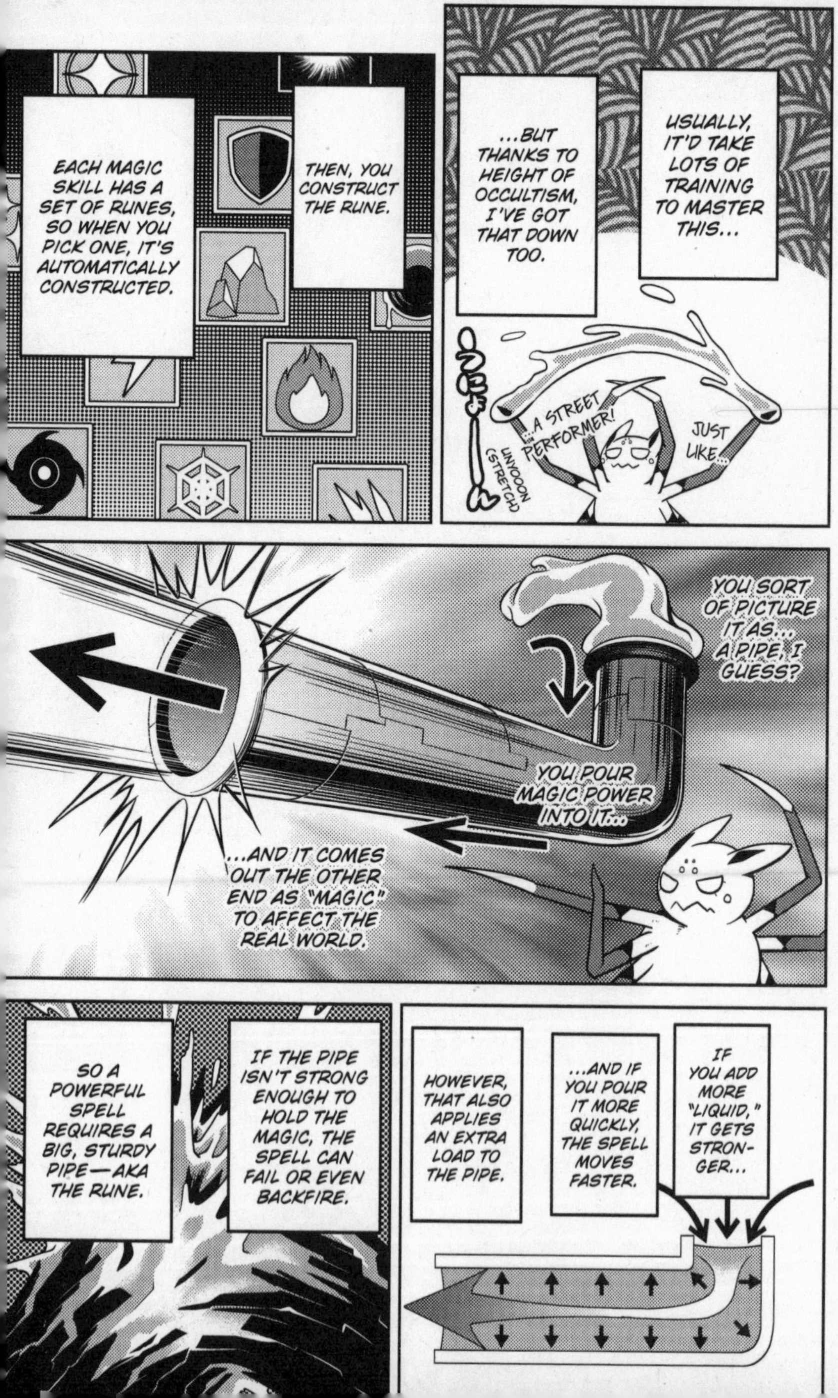
USUALLY, IT'D TAKE LOTS OF TRAINING TO MASTER THIS...
...BUT THANKS TO HEIGHT OF OCCULTISM, I'VE GOT THAT DOWN TOO.
JUST LIKE...
...A STREET PERFORMER!
UNYOOON (STRETCH)
THEN, YOU CONSTRUCT THE RUNE.
EACH MAGIC SKILL HAS A SET OF RUNES, SO WHEN YOU PICK ONE, IT'S AUTOMATICALLY CONSTRUCTED.
YOU SORT OF PICTURE IT AS... A PIPE, I GUESS?
YOU POUR MAGIC POWER INTO IT...
...AND IT COMES OUT THE OTHER END AS "MAGIC" TO AFFECT THE REAL WORLD.
IF YOU ADD MORE "LIQUID," IT GETS STRONGER...
...AND IF YOU POUR IT MORE QUICKLY, THE SPELL MOVES FASTER.
HOWEVER, THAT ALSO APPLIES AN EXTRA LOAD TO THE PIPE.
IF THE PIPE ISN'T STRONG ENOUGH TO HOLD THE MAGIC, THE SPELL CAN FAIL OR EVEN BACKFIRE.
SO A POWERFUL SPELL REQUIRES A BIG, STURDY PIPE—AKA THE RUNE.

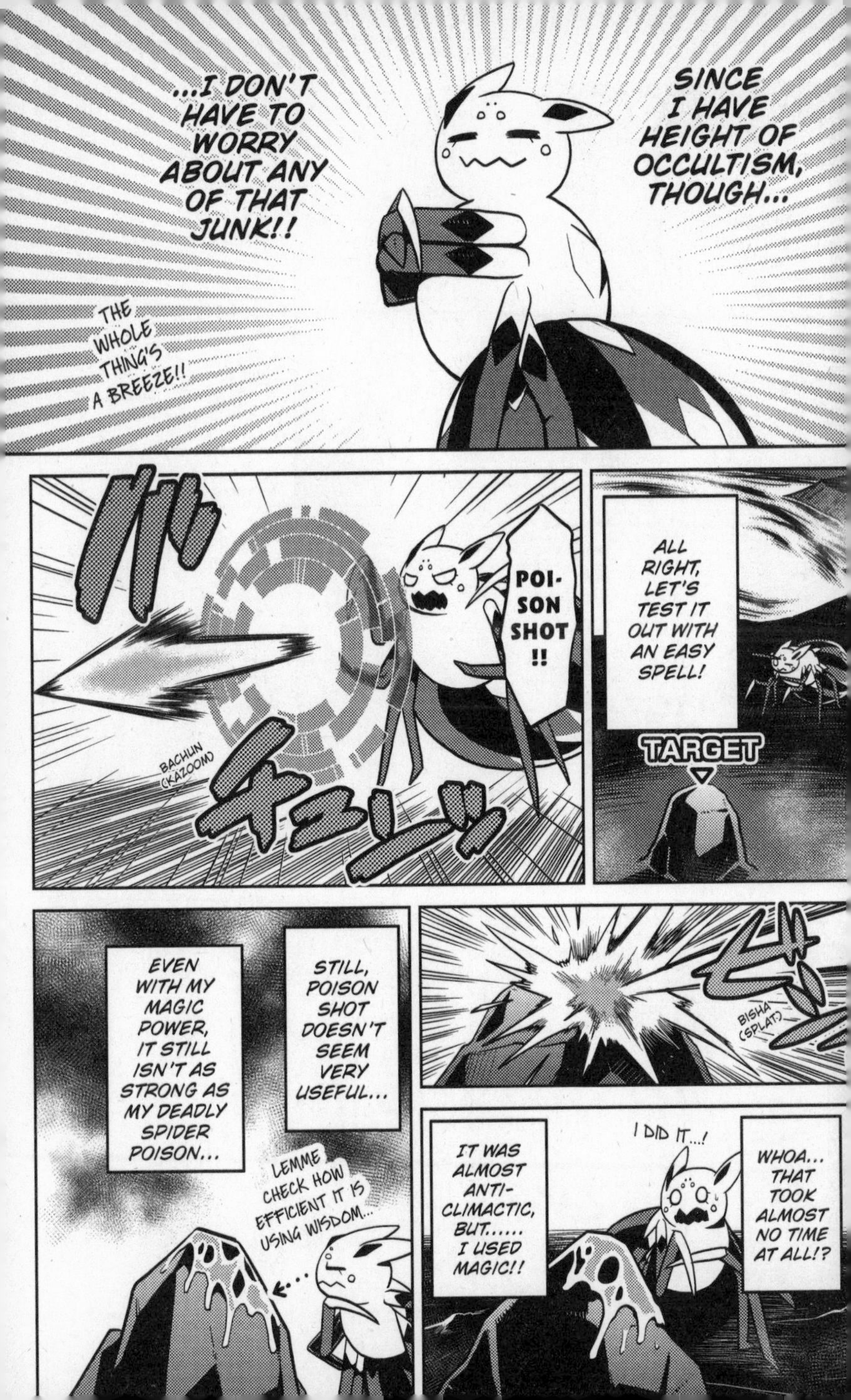
SINCE I HAVE HEIGHT OF OCCULTISM, THOUGH...
...I DON'T HAVE TO WORRY ABOUT ANY OF THAT JUNK!!
THE WHOLE THING'S A BREEZE!!
ALL RIGHT, LET'S TEST IT OUT WITH AN EASY SPELL!
TARGET
POI-SON SHOT!!
BACHUN (KAZOOM)
BISHA (SPLAT)
WHOA... THAT TOOK ALMOST NO TIME AT ALL!?
I DID IT...!
IT WAS ALMOST ANTI-CLIMACTIC, BUT...... I USED MAGIC!!
STILL, POISON SHOT DOESN'T SEEM VERY USEFUL...
EVEN WITH MY MAGIC POWER, IT STILL ISN'T AS STRONG AS MY DEADLY SPIDER POISON...
LEMME CHECK HOW EFFICIENT IT IS USING WISDOM...
...

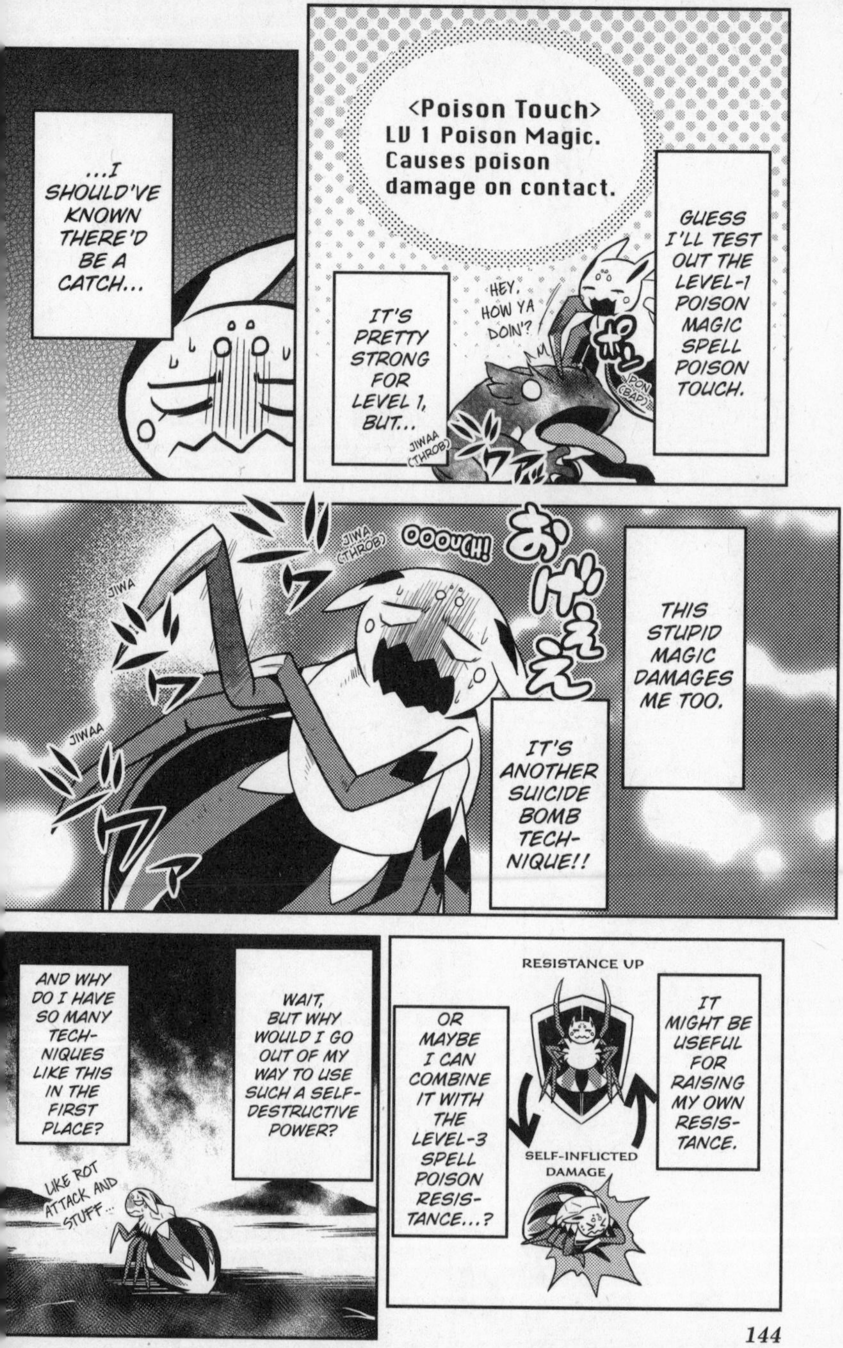

<Poison Touch>
LV 1 Poison Magic. Causes poison damage on contact.
GUESS I'LL TEST OUT THE LEVEL-1 POISON MAGIC SPELL POISON TOUCH.
HEY, HOW YA DOIN'?
PON (BAP)
IT'S PRETTY STRONG FOR LEVEL 1, BUT...
JIWAA (THROB)
...I SHOULD'VE KNOWN THERE'D BE A CATCH...
THIS STUPID MAGIC DAMAGES ME TOO.
OOOUCH!!
JIWA (THROB)
JIWA
JIWAA
IT'S ANOTHER SUICIDE BOMB TECH-NIQUE!!
IT MIGHT BE USEFUL FOR RAISING MY OWN RESIS-TANCE.
RESISTANCE UP
SELF-INFLICTED DAMAGE
OR MAYBE I CAN COMBINE IT WITH THE LEVEL-3 SPELL POISON RESIS-TANCE...?
WAIT, BUT WHY WOULD I GO OUT OF MY WAY TO USE SUCH A SELF-DESTRUCTIVE POWER?
AND WHY DO I HAVE SO MANY TECH-NIQUES LIKE THIS IN THE FIRST PLACE?
LIKE ROT ATTACK AND STUFF...

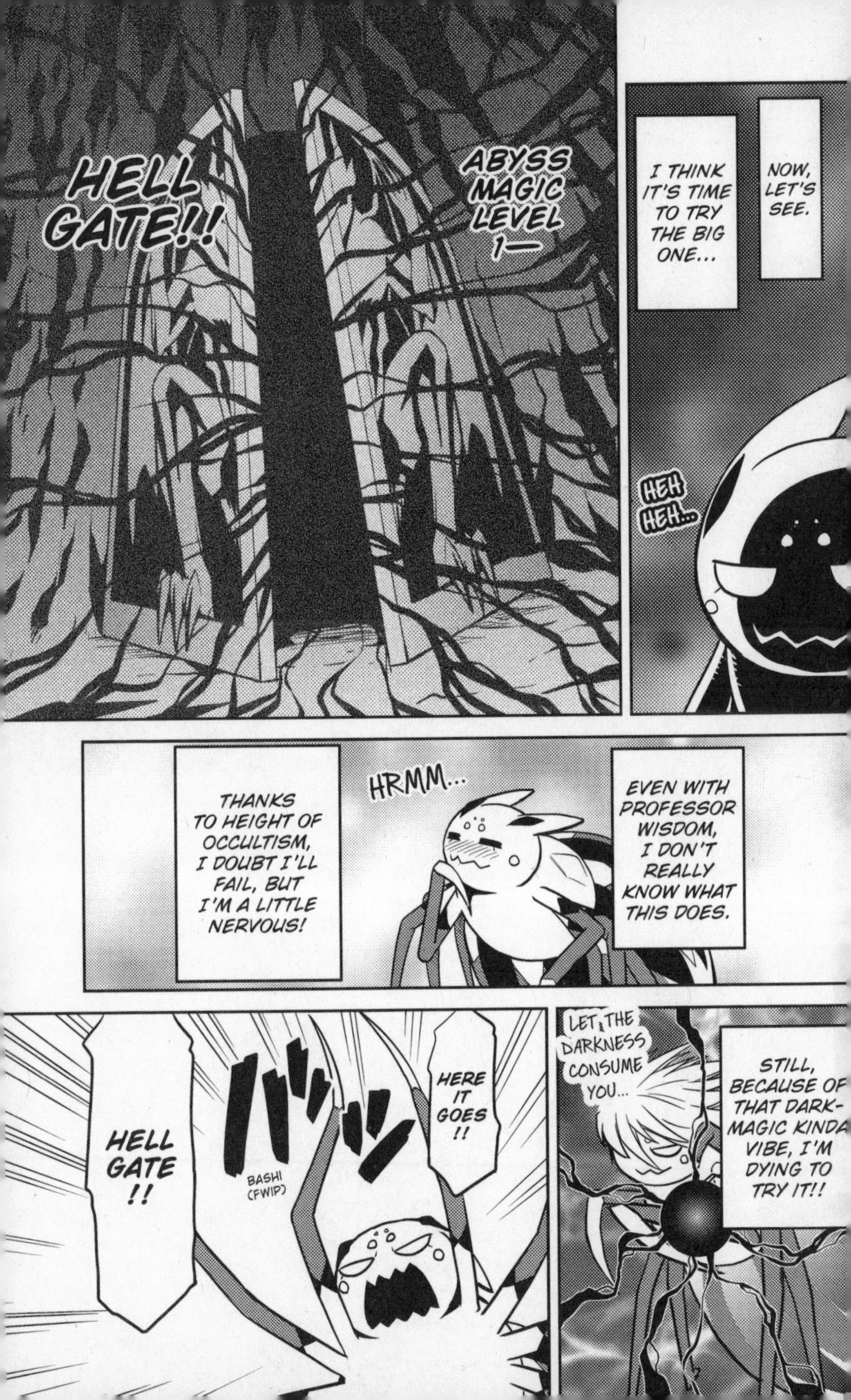
NOW, LET'S SEE.
I THINK IT'S TIME TO TRY THE BIG ONE...
HEH HEH...
ABYSS MAGIC LEVEL 1—
HELL GATE!!
EVEN WITH PROFESSOR WISDOM, I DON'T REALLY KNOW WHAT THIS DOES.
HRMM...
THANKS TO HEIGHT OF OCCULTISM, I DOUBT I'LL FAIL, BUT I'M A LITTLE NERVOUS!
STILL, BECAUSE OF THAT DARK-MAGIC KINDA VIBE, I'M DYING TO TRY IT!!
LET THE DARKNESS CONSUME YOU...
HERE IT GOES!!
BASHI (FWIP)
HELL GATE!!

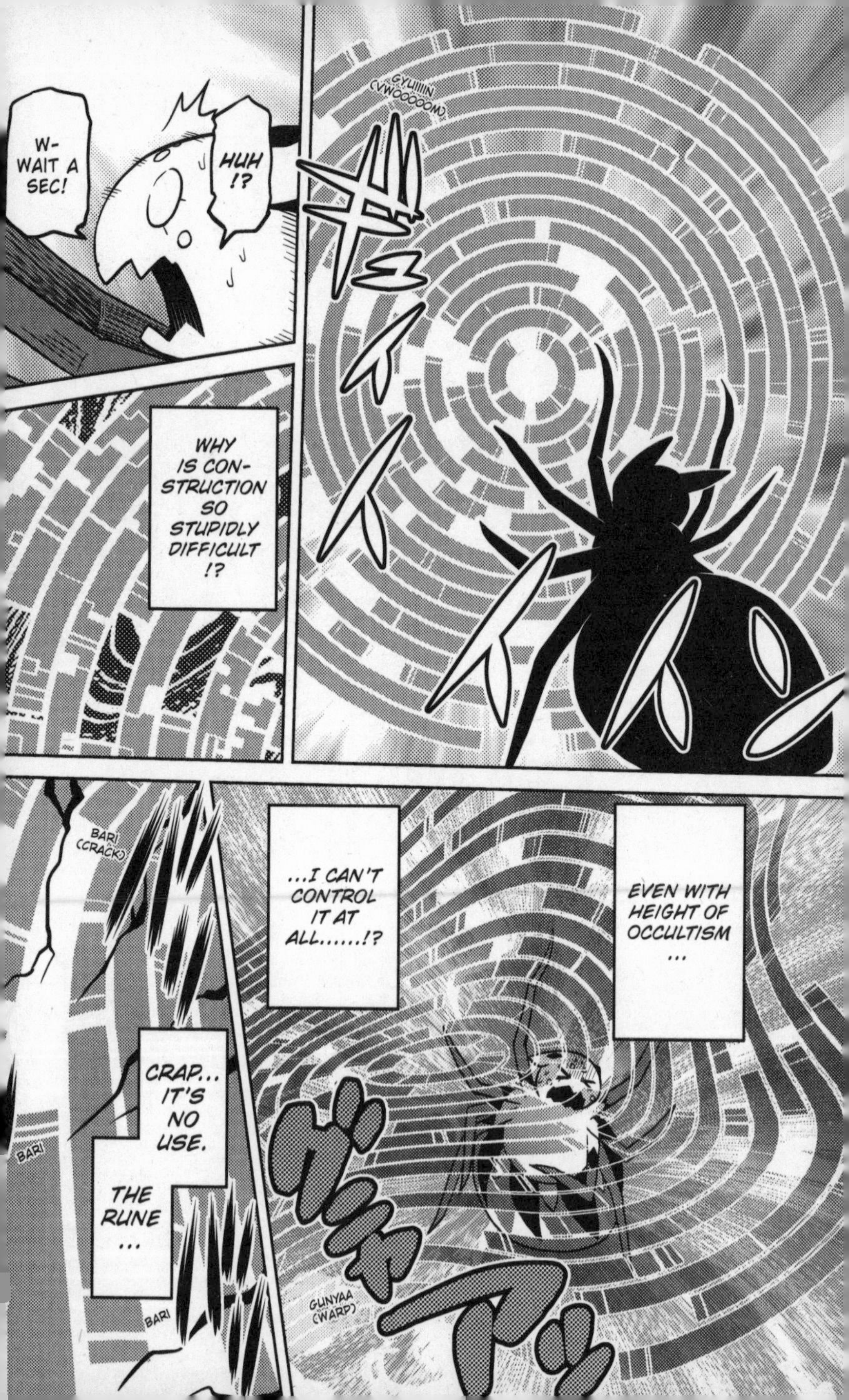
GYUIIIIN (VWOOOOOM)
HUH !?
W-WAIT A SEC!
WHY IS CON-STRUCTION SO STUPIDLY DIFFICULT !?
EVEN WITH HEIGHT OF OCCULTISM ...
...I CAN'T CONTROL IT AT ALL......!?
GUNYAA (WARP)
BARI (CRACK)
CRAP... IT'S NO USE.
THE RUNE ...
BARI
BARI

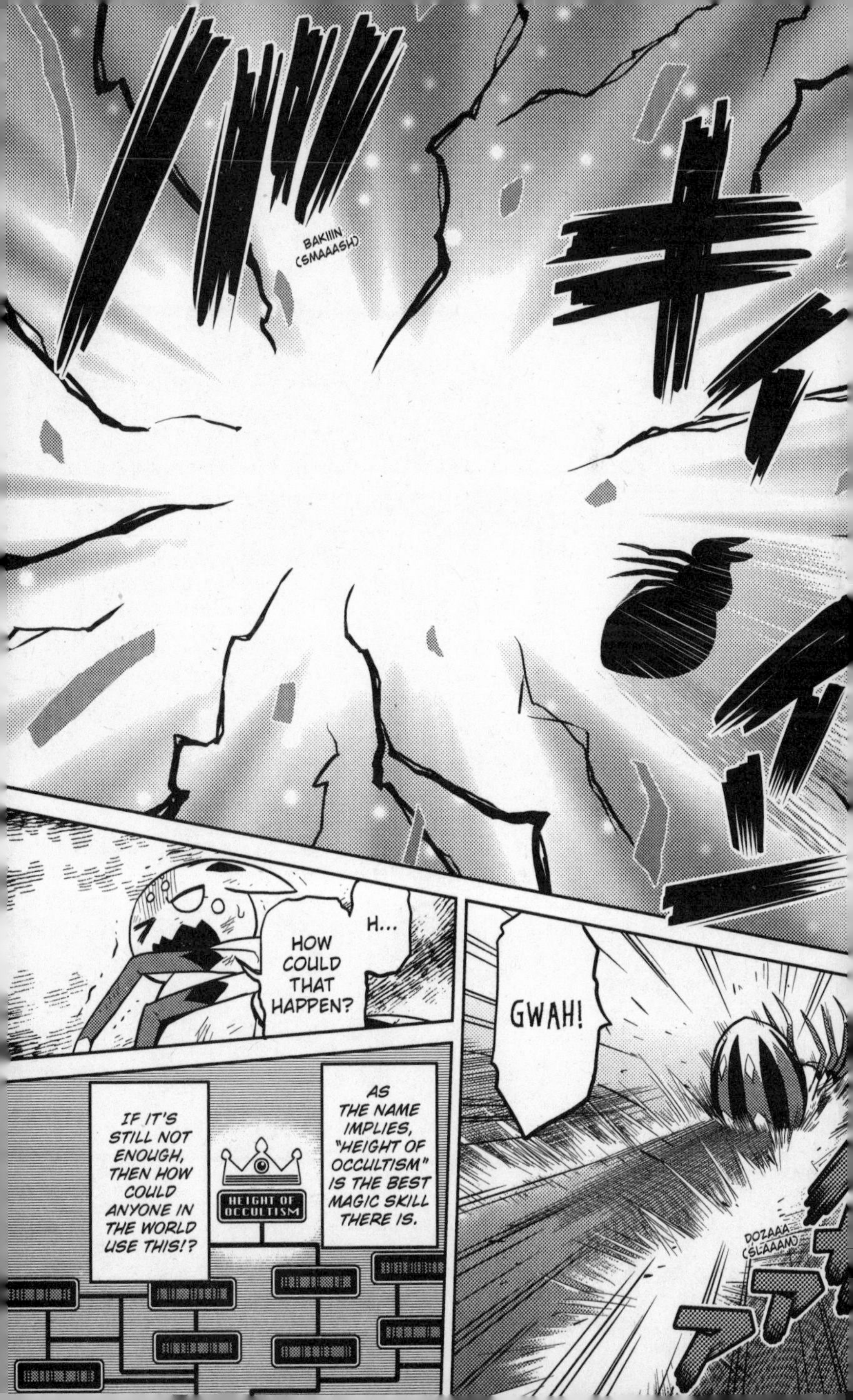
BAKIIIN (SMAAASH)
GWAH!
DOZAAA (SLAAAM)
H...
HOW COULD THAT HAPPEN?
AS THE NAME IMPLIES, "HEIGHT OF OCCULTISM" IS THE BEST MAGIC SKILL THERE IS.
HEIGHT OF OCCULTISM
IF IT'S STILL NOT ENOUGH, THEN HOW COULD ANYONE IN THE WORLD USE THIS!?

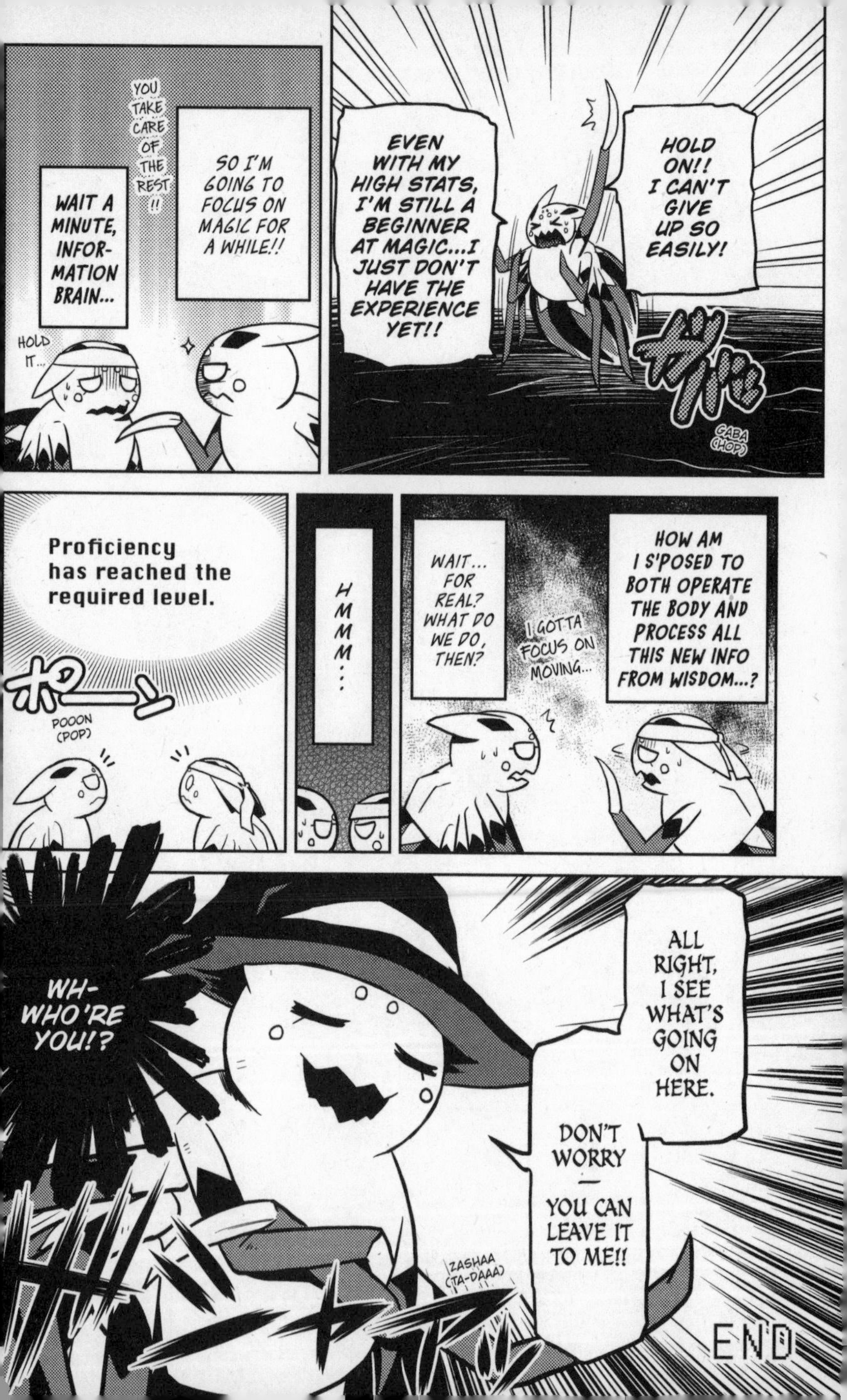
HOLD ON!! I CAN'T GIVE UP SO EASILY!
EVEN WITH MY HIGH STATS, I'M STILL A BEGINNER AT MAGIC...I JUST DON'T HAVE THE EXPERIENCE YET!!
GABA (HOP)
SO I'M GOING TO FOCUS ON MAGIC FOR A WHILE!!
YOU TAKE CARE OF THE REST!!
WAIT A MINUTE, INFOR-MATION BRAIN...
HOLD IT...
HOW AM I S'POSED TO BOTH OPERATE THE BODY AND PROCESS ALL THIS NEW INFO FROM WISDOM...?
I GOTTA FOCUS ON MOVING...
WAIT... FOR REAL? WHAT DO WE DO, THEN?
HMMM...
Proficiency has reached the required level.
POOON (POP)
ALL RIGHT, I SEE WHAT'S GOING ON HERE.
DON'T WORRY — YOU CAN LEAVE IT TO ME!!
ZASHAA (TA-DAAA)
WH-WHO'RE YOU!?
END

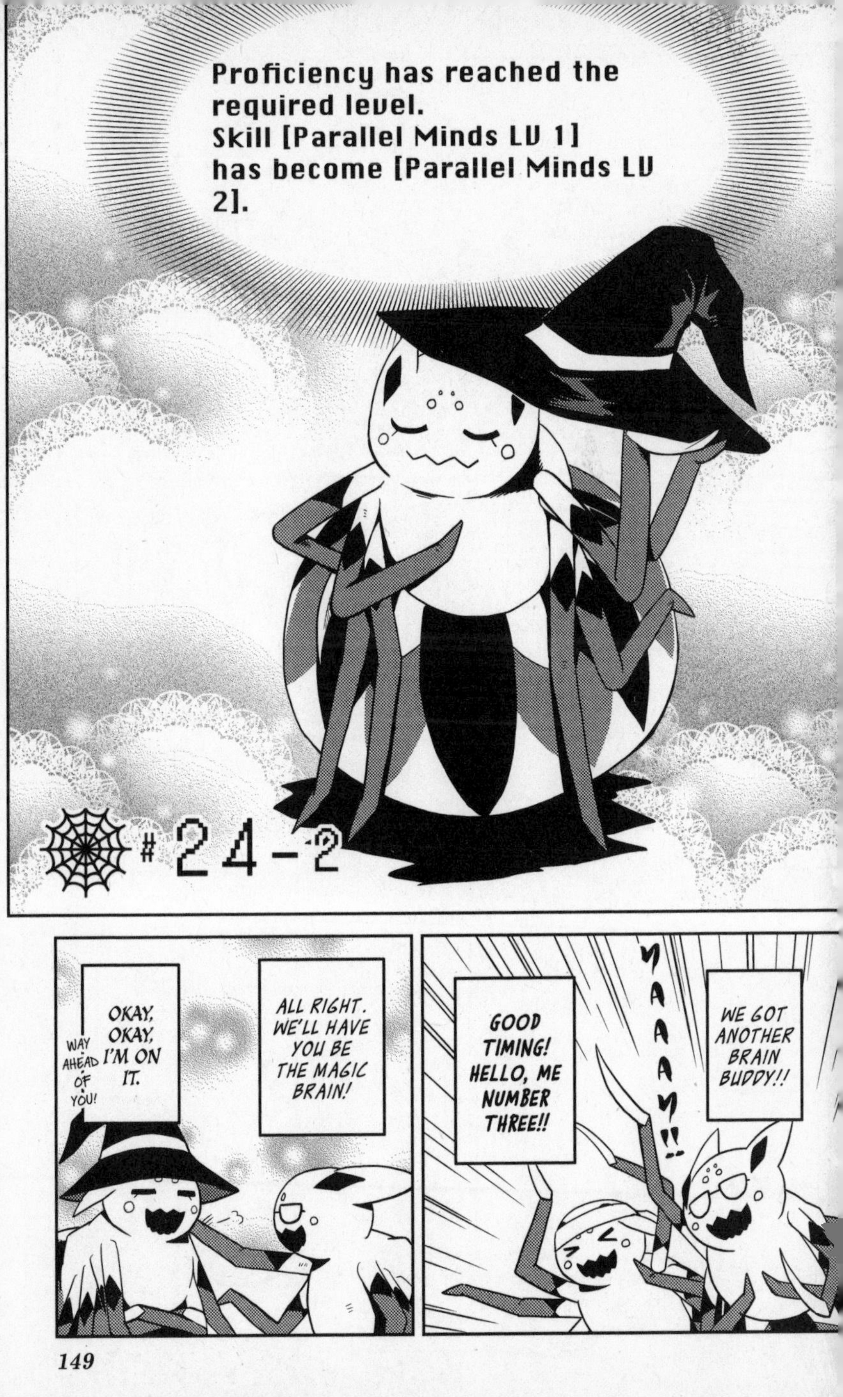
Proficiency has reached the required level.
Skill [Parallel Minds LV 1] has become [Parallel Minds LV 2].
#24-2
WE GOT ANOTHER BRAIN BUDDY!!
YAAAAY!!
GOOD TIMING! HELLO, ME NUMBER THREE!!
ALL RIGHT. WE'LL HAVE YOU BE THE MAGIC BRAIN!
OKAY, OKAY, I'M ON IT.
WAY AHEAD OF YOU!

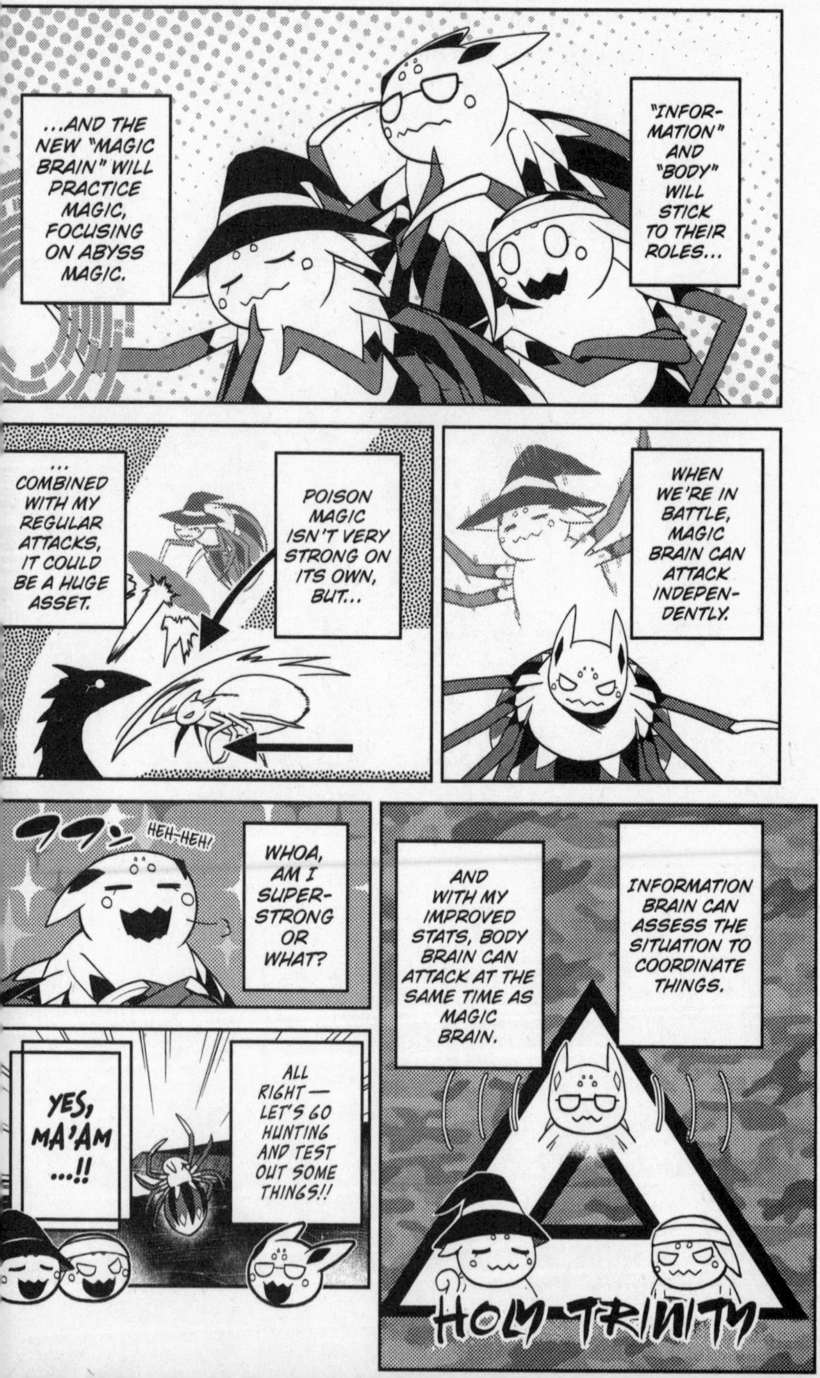
"INFORMATION" AND "BODY" WILL STICK TO THEIR ROLES...
...AND THE NEW "MAGIC BRAIN" WILL PRACTICE MAGIC, FOCUSING ON ABYSS MAGIC.
WHEN WE'RE IN BATTLE, MAGIC BRAIN CAN ATTACK INDEPENDENTLY.
POISON MAGIC ISN'T VERY STRONG ON ITS OWN, BUT...
...COMBINED WITH MY REGULAR ATTACKS, IT COULD BE A HUGE ASSET.
INFORMATION BRAIN CAN ASSESS THE SITUATION TO COORDINATE THINGS.
AND WITH MY IMPROVED STATS, BODY BRAIN CAN ATTACK AT THE SAME TIME AS MAGIC BRAIN.
HOLY TRINITY
WHOA, AM I SUPER-STRONG OR WHAT?
HEH-HEH!
ALL RIGHT—LET'S GO HUNTING AND TEST OUT SOME THINGS!!
YES, MA'AM...!!

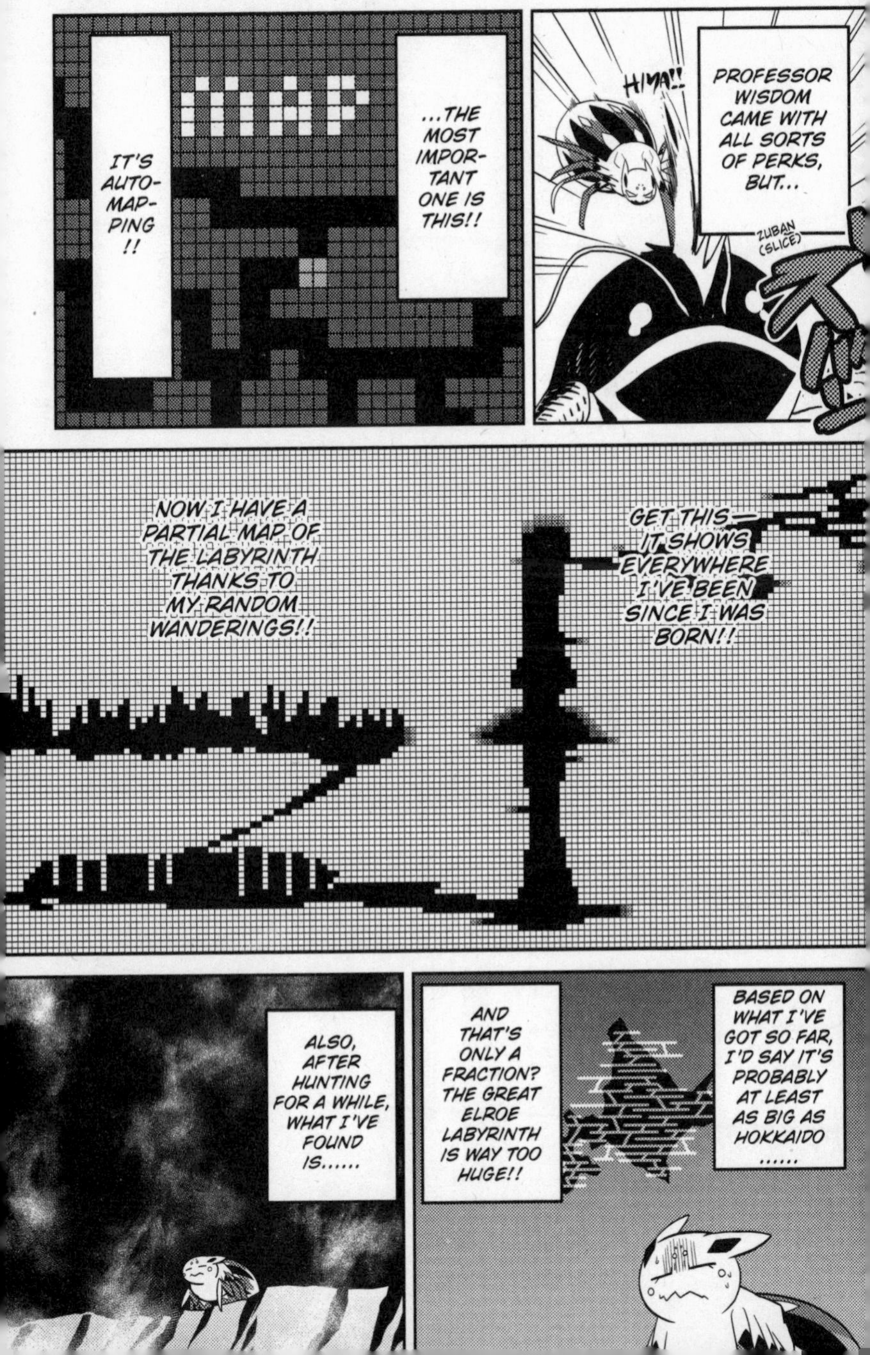
PROFESSOR WISDOM CAME WITH ALL SORTS OF PERKS, BUT...
HIYA!!
ZUBAN (SLICE)
...THE MOST IMPORTANT ONE IS THIS!!
MAP
IT'S AUTO-MAPPING!!
GET THIS—IT SHOWS EVERYWHERE I'VE BEEN SINCE I WAS BORN!!
NOW I HAVE A PARTIAL MAP OF THE LABYRINTH THANKS TO MY RANDOM WANDERINGS!!
BASED ON WHAT I'VE GOT SO FAR, I'D SAY IT'S PROBABLY AT LEAST AS BIG AS HOKKAIDO......
AND THAT'S ONLY A FRACTION? THE GREAT ELROE LABYRINTH IS WAY TOO HUGE!!
ALSO, AFTER HUNTING FOR A WHILE, WHAT I'VE FOUND IS......

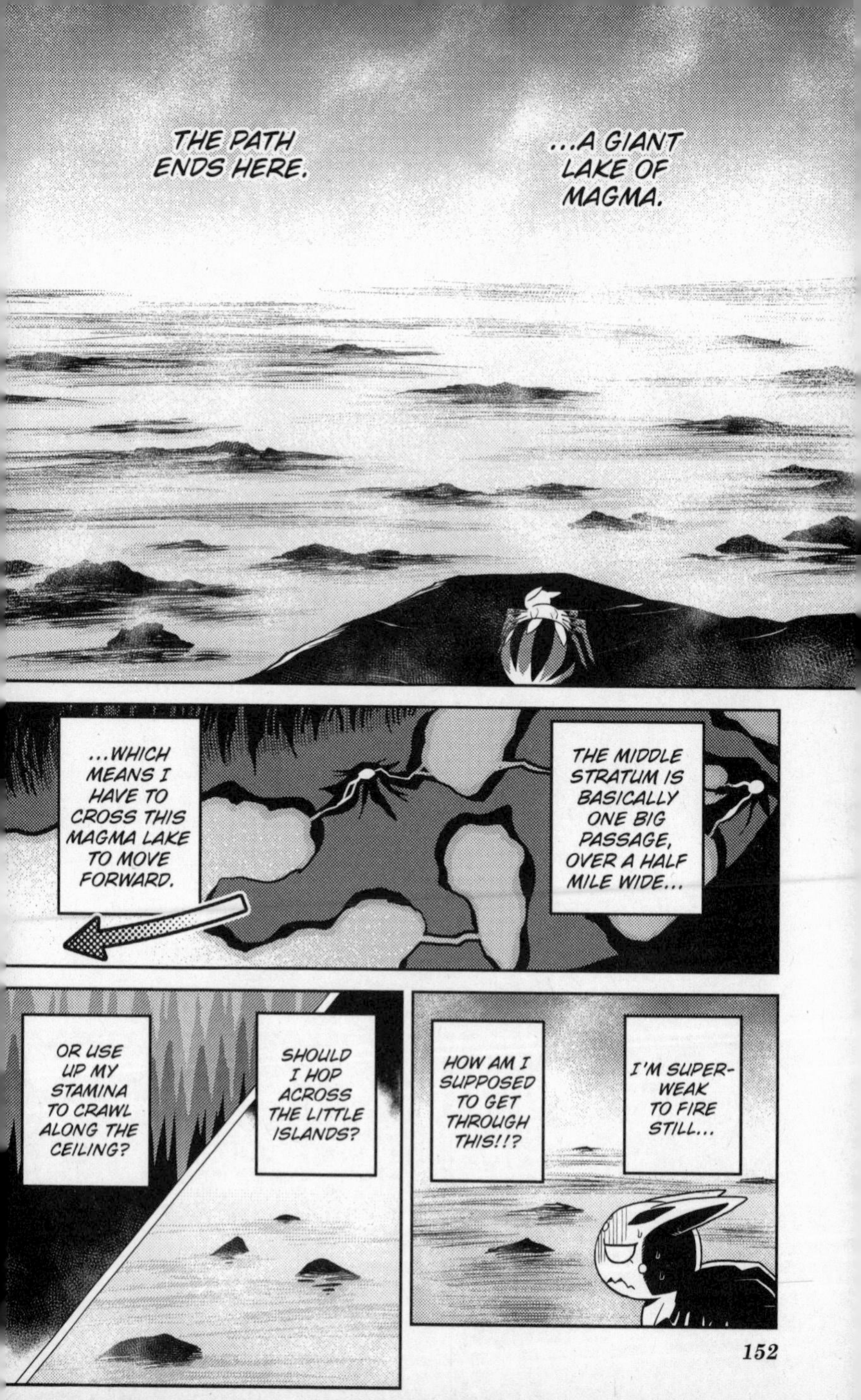
...A GIANT LAKE OF MAGMA.
THE PATH ENDS HERE.
THE MIDDLE STRATUM IS BASICALLY ONE BIG PASSAGE, OVER A HALF MILE WIDE...
...WHICH MEANS I HAVE TO CROSS THIS MAGMA LAKE TO MOVE FORWARD.
I'M SUPER-WEAK TO FIRE STILL...
HOW AM I SUPPOSED TO GET THROUGH THIS!!?
SHOULD I HOP ACROSS THE LITTLE ISLANDS?
OR USE UP MY STAMINA TO CRAWL ALONG THE CEILING?

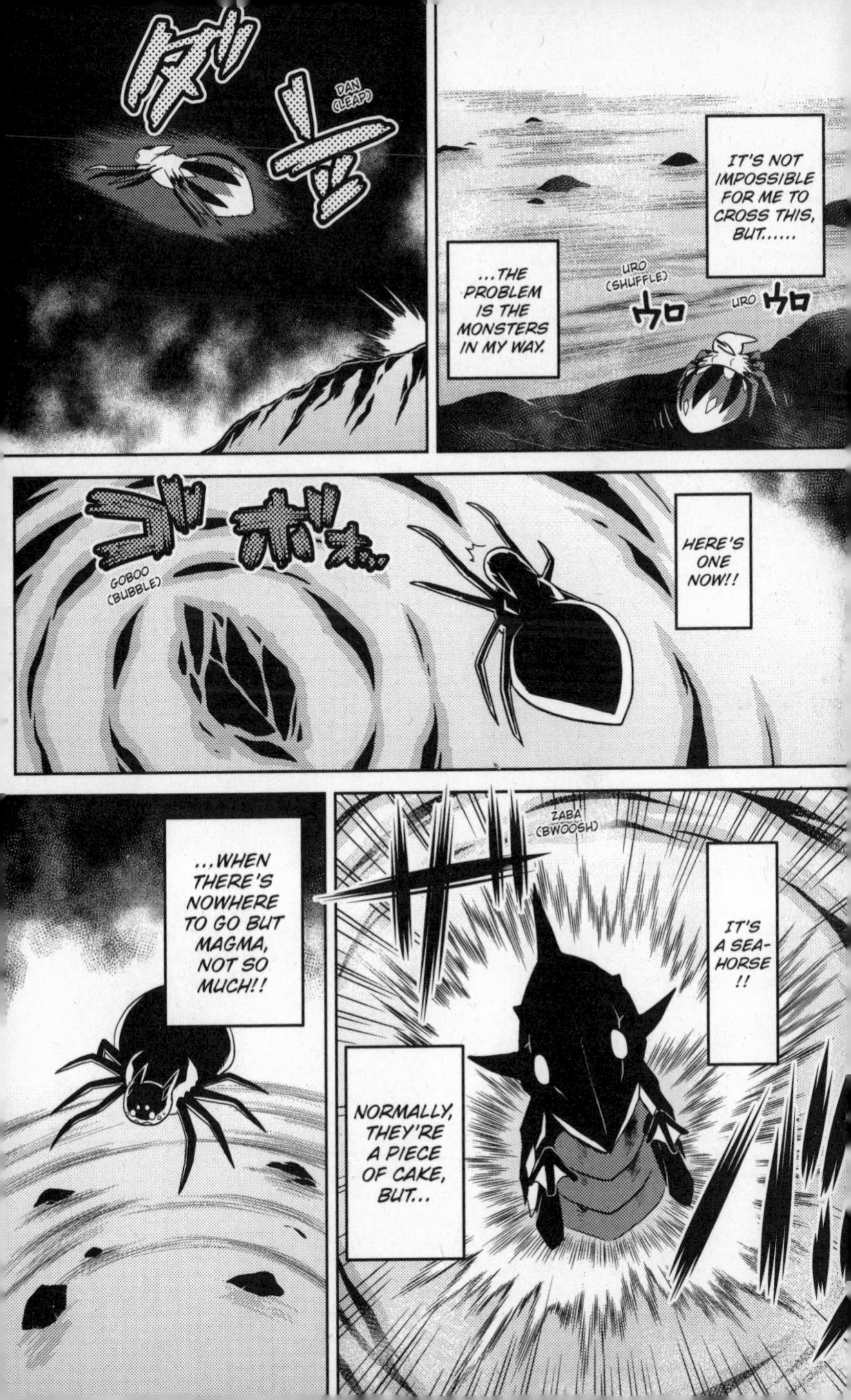
IT'S NOT IMPOSSIBLE FOR ME TO CROSS THIS, BUT......
URO ウロ
URO (SHUFFLE) ウロ
...THE PROBLEM IS THE MONSTERS IN MY WAY.
DAN (LEAP)
HERE'S ONE NOW!!
GOBOO (BUBBLE)
ZABA (BWOOSH)
IT'S A SEA-HORSE!!
NORMALLY, THEY'RE A PIECE OF CAKE, BUT...
...WHEN THERE'S NOWHERE TO GO BUT MAGMA, NOT SO MUCH!!

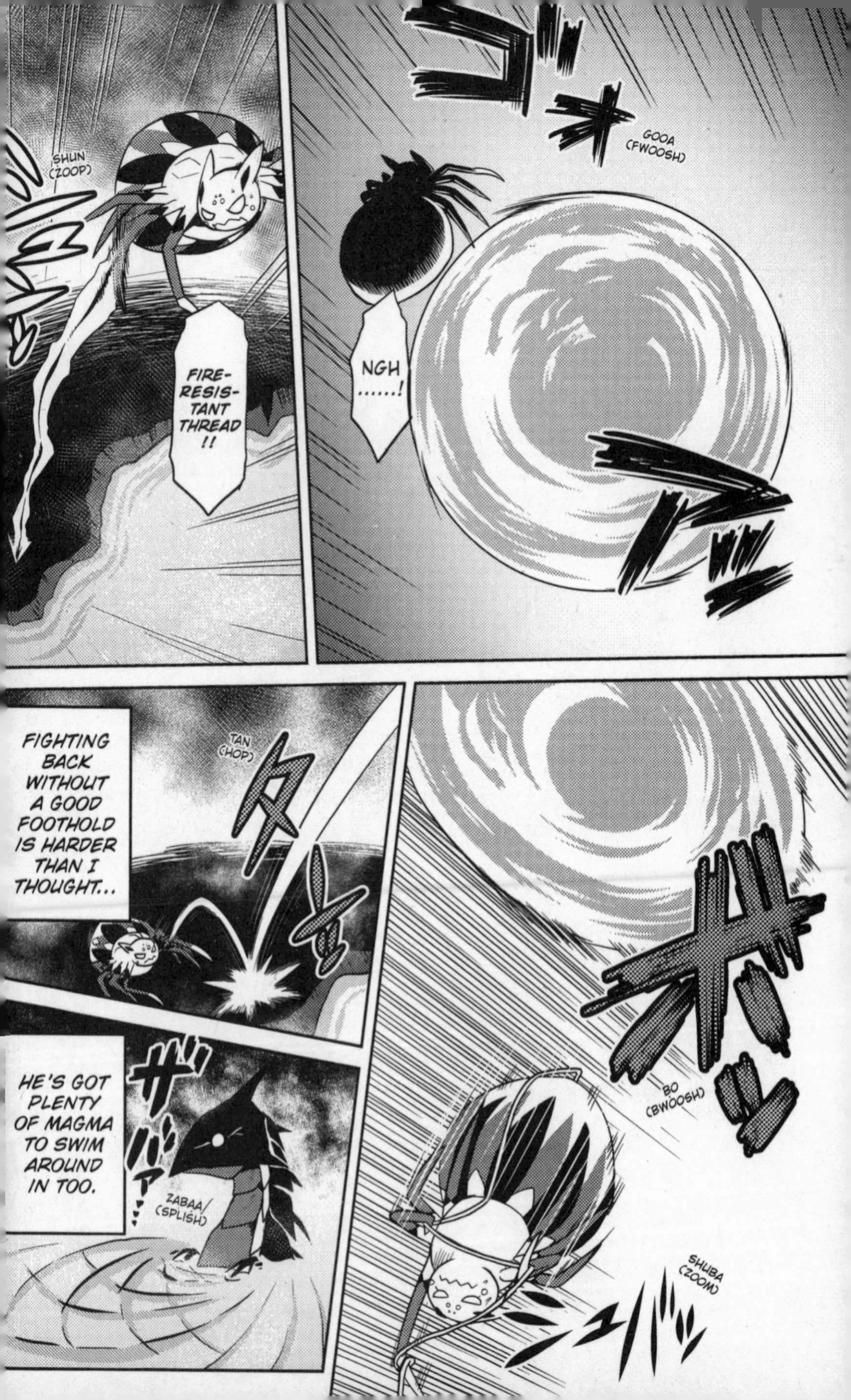
GOOA
(FWOOSH)
NGH
......!
SHUN
(ZOOP)
FIRE-RESIS-TANT THREAD
!!
BO
(BWOOSH)
SHUBA
(ZOOM)
FIGHTING BACK WITHOUT A GOOD FOOTHOLD IS HARDER THAN I THOUGHT...
TAN
(HOP)
HE'S GOT PLENTY OF MAGMA TO SWIM AROUND IN TOO.
ZABAA/
(SPLISH)

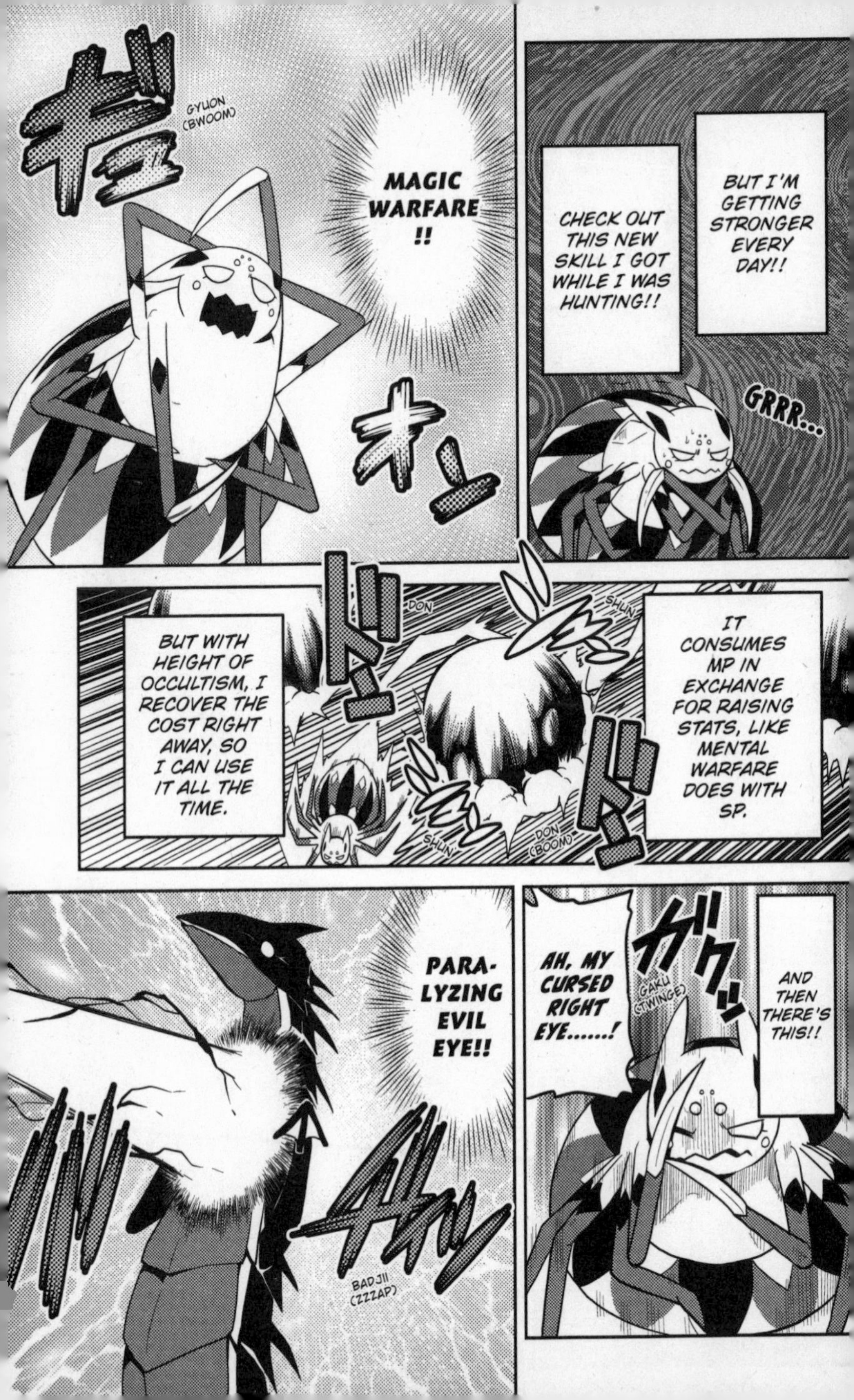
BUT I'M GETTING STRONGER EVERY DAY!!
CHECK OUT THIS NEW SKILL I GOT WHILE I WAS HUNTING!!
GRRR...
MAGIC WARFARE !!
GYUON (BWOOM)
IT CONSUMES MP IN EXCHANGE FOR RAISING STATS, LIKE MENTAL WARFARE DOES WITH SP.
SHUN
DON
BUT WITH HEIGHT OF OCCULTISM, I RECOVER THE COST RIGHT AWAY, SO I CAN USE IT ALL THE TIME.
DON (BOOM)
SHUN
AND THEN THERE'S THIS!!
GAKU (TWINGE)
AH, MY CURSED RIGHT EYE......!
PARA-LYZING EVIL EYE!!
BADJII (ZZZAP)

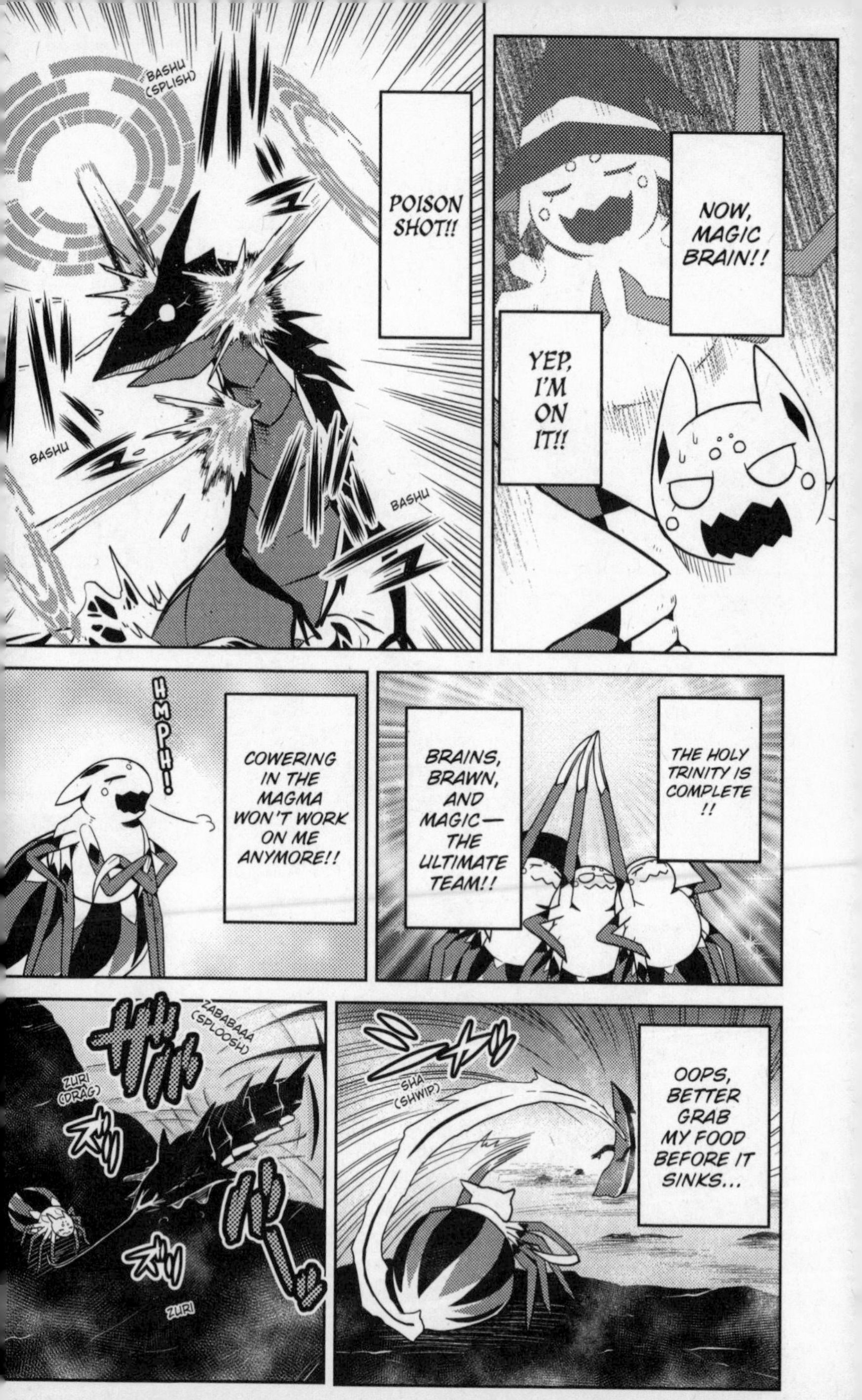
NOW, MAGIC BRAIN!!
YEP, I'M ON IT!!
POISON SHOT!!
BASHU (SPLISH)
BASHU
BASHU
THE HOLY TRINITY IS COMPLETE!!
BRAINS, BRAWN, AND MAGIC—THE ULTIMATE TEAM!!
HMPH!
COWERING IN THE MAGMA WON'T WORK ON ME ANYMORE!!
SHA (SHWIP)
OOPS, BETTER GRAB MY FOOD BEFORE IT SINKS...
ZABABAAA (SPLOOSH)
ZURI (DRAG)
ZURI

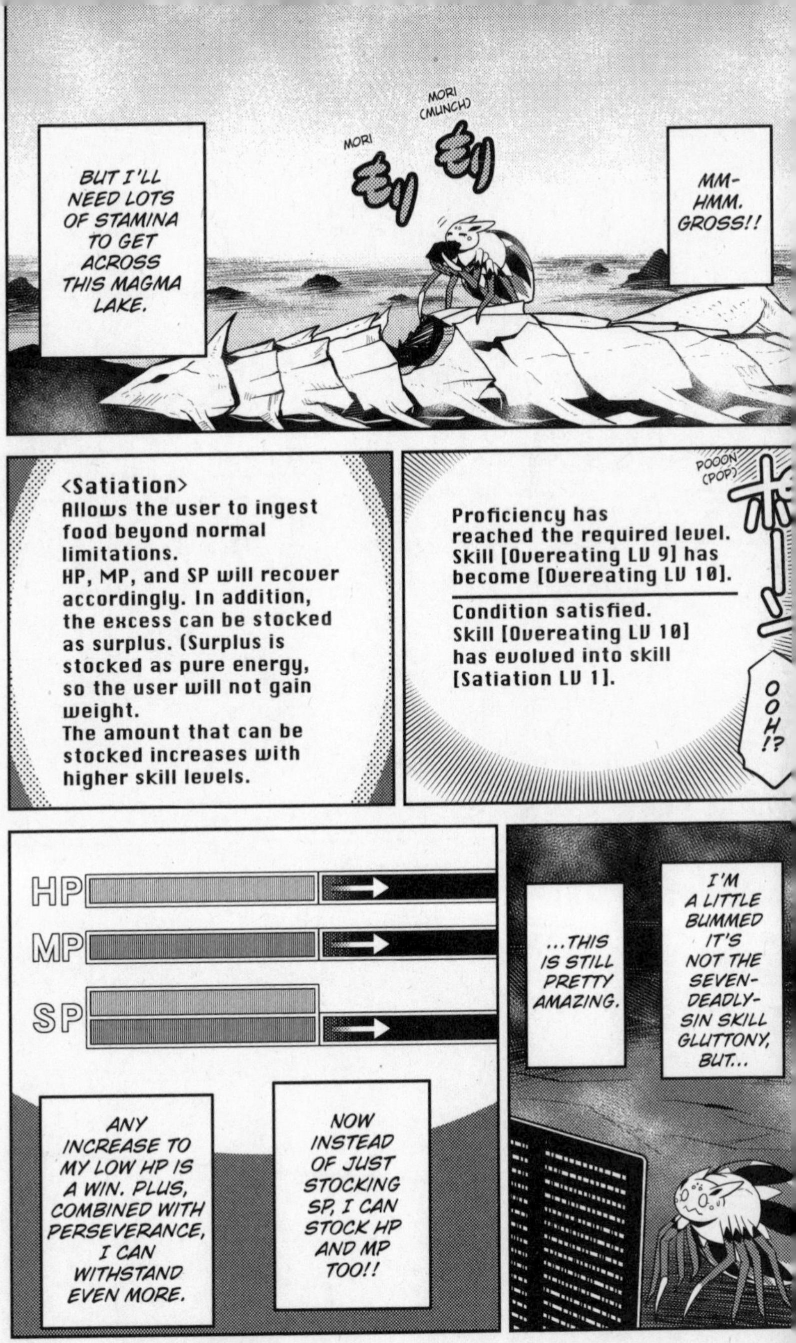
MM-HMM. GROSS!!
MORI (MUNCH)
MORI
BUT I'LL NEED LOTS OF STAMINA TO GET ACROSS THIS MAGMA LAKE.
POOON (POP)
OOH!?
Proficiency has reached the required level. Skill [Overeating LV 9] has become [Overeating LV 10].
Condition satisfied. Skill [Overeating LV 10] has evolved into skill [Satiation LV 1].
<Satiation>
Allows the user to ingest food beyond normal limitations. HP, MP, and SP will recover accordingly. In addition, the excess can be stocked as surplus. (Surplus is stocked as pure energy, so the user will not gain weight. The amount that can be stocked increases with higher skill levels.
I'M A LITTLE BUMMED IT'S NOT THE SEVEN-DEADLY-SIN SKILL GLUTTONY, BUT...
...THIS IS STILL PRETTY AMAZING.
HP
MP
SP
NOW INSTEAD OF JUST STOCKING SP, I CAN STOCK HP AND MP TOO!!
ANY INCREASE TO MY LOW HP IS A WIN. PLUS, COMBINED WITH PERSEVERANCE, I CAN WITHSTAND EVEN MORE.

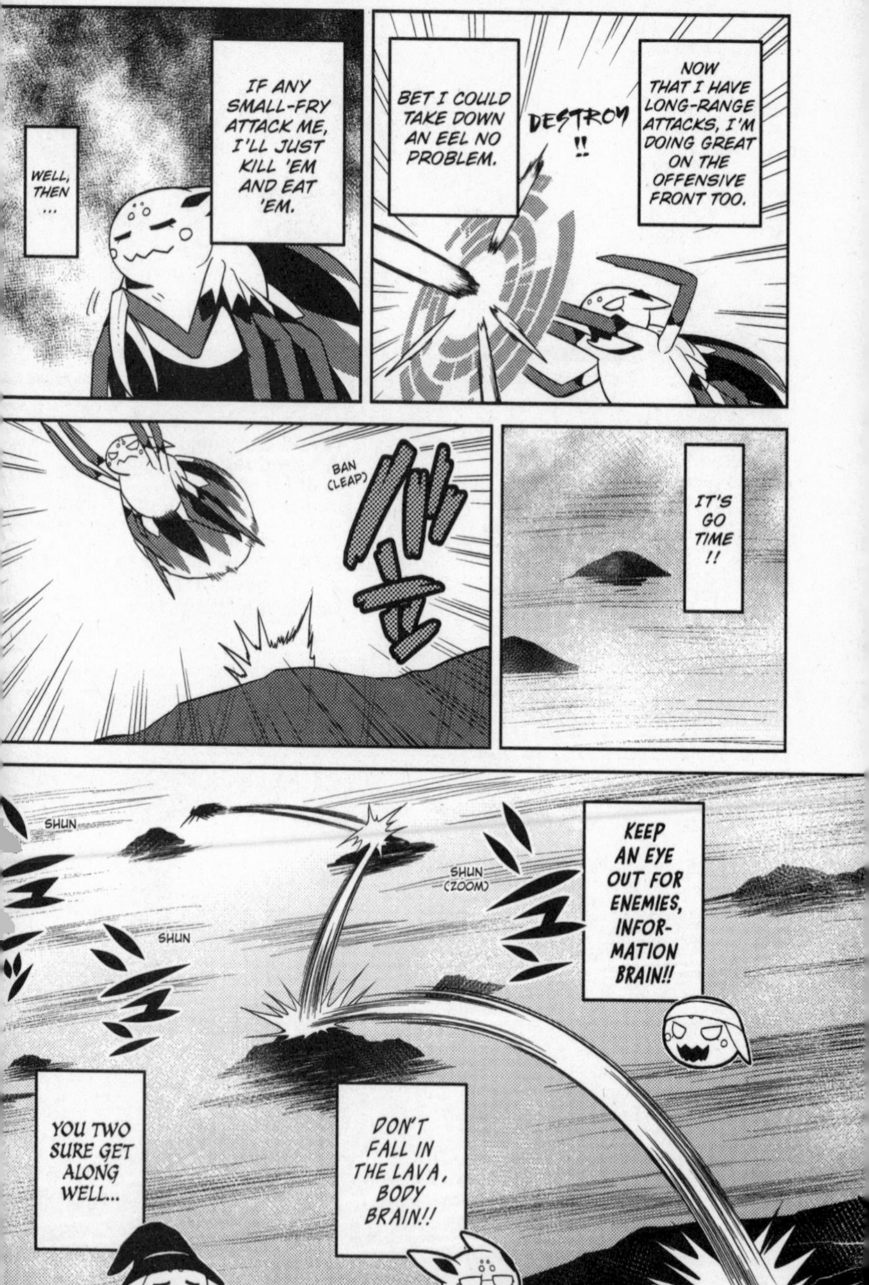
NOW THAT I HAVE LONG-RANGE ATTACKS, I'M DOING GREAT ON THE OFFENSIVE FRONT TOO.
DESTROY!!
BET I COULD TAKE DOWN AN EEL NO PROBLEM.
IF ANY SMALL-FRY ATTACK ME, I'LL JUST KILL 'EM AND EAT 'EM.
WELL, THEN...
IT'S GO TIME!!
BAN (LEAP)
KEEP AN EYE OUT FOR ENEMIES, INFORMATION BRAIN!!
SHUN (ZOOM)
SHUN
SHUN
DON'T FALL IN THE LAVA, BODY BRAIN!!
YOU TWO SURE GET ALONG WELL...

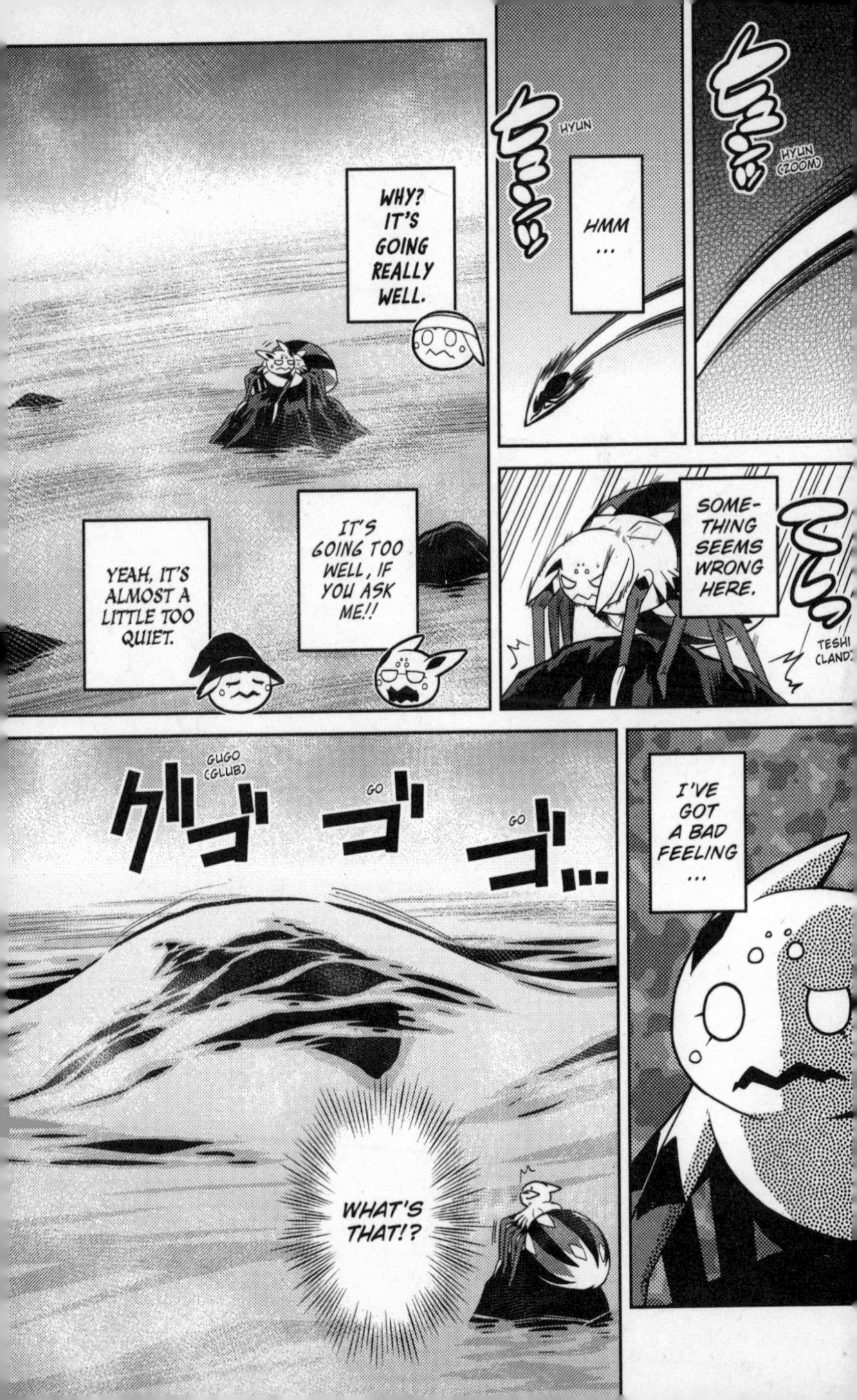
HYUN (ZOOM)
HYUN
HMM...
SOMETHING SEEMS WRONG HERE.
TESHI (LAND)
WHY? IT'S GOING REALLY WELL.
IT'S GOING TOO WELL, IF YOU ASK ME!!
YEAH, IT'S ALMOST A LITTLE TOO QUIET.
I'VE GOT A BAD FEELING...
GUGO (GLUB)
GO
GO
WHAT'S THAT!?

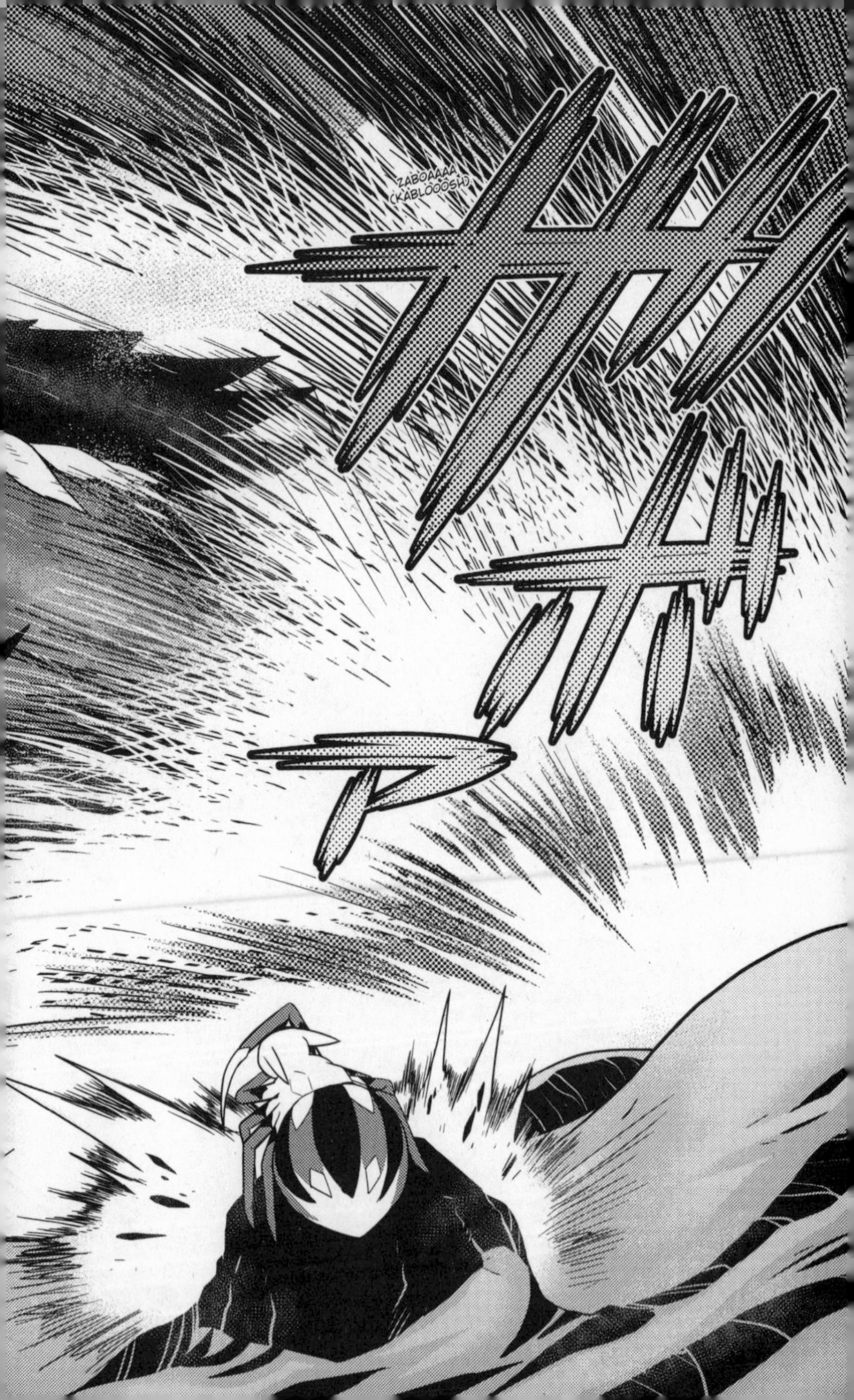
ZABOAAAA
(KABLOOOSH)

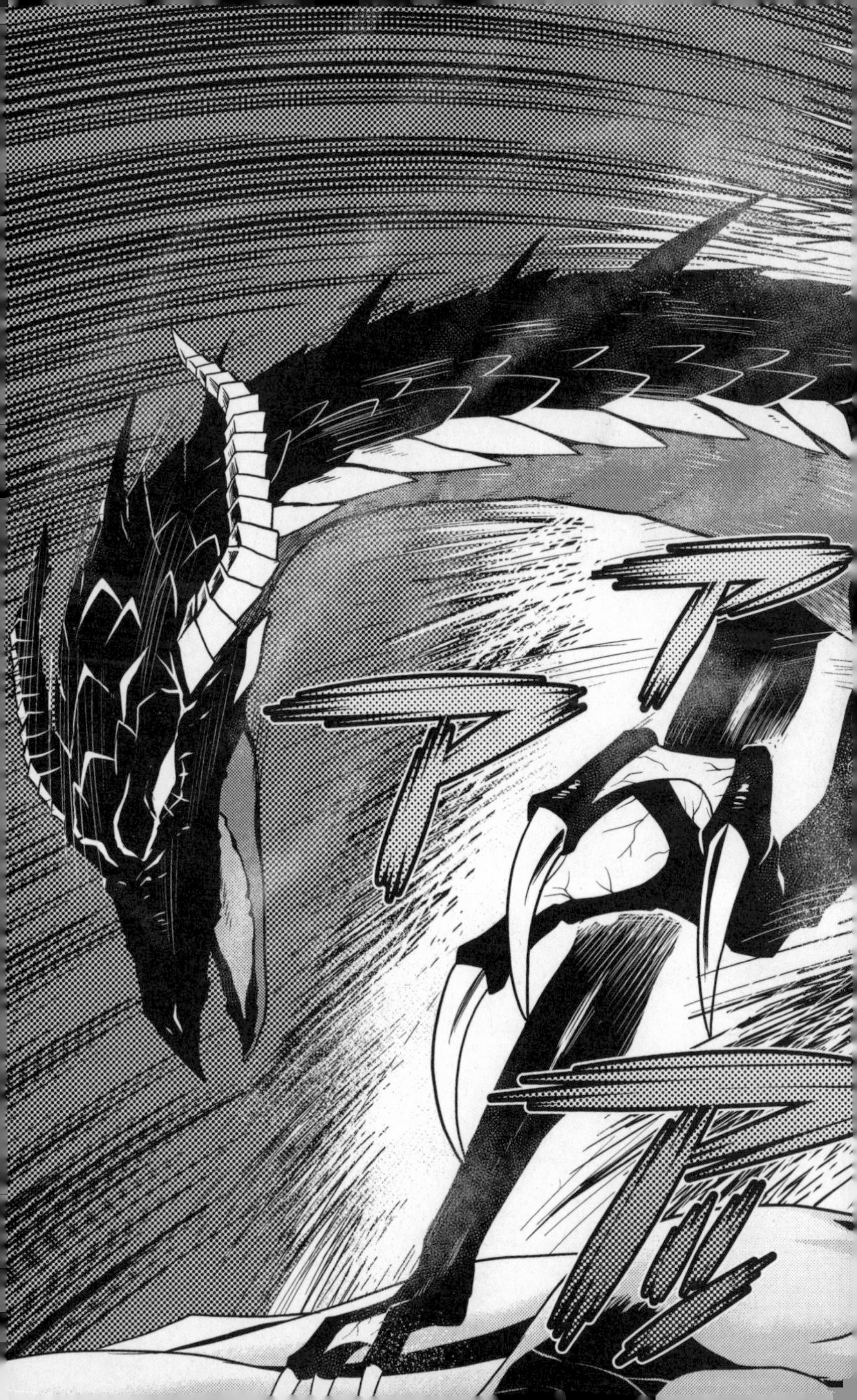

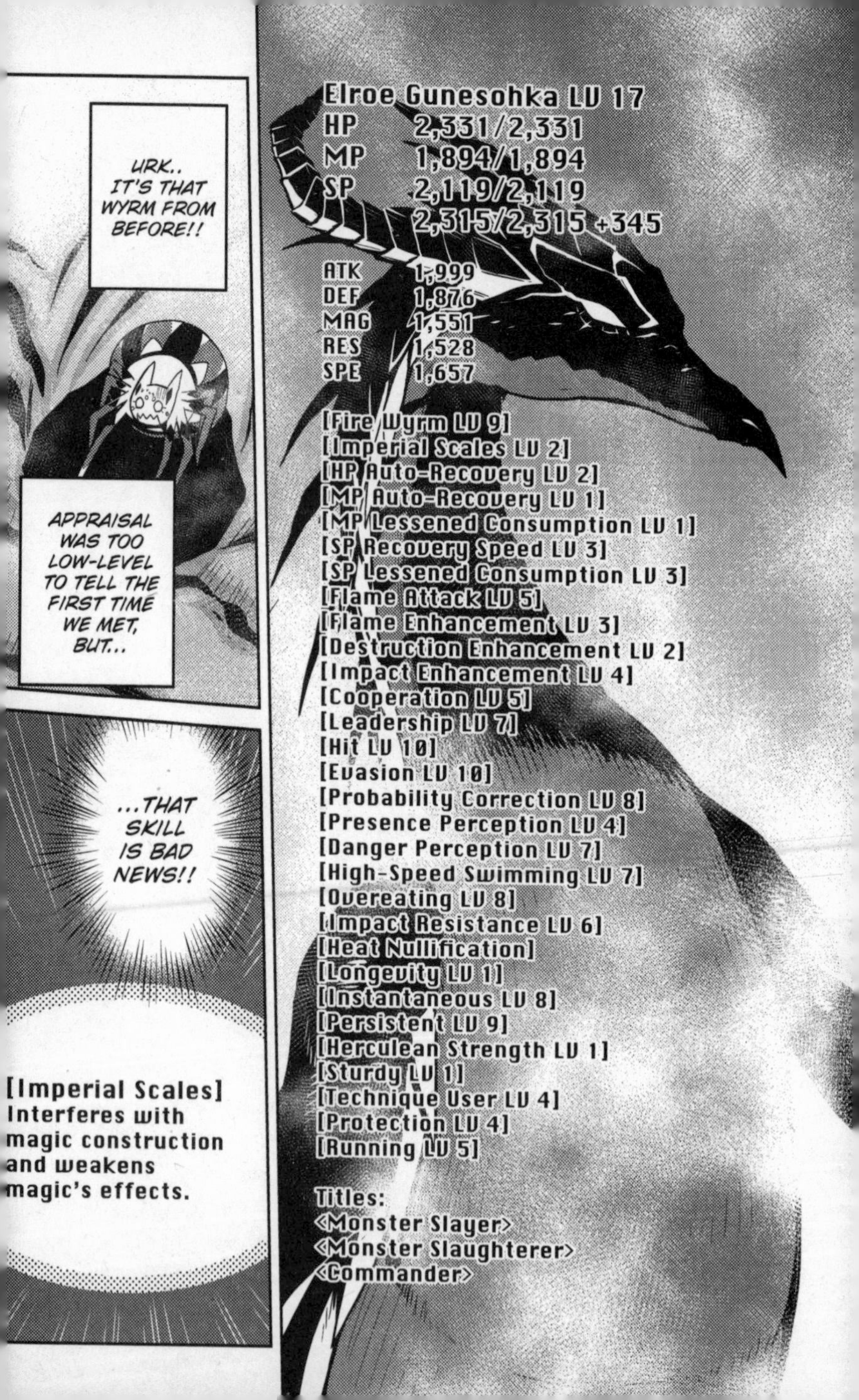
Elroe Gunesohka LV 17
HP 2,331/2,331
MP 1,894/1,894
SP 2,119/2,119
2,315/2,315 +345
ATK 1,999
DEF 1,876
MAG 1,551
RES 1,528
SPE 1,657
[Fire Wyrm LV 9]
[Imperial Scales LV 2]
[HP Auto-Recovery LV 2]
[MP Auto-Recovery LV 1]
[MP Lessened Consumption LV 1]
[SP Recovery Speed LV 3]
[SP Lessened Consumption LV 3]
[Flame Attack LV 5]
[Flame Enhancement LV 3]
[Destruction Enhancement LV 2]
[Impact Enhancement LV 4]
[Cooperation LV 5]
[Leadership LV 7]
[Hit LV 10]
[Evasion LV 10]
[Probability Correction LV 8]
[Presence Perception LV 4]
[Danger Perception LV 7]
[High-Speed Swimming LV 7]
[Overeating LV 8]
[Impact Resistance LV 6]
[Heat Nullification]
[Longevity LV 1]
[Instantaneous LV 8]
[Persistent LV 9]
[Herculean Strength LV 1]
[Sturdy LV 1]
[Technique User LV 4]
[Protection LV 4]
[Running LV 5]
Titles:
<Monster Slayer>
<Monster Slaughterer>
<Commander>
URK.. IT'S THAT WYRM FROM BEFORE!!
APPRAISAL WAS TOO LOW-LEVEL TO TELL THE FIRST TIME WE MET, BUT...
...THAT SKILL IS BAD NEWS!!
[Imperial Scales] Interferes with magic construction and weakens magic's effects.

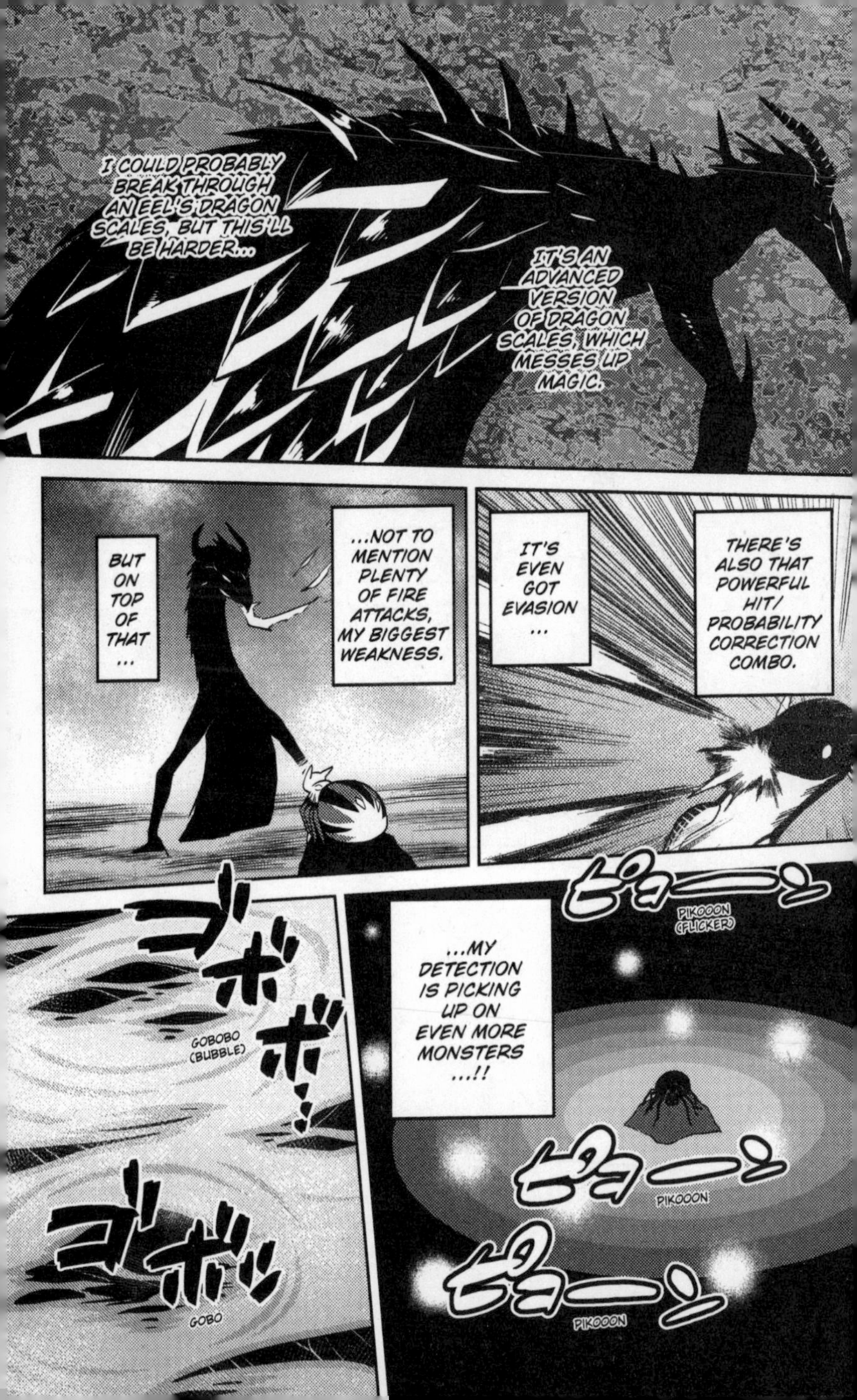
IT'S AN ADVANCED VERSION OF DRAGON SCALES, WHICH MESSES UP MAGIC.
I COULD PROBABLY BREAK THROUGH AN EEL'S DRAGON SCALES, BUT THIS'LL BE HARDER...
THERE'S ALSO THAT POWERFUL HIT/PROBABILITY CORRECTION COMBO.
IT'S EVEN GOT EVASION...
...NOT TO MENTION PLENTY OF FIRE ATTACKS, MY BIGGEST WEAKNESS.
BUT ON TOP OF THAT...
PIKOOON (FLICKER)
...MY DETECTION IS PICKING UP ON EVEN MORE MONSTERS...!!
PIKOOON
PIKOOON
GOBOBO (BUBBLE)
GOBO

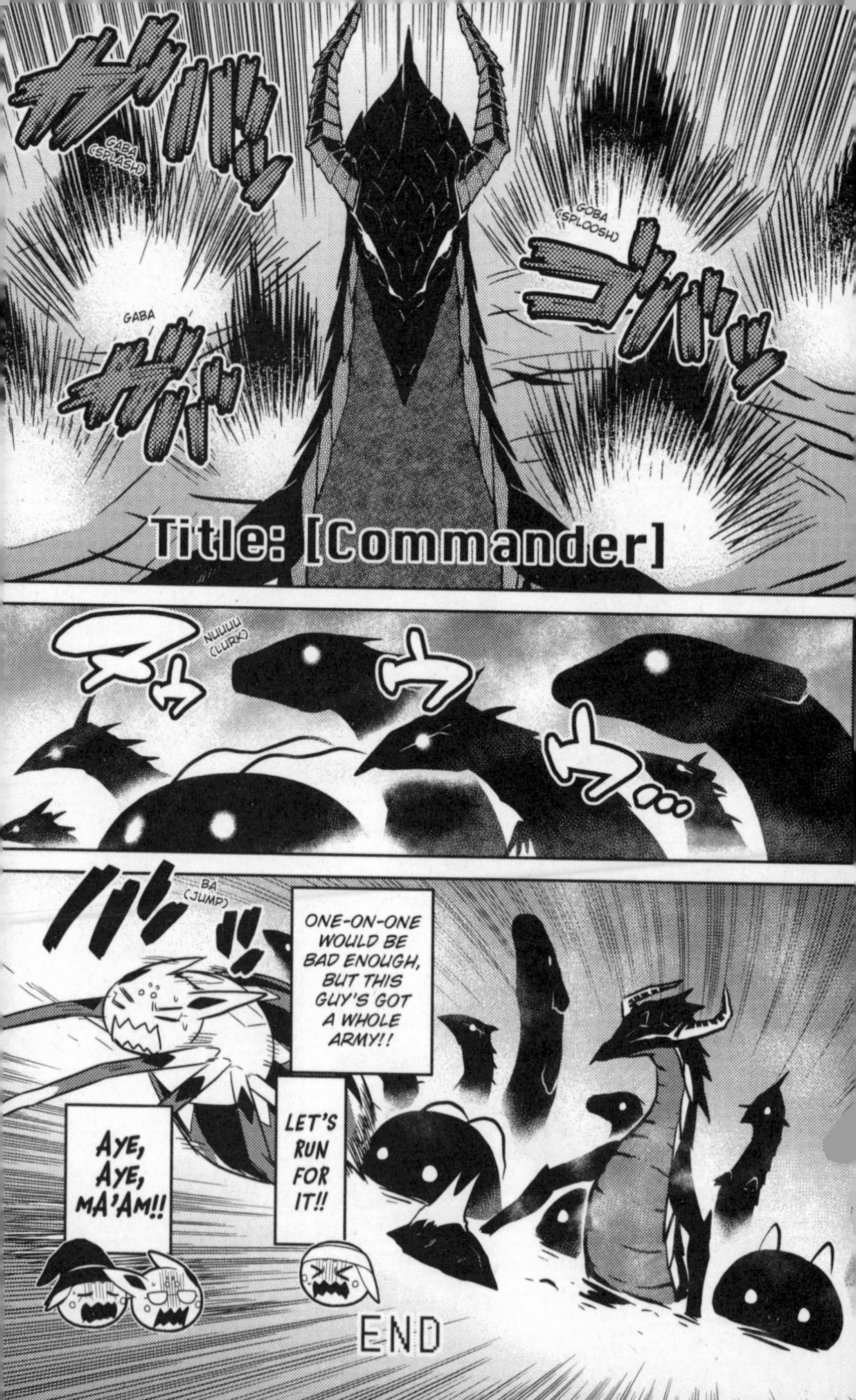
GOBA (SPLOOSH)
GABA (SPLASH)
GABA
Title: [Commander]
NUUUU (LURK)
ONE-ON-ONE WOULD BE BAD ENOUGH, BUT THIS GUY'S GOT A WHOLE ARMY!!
BA (JUMP)
LET'S RUN FOR IT!!
AYE, AYE, MA'AM!!
END

Bonus Short Comic
ANOTHER REINCARNATION #2

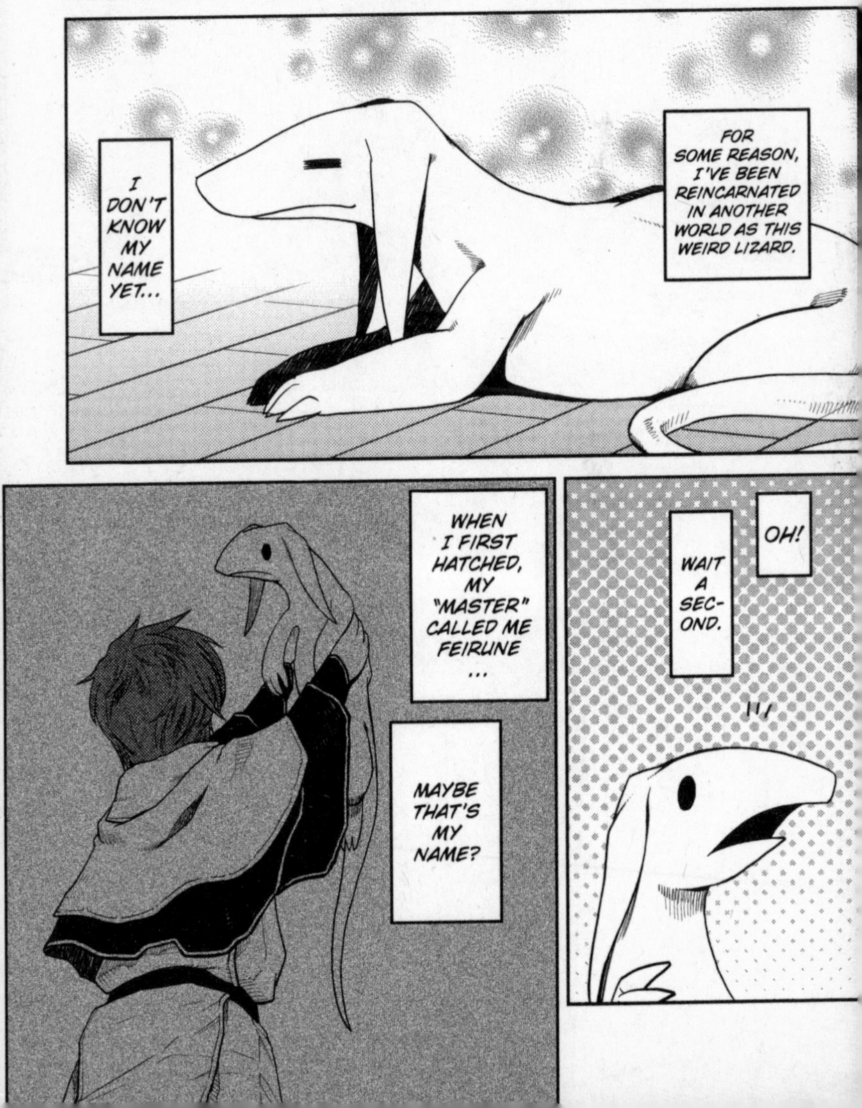
FOR SOME REASON, I'VE BEEN REINCARNATED IN ANOTHER WORLD AS THIS WEIRD LIZARD.
I DON'T KNOW MY NAME YET...
OH!
WAIT A SEC-OND.
WHEN I FIRST HATCHED, MY "MASTER" CALLED ME FEIRUNE ...
MAYBE THAT'S MY NAME?

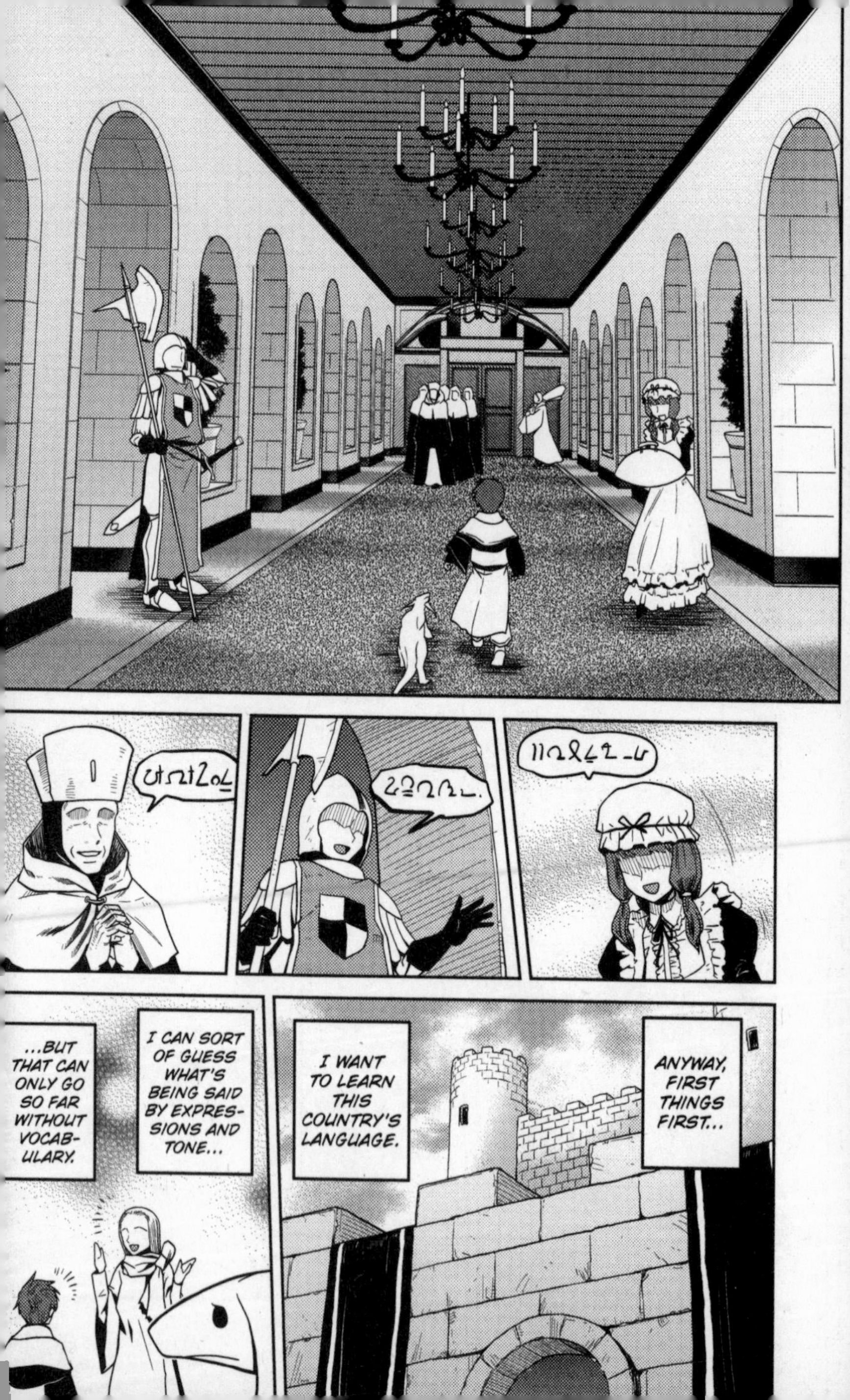
ANYWAY, FIRST THINGS FIRST...
I WANT TO LEARN THIS COUNTRY'S LANGUAGE.
I CAN SORT OF GUESS WHAT'S BEING SAID BY EXPRES-SIONS AND TONE...
...BUT THAT CAN ONLY GO SO FAR WITHOUT VOCAB-ULARY.

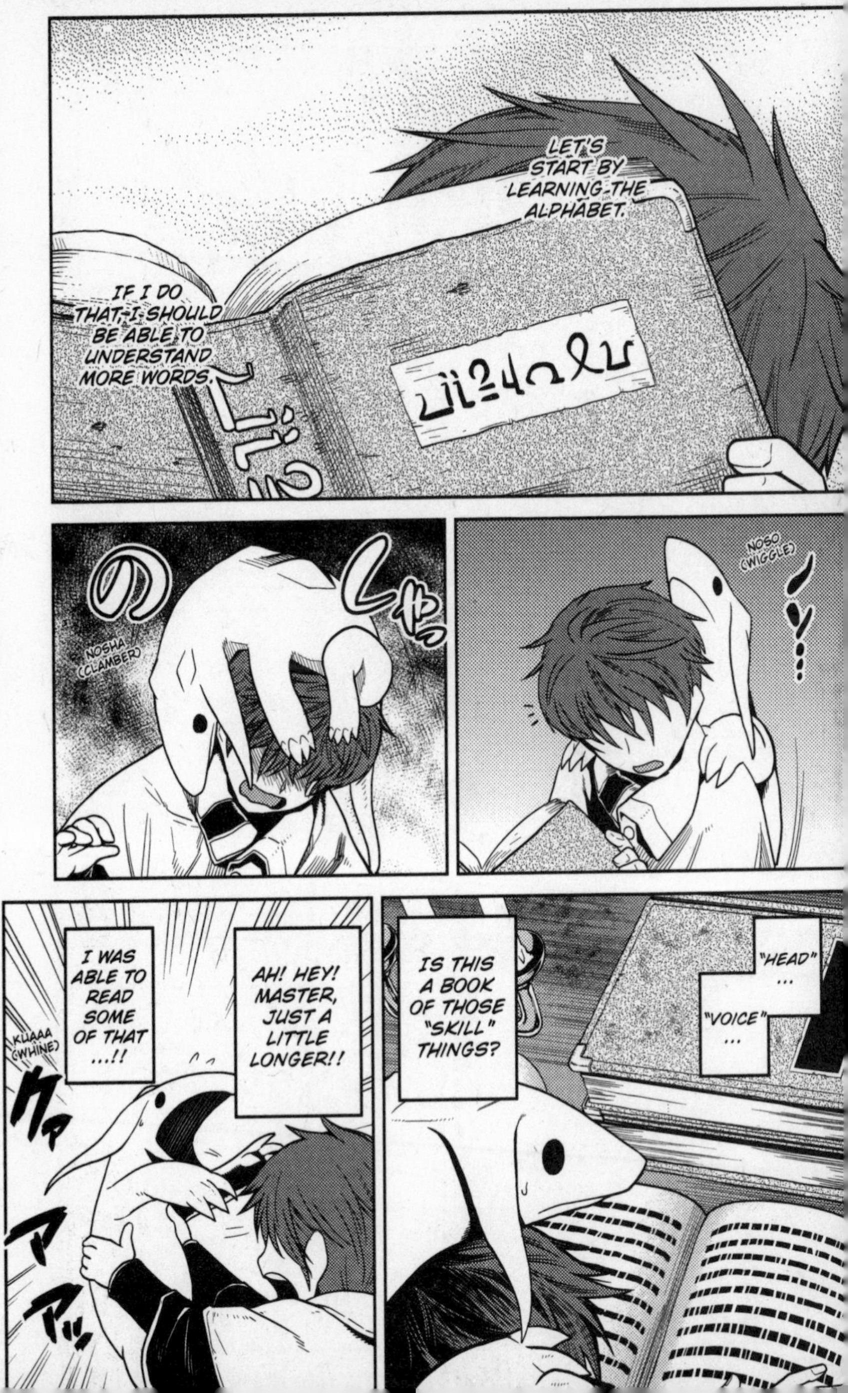
LET'S START BY LEARNING THE ALPHABET.
IF I DO THAT, I SHOULD BE ABLE TO UNDERSTAND MORE WORDS.
NOSO (WIGGLE)
ノソ…
のしゅ
NOSHA (CLAMBER)
"HEAD"...
"VOICE"...
IS THIS A BOOK OF THOSE "SKILL" THINGS?
AH! HEY! MASTER, JUST A LITTLE LONGER!!
I WAS ABLE TO READ SOME OF THAT ...!!
KUAAA (WHINE)

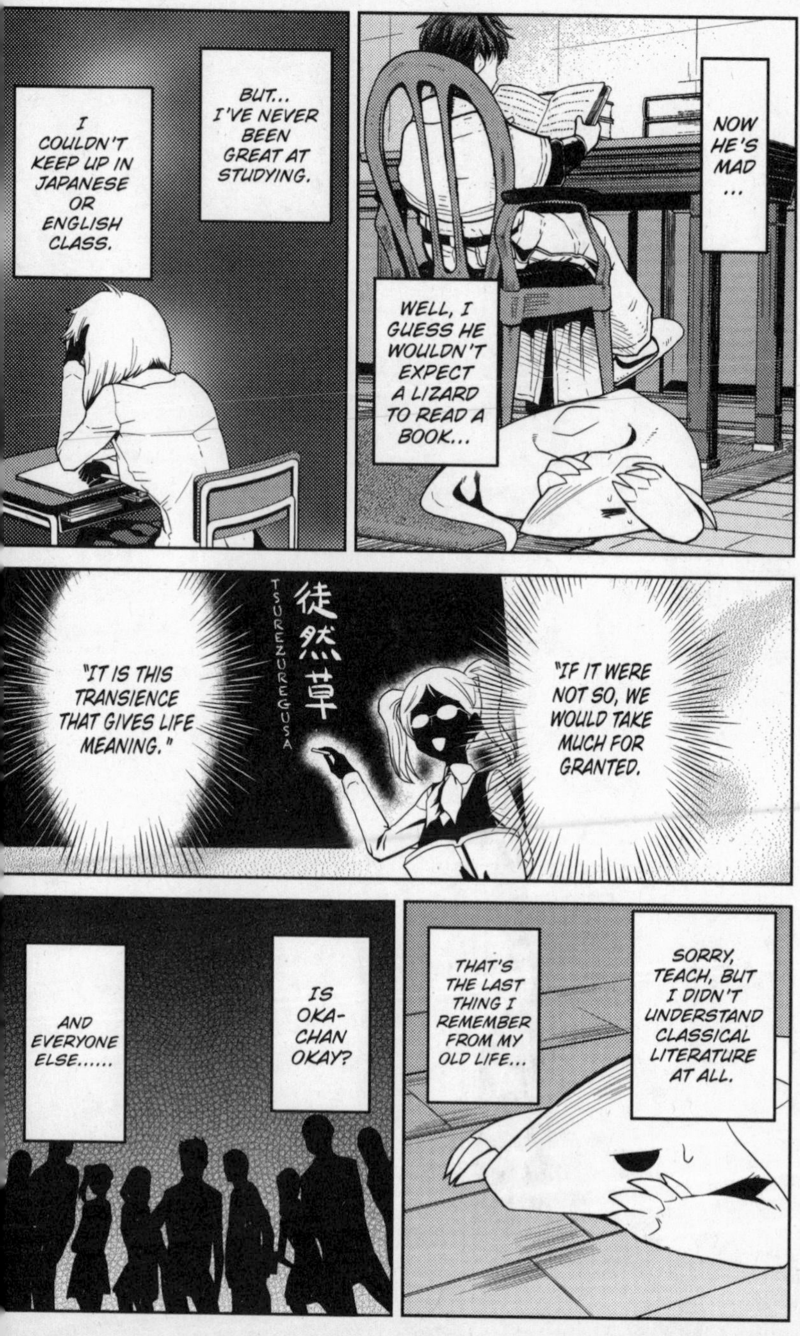
NOW HE'S MAD ...
WELL, I GUESS HE WOULDN'T EXPECT A LIZARD TO READ A BOOK...
BUT... I'VE NEVER BEEN GREAT AT STUDYING.
I COULDN'T KEEP UP IN JAPANESE OR ENGLISH CLASS.
"IF IT WERE NOT SO, WE WOULD TAKE MUCH FOR GRANTED.
徒然草
TSUREZUREGUSA
"IT IS THIS TRANSIENCE THAT GIVES LIFE MEANING."
SORRY, TEACH, BUT I DIDN'T UNDERSTAND CLASSICAL LITERATURE AT ALL.
THAT'S THE LAST THING I REMEMBER FROM MY OLD LIFE...
IS OKA-CHAN OKAY?
AND EVERYONE ELSE......

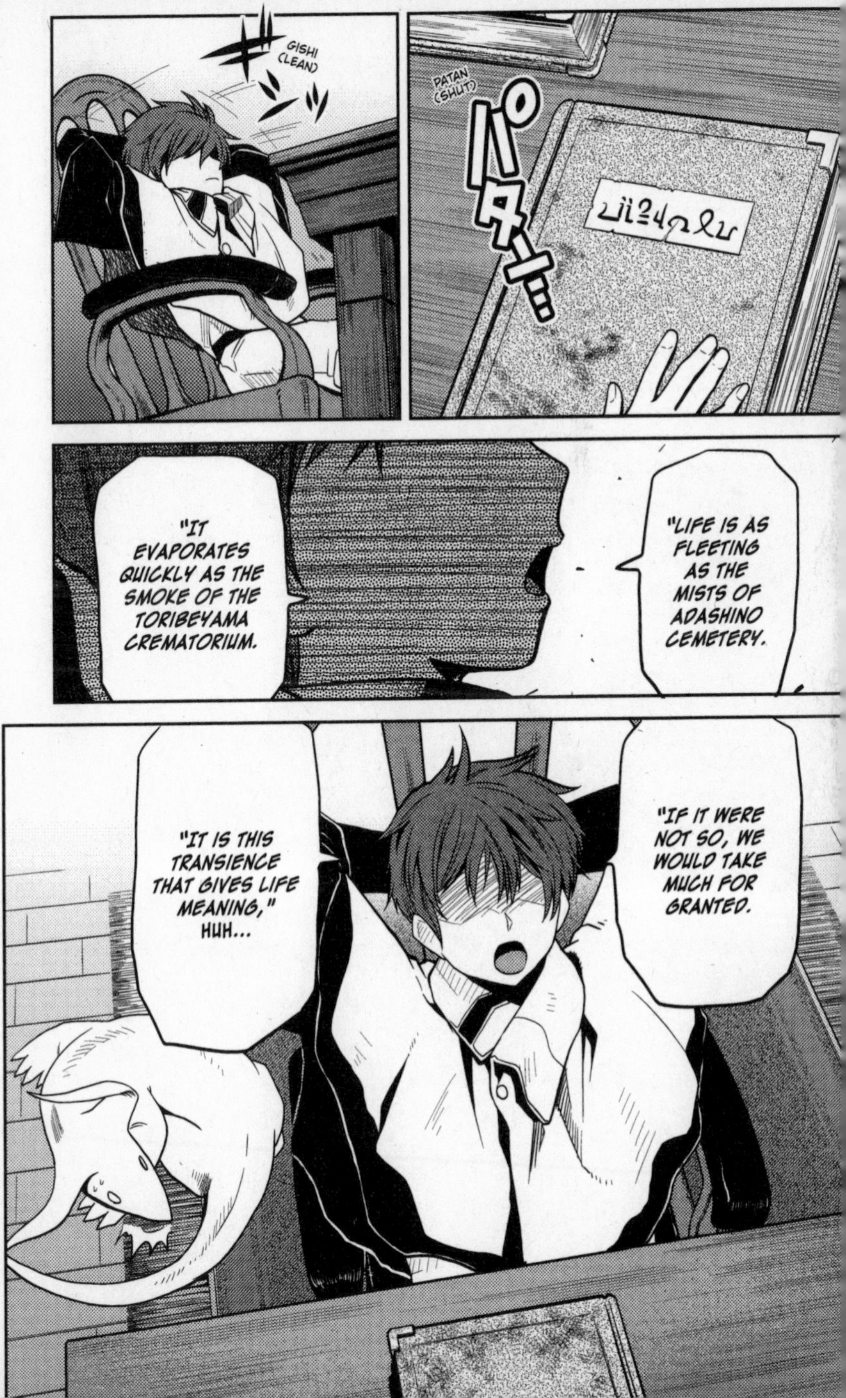
PATAN (SHUT)
GISHI (LEAN)
"LIFE IS AS FLEETING AS THE MISTS OF ADASHINO CEMETERY.
"IT EVAPORATES QUICKLY AS THE SMOKE OF THE TORIBEYAMA CREMATORIUM.
"IF IT WERE NOT SO, WE WOULD TAKE MUCH FOR GRANTED.
"IT IS THIS TRANSIENCE THAT GIVES LIFE MEANING," HUH...

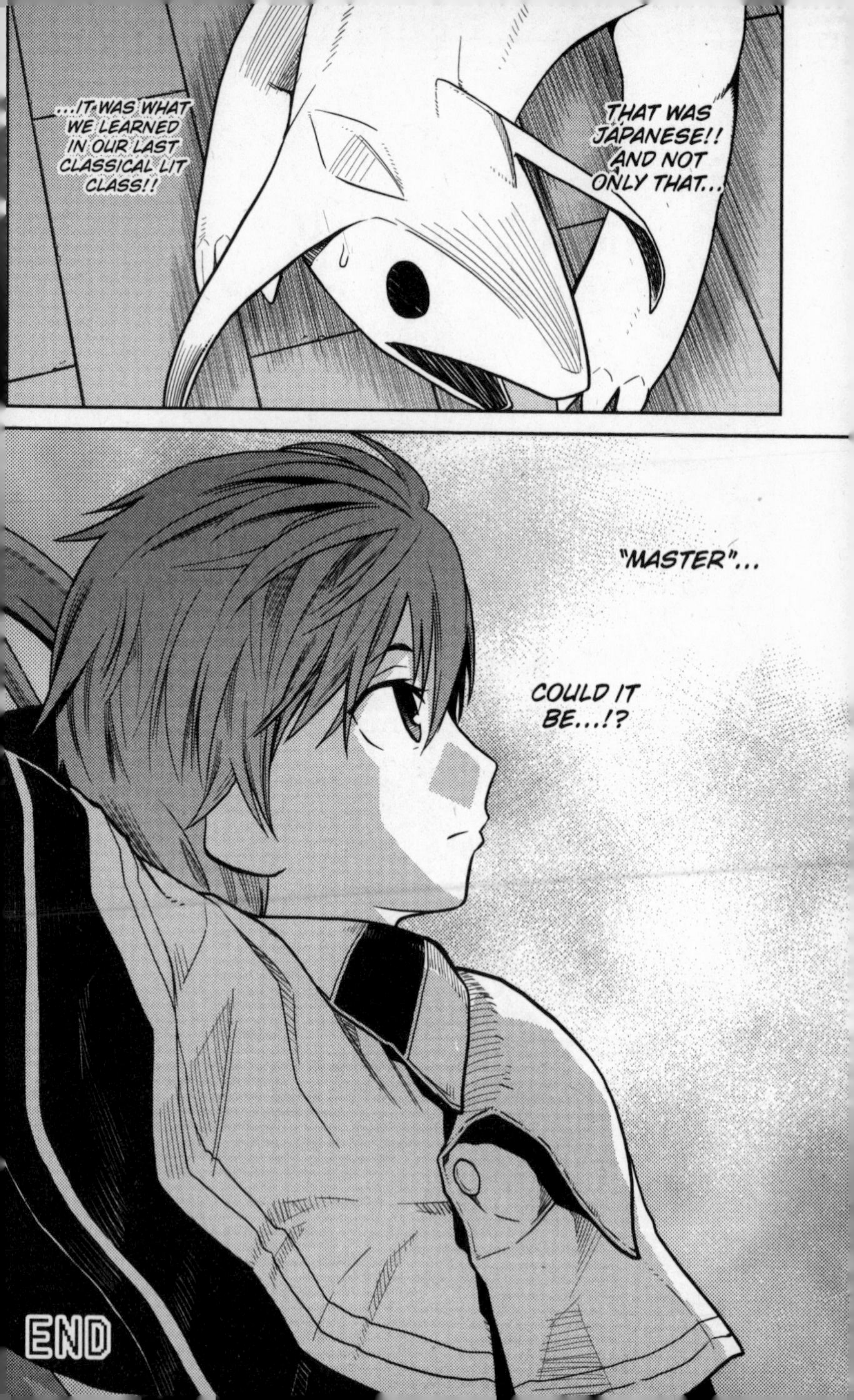
THAT WAS JAPANESE!! AND NOT ONLY THAT...
...IT WAS WHAT WE LEARNED IN OUR LAST CLASSICAL LIT CLASS!!
"MASTER"...
COULD IT BE...!?
END

AFTERWORD

ORIGINAL CREATOR:
OKINA BABA

I DON'T NEED PARALLEL MINDS, BUT I COULD CERTAINLY USE A SECOND BODY...I'M THE CREATOR OF THE ORIGINAL LIGHT NOVELS, OKINA BABA, AND THAT IS THE KIND OF SILLY THOUGHT ON MY MIND TODAY.

I MEAN, WOULD YOU REALLY WANT ANOTHER SELF TALKING TO YOU IN YOUR HEAD?

YOU KNOW HOW THERE ARE TIMES WHEN YOU THINK YOU'RE DOING SOMETHING COOL, BUT, REMEMBERING IT LATER, YOU GET REALLY EMBARRASSED?

CAN YOU IMAGINE IF THERE WAS A VOICE IN YOUR BRAIN MAKING FUN OF YOU THE WHOLE TIME? TH-THAT WOULD BE TERRIFYING!

BUT I GUESS IN KUMOKO'S CASE, BOTH PARTS OF HER BRAIN ARE ALREADY MASS-PRODUCING EMBARRASSING MEMORIES.

MAYBE I'D END UP LIKE THAT TOO.

THAT WOULD BE TERRIFYING IN A DIFFERENT WAY!

SO, ANYWAY, MY FAVORITE PART ABOUT VOLUME 4 IS GETTING TO SEE KUMOKO'S ONE-WOMAN COMEDY DUO.

ALSO, THE CATFISH ARE CUTE.

WHAT'S UP WITH THAT?

THAT'S GOTTA BE AGAINST THE RULES.

KIRYU-SENSEI MADE THEM PRETTY CUTE IN THE NOVEL ILLUSTRATIONS TOO...I MADE JOKES ABOUT IT, BUT IN THE END, I STILL LET IT SLIDE.

CUTENESS IS ALWAYS PERMISSIBLE!

CUTENESS IS JUSTICE!

THANKS FOR LETTING ME RAMBLE HERE, KAKASHI-SENSEI!

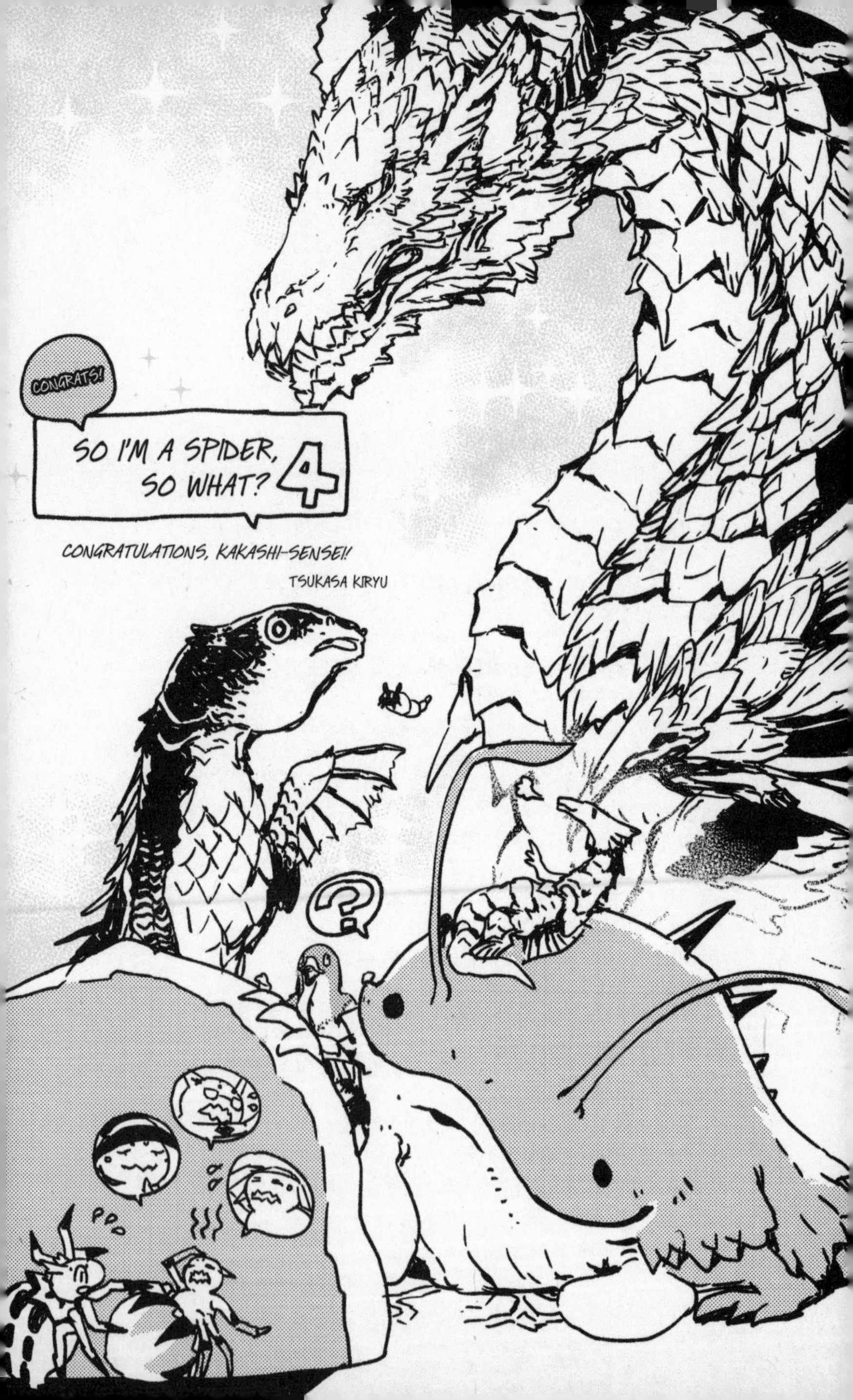

CONGRATS!
SO I'M A SPIDER, SO WHAT? 4
CONGRATULATIONS, KAKASHI-SENSEI!
TSUKASA KIRYU

STAFF LIST

The author

ASAHIRO KAKASHI

Assistants

TERUO HATANAKA

REI HASEKURA

MIMASAKA

Design

R design studio

(Shinji Yamaguchi, Akira Hayafuji)

You're reading
the wrong way!
Turn the page to read
a bonus short story by
So I'm a Spider, So What?
original creator,
Okina Baba!

Before I even think about going out into the world and spreading the truth, I gotta work on surviving in the Great Elroe Labyrinth.

【I think archaeology might be a pretty advanced field of study. The kind you can only do in times of peace.】

Yeah, probably.

It's certainly not for a solitary monster like me.

I guess we all learned a lesson today.

Contemplating history won't fill a monster's stomach.

Instead, I'll take out my frustrations on the nearest catfish and make a delicious meal of it.

"It's biologically significant"?

That doesn't matter!!

[The end]

the Upper and Lower Stratums, too.

So maybe the entire Great Elroe Labyrinth used to be totally filled with seawater.

That'd make the Middle Stratum an area that used to be an underwater volcano, right?

I know there are lots of monsters that don't look like sea creatures at all, but let's just say those guys came in after the labyrinth turned into a cave system.

If that's true, then the sea creature–type monsters have inhabited the labyrinth the longest.

In other words, they're a pretty big deal.

Hmm. So I guess the catfish is actually a historically important ancient creature, from a biological perspective.

Despite its stupid-looking face.

Still, isn't this kind of a huge discovery?

In my old world, you could've totally made a two-hour TV special about this, at least.

If I tell the world about this discovery, will my name go down in history as a super-important archaeologist?!

【Uh, hey, information brain?】

What is it, body brain?

【I hate to burst your bubble and all, but we don't actually know if your "discovery" is true.】

Well, I guess not, but I'm positive it's at least mostly true!

【Uh-huh. But even if it is, who are you going to tell, exactly?】

What do you mean, "who"...?

【Look. Here: Middle Stratum. Monsters: tons. People: none. Understand?】

......

【Not to mention... Me: monster. Humans: kill spiders. No mercy. Understand?】

......Oh Jesus.

That's right.

I'm a complete loner monster.

So I'm a Spider, So What?
The Middle Stratum Sea Theory
Okina Baba

I've gotten pretty used to the Middle Stratum by now.

This means I can finally relax a little, and relaxing means I now have time to overthink things.

And while I'm overthinking things, something occurs to me.

Did the Middle Stratum used to be part of the sea?

I'm serious.

Take the monsters that live here, for instance.

Seahorses. Catfish. Eels.

They're all sea creatures!

Frogs?

Well no, they're not sea creatures, but they are amphibious, so...

Anyway, going waaay back, I recently remembered that this Great Elroe Labyrinth apparently connects two continents.

Which must mean it's underneath an ocean, right? So it's not inconceivable that this place was underwater a long time ago.

That means my Middle Stratum Ocean Theory totally holds water. (heh-heh)

Let's say the labyrinth used to be part of the ocean.

Then it became a hollow space after the seawater, for some unknown reason, went away.

The handful of creatures that got left behind must have evolved really quickly or something, eventually becoming the monsters in the Great Elroe Labyrinth!

How's that for a genius proposal?!

When you think about it, there were sea creature–ish monsters in

So I'm a Spider, So What?

4

Art: **Asahiro Kakashi**

Original Story: **Okina Baba**

Character Design: **Tsukasa Kiryu**

Translation: Jenny McKeon ✖ Lettering: Bianca Pistillo

Kumo desuga, nanika? Volume 4
© Asahiro KAKASHI 2017
© Okina Baba, Tsukasa Kiryu 2017
First published in Japan in 2017 by KADOKAWA CORPORATION, Tokyo.
English translation rights arranged with KADOKAWA CORPORATION, Tokyo, through TUTTLE-MORI AGENCY, INC.

English translation © 2018 by Yen Press, LLC

Yen Press
1290 Avenue of the Americas
New York, NY 10104

Visit us at yenpress.com
facebook.com/yenpress
twitter.com/yenpress
yenpress.tumblr.com
instagram.com/yenpress

First Yen Press Edition: October 2018

Yen Press is an imprint of Yen Press, LLC.
The Yen Press name and logo are trademarks of Yen Press, LLC.

Library of Congress Control Number: 2017954138

ISBNs: 978-1-9753-0209-2 (paperback)
978-1-9753-0210-8 (ebook)

10 9 8 7 6 5 4 3 2

WOR

Printed in the United States of America